Born and brought up in Scotland, Reay Tannahill would have liked to go either to art or drama school but fell victim to the traditional Scots passion for formal education and found herself instead at the University of Glasgow, from where she emerged with an MA in history and a postgraduate certificate in social sciences.

After a varied early career – as a probation officer, advertising copywriter, newspaper reporter, historical researcher and graphic designer – she was asked by the Folio Society to write a short, illustrated study of Regency England. This allowed her to combine her interests in art and history and was followed by *Paris in the Revolution*, *The Fine Art of Food*, *Food in History* and *Sex in History*. Having spent twelve years researching and writing these last two books (translated into eleven languages), Reay Tannahill felt that a change was called for and embarked on her first historical novel, *A Dark and Distant Shore*, which was an instant bestseller. Since then she has written a further six critically acclaimed bestsellers: *The World, the Flesh and the Devil*, *Passing Glory*, *In Still and Stormy Waters*, *Return of the Stranger*, *Fatal Majesty* and *The Seventh Son*.

REAY TANNAHILL

The

Seventh
Son

review

First published in Great Britain in 2001 by
HEADLINE BOOK PUBLISHING

First published in paperback in 2002 by REVIEW
An imprint of Headline Book Publishing

10 9 8 7 6 5 4 3 2 1

ISBN 0 7472 6849 5

Typeset in PoliphilusMT by
Letterpart Limited, Reigate, Surrey

Printed and bound in Great Britain by
Mackays of Chatham plc, Chatham, Kent

HEADLINE BOOK PUBLISHING
A division of Hodder Headline
338 Euston Road
LONDON NW1 3BH

www.reviewbooks.co.uk
www.hodderheadline.com

This book is dedicated, with affection,
to Gloria McFarlane and Richard Rees

Contents

EDWARD III (1312-77)

Edward,
Prince of Wales
'The Black Prince'
(d.1376)

Lionel
Duke of Clarence
(d.1368)

Blanche of Lancaster m. John of Gaunt who m. (3) Catherine
(d. 1369)   Duke of Lancaster   Swynford
                   (d.1399)   (d. 1403)

RICHARD II
r.1377-99

Philippa
(d.1382)
m. Edmund Mortimer
3rd Earl of March

HENRY IV
r.1399-1413

John Beaufort
Earl of Somerset
(d.1410)

John Beaufort
1st Duke of Somerset
(d.1410)

Roger Mortimer
Earl of March
(d.1398)

HENRY V
r.1413-1422
m. Catherine de Valois who m. (2) Owen Tudor
(d.1437)   (exec.1461)

Henry
3rd Duke
(exec.1464)

Anne Mortimer
m. Richard
Earl of Cambridge
(d.1415)

HENRY VI
r.1422-61, 1470-1
m. Margaret of Anjou
(1430-82)

Richard
Duke of York
(1411-60)
m.Cicely Neville
(c.1415-95)

Jasper Tudor
(d.1495)

Edmund Tudor
Earl of Richmond m. Margaret Beaufort
(d.1456)   (1443-1509)
                        m(1) John de la Pole
                        (marriage dissolved)
                        m(3) Sir Henry Stafford
                        m(4) Thomas Lord Stanley

Edward of Lancaster
Prince of Wales
(1453-71)
m. Anne Neville
(1456-1485)

HENRY VII
(1457-1509)
r.1485-1509
m. Elizabeth of York
(1466-1503)

Anne
(1439-76)
m(1) Henry Holland
Duke of Exeter
div.1472
m(2) Thomas St Leger
exec.1483

EDWARD IV
(1442-83)
r.1461-70, 1471-83
m. Elizabeth Woodville
(1437-92)

Edmund
Earl of Rutland
(1443-60)

Elizabeth
(1444-?1504)
m. John de la Pole
Duke of Suffolk
(d.1491)

John
Earl of Lincoln
(1464-87)

Margaret
(1446-1503)
m. Charles
Duke of Burgundy
(d. 1477)

Elizabeth of York
(1466-1503)
m. Henry VII

Mary
(1467-82)

Cicely
(1469-1507)
m(1) John
Viscount Welles
m(2) Thomas Kyme

EDWARD V
(1470-?83)

Margaret
(b.&d.1472)

Richard
Duke of York
(1473-?83)

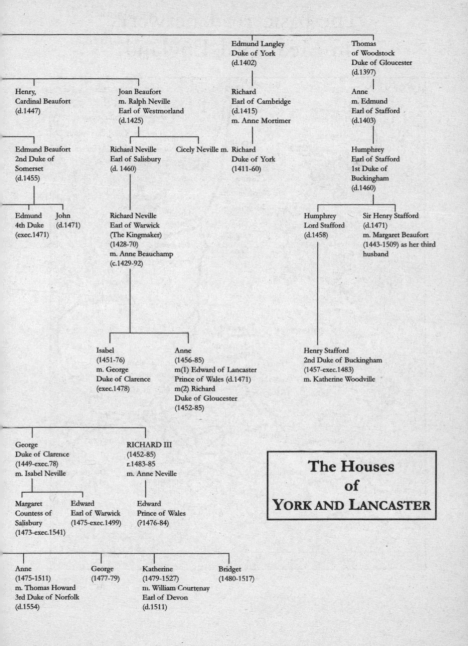

The Houses of YORK AND LANCASTER

The basic road network
in Mediaeval England

——	Major routes
– – –	Secondary routes
–·–·–	Watling Street

Berwick

Alnwick

Newcastle
Carlisle
Barnard
Castle   Darlington
Northallerton   Scarborough
Middleham
                    Sheriff
York   Hutton
Towton   Beverley
Pontefract
            Doncaster

                Nottingham

Shrewsbury   Tamworth   Leicester
            Bosworth
            Warwick   Northampton
Worcester   Towcester
        Tewkesbury   Woodstock
St David's   St Albans
    Brecon   Gloucester   Barnet
                    Oxford   London
Milford   Wallingford
Haven
        Bristol   Rochester
            Salisbury   Canterbury
                        Windsor
                    Winchester   Dover
            Dorchester
    Exeter   Portsmouth
Plymouth   Poole

0   km   100

0   miles   50

Introductory Note

Some readers like to go straight into a novel, others — especially where history is concerned — prefer to know exactly where they are before they begin. This page and the next are intended for those of the latter persuasion. The former can safely skip them, since most of the information is also contained in the book's text, distributed on a need-to-know basis.

What were the Wars of the Roses all about?

The foundations of the fifteenth-century Wars of the Roses were laid a century beforehand when King Edward III of England (1312-1377) fathered five sons. The eldest was Prince Edward, known as the Black Prince, while the younger, in order of seniority, were the dukes of Clarence, Lancaster, York, and Gloucester. The two eldest sons, Prince Edward and the duke of Clarence, both died before their father, Prince Edward leaving one son of his own, who duly succeeded to the throne as Richard II, and the duke of Clarence leaving only a daughter.

During the quarter-century after Edward III's death, the

legitimate heir Richard II was deposed and murdered by his cousin Henry, who was the child of Edward's *third* son, the duke of Lancaster, and who ascended the throne as Henry IV.

King Henry IV and his successors, Henry V and Henry VI, were thus known as Lancastrians, their house coming to be symbolised by the red rose.

Henry VI was gentle, spiritual and politically incompetent, a king who by the 1450s seemed to invite overthrow. And there was a rival prepared to make the attempt – Richard, duke of York, who had almost as good a claim to the succession as Henry, being descended on his father's side from Edward III's fourth son, and on his mother's from Edward's second son. The Yorkist symbol came to be the white rose.

Before the book opens...

In the last days of 1460, the duke of York and his second son, Edmund, were killed in battle against a royal army composed mostly of northerners and controlled by Henry VI's queen, the dazzling and formidable Margaret of Anjou, but within a few weeks they had been avenged by Edward, the 19-year-old eldest of York's sons, who sealed his triumph by having the defeated Henry VI deposed and imprisoned, and being declared king in his stead as Edward IV.

Edward's first decade as king was unsettled, ending in exile after his betrayal both by the man who had originally helped him to his throne – Richard Neville, earl of Warwick – and by his own brother, George, duke of Clarence. By the spring of 1471, however, Edward had returned from exile and recovered the throne, with Henry VI and Warwick both dead and Margaret of Anjou's armies decisively defeated.

George, duke of Clarence, made his submission to Edward and was welcomed back and rewarded, but it was the youngest of the three brothers – eighteen-year-old Richard, duke of Gloucester, who had remained loyal throughout – in whom Edward now reposed his trust, endowing him with important political and administrative responsibilities.

Now read on...

Chapter One

1471

1

'SAPPHIRES for my bride-to-be and a severed head for the king my brother,' said Duke Richard cheerfully. 'As St Paul pointed out, gifts may vary but the spirit is the same. In the present instance, a spirit of goodwill.'

Francis Lovell, on horseback beside him, gave a faint splutter of laughter. Although not as well versed in the scriptures as Richard, he doubted whether the kind of gifts St Paul had had in mind would have included a head, newly detached from the body of a traitor and then parboiled with bay salt to preserve it for its journey to London. But Richard's brother, the king, would no doubt receive it with gratitude and order it to be impaled on London Bridge as a warning to others who might think of betraying his trust.

Richard, as if he knew what Francis was thinking – which he probably did – grinned at him. Then, suddenly, he knitted his brows. 'I've just thought of something. Anne does have blue eyes, doesn't she?'

He had known his bride-to-be for half a dozen years but

1

Francis nobly refrained from pointing it out and merely said, 'Yes, she does. The sapphires will suit her very well.'

Richard was not in the least abashed. 'Oh, good.'

'Now,' he glanced round the courtyard of the tall stone keep that was Middleham castle and raised a gauntletted hand in a signal to his Master of the Horse. The high curtain wall of the castle had the effect not only of concentrating the pungent smells of the hundred mounted and liveried men milling around in the courtyard but of amplifying the gossiping voices, the clanking of arms, and the whinnying of horses into something resembling war in heaven. 'Let us go before we all suffocate or become deaf beyond hope of redemption.'

Since everyone knew that the young duke of Gloucester did not like to be kept waiting, there was an immediate flourish of trumpets calling the escort to order and the chaos of a moment before transformed itself into an orderly file moving out through the gatehouse, across the drawbridge, and downhill towards the river crossing that would take them into the heart of the Yorkshire Dales.

2

THE SEPTEMBER LANDSCAPE came as a relief to the senses, wide and clean and austere under the morning sun, a gentle wind blowing the scents of warm moorland to the riders' nostrils even though early frosts had already tinged the grass with amber and the bracken with scarlet. Small flocks of migrating birds fluttered restlessly over the rugged hillsides, their calls drowned by the disciplined clamour of Richard's escort – gentlemen, yeomen and grooms, all wearing his badge of a white boar on their sleeves. The trumpeter, leading the cavalcade, raised his head every few moments to shatter the air with a series of blasts designed to advertise his master's coming to the dozen miles of empty valley that lay ahead of them.

'His enthusiasm will soon wear off,' Richard said absently after half an hour, then, 'Look,' he went on, his eyes on a small scythe-winged hawk skimming over the trees along the river bank, 'a hobby falcon. That explains why all the little birds have vanished into cover. What is a hobby doing as far north as this, I wonder?' Hawking was one of Richard's passions.

War was the other, and Francis, with the optimism of his sixteen years, expected that Richard, two years his senior, would grow out of it now that the country was at peace, now that the House of York had finally triumphed over that of Lancaster.

It was hard to imagine an England no longer at war with itself, but Francis, a gentle soul despite the knightly upbringing he had shared with Richard, could think of few prospects more pleasing.

3

IT TOOK THEM ten days, pushing along at Richard's usual ferocious pace, to reach London, and at what felt like every league along the way there was a battlefield to serve as a reminder of the late wars, the wars that had transformed Richard from the insignificant youngest son of a rebel lord into a royal duke, brother of England's now undisputed king, Edward IV.

Richard had fought in Edward's last two, decisive battles at Barnet and Tewkesbury and, as a reward, had been appointed as the king's representative in the north of England.

Francis knew that he was having some difficulty in establishing his authority and convincing the dour northerners that he was one of them at heart. It was his primary reason for wanting to marry

Anne, whose family had dominated the north for more years than anyone cared to remember. Although her father, Richard Neville, earl of Warwick, had become the *late* earl of Warwick as a consequence of betraying Edward, most northerners remained loyal to the Nevilles. By marrying Anne, Richard hoped to buy their loyalty or, at the very least, their acceptance. He also had his eye on the Warwick estates.

But Edward's and Richard's self-centred middle brother, George, duke of Clarence, was making difficulties. Already married to Anne's elder sister, Isabel, George was determined to claim the Warwick estates for himself.

It was not hard to tell that George's intransigence was very much on Richard's mind as they rode south, and when they reached Coventry he regaled Francis with the tale of what had happened when he had last seen the place a few months earlier. It had been there that George, until then in treasonable alliance with Warwick – who had set him up as a potential alternative king – had seen the error of his ways and decided to make his submission to Edward.

'If it could be called submission,' remarked Richard caustically. 'Certainly, he went down on his knees. Certainly, he brought with him four thousand men he had raised in the West country to reinforce Edward's army. Certainly, he promised to be a good boy in future. But at no point did he bend his neck. My brother the king, however, chose to let it pass. It is his habit to be generous and forgiving, to think well of people . . .'

'Or to hope for the best,' Francis murmured under his breath.

'. . . until they give him an unequivocal reason to think otherwise. I hope George *will* have enough sense to behave himself.'

It was said in a tone suggesting that Richard thought it unlikely. Brotherly love had never been a feature of his and George's relationship. George was big, handsome and utterly unreliable

4

except in terms of his own self-interest, and Francis knew that there was going to be a major clash between the two when Richard reached London.

A clash over the marriage on which Richard was determined.

4

IN THE CITY of London, in the Great Hall of the mansion close by St Paul's where her father had lived in a style famous for its ostentation, fifteen-year-old Anne Neville said, 'But I don't see why not. Richard would be a very good match for me.' She glanced up uncertainly. 'Wouldn't he?'

Anne was small, fair and fragile, and George, duke of Clarence, was very large. It made her nervous.

'No.'

'I don't know *why* you're against it. I want to marry him and he wants to marry me. And the king has given his permission.'

Her brother-in-law said austerely, 'It's a matter of property and family alliances. It's complicated and you wouldn't understand, even if I explained it to you. Anyway, it is not for you to decide who you should marry.'

He really was the most exasperating man. 'But I have to marry *some*one! And soon! I've been a widow for four whole months. I quite like Richard, and if I don't marry *him*, you or the king might make me marry someone I don't like at all.'

She forced herself to gaze up at George beseechingly. His good looks, height and splendid physique gave him a presence almost as striking as that of his brother the king, but his charm was a more debatable quantity. Indeed, 'domineering' was the word that had sprung to Anne's mind the first time she had met him and nothing had caused her to change her opinion since. She couldn't imagine how Isabel, compliant though she was, could bear to live with him.

As usual, he resorted to repeating himself, as if saying something often enough gave it the force of revealed truth. 'This is a most improper conversation. Who you marry is no concern of yours. Marriage is a business arrangement. *Liking* people doesn't enter into it.'

Anne was a sweet-natured and amenable girl who was quite used to being ordered around in the interests of property and family alliances, even if she was getting rather tired of it. Her father, fearsomely ambitious, had married Isabel off to George because it had seemed to him advantageous to be father-in-law to King Edward's brother and heir. Unfortunately, the king had disagreed, and there had been a general falling out.

Her father, undismayed, had therefore arranged for Anne herself to be married to the son of the king from whom Edward had usurped the crown, Henry VI. He and George had then succeeded in driving Edward into exile and restoring the imprisoned Henry VI to the throne.

George hadn't liked Henry's restoration at all, because it had reduced him from being the king's brother and heir to just an ordinary member of the nobility. So he had transferred his allegiance back to Edward when his brother had reappeared from exile.

Edward had regained the throne, and George behaved as if his own double dealing had been all that had made it possible. It didn't, of course, occur to him that Isabel and Anne might not take kindly to his boasting about how clever he had been in bringing about the deaths of their father, the earl of Warwick; Anne's husband, the prince of Wales; and her father-in-law, the saintly and incompetent King Henry VI.

Anne sighed. She *did* want to marry someone she liked this time because, truthfully, she hadn't in the least enjoyed being married to the prince of Wales who, exciting at first, had turned out to be as arrogant and objectionable as he was goodlooking, always waving a sword around and talking about the traitors he intended to slaughter. He had been seventeen when he was killed at the battle of Tewkesbury in May. Anne didn't think he would have made a very good king if he had survived.

George said, 'Anyway, I can't imagine why you like Richard. He's fathered two bastards to my certain knowledge and there's a lot of unpleasant gossip about him. I have it on good authority that it was he who cut down your husband when he was fleeing from the field at Tewkesbury. And it was he who ordered Somerset and the others to be dragged out of sanctuary in the abbey and executed a few days later. And afterwards, he was at the Tower of London when King Henry died, and when he later went to see the body lying in state at the Black Friars it began to bleed again. And you know what *that* means!'

Corpses were known to bleed afresh in the presence of their murderer. Anne frowned. 'But you were . . .' she began, and then saw that Isabel was biting her lip and giving a tiny, sharp shake of her head that conveyed as clearly as words, 'Don't say it!'

So, instead of going on, 'You were there, too, when King Henry died,' she said, 'I don't know who killed my husband, of course, but killing people is what battles are about. And it was Richard's *duty* as Constable of England to execute traitors like Somerset. And if King Edward didn't blame him for that, I don't see why you should.'

She couldn't believe she was standing up to George like this but, on the principle that she might as well be hanged for a sheep as for a lamb, went on, her delicate complexion heightened, 'Anyway, men always do that kind of thing. My father often executed people he didn't like, and he didn't have the excuse of acting on the king's behalf. And even if Richard *did* all those things, which I don't believe, he probably did them because the king told him to.'

There was a vibrating silence. George, his face scarlet, scrutinised the magnificently carved, painted and gilded ceiling while Isabel went back to her embroidery – a sash with George's heraldic emblem of a bull, endlessly repeated – and began stitching away as if her life depended on it.

'That is quite enough,' George said at last.

'Yes, George.'

'The king has confided you to my care, and I will not permit you to marry the duke of Gloucester.'

'But . . .' It was a stupid situation. The king had given Richard permission to marry her, but her guardian – the king's other brother – was determined that he shouldn't. She couldn't guess how it was all going to end, but there was nothing she could do to influence events. Wearily, she said, 'No, George.'

He couldn't bear not to have the last word. Looking down at her, he said, 'And don't delude yourself that he has any feelings for you. He only wants to marry you for your property and family connections.'

It took her a great effort of will to resist the desire to shriek, 'But that is what you keep telling me marriage is supposed to be *about*!'

5

TOWCESTER, St Albans, Barnet . . .

'Only Tewkesbury missing,' Francis volunteered as they descended Highgate Hill and saw the whole of London spread out before them, its skyline dominated by St Paul's and a forest of

church towers and spires. Londoners were nothing if not sup-
portive of their religion.

Richard looked blank for a moment, and then said, 'Well,
we're not going all the way round by the west just for the pleasure
of revisiting yet another battlefield.' It was one of his more
endearing traits that, unlike many people, he never laughed at
Francis's occasional stammer, or showed contempt or impatience,
or tried to help him out. He had said once, 'You'll probably grow
out of it when you accept that there's nothing wrong with being
more of a scholar than a warrior.' Francis had blushed – something else he hoped he would grow out of, although at present all
he seemed to be growing out of was his clothes.

'As it happens,' Richard said now, 'I wasn't thinking of battles.
I was remembering ten years ago when my brother made his
formal entry into London for his coronation. I was eight and
George was eleven, and Edward had just inducted us as Knights
of the Bath, so we rode in the procession to Westminster in our
beautiful new blue gowns with their white silk trimmings and felt
very mature and important.'

'Were there minstrels, and cloth-of-gold, and c-c-conduits
flowing with wine?'

'Of course! No expense spared. Fortunately, the city merchants
paid for most of it. Unfortunately, they didn't repeat the effect
when Edward made his ceremonial re-entry last April. It wasn't
parsimony, as it happens, just that they always prefer to be on the
winning side, and this time they'd taken too long arguing over
which the winning side was likely to be to have time to arrange for
the pageantry. Wine and cloth-of-gold would have been wasted on
Henry if things had gone the other way.'

'Does your b-b-brother hold it against them?'

'No, he can't afford to. Too much depends on his being able to
borrow money from them.'

There was no hint of criticism in his voice, but Francis couldn't resist saying, 'Whereas you detest being beholden to anyone.'

Richard gave a shadowy smile and evaded the issue. 'The immediate question is, whom shall we go and visit first. Brother Edward? Or brother George?'

6

THE QUEEN SAID, 'As you know, my lord, I cannot love your brothers as dearly as you do yourself . . .'

'Naturally not,' the king replied abstractedly, his mind on the problem of how to finance his proposed invasion of France. 'Don't *you* have any ideas, Hastings?'

Hastings, the friend and mentor who held the post of Edward's lord chamberlain of the household, grimaced helplessly, all the expression lines of his forty-one years coming into play. They were pleasant lines, because although the first of his guiding principles was to make money, the second was to make himself liked by everyone. 'Parliament could vote a special tax to pay the longbowmen. Or we could try raising benevolences.'

'Not as a first step. People don't enjoy having loans forced out of them.'

The queen, who detested Lord Hastings – suspecting him, with some justification, of being her husband's whore-finder – was not accustomed to being ignored. She did not frown because it was ageing. She merely raised her voice slightly and amended her tone from genteelly gracious to shrewishly piercing. 'But I believe that my opinion is not without value.'

Edward's attention was caught and he smiled at her indulgently, thinking how pretty she always looked – the perfect ice maiden, though at thirty-four, twice married, and pregnant for the seventh time, perhaps 'maiden' was not the appropriate word. But elegant she was, with her Nordic fairness and the royal sense of style she had so swiftly developed after their clandestine marriage of seven years before. She reclined, now, in a gaily painted litter draped and cushioned with cloth-of-gold, four of her ladies-in-waiting on horseback around her. He would have liked to jump in and join her; he had never made love in a horse litter. His loins gave an interested twitch.

They were spending a few days at one of Edward's favourite residences, Eltham Palace in Kent, where he was planning major building works, but on this particular day he had chosen to ride out to survey its three deer parks and decide which to enclose and which to enlarge. It was a soothing way of passing the time and Edward, after three years of almost unbroken campaigning, was disinclined to expend more energy than necessary except in the pleasurable exercises of the bedchamber – or the horse litter.

He put temptation reluctantly aside. He was a big man and vigorous in bed. The litter probably wouldn't take the strain, although it might be worth trying some time. Urbanely, he said, 'Your opinion is always of value, my love. And with ten brothers and sisters of your own, I would not expect you to feel for George and Richard as I do.'

'No. Nor do I have a nature as forgiving as yours. I do not believe that George has mended his ways. Until our son was born last year, George was publicly recognised as your heir and I believe he still thinks of himself as such. I fear for little Eddie's safety.'

Delicately, she touched a handkerchief to her eyes while waving aside the reassurances trembling on her husband's lips. 'No, no. I am aware that you have arranged for every precaution to be taken. But George is setting himself up against you. Again.

His opposition to the marriage between Richard and Anne Neville . . .'

'For which I have already given Richard permission,' the king interrupted defensively.

'. . . is based on pure greed. He is determined that his wife should hold on to *all* the Warwick estates, instead of sharing them with Anne. I believe you must force him to share.'

Edward's high, smooth forehead furrowed slightly. 'It's difficult, my love. I did grant them to the Lady Isabel, after her father was killed, and I would prefer not to offend George by taking them away again . . .'

'It should be George's concern not to offend *you* more than he has done already. But you *must* make him behave. If you force him to share the Warwick lands, he will no longer be able to *afford* to look like a king in waiting, which he does. I find the royal way in which he conducts himself really quite shocking!'

Edward said, 'He doesn't do so in my presence.'

'Perhaps you don't see it, because you don't want to. You are far too soft-hearted.'

'I'm fond of George, and if sometimes George appears not to reciprocate, that is just George's way. He has not quite grown up yet.'

She gave a tinkling laugh. 'He is twenty-one years old! Richard is eighteen and far more mature. You *must* favour him over George.'

The king turned to Hastings. 'William . . .'

Hastings had been hoping not to be involved because, for once, he was in agreement with the queen. George was pompous, arrogant and dangerous, but Edward could not be persuaded to see it, or to admit to seeing it. On the other hand, the queen's complaint about George's royal pretensions was laughable, coming from a woman who was little more than a *parvenue* but demanded the kind of subservience normally accorded only to those in whose veins ran the bluest of blue blood.

'Sire?'

'Should we favour Richard?' the king asked.

Hastings was cornered. 'He has been unfailingly loyal to you, sire. Although you have already rewarded him, you have given far greater reward to George, who has *not* been loyal to you. Richard may well feel that he has been unjustly treated.'

Edward's golden-brown eyes looked absent. 'I do not believe that there is anything at my disposal that I can afford to bestow on him without undermining my own finances. A rich marriage for him would certainly be the most convenient solution.'

Trying for the lighter touch, Hastings offered, 'Very true. And the Lady Anne appears to be the only candidate, since the queen's brothers have already appropriated to themselves all the other great heiresses in the realm.' Then, aware of being skewered by the queen's pale gaze, he added hurriedly, 'I merely mention it. However, I understand that Henry Stafford is close to death, which will make a widow of that clever wife of his, the Lady Margaret Beaufort. *She* might be available.'

Diverted, the queen exclaimed, 'Invite that woman into the royal family? Never!'

Privately, Hastings cursed himself for his stupidity, because 'that woman' might have become queen of England in her own right, had it not been for a general prejudice against women rulers. She also had a son by a previous marriage who, through his father, had a different though more distant claim to the throne. It was astounding how many potential claimants there were, if one stopped to think about it.

'Elizabeth, my dear!' Edward said in mild rebuke. And then, with a sigh, 'I suppose I have no choice but to order George to agree to Richard's marriage. If only the two of them could be persuaded to resolve the inheritance issue between themselves! But I expect I shall end by setting up a formal review so that they can argue it out in front of lawyers. George won't like that. If I know anything, he'll go on complaining about it for years!'

7

RICHARD, having installed his household in the great waterside palace known as Baynard's Castle, the family home by the Thames, immediately despatched his serjeant of the stable to deliver the head of the Bastard of Fauconberg, which had survived its journey well, to the royal palace at Westminster, then himself set out, with Francis and a small bodyguard for company, for the Warwick mansion next to St Paul's.

Long familiar with the city, he barely glanced around him as the trumpeter cleared a path for him and bonnets were doffed towards him, but Francis looked with interest at the tradesmen's tiny houses, unable to imagine how people could actually live in them, and tried to assess the worth of the goods set out on the stalls in front.

Blocking their path ahead was a lumbering convoy of carts laden with firewood, hay and straw being carried up from the wharves, and the inevitable moment came when the straw bulging over the sides of one cart swept a merchant's entire stock of linen and ribbons off his stall on to the filthy ground. At once, a fist fight broke out which within seconds developed into a small riot. Knives began flashing and Richard was just saying, a disquieting gleam in his eye, 'We will have to do something,' when a sheriff arrived with his serjeants and yeomen, cuffed the ears of the belligerents, and dragged a random few of them off in the general direction of the pillory at Ludgate in the city wall.

Slightly deflated, Richard said, 'Well, that's swift retribution, if you like! My brother's campaign to impose law and order is obviously having an effect.'

As they approached Ludgate, the houses became larger and more imposing, and the late earl of Warwick's proved to be the most imposing of them all. Warwick's household had been so large that it was not uncommon for as many as six whole oxen to be consumed at breakfast.

The Great Hall of the mansion, which was stonewalled, whitewashed, tapestry-hung and as vast as its name implied, proved to be very full of people. Such halls had long been the focus of life in England's castles and mansions, the place where the lord kept open house for his followers, retainers and any other respectable persons who chose to present themselves, but it was becoming increasingly fashionable for the nobility to retire into their new Great Chambers, which could be entered only by invitation. George, it seemed, had chosen not to adopt the new ways, no doubt because a crowded Great Hall was an index of popularity and power – which ministered to his vanity.

Scanning the hall, Francis observed a chaplain who appeared to be testing the pitch of half a dozen choirboys, although how he could hear their piping voices in the general babel Francis could not imagine. Further over, dictating to a seated clerk, was a grey-faced gentleman with an armful of papers who looked as if he might be the household receiver, or rent collector. A jester was prancing around tapping people on the shoulder with his bauble and presumably telling them jokes, while a melancholy-looking fellow over in one corner was grinding away on a hurdy-gurdy. And everywhere, brightly clad knights and gentlemen were engrossed in conversations that seemed to entail a great deal of shouting and gesticulating.

Close by the far window was a small group of women, the only women in the room. Seated on a hard stool was a slender dark girl, languidly occupied with distaff and spindle. Three drab, middle-aged gentlewomen stood by, their hands folded subserviently. And in the centre, partly obscured from Francis's sight by a plump, curly-haired gentleman who was clearly offering her a special price on the lengths of velvet draped over his arm, was George's wife, the Lady Isabel. No sign of the Lady Anne.

And then the steward was leading them across to George, who with apparent relief dismissed the stout bishop with whom he had been conversing, but whose jovial welcome to his brother was as false as a harlot's vows of love.

Towering over the compact and neatly built Richard, George said, 'You look well, young Diccon. What news of the frozen north?'

'Thawing nicely. Lord Lovell here has been complaining of the heat.'

George floundered. 'Er, Lovell?' He stared at Francis as if he were a spirit that had strayed in from elfland, although even if he had no memory for faces he certainly knew – he was that kind of man – that the ninth Baron Lovell was one of the wealthiest young peers in England.

Francis straightened up his lanky length and did his best to look it.

'Ah, yes, Lovell. How are you? You've grown.' Without waiting for an answer, George turned back to Richard, but before he could say more Richard resumed with the bland amiability of one who did not expect to be denied, 'We have come to see the Lady Anne.'

'She's not here.'

Richard was silent for a moment. Then, 'In what sense?'

'What do you mean, "In what sense?" I said, she's not here.'

'She is supposed to be living here under your guardianship. Has she gone out to visit friends? Or to buy ribbons from the mercer? Or has she ceased to live here?'

'That's it. She doesn't live here any more.'

'So where *does* she live?'

'Don't know. How should I know?'

Richard's lips tightened but, when he spoke, his voice was relaxed. 'Don't play the fool, George. I know you have a brain in that big handsome head of yours, even if you choose to pretend otherwise.'

This tribute left George unmoved. 'Don't know where she is. She took herself off without a word to anybody. Didn't want to see you.'

It was an unlikely story. After a moment, Richard turned away to the great oriel window and stood looking out through the leaded panes.

Superficially, both men appeared calm and controlled. Francis knew that discipline and propriety had been the watchwords of their mother, the exquisite but terrifying Duchess Cicely, who had ruled their early upbringing with a rod of iron. But George's fists were clenching and unclenching at his sides, while Richard was fidgeting with the dagger at his belt, twitching it an inch out of its scabbard and pushing it back again, which might have been taken as a sign of irritation except that Richard's fidgets were more often a sign of surplus energy than of nervous tension.

Richard said, 'I know you don't want me to marry Anne, but make no mistake about it. Inheritance or no inheritance, I am determined on it.'

'Rubbish. It's not her you want. It's her claim to the Warwick titles and estates. And you can't have *them*, because I've got them. If you knew where she was, I wouldn't put it past you to run off with her.'

The noise in the Great Hall did not abate, but the silence

17

within their little group was almost palpable. And then Richard's shoulders shook, and when he turned back to face George he was laughing. Genuinely. 'Run off with her? Oh, no. I propose doing things correctly. There have been quite enough clandestine marriages in our family already and I have no intention of starting another war, as yours and Edward's did.'

George's handsome nostrils flared. His own marriage to Warwick's elder daughter had sealed his alliance with Warwick; it had been a direct act of rebellion against Edward, who had forbidden it. And it was Edward's own secret marriage to the seductive but humbly born widow, Dame Elizabeth Grey, née Woodville, in place of the French royal bride Warwick had been negotiating for him, that had alienated Warwick from him in the first place.

George exploded, 'I don't know what you mean. Nothing clandestine about *my* marriage. Isabel's father gave us his blessing and we were married in public by an archbishop of the church!'

It might have sounded convincing to someone who didn't know that the 'public' marriage had taken place not in England but in Calais, and that the archbishop in question had been the earl of Warwick's brother.

Richard's lips twitched and he said, 'Of course,' in a soothing tone which incensed George even more.

Francis studied the pair of them with amusement, George eye-catchingly splendid in a calf-length, ermine-trimmed robe of deep rose over a bright blue tunic, with a roll-brimmed blue hood on his head; Richard in his modish rust-coloured, wide-shouldered and extremely – some said indecently – short tunic above dark grey fitted hose and the new duckbill-toed shoes, his bowl-shaped green hat tipped jauntily forward over his nose. It was easy to understand that Richard, less impressive physically than George and never allowed to forget it, should compensate by running intellectual rings round his brother.

The duchess of York had borne her husband twelve children and lost five of them, including three sons, in infancy. Of the seven who had survived, four had been sons, the eldest of them Edward and the youngest, ten years later, Richard. Edward and George were both spectacularly tall, fair, handsome and beautifully muscled; so, reputedly, had been the second brother, Edmund, killed at Wakefield.

But Richard, born three years after George, came from a different mould. Several inches shorter than his elders, he was brown-haired rather than fair, lithe rather than muscular, brimming with physical and mental energy. The elder brothers seemed to have inherited their looks, on a grandiose scale, from their mother's side of the family, but it was generally held that Richard was the image of his father, except for one fundamental difference. Whereas the duke of York had been of a rash disposition and had paid for it with his life, his youngest son was the opposite, a thinker, a planner – a cautious and careful young man. Only Francis knew that he was not invariably as cool as he chose to appear. In the past and in an occasional burst of boyish mischief, he had proved capable of casting it all to the winds.

Now, he said, 'I am sorry that the Lady Anne prefers not to see me. Perhaps, if I could meet her, I could persuade her to take a different view. You are sure you have no idea where she is?'

'None at all.'

George's air of innocence was so elaborate that no one could possibly have believed him.

Richard said carelessly, 'Never mind. Lovell will find her.'

A startled Francis reflected that it was just as well he was not expected to open his mouth. There wasn't a letter in the alphabet that would not have had him stuttering like a kettledrum.

Just then came the sound of a flute being blown by a youthful yeoman who had appeared in the doorway, signalling to everyone that the room was to be cleared to enable the trestle tables to be set up for supper.

George did not invite Richard and Francis to stay.

'We must pay our respects to the Lady Isabel before we leave,' Richard said, unexpectedly striding off towards the little group of women with George hot on his heels. Francis followed more slowly, reflecting that while George was preventing Richard from asking the Lady Isabel about her sister's whereabouts, he himself might take the opportunity of questioning the girl with the distaff, whom he vaguely remembered from Middleham in the days when Richard and he had been among the youthful nobles who had been boarded out there for their knightly education.

He remembered her name just in time, and murmured, 'Constantia?'

She looked up from tucking her distaff into her belt. 'Don't you mean C-c-constantia?'

'No, I don't, you wicked girl. Where is the Lady Anne?'

Her mischievous expression vanished. 'I can't tell you. I daren't! Duke George is watching.' She dropped her spindle and bent to pick it up at the same moment as Francis did. In the confusion of apologies following the crashing of their heads, Francis heard her whisper, 'Sir John . . .' But then George was looming over them, saying, 'All well?'

The Lady Isabel had disappeared, and Richard was standing chewing his lower lip as he always did when he was thinking hard. 'Time to take our leave, Lovell,' he said.

George escorted them every step of the way to where their horses and servants awaited them, and then stood watching them ride off.

'WHY ME? And why "Lovell"?' Francis demanded.

'George doesn't understand friendship, only the master and servant relationship.'

'Oh. Thank you.'

'He gave me no opportunity to speak to Isabel. Did you have any luck with the girl?'

'Was it obvious?'

'To me, but probably not to George.'

'All she managed to say was, "Sir John . . .", before we were interrupted.'

'Well, well. At least it reduces the list of possibilities, but how many Sir Johns can *you* think of?'

Francis counted on the fingers of his gauntlet. 'Mmm. Seventeen?'

'Clever of you. I can only make fifteen. Now, let us consider. Since George is behind it all, we can safely assume that Anne has not gone rushing off to a member of her own family. So that rules out the Nevilles and their assorted kin, including the Beauchamps and Despensers.'

'Her mother-in-law?'

Raising an eyebrow, Richard said, 'To languish with her in prison in the Tower? I doubt it.'

'I wasn't thinking of Margaret of Anjou herself, more about supporters who could have been kind to Anne when they were in France. Like Sir John Fortescue.'

'Certainly, he's a kindly man. And a "Sir John", too! But let us first look at George's retainers. Those to whom he could say, "Look after the Lady Anne for me. Keep her hidden." '

'Hidden?'

'No point in placing her where she could be recognised by

anyone who dropped in for a cup of ale.'

Francis was slightly shocked. 'You're not suggesting she might be locked up somewhere?'

Richard gave him no immediate answer because his gelding shied, startled by a dog darting out from a dark alley. But as Richard brought him back under control, the torches over the merchants' booths lit a spark in his grey eyes. 'If she is locked up, George will pay for it, and so will Sir John, whoever he may be. We'll try Kemp first. He has a house in Paternoster Row. Then Strensham, in Basinges Lane, and Harewell, over by Bucklersbury. After that, if need be, we can take further thought.'

9

'ARE YOU managing, my lady?' enquired Sir John's wife a little tremulously.

'No, I am not,' Anne snapped, in no mood for mincing words. But then she giggled. Mincing words, mincing almonds, what was there to choose? Putting down her cleaver, she wiped her hands on her skirts and said, 'I know I offered to help prepare the food for your babies, but I cannot make the almond milk without help.'

'Oh, dear! What shall we do? Cow's milk is very bad for them.'

How was it possible, Anne wondered, for a woman to be so helpless? Presumably she was accustomed to leaving everything to the children's nurse, which would be fine except when the nurse fell ill, as she had done now.

With some exasperation, she said, 'It takes *pounds* of almonds to make as much milk as the babies need. I have chopped them as best I can, but I am not strong enough to grind them. Unless the milk is to be very weak the yeoman powderer will have to pulverise them with his giant pestle and mortar.'

'But those are for salt.' Her ladyship sounded perfectly vacant.

'They can be used for other things.'

Doubtfully, 'Can they? Perhaps I should ask the clerk of the kitchen.'

'Perhaps you should.' Anne had to raise her voice because there was suddenly a great deal of noise coming from the passage leading between the main kitchen and the Great Hall, the noise of men shouting angrily. The two women peered out from the nursery pantry and, like everyone else in the kitchens, stared open-mouthed towards the archway where a mass of struggling bodies seemed to be fighting to get through.

It didn't last long. After a few moments, the bodies disentangled themselves and shook themselves down.

Anne said, 'Ooooh,' and hastily began tucking her hair into her cap.

One man was still shouting, 'You have no right to break in like this. How dare you!' while another and much younger one ostentatiously restored his dagger to the scabbard at his belt, surveyed the kitchens and, ignoring the irate porter, strolled across to Anne to smile at her charmingly and bow over her small, greasy hand. He was a very attractive, dangerous-looking young man.

'My lord duke,' she said weakly, smiling back. 'What an unexpected pleasure.'

He tilted his head in acknowledgement, then, glancing at Sir John's twittering lady, said, 'No doubt someone will explain to me why my bride-to-be, the future duchess of Gloucester, should be hidden away in this vulgar establishment, employed as a *kitchen maid*!'

Richard had always behaved and sounded older than he was, but now he excelled himself. Even the king could not have been more majestic.

Anne caught sight of Francis Lovell and, meeting his eye, saw that he was having as much difficulty in sustaining his gravity as she was.

Pink-cheeked with suppressed hilarity, she fixed her gaze on Richard and said, 'My lord duke, you mistake the situation . . .'

10

NOTHING would convince him.

'Employed as a *kitchen maid*!'

He and Francis stood guard over her while a servant was despatched to pack her belongings.

'It had nothing to do with George. He wanted me out of the house in case you came to take me away . . .'

'Three boxes. Is that everything?'

'I think so. But I was in the kitchen from choice. It was preferable to sitting in that woman's chamber and listening to her tedious conversation . . .'

'Not Baynard's Castle, I think. My mother is not in residence to lend respectability. And you cannot go back to my brother's. Kitchen maid, indeed! I will take you to sanctuary in St Martin's le Grand. I understand that their guest lodgings are well appointed. You will be safe and comfortable there until I can make arrangements for our marriage. Are you ready?'

'Yes. But I should say goodbye to my hostess . . .'

'Unnecessary.'

Her submissiveness vibrant with sarcasm, which Richard entirely failed to notice, Anne said, 'Very well, my lord.' Francis winked at her conspiratorially as he tossed the porter a gold noble. The man had only been doing his duty in trying to keep them out.

Richard said, 'The next thing is to deal with George.'

Chapter Two

1472

1

HIGH-HANDED though Richard could be when dealing with opposition, his quarrel with George was not of a kind that could be resolved by simply bursting into the Warwick mansion with a body of armed men at his heels.

Assuring himself of the person of the Lady Anne had been only the first stage, though it had been one that had given him more pleasure than he expected — largely because the Anne of today was such an improvement on the Anne of yesterday.

He had remembered her, from his years in the household of the earl of Warwick before that gentleman's break with Edward, as a pale and nondescript little girl, a most unlikely daughter for the overpowering earl and his scarcely less overpowering lady. So, when he had stormed off from George's in search of her, he had done so in the resigned knowledge that a colourless wife was the price he had to pay for the power and possessions he so desperately needed. It had startled him a good deal to discover that she had changed almost beyond recognition, that there was now some-thing very taking about her, something which owed little to the neat prettiness of her features, her soft fair hair, her blue eyes and dainty figure. The episode in the kitchen might have been over-heated, in all senses, but he had still been aware of the sweetness of her expression, the sparkle of fun, the look of candid innocence. He had found himself liking her – a most unexpected bonus.

Now, having assured himself of the lady, he had to assure himself of her property. And that was a matter of some legal intricacy, since the 'Warwick inheritance', though vast, was not a single entity. Part of it was entailed, which meant that the law required it to pass from Warwick himself to his male next of kin. Part also consisted of estates which he had enjoyed in the rôle of husband to his countess, whose personal inheritance they were and which should have reverted to her when she became a widow. Strictly speaking, only the third and final part was available to be divided between his two daughters.

Or should have been.

But Warwick had been attainted for treason, and all his estates had passed to the crown. Whereupon Edward had used them to pay off his brothers for their help in restoring him to the throne. With a nod towards testamentary disposition, he had granted George's wife Isabel all the estates to which she might be assumed to have hereditary expectations. And to Richard he awarded the property belonging to the entail. Anne's rights, and her mother's, were ignored.

But, now, with Richard anxious to marry Anne for the half-share she should have had, as well as for the power of the Neville name, George was flatly refusing to part with anything. Royal grant, he maintained, took precedence over testamentary probability.

It was not, of course, as simple as that, and for weeks Richard's and George's attorneys had a highly enjoyable and profitable time, blessed by clients who failed to appreciate that their own inspirational meddling contributed nothing beyond extra noughts on their bill.

Just before Christmas, Francis decided that it was time he paid attention to his own affairs for a change — which included becoming better acquainted with his wife, to whom he had been distantly married for five years. It had been a match arranged in their childhood, and Nan, although now of an age to consummate the marriage, was still resident at her parents' home in the north and refusing to leave it. Francis knew he ought to do something about taking her to his family home at Minster Lovell in Oxfordshire, but it was desperately in need of repairs and improvements and he thought it might be unkind to insist.

Richard, asked for advice, said merely, 'You must do as you think best.'

When Francis returned to London in January, deep in gloom over the bigotry of his mother-in-law and hoping that her daughter hadn't inherited it — it was hard to tell, since she had done little but blush and look helpless — Richard greeted him briskly.

'I hope things went well? Now, pay attention. Edward has summoned George and myself to Sheen next month. He says he has been much irritated by public gossip and reports of violence involving our retainers, and that it is time for us to argue our cases before himself and his council.'

Francis knew better than to ask, 'Are you prepared?' Richard was always prepared.

2

THEY WENT by barge to the palace of Sheen, the delightful residence on the banks of the Thames begun by Henry V and completed by his son, three leagues upriver from London.

The scene that met them when, having landed at the water gate, they entered the hall of the royal lodgings, was less delightful. A platform had been erected at the end of the hall and five men sat lined up on it, the king in the centre under his canopy of state, wonderfully handsome and stately in a gold-on-black damasked robe over a gold-embroidered black tunic, and with a jewelled gold coronet on his fair head. The royal chamberlain, Lord Hastings, was on his right, pink-faced and white-haired, his wide mouth bracketed by deeply carved smile lines; and the royal steward, Lord Stanley, was on his left, a big, deceptively soldierly looking man with morose eyes, a large nose, and a small mouth. The two outer chairs were occupied by the queen's brother, Anthony Woodville, Earl Rivers, whose resemblance to her was striking, and a small, mean-faced bishop whom Francis failed to recognise.

'John Morton, bishop of Ely,' Richard murmured. 'A Lancastrian until last year, and a very sharp little lawyer who specialises in disputed wills. Edward admires his ability, if not his personality.'

Below the platform was a large square green-baize table strewn with document rolls and surrounded by officials wearing parti-coloured gowns of blue and white or brown and green. At the end of the table furthest from the king and facing him were already congregated Richard's and George's attorneys, distinguished by the coarsely woven white mesh cauls they wore on their heads.

There was to be no time wasted on the courtesies. As soon as George appeared with, like Richard, only one gentleman in attendance, there was a flourish of trumpets and the king declared the council in session.

'It appears to us unseemly,' Edward began in a very haughty way, 'that a dispute between two of the greatest nobles in the realm should have become the subject of common gossip and speculation. It is also unacceptable that men wearing the white boar badge of Gloucester and the black bull badge of Clarence should be unable to meet in the streets without resorting to fisticuffs or worse.'

Richard listened virtuously, but George, to the king's obvious exasperation, allowed his eyes to wander around the chamber, studying the people, the tapestries, the painted ceiling, and at one point sniffing audibly as if trying to identify the powerful smell of damp that was natural to a building standing on the banks of a tidal river. It caused several of those present also to sniff enquiringly, though less brazenly.

Francis thought what a rash fellow he was. After his treachery of the years 1469-71, when he had sought not only his brother Edward's crown but his life, he should have thought himself lucky to be still alive and free. A sensible man would have lain low, behaving quietly and responsibly for a while at least. But not George.

The king said, 'This being an advisory council, not a court of law, we are not bound by the formalities. Let the duke of Clarence begin the proceedings by stating his case.'

George cleared his throat sharply. 'The dispute concerns my ward, the Lady Anne Neville. The lady having been married outside this kingdom and then widowed, but being still of tender years and having no guardian, was put in my care by you, sire, because of my relationship to her as the husband of her sister, the Lady Isabel.'

He stopped for breath. Then, 'It is the responsibility of a guardian to arrange a suitable marriage for his ward . . .'

The king intervened. 'As I understand it, the Lady Anne is fifteen years old and therefore well above the legal age of consent. According to both secular and canon law' – he glanced at Bishop

Morton — 'she is entitled to reject a marriage that does not find favour with her.'

The bishop nodded, thin-lipped and narrow-eyed.

George was all injured innocence. 'I know that. But I am not trying to enforce an unwanted marriage on her. Rather the opposite. What I am doing is fulfilling my legal duty as her guardian by refusing permission for a marriage of which I cannot approve.'

The king glanced at Bishop Morton again, and the bishop said, 'It is a point well made. Perhaps you would be so good as to amplify it?'

Inaudibly, except to Francis, Richard breathed, 'Go on, George. Commit yourself.'

George's attorney rose on tiptoe to murmur in his ear but George shook his head and replied loftily, 'The proposed marriage is with Richard Plantagenet, duke of Gloucester, whom I believe to be a wholly unsuitable match for the Lady Anne.'

Briefly, there was silence. It was broken by the queen's brother, who was generally held to be a kindly, serious and honourable man — temperamentally so unlike his grasping and widely unpopular Woodville kin that he was whispered to be a changeling. He was just thirty years old, haggardly handsome, exactly of an age with the king and a dozen years younger than the other royal favourite, Lord Hastings, who was sitting next to him trying to look judicious but succeeding only in looking as if he could have done with an extra hour or two in bed that morning. As was the way with royal favourites, the two men detested each other.

With the studied air of nonchalance that characterised all his dealings, Lord Rivers said, 'Perhaps we may ask about the duke of Clarence's reasons for regarding the duke of Gloucester as an unsuitable match for his ward?'

It opened the gates for discussion of the real issue, the

inheritance. Francis could see Richard thinking, 'Thank you.'

George reacted badly. Rivers might be the queen's brother, but he was very much George's inferior in rank. 'No, you may *not* ask. I have made my decision on perfectly good grounds and I will not have my judgement questioned!'

'Oh, but you will,' said the king tartly. 'You have caused a great deal of trouble by disobeying our royal wish that the marriage should take place, and we require you to explain yourself.'

3

NO ONE could have described George's expression as that of a dutiful subject arraigned before his king. Upstanding, handsome, splendidly dressed in damasked blue, he was still unmistakably a younger brother resentful at always coming second.

'Now, see here, Edward,' he blurted, but before he could go any further the king stopped him with a sharp, 'Enough!'

When Edward took that tone, even George paid attention. He paused, turned to his chief attorney, and held out his hand for a roll of papers. He disguised his discomfiture well, Francis thought, even if there was a petulant twist to his lips as he turned back to the bench.

'Very well. I believe the character of the said duke of Gloucester to be such that he would not take properly tender care of a nobly born and gently reared young woman.'

Taking tender care of a young wife was such an unlikely qualification for a husband that smothered smiles were apparent all round the table. Wives were contributors of marriage portions and bearers of heirs, no more, unless a man were unnaturally lucky. And a wife whose husband treated her civilly and did not beat her could think herself equally lucky. What was Clarence talking about? Richard of Gloucester was a tough, loyal, sensible young man, a man of his time. What more could a young woman ask for?

'You will have to do better than that,' said the king. He had had to threaten his own wife with a dagger before she accepted him, and their marriage had been both successful and fruitful. Having a selective memory, he had forgotten that what had brought the dagger into play had been her resistance not to becoming his wife, but to becoming his mistress.

George said, 'Very well. The Lady Anne has been used to live in the greatest luxury, first as daughter of the earl of Warwick, the wealthiest noble in the land, and subsequently in my own care.'

'Kitchen maid,' Richard muttered, not quite under his breath. A few lips twitched among the officials at the table. The story had already gone the rounds.

'I do not believe,' George went on, plunging deeper into the mire, 'that the duke of Gloucester is sufficiently well endowed with titles and estates to maintain her in the style to which she is accustomed.'

The king and his four advisers stared disbelievingly at him for a moment. Then the king said, 'That can be remedied easily enough.'

'No, it can't. Not if I have anything to do with it!' George met his brother's eyes unflinchingly, secure in his own illicit power. He had rebelled against Edward before, and everyone knew that he would do so again if thwarted. Edward had been dethroned once, and the threat of a repetition ought, George was convinced, to be enough to frighten him into favouring George himself over Richard, who was, and probably would always remain, selflessly loyal.

He thought he had won when Edward said, 'I believe this might be a suitable moment for us to retire and refresh ourselves with a cup of wine. We will convene again when the bells ring for *sext*.'

4

THE KING and his councillors having departed the hall, servants appeared with leather jugs of ale and wooden drinking bowls for those left behind, who had already gravitated into small, gossipy groups. George threw a single, triumphant glance at Richard and then became immersed in conversation with his attorneys.

Richard said, to Francis's mild surprise, 'Let us go outdoors and breathe some fresher air.' It was a typically dull, cold and unpleasant February day, and the wide, brown, sluggish river smelled anything but fresh.

However, there was someone else enjoying the scene – the big-nosed, balding, expensively dressed but indefinably slovenly-looking royal steward, Lord Stanley, who had clearly just been relieving himself into the river. Francis, introduced to him and surprised by the limpness of his handshake, knew of him as the head of a powerful family with vast estates and followings in the Midlands and the North-West, a man with a reputation for wiliness and an amazing talent for ending up on the winning side, whichever side that happened to be.

'Can't talk now,' Stanley said. 'Everything's *sub judice*, wouldn't be proper.'

Richard nodded gravely. 'No.' He gestured around. 'The weather does not look promising.'

'Oh, I don't know.' Stanley glanced towards the sky. 'I think it will clear. You should have a more – ah – settled trip back to London.'

'Really?'

Stanley nodded and turned away.

Nothing could have appeared more innocent or uncontrived. Richard's eyes sparkled. 'Good. That sounds hopeful. Now let us wait for the noon bell to summon us back indoors.'

5

IT WAS Lord Stanley who re-opened the proceedings. 'It appears desirable to our lord the king that this council be reminded of the situation concerning the redistribution of what is known as the Warwick inheritance.'

George sighed gustily.

'Upon the death in battle of the late, traitorous earl of Warwick,' Stanley went on, 'George, duke of Clarence, in right of his wife, the Duchess Isabel, took arbitrary possession of the late earl's titles and lands, the duchess being the elder of the earl's two children, both daughters. Certain of the earl's estates – those legally entailed to his male next-of-kin – were exempt from this arrangement.

'However, the late earl, by bearing arms against the king when the royal banner was displayed, had been guilty of treason, which carries the penalty of forfeiture. The inheritance in its entirety, therefore, reverted to the king. Errr . . .'

Stanley held out a large hand and waggled his fingers, and after some frantic shuffling one of the officials at the green baize table handed a document roll up to him.

'Errr . . . Yes. The king, of his generosity and in recognition of the duke of Clarence's assistance in restoring him to the throne, then chose to grant the duke all those lands to which the duchess had hereditary expectations. The king similarly, in recognition of Richard, duke of Gloucester's loyal services, granted to him all that part of the Warwick inheritance entailed to Warwick's male next-of-kin.'

George interrupted, 'And *that* was ill-judged! Male Gloucester may be, but he's a long way from being next-of-kin. I'm nearer in line myself.'

Lord Hastings, on the platform, grinned mischievously, as if to say, 'Don't you wish you'd thought of that before!' while Stanley replied evasively, 'Certainly you were both kin through your mother, the sister of the late earl. But that is not the issue.'

'No, I agree. It isn't,' George said. 'The issue is that the king my brother granted me *everything* to which my wife had hereditary expectations, and I don't see why I should share it with anyone.'

Coolly, Richard's voice broke in. 'Careful, George. Royal grants can be taken away as easily as they are made.'

The king said acidly, 'Thank you, Richard.'

'It appears to me,' intervened little Bishop Morton, 'that there may be some question about the definition of the Duchess Isabel's "hereditary expectations". Am I correct in thinking that the duke of Clarence believes these to include the properties and titles which she *may* ultimately inherit from her mother, the countess of Warwick, when that lady is gathered to God?'

George said, 'Of course.'

'So that, although the countess's possessions *should* have reverted to her on the death of her husband, who had legal title to them only during his lifetime, the duke of Clarence has appropriated them on his wife's behalf.'

George said, 'Of course. The king my brother granted me *everything* to which my wife had hereditary expectations, and that includes what will naturally come to her when her mother dies.'

The king frowned. 'I did not intend the countess to be dispossessed of her rightful property in the meantime.'

'Then you should have been more careful, shouldn't you?'

George sounded as if this was a schoolroom squabble rather than a royal enquiry.

Francis shook his head to clear it, and glanced at Richard, whose face showed the same weary tolerance as everyone else's. George was always so convinced of his own rightness that he couldn't conceive of any sensible man thinking otherwise, which helped to explain his manner, even if it didn't justify it. It was a constant source of irritation to those around him that, although he had a perfectly good brain, he used it only in the context of his own obsessions. Richard had said once, 'George is like an attorney who knows everything about the law but fails to recog-nise that a brain can be useful for other, everyday things like deciding where to hammer in a nail on which to hang his hat.'

Richard stepped forward. 'May I speak, sire?'

'Do!'

'May I suggest that much of the present difficulty could be resolved if the matter of the inheritance were treated as just that, an orthodox inheritance dispute uncomplicated by royal grants – or their wording.' He smiled charmingly at Bishop Morton, who looked unimpressed.

But to others Richard sounded like a sensible man. Everyone knew that the uncertainty associated with royal grants was a perennial source of worry to the recipients. So if everything could be settled on the routinely legal basis of natural inheritance, the king's two quarrelsome young brothers might go away and let everyone else get on with their lives in peace.

'Let us, for the time being,' Richard went on, 'leave the matter of the countess of Warwick's possessions in abeyance. Let us also think further about the entail of the late earl's own possessions. His closest male kin is, of course, the young duke of Bedford, whose father, like Warwick, died a traitor and should therefore be forfeit.'

Francis, aware that Richard was no more interested than George was in the rights of young Bedford or the deprived countess of Warwick, wondered whether Richard wasn't, in fact, digging a pit for himself to fall into.

The bishop was shaking his head and grimacing disapprovingly – what a spiteful-looking little man he was, Francis thought – but his expression changed suddenly and his mouth rounded into an 'Ouch!' as Lord Stanley gave him a hearty kick on the shin, which Francis observed with pleasure from where he was standing, but which no one else seemed to notice.

Richard's words sounded perfectly rational, and Francis wondered if he himself was the only man present to whom they also sounded distinctly slippery. Young Bedford could probably fend for himself, but the countess, in sanctuary at Beaulieu, seemed to have no one to speak for her, although rumour had it that she was speaking quite vociferously for herself. It had not previously occurred to Francis, orphaned as a child and brought up in largely masculine company, that being a woman might be almost as difficult as being a man, in a different way, of course. So absorbed was he in this revelation that he almost missed what came next.

'. . . principles of natural justice,' Richard was saying. 'Then that part of the Warwick inheritance which is available for distribution to his heirs of the body ought properly to be divided between his two daughters, Isabel and Anne.'

The king and the members of his council nodded sagaciously. So, too, did the queen, now seated with her ladies behind but not quite hidden by a screen in the corner of the hall. No one asked Richard to define what he meant by 'available'.

Unbelievably, George laughed aloud. It did not appear to be a calculated response, more as if he had suddenly been struck by a clever and pleasing thought.

Richard raised a politely enquiring eyebrow.

George said, 'I withdraw my opposition to your marriage with the Lady Anne.' Everyone looked at him. 'But even if the law requires her to benefit from the Warwick inheritance – which I will resist with vigour, since that would mean my being deprived of what has been royally granted to me – you will have to be *legally* married to her. And you may find that a problem!'

6

A FEW DAYS LATER, the Lady Margaret Beaufort, interviewing her prospective fourth husband, said with deceptive naivety, 'And what, Lord Stanley, did the duke of Clarence mean by that?'

Stanley, much more interested in his own marital prospects than in Richard of Gloucester's, shrugged his heavy shoulders and said, 'Papal dispensations and that kind of thing.'

'And that kind of thing?' the Lady Margaret repeated, dropping her eyes to her little golden goblet with the daisy on its cover. In the course of her twenty-eight years, she had learned the knack of innocent enquiry. Usually, it brought her the answers she expected, but sometimes there was a small nugget of extra information that proved to be of value.

'Richard of Gloucester and Anne Neville are related several times within the prohibited degrees of affinity. Clarence had enough difficulty extracting a dispensation from Rome when he married Lady Isabel in sixty-nine, because they were first cousins and Lady Isabel was also his mother's godchild. In Richard's case, the same impediments apply, with the additional one that his brother and Lady Anne's sister are man and wife. So if he doesn't get a papal dispensation, he won't be properly married in the eyes of the church and won't have any rights in the Warwick inheritance at all, even if the king's council decides that the Lady Anne is entitled to part of it.'

Absently, she said, 'We have a new pope now. Perhaps he may be more flexible than the last.'

Stanley guffawed. 'I'm sure he will. He's a della Rovere, and that's a family that knows what the world is about. But while a *quid pro quo* will always buy flexibility, I doubt if young Diccon has any to offer.'

'I suppose not.'

They were at Margaret's favourite residence, the moated and castellated manor known as Woking Old Hall, set among orchards, gardens and a deer park, and conveniently accessible by river from London. Stanley had been reassured to discover how many servants there were and how well maintained everything was. The counting house had recently been reroofed and the stables repaired; there were sheep and cattle sheds, a poultry house and a fishpond. Inside the Hall, the walls were hung with fine tapestries representing not scenes of piety, which he would have expected, but Classical epics, tales of kings and heroes – the labours of Hercules, the lives of Samson, Saul, and Nebuchadnezzar.

There was no reason for him to know that the pewter and glass on the table and the magnificent canopy of crimson sarcenet under which he and Lady Margaret dined had been specially ordered for a visit from King Edward three years before and had been packed away and rarely used since. Lady Margaret brought them out only when she wished to impress, and it was seldom that she needed or desired to impress.

'However, let us discuss our own marriage.' Stanley smiled ingratiatingly and, not for the first time, Margaret wondered why she was proposing to marry a man almost ten years older than she was, twice her size and with half her intelligence. But she knew

41

the answer. He was powerful, and available, and she needed him.

She was a wealthy woman with lands scattered widely across the country, always under attack from others who claimed rights in them. Holding on to her estates took up almost as much time and effort as managing them. She had no intention of being caught in the same kind of trap as the unfortunate countess of Warwick, who had no powerful supporters and was being treated as if she were already dead because the dukes of Clarence and Gloucester wanted her possessions for themselves.

Margaret, on the other hand, wanted *her* possessions for her son, who had been born to her when she was thirteen years old and already a widow, under circumstances of such pain and torment that she could never bear a child again. Above all, she wanted his title back for him, the title of earl of Richmond which, because of his blood relationship to King Henry VI − his father, her then husband, had been Henry's half-brother − had been taken away from him some years before by King Edward and bestowed on the duke of Clarence. Who refused to part with it again.

She weighed up the question of how Clarence would react to the resolution of his dispute with the duke of Gloucester. If he won, there would be no holding him; he was not a generous man and would not be prepared to give up anything. If he lost, he would cling to what he had, unless the king chose to bring him to heel by further depriving him. In that case, Stanley's influence might well be decisive in retrieving the honour of Richmond for fifteen-year-old Henry, now in voluntary exile in Brittany. She had urged him to go, because she feared what the king might do if he stayed. The king's promises of safety and security were not to be trusted and she knew that Edward must think he had every reason to feel vindictive towards any potential Lancastrian claimant to his throne.

She had only a mild interest in the wellbeing of the Lady Anne

Neville, briefly wife to the late prince of Wales, one of her own multitude of nephews-by-marriage, and no feeling at all — other than a vague dislike — for Richard of Gloucester who, after Tewkesbury, had dragged her cousin Edmund Beaufort, duke of Somerset, out of sanctuary and executed him at the king's command. But she prayed devoutly that Gloucester would emerge triumphant, because George of Clarence badly needed to be cut down to size.

'. . . my lady must be guaranteed an income of not less than three hundred and thirty pounds a year from your estates in Cheshire and North Wales,' her receiver-general Reginald Bray was saying to Lord Stanley as she turned back to the business in hand.

'And you in return, my lord,' she intervened, 'will of course have a life interest in my own estates, which I hope may be expanded with the passage of time.'

Stanley had a fairly shrewd idea of what was on her mind, and nodded approval. She was a remarkable woman, refined of feature, gracious and charming in manner, more than conventionally pious, tiny in stature and looking as if a puff of wind would blow her away, but as strong-minded in pursuit of her own ends as any man he could think of. If they had both been younger, her personality might have posed a problem, but they were two mature and experienced people and, in any case, need not see more of each other than they wanted to. He suspected that the bedchamber would be out of bounds, but substitute wives were easy to come by at Edward's court. Edward was always looking for candidates to whom he could pass on his discarded mistresses.

Margaret, elegant in black velvet trimmed with ermine and pearls, her hair invisible under the face-framing widow's barbe, had the feeling that Stanley would soon fall into the habit of referring to her as 'my clever little wife'. Just as long as he did not do so in her hearing . . .

7

'I WILL MARRY Anne at Middleham immediately after Easter,' Richard said. 'In the village church. In style. Archbishop Neville can conduct the service. And that,' he added with satisfaction, 'should leave no one in any doubt that I am the true inheritor of all Warwick's power and influence in the north.'

The king and his council had chosen to ignore the niceties of the dispute over the Warwick inheritance and, on March 18th, had reached a decision that all of it, without exception, was in the king's gift and divisible according to his wishes. George was to give up some lands to the Lady Anne and, in return, received a promise that if the king, at some future date, were to take back any of the estates he held by royal grant, he would be suitably compensated. The dilemma of the countess of Warwick – alive, but treated by the law as if she were dead – was not confronted, and George continued to administer his share of her estates as his own. Richard would do the same with those transferred to Anne.

It was a compromise that satisfied no one except the king. 'Principles of division' were of limited usefulness to those more interested in the practicalities of it – practicalities such as who was entitled to collect rents from which estates without the risk of becoming embroiled in a fight.

Francis said, 'But Richard, what about the p⁄p⁄papal dispensa⁄tion for your marriage? *That* isn't going to arrive from Rome within the next t⁄t⁄two or three weeks.'

'No. The Curia is famously slow about such things.'

'Even if it is granted at all.'

Richard shrugged.

Francis grinned, remembering Richard lecturing George a few months earlier about his intended match with the Lady Anne. 'I propose doing things correctly,' he had said. 'There have been quite enough clandestine marriages in our family already.' And George had exploded, 'Nothing clandestine about *my* marriage. Isabel's father gave us his blessing and we were married in public by an archbishop of the church!' Did Richard recognise the irony of having that same archbishop preside over his own canonically clandestine marriage?

'So what are you going to d⁄d⁄do about it?'

'If it comes, well and good. If it does not, no one need know. We will simply behave as if it *has* come.'

8

ANNE was so relieved when Francis arrived to take her away from sanctuary at St Martin's le Grand and escort her home to Middle⁄ham that she disgraced herself by flinging her arms round him.

'What a delight to be going home! It's almost two years since my father took me to Margaret of Anjou's horrid, cold, poverty⁄stricken court⁄in⁄exile at Koeur to marry the prince of Wales. And then I was dragged along on their stupid invasion of England, which *anyone* could have seen was doomed to fail. And then I had to hide with her in that convent near Tewkesbury. And then I found myself as George's ward and having to do what he said. And now I have had six months of unbearable idleness in St Martin's, with only one five⁄minute visit from Richard — complete with entourage! — to enquire after my well⁄being. Oh, Francis! Where is my horse? Let us get on the road *at once!*'

He laughed back at her. 'I have a pretty little palfrey for you, and no, we are not going to ride north at a full gallop. Think of your dignity or, if not yours, think of Richard's.'

She had changed a good deal in her two adventurous years, from a fair, composed and rather anonymous little girl into a positive and lively-minded young woman. Francis liked the new version even when physical weariness began to take its toll. She had always had a delicate constitution.

At one point, he asked anxiously, 'Should I have brought a litter for you? I didn't think of it.'

'Certainly not.' Her smile reappeared. 'I can see that you have never travelled in a horse litter. You are jiggled around unmercifully, jarred by every bump in the road, made seasick by the swaying, and when the leading horse stops suddenly, the rear horse collides with the back of the litter and throws you to the floor. Bruises, bruises, bruises. Thank you, no. In any case, we are in a hurry. Has Richard gone ahead, or is he following us?'

'Following. He had arrangements to make.'

'And so have I! Clothes! After two years as a vagrant, I have nothing to wear. I *must* be suitably attired for my wedding.'

Francis said, 'I believe you will find, when the sumpter horses are unloaded, that there are some rolls of sarcenets and velvets and cloth-of-gold. Richard thought you might need them.'

She blinked at him for a moment then, sounding as if she were holding back tears, managed, 'How kind of him. I feel as if no one has been kind to me for years.'

Francis said nothing. Kindness had not been at the top of Richard's list of priorities. As Anne's husband at Middleham, he would be publicly seen as Warwick's heir. This marriage was, to him, the ultimate symbol of his new power in the north and he was determined that it should be splendid.

9

IT WAS such a delightful spring day when the marriage was solemnised between the duke of Gloucester and the Lady Anne Neville that although she knew perfectly well that marriage, even lacking a papal dispensation, was a sacrament as well as a business arrangement, it was as much as Anne could do not to twinkle cheerfully at everyone within range.

She did not have any maidenly fears as to what the night would bring; had not done so even on the occasion of her first wedding. She supposed that having been reared in the countryside might have something to do with it; one could hardly remain ignorant of how domestic animals waxed fruitful and multiplied. But there was more to it than that. Although she herself was one of only two children, her father had been one of ten and her great-aunt – Richard's mother, the saintly Duchess Cicely – had been the eighteenth child of her father and had herself borne her husband twelve infants. So the act of marital intimacy, Anne had reassured herself, could not be so very shocking. And indeed it hadn't been shocking with the prince of Wales. But Jesu! it had been dull. She hoped that Richard, who was good at everything, would be good at that, too.

When they met at the church door, he nodded approvingly at her sky blue velvet robe with its trimming of cloth-of-gold, the deep V of its neckline displaying to perfection the wonderful sapphire necklace he had given her six months before. On her head was a tall, pointed hennin draped with fragile blue sarcenet. She and the sempstresses and her ladies-in-waiting had been stitching away all night and had finished only an hour before the ceremony, but it had been worth it. She smiled with mock graciousness at her husband-to-be and nodded approvingly back at his own blue doublet embroidered with the white roses of

York, surmounted by a long gown of darker blue cloth-of-gold damasked with the insignia of the Order of the Garter and lined with white satin. He was a handsome, hard-looking young man and, since she herself was small and slender, his lack of height did not trouble her.

And then the proceedings began on the steps of the church, with hundreds of Yorkshiremen, their dogs and their horses as far from silent witnesses.

Richard did not raise his voice as he spoke of the dower his wife would receive from him − £133 a year − and held out to her an open book on which rested a gold ring. The parish clerk waved his aspersion, sprinkling it and them with holy water, and then she placed her right hand in Richard's and he slipped the ring on and off the thumb, the forefinger and the middle finger, murmuring in turn, 'In the name of the Father, the Son, and the Holy Spirit,' before placing it finally on the fourth finger where it was destined to remain.

'With this ring, I thee wed, with this gold I thee honour, and with this dowry I thee endow.' And then it was time for them to turn away into the church for prayers and Mass and a final blessing of their marriage.

Anne's uncle, George Neville, Archbishop of York, was forty years old, a clever, ambitious and learned man and an astute politician. Anne was pleased that he had agreed to conduct the ceremony, because she was fond of him and knew that Richard was, too.

Afterwards, with Richard walking by her side and the church bells still gaily ringing, she was carried back the short distance to the eastern gate of the castle in a ridiculously extravagant litter draped with garlands of gilded leaves and enamelled flowers.

The wedding feast was a splendid affair. Richard and Anne sat under a bright red canopy of state on a dais at the end of the

Great Hall with, at right angles to it, long tables for their most distinguished guests. Of Richard's immediate family, only one was present, his eldest sister, the duchess of Exeter; a somewhat inappropriate guest, Richard remarked with a hint of sourness, since she had just divorced her husband in order to marry her lover. The duke and duchess of Clarence, cynically invited, had chosen not to attend, while the king – who customarily kept the feast of St George, on April 22nd, at Windsor – had sent Lord Hastings to represent him.

Of Anne's family, there was a huge assortment of uncles, aunts and cousins, including her dislikable Aunt Alice FitzHugh and the limp little daughter who was Francis Lovell's wife. Aunt Alice, an unregenerate Lancastrian, detested the House of York and therefore loathed Richard – and Francis by association. Anne reflected that she must make an effort to help Francis sort out his domestic situation; he needed help, and she was as fond of him as if he were the brother she had never had.

But the vast majority of the guests were men who had previously supported her father, the earl of Warwick, and whom Richard hoped now to draw into his sphere of influence. Glancing along the tables, Anne saw Percies of Northumberland, Nevilles of Westmorland, Beauchamps, Scropes and Greystokes, and guessed that lesser members of the same families were seated with an assortment of judges, lawyers, clergy, aldermen and squires at further tables in the Great Chamber, through the doorway from the Great Hall.

There were carved wooden partitions at the far end of the Hall, screening off the pantry and the buttery. The kitchens were on the floor below, and Anne had almost forgotten how many cold draughts and cooking smells came sweeping up the staircase along with the gentlemen waiters as the dishes were brought in in procession, with the marshal of the hall shouting 'By your leave, my masters!' and everyone standing up and taking off their hats and waiting while the server and carver and cupbearer went on bended knee before the bridal pair.

It was a lavish feast. In the first course there were venison with frumenty, roast beef, roast swan, lampreys in galantine sauce, a custard with dates and prunes. Then came an interval when the company was entertained by acrobats and tumblers, mummers, jesters and musicians, and afterwards the second course offered a soup of chicken in almond milk, roast pig, roast crane, roast rabbit, chicken glazed golden with egg yolks, spicy fish pie, and – to Anne's relief, since her appetite had deserted her – some light and fragile little pastry fritters filled with raisins of Corinth.

'Sumer is icumen in,' warbled the singers, almost inaudibly in the rising din of hundreds of well-fed guests gossiping about politics, and rents, and the wickedness of the Scots on the other side of the Border.

After three hours, it was time to clear the boards and, meditatively, when the archbishop had pronounced the grace after meat, Anne watched the castle almoner march round the Hall with his basket, collecting the bread trenchers soaked with sauces and drippings from the dishes for which they had served as platters, for distribution as alms to the poor. She was beginning to feel the effects of lack of sleep and wondered whether she could slip away for a brief rest during the hours of sport and dancing that lay ahead. The prospect of thereafter sitting through a lengthy supper did not appeal to her at all, but was unavoidable.

She shuddered slightly, and Richard interrupted his conversation with her Uncle George – reminiscing about the famously ostentatious feast he had held to celebrate his enthronement as archbishop of York – to raise an enquiring eyebrow. 'I am finding all this a little tiring,' she confessed, and he said, 'You will have to get used to it.'

'What? To getting married?'

'To great banquets.' He grinned and turned back to her uncle. 'As I remember, your guests and their servants numbered well over two thousand people . . .'

10

THE DAY ended at last. The Compline bell rang and Richard and she, their hair full of the seeds, symbols of fertility, that had been showered upon them, went publicly to bed. The bedclothes were drenched with incense and holy water but the guests crowding into the chamber also brought with them an overpowering smell of wine and ale. The ever-present jester pranced up to the great fourposter and tapped Richard and Anne in turn with his bauble, his badge of office, chirruping something that was no doubt intended to be witty. Anne could not hear him above the noise, but did not feel that she had missed anything. As jesters went, he was not a very good one.

At last, in response to calls for silence, the noise diminished, and Archbishop George raised his voice and his hands to bless the marriage bed. 'God of Abraham, Isaac and Jacob, bless these young people and sow in them the seed of eternal life, that it may spread throughout the length of days and down the ages . . .'

It was some time before they were left alone, but when everyone had been more or less forcibly ejected from the room, Anne leapt out of bed, exclaiming, '*What* a relief.'

'I beg your pardon?'

'These seeds. Spread throughout the length of days, indeed! They're spread throughout the whole length of the bed. I feel as full of perforations as a sieve.'

Together, they brushed the seeds out and, since they were both in a reprehensibly frivolous state of mind, ended by laughing so much that there was no trace of embarrassment when they fell into each other's arms.

She had been right in guessing that Richard would prove less dull in bed than her first husband. Since he had already fathered two bastards – she must ask him about those some time, but not quite yet, perhaps – he had presumably had more experience.

Somewhere in the middle of the night, lying with her head on Richard's shoulder and his arm around her, Anne murmured, 'How lovely it is to be home.'

'Home?' Richard repeated drowsily. 'What do you mean by "home"?'

'The place where you belong! Where you always come back to. Where you *know* you will be more contented than anywhere else in the world. You know perfectly well what I mean!' Then, suddenly tentative, 'Don't you?'

He chuckled. 'I know the theory, but the practice has always managed to escape me.'

She cocked her head enquiringly.

He had no desire to talk, and he smoothed one hand tantalisingly down the length of her body as he said, 'My first eight years were spent at Fotheringhay, which my mother loved. But since then, through no particular fault of mine, it has been two months here, four months there, six months somewhere else.'

'You had four years here at Middleham, learning to be a knight,' she pointed out.

'Yes – and being a member, however junior, of your father's train meant that, everywhere he went, I went too. If you think back, you will remember that he was very rarely here.'

'That's true, I suppose. Oh, *poor* Richard! To have been nothing but a vagabond all your life. Something will have to be done . . .'

'Undoubtedly.' He moved, purposefully.
'*Richard!*'
All in all, it was a most enjoyable night.

11

A FEW DAYS LATER, the king arrested Archbishop Neville and deported him to prison in Calais, England's foothold in France.

Richard was annoyed. It was not only that he had a personal liking for the politically unprincipled but intellectually stimulating archbishop, but that by imprisoning the most distinguished member of the Neville family Edward seemed to be undermining Richard's attempts to reach a *modus vivendi* with the traditional Neville supporters in the north.

No formal statement was issued from court, but rumour had it that Edward proposed absorbing the revenues of the see of York into the royal treasury; that he had taken personal possession of the archbishop's extensive store of worldly goods; and that he had ordered the precious stones to be removed from the archbishop's magnificent, jewelled mitre and used to make a new crown for himself.

'Oh, dear!' Anne said. 'Uncle George will be *miserable* in that dreadful place, with not even his books to console him. Can you not speak to your brother on his behalf?'

It was then she discovered that Richard, though he didn't usually allow it to show, was somewhat in awe of his brother. 'I'm sure he has good reasons of policy for what he has done. I just wish he would tell me what they are!'

No explanations were forthcoming, so in September Richard despatched Francis to London to discover tactfully what was going on.

Francis soon discovered that a great deal more was going on than met the eye, but it was not easy to make sense of it. Although he himself had gained greatly in assurance over the preceding year, had more or less stopped stammering and blushing, and had even stopped growing, he couldn't − or not without a juvenile giggle − imagine himself saying outright to the king, 'Please, sire, your brother of Gloucester wants to know what is going on.'

Unfortunately, Lords Hastings and Stanley, the sources on whom he had been relying, both proved to be suffering from an acute attack of discretion, partly explained by the presence at court of the seigneur de Gruuthuse.

It was de Gruuthuse, as Burgundian governor of Holland, who had taken Edward and Richard under his wing when they had fled to the Low Countries almost two years before, but this return visit, Francis discovered, was not simply a return of hospitality. Edward had reached the limit of his patience with King Louis XI of France, a sly and clever man who amused himself by trying to manipulate English affairs; any traitor who fled from England could be assured not only of a welcome from Louis but, if required, of practical assistance with men and money. Now, Edward intended to teach him a lesson by invading France, but wanted first to be assured of support from the independent duchies of Brittany and Burgundy, who weren't fond of Louis, either.

The diplomatic situation was delicate, and talking about it was frowned on, although Francis soon learned that the wheels of diplomacy had been well oiled with gifts to the seigneur de Gruuthuse − among them a pretty but pointless crossbow strung with silk, and a gold cup garnished with jewels and containing that most valued specific against poison, a piece of unicorn horn. It was seven inches long − a *very* expensive statement of goodwill.

As for Archbishop Neville, he, it seemed, had suffered from

being on the fringes of the French manoeuvres.

Or so Francis eventually discovered from no less a person than the queen, who deigned to receive him during the dancing that followed a spectacular banquet in her Great Chamber at Windsor.

On one knee before her, he began by expressing his admiration of the chamber.

'Yes,' she said a little pettishly, 'it is very fine when all the candles are lit, but it needs more daylight. The king has agreed to have a bay window added for me. Do you have large windows at – Minster Lovell, is it?'

'Not at present, though I too hope to embark on building works . . .'

He risked rising to his feet, since it was abundantly clear that she had no interest in him or Minster Lovell. Her eyes were on her six-year-old daughter, the Princess Elizabeth, who was executing a stately *basse danse* with the young duke of Buckingham.

Francis knew where his duty lay. 'The princess your daughter is a very lovely and very accomplished little girl. You must be proud of her.'

He was horrified to see tears come to the queen's eyes, eyes that he now observed to be brown rather than the blue her fairness would have suggested.

'Yes,' she said. 'I also have two other lovely little girls.' Then, her voice becoming uneven. 'I had three, but my new baby Margaret has been taken from me, only a few weeks after she was born.'

Francis, as cowardly as any other man in the face of a woman's emotions, resisted the desperate instinct to look around for escape. But he was rescued just as he had begun to blurt, 'Oh, dear, how sad,' by a female voice which turned out to belong to a very small lady in brown velvet and pearls who had materialised at the queen's side.

'Madame, you are distressed. May I be of help?'

Francis was startled to see the queen's pathetic expression freeze and then reshape itself into one of unmistakable loathing. He wished even more devoutly that he were elsewhere.

'Ah, Lady Margaret,' the queen said acidly. 'You are going to raise my spirits by reminding me how fortunate I am to be the mother of six living children, and perhaps others in the future, when you have only one child and no hope of more.'

The solicitude on Lady Margaret's small pointed face did not abate. 'No, madame, I know what bereavements you have suffered . . .'

'I have been bereft of my mother, too, this year. Did you know? Her death hastened by your own unprincipled acquisition of her dower rights in the Kendal estates.'

'I think not, madame. It is not earthly troubles but the grace of Our Lord that decides when His lambs are gathered unto Him.'

The queen having thus been reduced to speechless fury, the lady turned to Francis and said, 'You're young Lovell, I hear. I knew your father.' It was more than Francis had done. 'You have come from Middleham. And how is my niece?'

Only then did Francis realise that this must be the Lady Margaret Beaufort, now the wife of Lord Stanley. Laboriously, he worked it out. As the erstwhile widow of the half-brother of the late King Henry VI, she would be aunt by marriage to Henry's son, Edward of Lancaster, the late *soi-disant* prince of Wales, to whom Anne had been briefly married. Which did make Anne a niece. Of sorts.

'She is well and happy, I believe.'

'I was sorry to have missed the wedding ceremony, but my own nuptials were close upon me and I was much engaged.'

While Francis tried to remember whether Lady Margaret had even been invited, the queen found her voice again, directing it at

Francis. 'It was a disappointment to the king that Duke Richard should have invited that traitor, Archbishop George Neville, to conduct the ceremony.'

Since the archbishop had been brother to Richard Neville, earl of Warwick, who had not only rebelled against the queen's husband but executed her father and one of her brothers without trial, it was not to be expected that she would be an admirer of the Nevilles. But to call the archbishop himself a traitor? He was surely too clever for that.

'Traitor?' Francis said.

'The earl of Oxford is his sister's husband. An implacable opponent of the king, as I am sure you know, and at present in France harassing our garrison in Calais.' Francis did know, since the earl of Oxford had been attainted and Edward had generously granted all his possessions to Richard. 'The archbishop,' the queen went on, 'was in secret communication with him.'

The small lady in brown said, in a tone full of meaning, 'And so, it is believed, were others.'

She and the queen, in sudden accord, glared across the room at George, duke of Clarence, who was occupied in giving the king and the seigneur de Gruuthuse the benefit of his opinion on some matter on which they were probably better informed than he. They were bearing it well.

It was a release when the little Princess Bess came prancing across the room towards her mother, followed by the duke of Buckingham, a tall, supercilious, handsome boy of about seventeen.

'Ah, nephew!' said the Lady Margaret, and Francis had to begin working things out all over again. This one was not too difficult. Lady Margaret's recently deceased third husband had been the younger brother of this boy's father.

The queen said, 'Your lady wife seems to have deserted us. It is not acceptable, without making a formal farewell. Has she been taken ill?'

'I shouldn't think so,' said the duke airily. 'I would have heard if there had been anything wrong.' His lady wife happened to be one of the queen's sisters, and he had been married off to her, willy nilly, when he was ten. Rumour had it that he detested her, and all her kin.

But it occurred to Francis that there might be a further reason why he and the queen were eyeing each other with dislike. Buckingham, besides being head of the richest and longest-established of the great landowning families and therefore Edward's mightiest subject, was also of royal blood and all too aware of it. It made the king nervous and frightened the queen, obsessive about the possibility, however remote, of competition threatening her two-year-old son, the heir to the throne.

Francis felt mildly faint. He had sometimes regretted having few relatives of his own, but that regret was suddenly swept away in a flood of purest gratitude.

12

RICHARD was chewing his lower lip in a way that had become familiar to Anne during the six months of their marriage. It meant that he was concentrating hard and would not even hear her if she said anything, or not if she said anything domestic and unimportant. He would hear, soon enough, if she told him that the Scots were at the gates.

She smiled at his secretary, who had glanced up from his busy scribbling to Richard's dictation, and went away.

'You are very occupied these days,' she remarked that afternoon, as they rinsed their hands before sitting down for supper in the

Great Chamber. For once, there were no guests of note to share their board – with the approach of winter the number of travellers seeking hospitality always diminished markedly – so that they were able to converse sensibly while they ate, interrupted only by the ceremonial bringing and taking away of dishes that were an inescapable adjunct of life in the household of a royal duke.

He said, 'Yes. If you are interested, I am endeavouring to make sense of the possessions that have been so generously bestowed on me by the king my brother. You know how scattered they are – from your father's estates here in the north to the others forfeited from the earl of Oxford and the leaders of the Lincolnshire rebellion, which are mainly in Essex and the eastern counties.'

Anne had been pleased and surprised that Richard found it possible to talk to her as if she were a rational human being, rather than just a wife. She had thought at first that it might be because, in his early youth, he had been brought up in a house full of sisters, ruled over by their dauntless mother, the Duchess Cicely. But then she reflected that the same could hardly be said for George, three years older, who had been there too.

She had mentioned it to Francis, who had said, 'It's just how Richard is made. True friendship is a rare commodity on the upper levels of society – too many people have too many axes to grind – and Richard values his friends accordingly.'

'Even if they happen to be women? Or wives?'

Francis had laughed. 'I don't think he even notices.'

'Oh, yes, he does!'

But the marriage bed, she had to admit to herself, was more a friendly than a passionate place. Pleasure certainly, and affection, perhaps, but not much more. Neither her nor Richard's emotions were engaged, but that was no bad thing. It left them both their independence of spirit. It meant, too, that when Richard was away, as he increasingly was – trying to establish a working relationship with Henry Percy of Northumberland, settling local disputes, carrying out civic duties in York – they missed each other, but not to distraction.

Now, Richard went on, 'Add the offices of Constable and Admiral of England – I am almost grateful that I had to soothe George by relinquishing the post of Great Chamberlain to him – and you will see that I can't possibly administer them all. What I am trying to do, for a start, is put the records in order. Rights, titles, old documents, petitions, patents, and so on. Did your father, for example, allow his entitlements over knights' fees to lapse?'

'Goodness! *I* don't know.'

'I didn't think you would,' he said, his mouth turning down in mock dejection, and signalled to his cup bearer. He took a long, grateful gulp of ale. 'Ugh, how I dislike salt cod. Why am I eating it?' It was a fish day and the kitchens seemed not to have soaked the cod in as many changes of water as they should have done.

Anne said, 'This blandesorre of pike is good. Why don't you try it?' but Richard had already moved on.

'Once everything is written down I will be able to assess what has to be done to bring in a worthwhile income. George has four thousand five hundred pounds and does scarcely anything for it. I have nothing like that, yet the king is anxious for me to try and bring some order and unity into this lawless north.' He frowned. 'I cannot possibly do it without adequate funds.'

Anne's blue eyes danced. 'Perhaps I could help.'

Her husband eyed her suspiciously. 'Yes?'

'We-e-ll, if all else fails, I could always find paid employment as a kitchen maid, couldn't I?'

Chapter Three

1472-74

1

'POOR, helpless old lady? Ha!' With the hilt of his sword, Richard hammered on the door of the convent at Stratford le Bow. 'If she were poor, I would not be interested in her. And sixty years old she may be, but she has shown herself far from helpless. Open up! Open up!'

The door at last creaked open on the stately figure of the prioress, a heavy ring of keys in her hand and a very small nervous-looking nun, probably the gatekeeper, peering over her shoulder.

Fixed with a steely gaze that reduced him from a responsible twenty-year-old (plus a few weeks) to an obstreperous ten-year-old, even Richard was momentarily silenced. 'And who is it,' enquired the prioress, 'who so gracelessly demands entry to God's house of women?'

Pulling himself together, Richard said, 'I am Richard, duke of Gloucester,' and then, since this produced no softening of the lady's stare, added sulkily, 'brother to the king.'

'Indeed? Then you should know better than to hammer at gates.'

'I do so only when necessary.' Richard dismounted and tossed his reins to a groom. 'You have a guest here, I believe? The dowager countess of Oxford. I wish to speak to her.'

Without turning her head, the prioress said, 'Sister Aquilina, go and ask whether her ladyship is prepared to receive this — ah — gentleman.'

'Yes, Mother.' The little nun scurried away.

Silence reigned, except for the shifting of horses and rattling of harnesses. By the time the little nun returned, Richard was breathing heavily through his nose.

The nun whispered, the prioress inclined her head and stood aside, and Richard entered with Francis, Jocky Howard, John Pilkington, and others of his entourage at his heels.

2

IT WAS a very small Benedictine convent, and the dowager countess of Oxford had no doubt paid handsomely for the privilege of her private room, which contained a spartan white bed, a clothing chest, a pair of coffers, a wall shrine, a magnificent candelabrum, a shelf of parchments, and about a dozen lapdogs.

Warding off a pair of the yapping little beasts, Richard said without preamble, 'Madame, the king our master has awarded me the custody of yourself and your possessions. I have come to . . .'

The countess, clutching the crucifix at her breast, stopped him short. 'Oh, blessed Jesu, help me!' she wailed. 'Oh, blessed Lady, succour me!' and burst into a flood of noisy tears.

The dogs joined in.

Lord Howard bellowed, 'Silence!' but it had no effect.

Richard waited for a few moments and then, through the uproar, coldly made himself heard. 'The coffers and the parchments.'

Elbowing their way across the crowded little room, Sir John Pilkington and his servant possessed themselves of the required items and turned back towards the door, provoking cries of, 'No! No!' and an intensified volume of tears and prayers from her ladyship matched by a cacophony of howling from the dogs. Lord Howard swore coarsely as a set of teeth embedded themselves in his expensively booted calf and Pilkington's servant staggered under his load as he tried to aim a kick at one of the pack.

Francis bent to pick up a new-looking puppy, white and curly as a spring lamb, who appeared to be barking mainly because that was what dogs were supposed to do. It licked his cheek and settled contentedly in his arms, and he wondered whether the countess might be persuaded to part with it.

The commotion showed no sign of dying down and Richard said at last, 'This is impossible. My lady, you must come with us to Stepney, where my household is lodged, so that we may discuss matters sensibly.'

An audience had gathered in the snowy yard outside the convent, and the countess played to it unmercifully. 'Oh, blessed Jesu, help me! Oh, blessed Lady, succour me! Oh, Lord, in Thy goodness, have pity on this poor defenceless old lady.' But Francis noticed that she was sufficiently spry to mount her horse unaided. He sensed that the prioress was not sorry to see them go, especially when the dogs poured out of the gate after them, but there was some shouting from the idlers and a few stones were thrown. Rumours flew ahead and the number of bystanders and missiles steadily increased along the three slushy miles of their route back to London.

Richard was not used to being unpopular and by the time they reached Stepney he was in a furious temper.

3

'IT'S LIKE sitting under the Aysgarth Falls,' he said, when he had recovered himself. 'The woman never stops. If her husband had not been executed for treason, he must certainly have drowned.'

'Perhaps,' Francis offered, 'it explains why her son has taken to piracy.'

'Perhaps. But how am I to talk to her?'

'Lock up the dogs, for a start.'

'I have done so, but now she is howling because she has been parted from them. No, I will have to speak to her in private, with no one present but the lawyers. If there is no one to impress, perhaps she will moderate her lamentations. You may lurk behind the arras, if you wish. In fact, I'd be grateful if you did. It would be useful to have a witness to confirm my memory of what is said.'

'An unprejudiced observer?'

'Naturally.'

The shallow space between the arras and the wall was, in fact, already somewhat overcrowded when Francis slipped into position. Richard's chamberlain, Pilkington, was there, as were his retainers Sir James Tyrell and William Tunstall. After a moment or two, big Jocky Howard also came pushing in. Everyone frowned at everyone else, as if to say, 'Shhhh!' but Francis consoled himself with the thought that, if the countess did resort to weeping and wailing and gnashing of teeth, even a riot behind the arras would pass unnoticed.

She began, predictably enough, by demanding to know how

the duke of Gloucester could be so heartless, so cruel, so un-Christian, as to wish to deprive a poor, helpless, defenceless old lady of what little she possessed. Through a gap in the stitching of the arras, Francis saw that the kerchief with which she dabbed her eyes was of sufficient size to do duty as a Thames bargee's sail. It did not augur well.

'Let us leave my heart and my Christianity out of it,' Richard said. 'What we are concerned with is legality.'

The countess quavered, 'But you have no legal rights over my property.'

Cordially, Richard said, 'You have certainly done your best to make that so. As I understand it, as soon as it became apparent to you that your son had chosen the losing side in the recent wars and would most certainly be attainted and forfeited, you took swift action to protect your own estates. That does not seem to me, if I may say so in passing, to be the action of a "helpless" or "defenceless" old lady.'

'Yes, but . . .'

'Knowing that, on your death, your possessions would automatically pass not to your forfeited son, the earl of Oxford, but to myself, to whom they have been granted by the king, you issued leases on all your properties in such a way as to place them in trust – "enfeoffed to use" is the expression, as I am sure you remember – which, as the law stands, would enable you to bequeath them by Will instead of having them confiscated.'

Francis would have expected her to deny all personal knowledge of this legal trickery, to claim that she had acted on the advice of her attorneys without understanding the ins and outs of the case.

However, she made the mistake of saying, 'But the trust would in any event be invalidated if I chose to bequeath my estates by Will to an attainted person such as my son, the earl.'

Richard's satisfaction showed in his voice. 'Precisely. But you could bequeath them to a third party who might then convey them by some further trickery to your son. And that, I am sure, is what you intended.'

It was strange that she had such a quiet speaking voice but such a piercing howl. The arras wavered slightly as the eavesdroppers clapped their hands to their ears.

'I intended – oh, blessed Jesu, help me! – nothing against the law. I made only the arrangements that my attorneys recom~ mended. Oh, blessed Lady, succour me!'

'Then, if you intended nothing against the law, you must alter your arrangements so that they conform with the law.'

'No. I have done nothing wrong. *You* shall not have what belongs to me and my family. My sons would never forgive me.'

'You, and they, should have thought of that before. What you must now do is arrange for your lessees to release their rights in your estates to me.'

'Never!'

Everyone waited patiently for the flood to subside, although Francis was conscious of Jocky Howard, beside him, muttering impolitely under his breath. Francis himself couldn't decide whether to be sorry for the old lady, or not.

Richard said, 'This must be considered rationally. Then you will see that it is your only choice.'

'Never!'

With seeming irrelevance, Richard remarked, 'I cannot stay in London for very much longer. I must return to the north. If you have not, by the time I leave, been persuaded to review your position, then you will have to come with me so that we may continue our discussions.'

Her screech surpassed anything that had gone before. 'Such a journey in this great cold, through frost and snow! At my age!

I should not live to see the end of it. And my poor little dogs! And how would I be treated there if I did survive such jeopardy? Oh, cruel, cruel! You cannot force me to come with you.'

'The king has given me custody of your person as well as your estates. I can certainly force you to come with me, though I would much prefer not to. I would rather we settled things amicably here and now.'

'*Amicably!* How can I live if you take everything away from me?'

'I have no intention of leaving you destitute.'

Neither Richard's nor the countess's attorneys had so far raised as much as a murmur, but they came into their own when the haggling began.

4

IN THE end, it was settled that the countess herself and her lessees – willingly or by chancery suit if necessary – should release their rights to Richard and, by due process of law, confirm his title. In return, Richard agreed to pay the countess an annuity of £350 per year for life, to meet her outstanding debts of £240, and to advance the career of one of her sons who was studying divinity at the university of Cambridge.

'She can have her dogs back, too,' Richard said.

Just then a servant from Middleham arrived, bearing letters for him.

'How long since you left Middleham? Were the roads bad?' Richard demanded.

'Terrible, my lord. I have been in and out of snowdrifts all the way. It has taken me fourteen days.'

The only benefit of letters travelling so slowly was that most crises had resolved themselves by the time the recipient learned of them.

'Ah,' Richard said, opening one of the missives. 'Something from Anne.'

Francis could make nothing of the variety of expressions that chased one another over Richard's face as he scanned the single sheet – the widening of the eyes, the softening of the taut skin, the slight loosening of the uncompromising mouth, and finally the eyebrows snapping together into a heavy frown.

'God's bones! Not *another* old lady!'

5

ANNE WAS pregnant, sick and frightened. She should have been delighted, but she could not forget Isabel going into labour two years before with her first baby, aboard the ship on which George had been forced to flee from England. The ship, swooping and lurching in the rough April waters, had been greeted by cannon fire from Calais, and Isabel had screamed with seasickness and pain and terror as she gave birth to the baby girl who had died within hours. Anne and their mother had watched, helpless, as the physician who accompanied them showed how little he knew of midwifery.

Anne didn't expect to be aboard an overgrown cockleshell when the time came to give birth, but Isabel hadn't expected it either.

Now, mildly shocked at herself – she was, after all, a twice-married lady of almost seventeen – she discovered that she wanted her mother.

And wrote to Richard to say so.

6

FRANCIS was envious when he heard why. Thanks to his own mother-in-law, he had not yet been permitted even to consummate his marriage, and although Anne had spoken sternly to both her Aunt Alice and her cousin Nan, Francis's wife, it had been to no avail. Nan was too delicate, she was told, to take on the full responsibilities of marriage, too sensitive to be removed from her home in darkest Yorkshire to the unknown perils of rural Oxfordshire.

Where Richard did no more than soften at the news of his impending fatherhood, Francis would probably have been throwing his bonnet in the air.

Afterwards, characteristically, Richard spent less time pandering to his own emotions, as he put it, than to exercising his mind over the countess of Warwick.

'I will need the king's permission to extricate her from sanctuary at Beaulieu and take her to Middleham. Which will annoy George, who will suspect me, once I have her "in my power", of intending to make her surrender *all* her possessions to me, thus depriving him of the use of them which he has illicitly continued to enjoy for these last eighteen months.'

'And that would never occur to you, would it?'

'Of *course* not,' Richard said.

7

IT TOOK too long.

Receiving Richard's petition, the king conveyed, charmingly but unequivocally, that he had more important things to worry about than the duchess of Gloucester wanting her mother.

It came to Richard as a not altogether welcome surprise to find an ally in the queen. She smiled at him patronisingly and, to Edward, said, 'It is the Lady Anne's first child, my lord, and she is not yet seventeen. Her need for support is understandable. I believe you should grant Duke Richard's petition.'

Then she dropped her gaze to her embroidery. She had told no one that she herself, at thirty-five, was newly pregnant for the eighth time and, since she found herself walking slowly and had become perceptibly hollow-eyed, the signs were that the child would be a boy. She intended to keep the news from the king for as long as possible. She knew that his wandering gaze had recently alighted on a merchant's wife, pretty Mistress Shore, whom she suspected of being cleverer than his usual women and perhaps clever enough to take advantage of her own incapacity by becoming an established rather than a passing fancy. It was the most tiresome aspect of being pregnant, to have to forbid one's husband one's bed. But they both needed another son, and could not afford to take any risks.

'The case of the countess of Warwick is not as simple as that,' Edward said patiently, aware that 'not as simple as that' was becoming something of a litany. His wife and her innumerable relatives were always ready to tell him what to do, and although he made concessions to them as often as he was able – they were, after all, part of his family – there were times when it would have been inept to do so. 'I want no more trouble from George, and he will certainly go off in another of his tantrums if he thinks young Diccon here is in a position to influence the countess over the disposal of her property.'

Elizabeth was not disturbed by the thought of George going off in a tantrum. Far from it. The more troublesome he became, the more likely it was that her normally tolerant husband would lose patience and banish him out of harm's way. To the Tower, perhaps. Or the fortress of Hammes, near Calais.

She had mentioned it to her brother Anthony, Earl Rivers, who had drawled, 'Not Hammes. Too easy for him to conspire with the French.'

'Well, something must be done. You know how I detest the man, and I cannot feel easy when he is running loose with his eyes still on the throne.'

There had been no need for her to say more. When next she heard a rumour of George being involved in something treason-able, she would know the source of the rumour. When next he behaved outrageously, she would know who had encouraged him. It was useful having a brother who made it his business to be trusted by everyone.

Richard said, 'I think, sire, that it might be politic to ask Parliament to make a final ruling on the countess's estates. Both George and I would accept that.'

His brother's fair face clouded. 'You might, but I doubt that George would if he suspected that Parliament was being manipu-lated. I take it that's what you're suggesting? When I think how tolerant of him I have been . . .'

'And how generous to him.'

'Too generous. And the only thanks I get is insolence and dabbling in treason. I hear rumours that he is still conspiring with the earl of Oxford and, through him, Louis of France.' Failing to observe the satisfied gleam in his wife's eyes, he concluded, 'As if I did not have enough to trouble me!'

It was one of Edward's talents that, however frequently he complained about his worries, he always succeeded in looking as if he did not have a care in the world. Tall, splendidly built, fair and handsome – save, perhaps, for his rather womanish rosebud mouth – he was the picture of majesty, friendly, assured, sympa-thetic, and as successful at charming men as he was their wives; all of which helped to mask the ruthlessness that was one of his most deeply ingrained characteristics.

His were talents that Richard himself, too wary to achieve instant rapport with strangers, sometimes envied. If they had been accompanied by more reliable judgement, Edward would have been the perfect king, but others often exercised judgement for him, and Richard had no high opinion of those who did – Hastings, boon companion; Stanley, shifty and self-interested; and the unctuous Anthony Rivers, brother to the queen and something of a moral enigma.

'In the meantime,' Edward said, 'the queen and Lord Rivers will soon be accompanying my son the prince of Wales to Ludlow, to set up his new household there. Even at two years old, a prince must begin learning to be a prince. I wish to extend royal control in Wales, which has never been reliably trustworthy, so I will join them at the end of May, and summon a conference of the local lords at Shrewsbury. But before then parliament has to be prorogued and I must hold a council to arbitrate on your dispute with Harry Percy of Northumberland over your spheres of influence in the north. I cannot spare you to go back to Middleham at this point.'

'All the more reason,' the queen interjected, 'for you to permit the countess of Warwick to go there to support her daughter in childbirth.'

Edward said, 'I'll think about it.'

8

HE THOUGHT about it until the beginning of June, when George, summoned to the conference at Shrewsbury, failed to turn up. 'That settles it!' Edward said, tight-lipped. 'If George cares nothing for my wishes, why should I care for his? Diccon, I still need you here, but you may arrange to have the countess of Warwick taken to Middleham.'

Richard sent James Tyrell to Beaulieu to collect the countess and escort her north – complaining all the way – but by the time she reached Middleham Anne had already borne her son. And lost him.

She had done everything the physicians advised, had eaten nothing salty or sweet or fatty; had drunk no ale; had walked as little as possible and ridden not at all. But she had felt ill, always, and the cruel headache never left her.

When she had been brought to bed, she had made her confession in case she died giving birth. The priest was shocked when she stoically managed a giggle and murmured, 'Not very reassuring, is it?' And then, of course, he had gone off to the church and set all the bells ringing to invoke the aid and favour of the saints. There was just time for her headache to become blinding before the birth pains began. The midwife, and Richard's old nurse Anne Idley, and every mature female Neville relative for miles around had warned her that she would have an agonising time because she was so slight and narrow-hipped. She had been prepared for that, but not for the succeeding agony of loss.

He had lived just long enough to be baptised, which all the women who had kept her company during her ordeal, praying and moaning with her throughout the long night and half the day, said was a great relief because it meant he would go to heaven.

She knew she should find solace in that but, somehow, she couldn't. More than anything, she wanted sympathy from some-one she really cared for. Richard, his constant attendance required by the king, could not spare the two or three weeks it would have taken him to travel from court to Middleham and back, and his letters showed characteristically little trace of emotion. Her sister Isabel wrote, but the letter was so carefully phrased that Anne guessed her sister had been in fear that George might read it.

And when her mother, whom she had not seen for two years, arrived in a state of weary snappishness after the discomforts of the journey, Anne's overwrought tears elicited little more than a brief embrace and a reminder that it was woman's fate to endure such torments as the good Lord decreed. Losing children was one of them.

'I do not know why I have been brought here,' she went on, returning to more important matters. 'My time in sanctuary has given me spiritual respite from the trouble and strife that marked the years of my marriage to your father, when he could think of nothing but power and how to achieve and maintain it. I cannot imagine that Middleham will be any more peaceful under the rule of young Richard of Gloucester. And I strongly object to being a pawn in this stupid game between him and George of Clarence, which I suppose is behind it all. What, oh blessed Jesu, have I done to deserve two such grasping sons-in-law? I take it you have no more influence over Richard than Isabel has over George? Well, we shall see what he has to say for himself . . .'

Vainly, Anne tried to stem the flow.

9

IT WAS six months before Edward's patience with George finally ran out. He had thought that awarding Richard control over the countess of Warwick – not being sufficiently acquainted with the lady to appreciate that 'control' was a meaningless concept where she was concerned — would force George to think, to realise that both his favour and his estates were at risk. To appreciate that good behaviour would be advisable.

But George, true to form, simply went on huffing and puffing, and declaring his intention of settling matters with young Diccon once and for all. There were other dark rumours, so that, when that perennial troublemaker, the earl of Oxford, subsidised by Louis of France, seized St Michael's Mount on the coast of Cornwall — strategically a very odd thing to do — most of the men of the king's court sent for their armour and waited for George to declare himself. No one had any doubt that he was meditating a renewed claim to the throne.

Edward said, 'Enough! George must learn that I do not make empty threats,' and Parliament dutifully passed an Act enabling the king to take back *all* the titles and estates he had given out to his various lords in the preceding years, unless he personally chose to sign provisos of exemption. He signed a proviso of exemption for Richard, but not for George.

By a stroke of the pen — or, more accurately, as Richard remarked, by *no* stroke of the pen — he deprived George of almost everything he had thought he owned, and not only on paper. This time, just to be sure that George paid attention, Edward appointed a commission to take physical possession of George's lands in the North Midlands, by force if necessary.

10

RICHARD, back at Middleham, said, 'I find it just a little odd that every single rumour of plot, counterplot or even local disaffection that comes to my ears should come with George's name attached. He must be as busy as a flea in a rat-run. Did you hear anything at court, Francis?'

Francis had just been in London for his own purposes. One of the estates he expected to inherit from his grandmother was Killerby on the River Swale, not far from Richmond, which was much in need of improvement, especially in its defences. It was near enough the Border to be at risk from Scots marauders, so he had a good case for asking the king to grant one of the official licences to crenellate that was necessary for any lord desirous of adding battlements to his property. The licence had been granted, so when Killerby became his there would be no hindrance to starting on the work, except finding the time, which was not easy. Although Richard was by no means demanding of those close to him, it was an undeniable fact that everyone's world revolved around him.

'I heard all the same rumours as you've heard, I suppose. They're common currency – so common, in fact, that I became inquisitive.'

'And?'

'I think – I *think* – that most of them are emanating from Anthony Rivers. I couldn't ask outright, of course, but I heard from someone, who had heard from someone, who had heard from someone else . . . Well, you know what I mean. I only succeeded in tracing two or three of the tales back to source, but that source was almost certainly Rivers.'

'You didn't, I take it, ask Rivers himself where *he* heard the stories?'

'No! I value my head and would prefer to keep it on my shoulders, thank you. Rivers is a bad man, despite appearances, and he carries a great deal of influence with the king.'

'You are becoming very perceptive, Francis.' Richard was silent for a moment, then, 'Perhaps I will write to Edward and ask him if he is quite sure of the truth of the rumours.'

He wrote, and after some delay received a reply in the person of Lord Hastings, who was in the North Midlands, already halfway to Middleham, inspecting his new estates — those that had been taken away from George by the Act of Resumption. Hastings's talent for acquisition was something to be marvelled at.

He was a delightful man. 'A real pleasure to have as a guest,' said Anne to Richard in one of their rare moments of privacy. She had discovered that there were only two things she disliked about being Richard's duchess. The first was that they were perpetually surrounded by people, hundreds of them, members of Richard's retinue and the ducal household, as well as a constant stream of visitors which all too often developed into a flood. That was the second thing she disliked, having to entertain the dullest collection of men it was possible to imagine. *They* thought they were interesting; sometimes even Richard thought they were interesting, especially if they were clever churchmen in search of sponsorship. But for Anne, essentially shy with strangers though learning to conquer it, three hours at table was three hours of torture.

Lord Hastings, bright and beaming and full of gossip, came as a welcome relief. Nothing very much was said at table, since nothing confidential *could* be said at table with so many ears on the prick, but afterwards, in a corner of Richard's Great Chamber, it was different.

'The king your brother,' Hastings told Richard merrily, 'has charged me with messages for you. I will try and quote his exact words. He said, "Tell young Diccon not to be so soft in the head. It is not *his* throne that is at risk." '

Anne, who had refused to be left out of what promised to be an intriguing conference, glanced at her husband and thought that it would be hard to find anyone less soft in the head than he.

There was a sardonic quirk at the corner of Richard's mouth. 'Unarguable. And what else?'

'Edward said, "Tell him one cannot afford to be gentle or mealy-mouthed with the opposition – with other claimants to the throne – even if they do happen to be members of the family." '

Richard laughed, 'Which, almost by definition, they are bound to be.'

Hastings twinkled at him. 'True enough. Though not always as close as brothers. But George is being an unmitigated nuisance and can hardly complain if Edward decides to teach him a really harsh lesson.'

'I understand that. What concerns me is whether George is being quite such a nuisance as he is painted.'

'Oh, yes,' said Hastings quickly. 'There is no doubt about it.'

It was, of course, Richard reflected, very much in Hastings's interest for George to be unpopular with the king. If George were to be forgiven, Hastings might find himself having to return the handsome new estates he had just acquired.

Just then, one of Anne's gentlewomen came to murmur that the youngest of Richard's pages had hurt himself, and would my lady please come and decide what was to be done.

Anne excused herself with reluctance. Bruised pages were an everyday occurrence, when small boys practised swordsmanship with inexpert energy and wooden weapons, and she would have preferred to stay where she was. But it was the duty of the lady of the house to care for the boys who were sent to her husband to learn the knightly virtues. If her own little son had lived, she didn't think she could have borne to send him away to be educated elsewhere.

'Anyway,' Hastings went on after she had left them, 'Edward has no wish to destroy George or drive him into the wilderness. If George shows himself even slightly amenable, he will be given another chance. Parliament still has to confirm the division of the Warwick inheritance, so perhaps we will then see whether he is prepared to be flexible.'

Richard said, 'Hmmm.'

'Don't fret,' Hastings went on cheerfully. '*You* won't come off worst. Now, tell me! Are there any good whorehouses in York?'

'Several,' his host replied, omitting to remark that he was doing his best to have them closed down. Richard was very straitlaced in some ways.

And then he looked up to discover that Anne had returned and had obviously overheard this exchange. Her blue eyes were enormous, and he couldn't quite tell whether with humour – or reproach.

11

'DISCUSSING compromises?' Anne exclaimed. 'You mean the king is *still* prepared to make concessions after all the trouble George has caused?'

'He could cause more,' Richard said. 'One thing you can be sure of with George is that he never learns. You have to admire him for consistency, if nothing else.'

'Humph!' said his mother-in-law.

She said a great deal more when, in May 1474, Parliament passed an Act to settle, once and for all, the division of the Warwick inheritance.

The Act recognised the right and title of the dukes of

Clarence and Gloucester, and their wives, to the inheritance of the late earl of Warwick — including the dowry lands of the countess of Warwick, the use of which the earl had enjoyed during his lifetime — and provided for its partition between them. To facilitate these arrangements, the widowed countess was barred from any claim or interest in her own inheritance, and was to be regarded as if she 'were now naturally dead'.

' "Naturally dead"!' she erupted. 'I have lived for forty-five years and might live for another forty-five yet. Though I pray to sweet Jesu that I do not. Have you' — she snapped at Richard — 'no knowledge of grace, no awareness of justice, no sense of family? I do not know how you dare act as you have done. It is theft, pure and simple. You and your appalling brother George have stolen everything from me, so that I have no residence, no land, no support for my remaining years. What am I expected to do for the rest of my life?'

Richard flashed a glance at Anne — who was clearly just about to say, 'You will always have a home here, mother' — and Anne obediently closed her mouth again and busied herself with distaff and spindle.

The countess had by no means finished. 'Do not pretend that you had no hand in this unprincipled division of my property, although I should have thought you were already amply endowed.' Her voice became heavily sarcastic. 'And what, as a matter of interest, are you proposing to do with the property you have stolen from me?'

Richard, whose most immediate concern was not what should be done with her property, but what should be done with *her*, had been considering the matter. Some of her lands he was anxious to have, to extend the concentration of his possessions in the north, but others were of little interest. Among the latter were two small estates in Suffolk, which had the overriding advantage of being a long way away from Middleham. Something in the West country would have been even better, but he had nothing there for which he did not already have plans.

Glancing out through the tall, narrow window, he saw that the sun was struggling through the rain clouds. It made no difference to the temperature within the twelve-foot-thick walls, and the air still smelled powerfully of sodden earth. If it was an augury, he couldn't tell what kind.

Carefully casual, he said, 'I am sorry if you dislike what has happened . . .'

'*Dislike!*'

'But neither your daughter nor I wish you to feel a prisoner at Middleham. That being so, I am prepared to make either Blaxhall or Burwash over to you. Whichever you choose. You would, I think, have to take up permanent residence there to be sure of collecting the rents that would provide you with the necessary income, but you should be able to live in comfort.'

She had not expected it, and was not grateful. For several days she waylaid and catechised him whenever the opportunity arose, so that in the end he said to Anne, 'If she asks me about my motives just once more, I will tell her the truth – and then pick her up bodily and transport her to Suffolk myself.'

'Oh, Richard! She's not as dreadful as that!'

'Is she not? Oh, by the way, the Act also covered a point that I have not yet told you about.'

She could see that he was being provocative, and said warily, 'Ye-e-es?'

'It was decreed that I should retain a life control in your share of the inheritance in the event of our divorce . . .'

Although she knew he was teasing her, she felt her heart miss a beat. It was desperately unlucky to talk of such things. 'Our *what*?'

'Don't! You sound like your mother.' Then, mellifluously, 'Though only if I do not remarry.'

She said, 'Well, that's something, I suppose.'

She had tried to match his tone, but he raised his brows enquiringly. 'Did I shock you? I didn't mean to do so.'

'No, it merely seemed odd to have our private life incorporated in an Act of Parliament.'

'It's called "covering all eventualities".'

'Is it? Well, I see no need for them to have bothered.'

'You don't view divorce as a possibility?'

He was teasing her again – she hoped. 'Why should I? I am an impeccably virtuous wife, and you are an impeccably virtuous husband.' She paused. 'I think.'

He knew she was remembering the whorehouses in York but, mischievously, felt no inclination to explain.

She had not asked about them, and did not do so now. She had always been desperately careful not to make demands on him. Nothing had ever been said, but her instincts told her that their good relationship depended on it.

More seriously, he said, 'The reason they "bothered", as you put it, is that the papal dispensation for our marriage has not yet been granted, so in a sense we are not really married at all . . .'

'You mean we're living in sin?'

'. . . which means that divorce or annulment would be ridiculously easy. It could be argued that, lacking the dispensation, the marriage does not exist.'

She shuddered. 'I don't think I like this conversation.'

'No. And that is why, despite Edward's dislike of English gold leaving the country, I am sending someone to Rome with a bribe large enough to buy not only a dispensation, but one backdated to the day of our marriage. Does that make you feel happier?'

'Much.'

He laid his hard, calloused horseman's palm against her cheek and said, 'Good. Then let us go to bed to celebrate.'

Chapter Four

1474-76

1

THE PARLIAMENT that had been summoned in 1472 was still sitting, off and on, almost three years later. It meant that Richard was in the south a great deal, and even when, in theory, he was at home, he was rarely at Middleham. When he had administrative or legal duties to fulfil in York, he stayed either with the Augustinian friars there, or in his own fortified manor house at nearby Sheriff Hutton. When he was fulfilling his rôle as steward of the Duchy of Lancaster beyond Trent, his headquarters were at the massive and scruffy royal castle of Pontefract. Sometimes, touring the countryside, hearing pleas, initiating enquiries, settling disputes, he would base himself at Barnard Castle in the north, which was also convenient as a centre for chasing away Scots reivers.

Increasingly, he won the supporters he needed. Increasingly, under the burden of responsibility, he became more demanding and less light of heart. Increasingly, the sheer force of his personality drew his intimate circle more tightly around him.

Anne felt it, like everyone else; had the sensation of becoming ever more dependent on him, more obsessed by him. Now, when he was away, she missed him badly, although she was constantly busy herself, in charge of castle and estates in his absence. There was at least one undeniable benefit of all his activity — there was never any lack of subjects to talk about when they were together, and there were still things to laugh about.

There was one occasion when he came riding back to Middleham on a dreary wet day with his hair grey, his face black, and his fur-lined russet hood and cloak reduced to a random patchwork in tasteful shades of mud. The odd thing was that everyone else in his entourage, though damp, was impeccably clean.

Dutifully, Anne curtsied and said, 'My lord.'

Equally dutifully, he bowed and said, 'My lady.' There was a comical gleam in his eye. 'No, I did not fall in a puddle.'

'I am so glad.' He appeared to be undamaged, and that was all that mattered. In the climate of the times, danger was everywhere and no man's wife lived free from the fear of it. 'A bath, perhaps?' she asked, and the question was enough to send one of the grooms scurrying off to tell the yeoman of the chamber to have an extra cauldron put on the kitchen fire.

'That's better,' she said, when he reappeared clean and smelling of rosewater an hour later. 'You were going to tell me what happened?'

'I have been down a mine. And then was rained on.'

'Down a . . . I beg your pardon?'

'You know what a mine is?'

'Yes, I suppose so. How exciting.'

He laughed. 'Tell her, Francis!'

Francis, lounging in front of the fire with a cup of spiced ale in his hand, said, 'You know there are copper deposits not far from here?'

She did, although she had no real idea of what a copper deposit was.

'Well, when we were at Barnard Castle, these miners turned up from Bohemia, asking for an interview with Richard.'

'All the way from Bohemia? Goodness! Did they speak English?'

'Of a sort. They said that they had found deposits of silver next to the copper and that, if Richard would cover the costs of hoisting, pumping and drainage machines . . .'

'Not to mention,' Richard interrupted blandly, 'furnaces and charcoal and a few other minor items . . .'

'They could guarantee to dig out substantial quantities of silver.'

'Which I could well do with,' Richard said. 'And so, come to that, could the king.'

'So Richard said, "Prove it",' Francis resumed. 'And they showed us a lump of ore.'

'What does ore look like?' Anne asked guilelessly.

Her husband grinned. 'You're guessing that we didn't know.'

'Oh, I'm *sure* you knew.'

Francis, feeling a little left out, went on, 'It could have come from anywhere, and Richard said that wasn't good enough. He wanted to see where the ore had come from. So we went trailing off to the mine and were shown baskets of the stuff being brought up from underground. Bits of rock with silvery streaks. Richard said that still wasn't good enough. There was nothing to prove that the ore was actually being dug out of this particular mine. They might just have brought a supply from somewhere else to fill the baskets, you see?'

'Yes, I do see, now that you point it out to me. So I suppose that Richard went down the mine himself, to discover what, if anything, was really being dug out.'

Francis took a deep breath. 'You two are well matched, aren't you?'

'And there wasn't any silver, of course. So what did you do?'

Richard said, 'I gave them a couple of gold nobles in recognition of their spirit of enterprise, and suggested that they might find a more gullible sponsor elsewhere.' His expression became angelic. 'In George, duke of Clarence, to be precise.'

'*Richard!*'

2

ANNE WAS worried about Francis, though not because he complained or showed any sign of being unhappy. In fact, he was his usual amiable, vaguely untidy, wryly amused self.

He said, 'I suppose I could petition the king to order my wife to come and live with me. Or I could kidnap her. The law entitles me to do so, but it hardly seems worth the trouble. She doesn't like me, and I don't like her much, either. I would prefer not to have to enforce my rights on her.'

Solemnly, Anne said she quite understood, though it was hard to imagine, in terms of anything other than farce, the considerate Francis trying to enforce his marital rights on Nan, who was a dismal, woebegone girl at the best of times and would probably weep tears by the bucketful throughout.

'But you need a wife,' she went on. 'Every man needs a wife. Who else' – her voice became dulcet – 'can give him good advice, incline him towards leniency, and champion the cause of those who come seeking favours?'

Francis raised an eyebrow. 'You've been at the etiquette books again. No, every man needs a *woman*, unless he has a possessive turn of mind and wants legitimate sons to whom he can pass on his estates. Which I'm not sure that I do. What, after all, is the purpose of "owning" land that, in the last analysis, belongs to the king anyway? Estates are nothing but a burden.'

She couldn't help but giggle. Having just inherited wide stretches of Yorkshire and Lincolnshire from his grandmother, Francis was feeling bowed down by the responsibility. He could easily afford to delegate their management to stewards and comp-trollers but, like Richard, was temperamentally incapable of leaving others to do what he saw as his own clear duty.

She said, 'We're not talking about estates. We're talking about wives.'

'Women. But if you're concerned on my behalf, don't be.' He blushed as he had not done for years. 'I have an – ummm – arrangement with a charming lady who – errr . . .'

'Oh, well, that's all right then.'

'Yes. Now, as to' – hurriedly he changed the subject – 'these building improvements Richard wants me to supervise here. I have found a master mason who has been well recommended. He will need space in the courtyard to set up the lodge for his apprentices and journeymen and tools. I will bring him to see you.'

Builders! Anne sighed. 'Heigh ho. What's a little more disrup-tion, here or there.'

'It will be worth it,' Francis assured her, 'when you have the new bay window in the Great Chamber, and the extra height in the north-west tower.'

'No doubt.'

3

RICHARD CONTINUED to be engrossed in rationalising his landholdings by every means in his power. Sometimes he was prepared to exchange immediate gains for future concessions; sometimes he held to the letter of the law; sometimes he compromised; sometimes he took a case to chancery for review; sometimes he even made deals enabling lands granted to him by the king to be returned to their attainted owners — for a consideration, of course. By diplomacy, too, reinforced by personal persuasiveness and an emphasis on reconciliation, he sold the idea of mutual advantage to most of the local lords, gentry and merchants so that, surprisingly soon, he came to exert personal dominance in the north.

'I owe a good deal of it to you,' he told his wife one day, when he was feeling particularly pleased with himself over some satisfactory transaction. She clapped a hand to her forehead. 'Recognition at last! And I thought you only married me for my money!'

'Not "only". I needed your hereditary rights, too, the traditional Neville ties of service and loyalty. They have given me far more leverage than royal grants ever could.'

'And?'

'And what?'

'*And* you owe a great deal to me for supervising your castle and your comfort, and dressing up as a gracious lady to accompany you to ceremonies in York, and being charming to the neighbours — and to you.'

'I cannot deny it. Indeed, I think perhaps it is time for us to retire for the night. Unless you have more interesting things to do?'

'No⁓o⁓o⁓o. I don't think so.'

Except when it was the wrong time of the month, she never refused him her bed, partly because she longed to conceive again, to give him the son she knew he must want, although he had never said so. She was certain that it was her fault that she was not conceiving, because Richard had fathered two bastard children before their marriage – John and Katherine, who had their own separate household at Sheriff Hutton, where Richard visited them. Anne knew nothing about their mothers; she was reluctant to ask, and Richard did not offer to tell her. She knew only that he was proud of them. He did say that, when they were older, he would take her to visit them, but she didn't believe that, if she remained barren, she could bear such an encounter. She felt tearful every time she thought about it.

And Richard was *so* good. He made love to her because he wanted to – she had no doubt about that – and was never rough but always considerate with her, as if her feelings, her enjoyment, mattered as much as his. For someone who was so energetic out of bed, he was wonderfully gentle *in* it.

Gradually, gradually, she was learning the complexities of his character, what lay under the hard and effective carapace that protected him from the outside world, the carapace that appeared to be toughening with the years. She worried about that, a little, but knew that men, like castles, needed strong defences if they were to survive.

4

UNFORTUNATELY, Richard was not perfect on all counts.

The country was buzzing with preparations for war. Edward's long-planned invasion of France, despite the English taxpayers' reluctance to pay for it, was destined to take place in the summer of 1475 and everybody knew about it, including the French.

Richard, who held the post of Lord High Admiral, had been practising for months. He had fitted out his own ships in the north and sent them off to do some quiet privateering.

It was pure bad luck, he maintained, that his *May Flower*

happened to capture a richly cargoed armed merchantman called *The Yellow Carvel*, which turned out to belong personally to King James III of Scotland. Upsetting the Scots didn't worry Richard at all, but Edward took a different view. For one thing, he was in the midst of negotiating a marriage between the king of Scots' year-old son and his own five-year-old daughter Cicely. For another, he did not want the Scots irritated into invading England while he and his army were away invading France. Richard was therefore told to behave himself, and a protesting Francis found himself despatched to Edinburgh on a formal embassy from the duke of Gloucester, laden with gifts and full of apologies for capturing the ship, stealing the cargo, and throwing the crew overboard.

Richard said he was too busy to go himself. He had indented to supply Edward with not only ten knights and one hundred esquires, but thirteen hundred archers, and proposed supervising the bowyers and fletchers personally to insure against his archers running out of weapons.

5

IT WAS a wonderfully impressive sight when Richard and his little army rode out from Middleham for the assembly point near Canterbury, Richard with his archers and lancers, his usual escort of gentlemen, a train of fifty reserve war horses for his own use, and a splendid cavalcade of cooks, pages, surgeons, chaplains, grooms, saddlers, and baggage animals laden with tents, arms and equipment. Rumour had it that the king had commissioned a portable wooden house for his own use and Richard had shaken his head and remarked that he feared that Edward had lost his stomach for serious campaigning.

Anne had done her best to be a helpful and strongminded wife, ensuring that her husband's armour was well polished and making a determined effort not to say fatuous things like, 'Look after yourself!' Unfortunately, trying to take an intelligent interest, she found herself instead asking fatuous questions such as, 'Do horses suffer from seasickness?' Richard quirked an eyebrow at her and didn't answer.

When they had all vanished into the scented summer distance, she found her knees shaking so much that she had to sit down.

It would be months before she saw Richard again.

If ever.

It didn't bear thinking about.

6

MARGARET BEAUFORT had turned pale as death and there was nothing she could do to disguise it.

'The duke of Brittany?'

Mention of Brittany always set her nerves jangling. When she had encouraged her son to flee from Wales to France four years earlier, he had landed by mistake in the independent duchy of Brittany and been received benevolently, to his and his mother's vast relief, by the duke. Edward had been displeased, and had tried to persuade his supposed ally, the duke, to surrender his uninvited guest – 'the only imp now left of Henry VI's brood' – but without success. All the duke would do was undertake to guard the young man so that he could do no harm to the House of York. The more often Edward asked, the more convinced the duke had become of the diplomatic value of his guest.

Relations between England and Brittany had been sufficiently erratic for Margaret to feel that her son was as safe as he could be anywhere. But now it seemed that Brittany was actively seeking English friendship and the formal alliance that it had been evading for years.

Stanley said, 'Yes, we've just drawn up a treaty. The duke is contributing eight thousand men to the war against France, and we are sending him two thousand longbowmen to strengthen his own forces. Oh!' Belatedly, he observed his wife's pallor. 'You're worried about young Henry, are you?'

'Yes.'

'Well, he hasn't been mentioned, if that's what you're thinking. Brittany hasn't volunteered to hand him over.'

Little went on at court that Stanley did not know about, and Margaret was partly reassured. On the other hand, Edward could be secretive when it suited him, and was unlikely to forget that his trusted steward, Thomas Stanley, was also stepfather to 'the imp' Henry. It was a nightmare, all of it.

So, even as she went about the business of taking a wifely interest in preparing her husband for war, supervising the embellishment of the sallet helmet he would wear on the march, purchasing crimson and blue sarcenet for his standards, instructing his deputy Master of the Horse on the purchase of mounts for him in Flanders, her concern was not for her husband, big, wily, unlovable, indestructible. It was entirely for her eighteen-year-old son — who was slight, innocent, much loved and in danger.

7

THE QUEEN was intolerably weary of the forthcoming war, a subject which had alternated with George, duke of Clarence, as her husband's main topic of conversation for more than three years. Raising money was all he thought about, some of it by taxation, some by personal exercise of the royal charm on the merchants of London, and some by exercise of that charm on the merchants' ladies. At least it seemed to have taken his mind off the luscious Mistress Shore – if 'mind' was the right word in the context.

Elizabeth had very little time for women, and not much more for men. She disliked seeing her twenty-four-year-old son Thomas, marquess of Dorset, competing for mistresses with that disgusting old libertine, William Hastings. And both of them encouraging her husband in his wenching. She could imagine all too well what they would get up to in France.

Well, at least they would all be out of the way for the next few months, playing at soldiers. It was to be the largest English army ever to invade France – eleven thousand fighting men and the same again of camp followers – and included almost all the nobility. There were five dukes, one marquess, four earls and a dozen barons, and there had been competition among them as to who could bring the largest force. George, duke of Clarence, had boasted that no one could match his one hundred and twenty men-at-arms and twelve hundred archers, but Richard of Gloucester had not only matched but surpassed him. Which had been mildly amusing.

It seemed unlikely that anything would go seriously wrong but, just to be on the safe side, she had insisted that the four-year-old prince of Wales be brought up from Ludlow to be made official head of state and keeper of the realm in the king's absence. She foresaw no difficulty in dominating the council that would act for him.

Since it was summer, and the weather fine, she decided she would accompany the king on his way to Canterbury and then to Dover. She could wear her new gold velvet with the white silk sleeves, and the flattering butterfly head-dress in white lawn over the jewel-embroidered cap . . .

8

THE duke of Brittany had not shown up at all, and the duke of Burgundy had turned up with no more than apologies, promises, and his personal bodyguard.

'Allies!' Edward snorted. 'What is the use of them?'

They had spent ten days loitering in a torrentially wet Calais waiting for Charles of Burgundy and, tempting though it was simply to turn around and go back home, Edward knew that he did not dare, not after all the money-raising, the boasting, the swaggering. He had to make some display of military might.

So he and his army marched. And went on marching. The downpour continued, the days passed, and the weeks, and nothing happened except that his troops became increasingly sickly, irritable and insubordinate.

King Louis was not even obliging enough to offer them battle. Instead, in the end, he invited them to a party.

It was not quite as simple as that, of course. There were negotiations first, with Louis having the advantage of already knowing how much it was likely to cost him to buy Edward off. He had learned the answer some weeks earlier, 'privately', from Garter Herald, who had conveyed that the best tactic would be for him to allow Edward to land in France, then send official envoys to him, and meanwhile make separate approaches to the English king's most influential advisers, including John, Lord Howard, and Thomas, Lord Stanley.

Edward's and Louis's representatives met in a village near Amiens. Edward's representatives said that their master would take his army home again if Louis would pay him, personally, £15,000 within fifteen days and £10,000 per annum thereafter for as long as they both should live. Louis's heir should marry Edward's first or second daughter and Louis should provide her with an income to the French equivalent of £60,000 per annum. Edward also required a secret agreement binding himself and Louis to come to each other's aid in the case of domestic rebellion.

Louis said, 'Yes.'

And privately budgeted for extra expenditure, as suggested, in the form of sweeteners for some of Edward's leading nobles, including Lords Howard, Stanley and Hastings.

Prior to the meeting between the two sovereigns at which the treaty was to be signed, Louis instructed the innkeepers of Amiens to provide free food, drink and women to any English soldier who asked for them, and for three or four days Amiens was so full of paralytic English fighting men that Edward had to have them forcibly thrown out of the town.

To Edward's annoyance, his brother Richard of Gloucester said thank you but he would prefer not to be a formal witness at the signing of the treaty.

'Really, young Diccon, must you be so holier-than-thou? George has no objections!'

Richard shrugged and went off to the cathedral, the largest church in France, 'higher than all the saints, higher than all the kings', a fitting shrine for the holy relic of St John the Baptist. The façade and the towers were barely completed, but the stone of the vast, vaulted nave, begun long before, seemed to Richard's restless spirit to be saturated with two hundred years of prayer and worship, and the light flooded like the gaze of God himself through the great rose windows. Richard, reared by a famously devout mother, the Duchess Cicely, briefly found peace in his soul.

The English army was drawn up in order and all the church bells of Amiens were echoing across the plain as Edward and Louis met on the bridge at Picquigny. A screen had been erected across its centre, broken by a trellis through which they could converse. 'Just like the confessional,' Francis remarked cheerfully, and Richard replied, 'Ha!'

King Louis, 'the universal spider', was recognisable from his immensely long and pointed nose and the meanness of his attire. There had been a famous occasion when he met Henry IV of Castile wearing a skimpy little jacket of cheap huckaback and a lamentable hat decorated with a brooch moulded from lead. He was little better dressed on this occasion. Edward, on the other hand, looked magnificently regal, if tending towards fat, in black cloth-of-gold and a black velvet hat adorned with a fleur-de-lys of precious stones. When he and Louis tried to embrace each other through the trellis, Richard turned away. 'I did not bring thirteen hundred archers all this way to witness a farce.'

'No,' Francis said. 'But for Louis to empty his treasury must be just as painful for him as losing a battle. This is a day he won't forget. And think of all the men who are alive and might have died.'

'Yes. And think, too, of the dishonour of being bought off without a blow struck.'

9

ANNE SAID, 'How delightful to see you again. Will you be staying long?'

He took her hands in his, so that she was forced to drop the overskirt which she had been holding fashionably bunched below her waist.

His hard grey eyes softening, he looked her up and down and said, 'How long should I stay?'

'Until some time between the Purification of the Blessed Virgin' – her husband gave a faint choke of laughter, and she blushed – 'and St Matthew's day.' Then, after a moment, breathlessly added, 'Please!'

It was mid-October, and she was five months gone with the child, five months during which she had seen nothing of Richard, and heard not much more. She did not expect him to pamper her in the days to come, nor sit by her bedside after she had – please, blessed Jesu! – given birth. She just wanted him to be there, somewhere. It would be enough to calm her fears, give her strength, bring herself and the child safely through their ordeal.

Agnes, one of her ladies, bobbed a curtsey and said, 'It is wonderful news to welcome you home, is it not, my lord duke?'

His mood broken by the intrusion, Richard said coolly, 'Indeed. Now, my lady, tell me what has been happening during my absence.'

'No, you first. I hear that the campaign was a success. No casualties at all?'

'None other than a few drunken revellers, and my troublesome former brother-in-law, the duke of Exeter, who fell overboard on the voyage home.'

'Oh, how dreadful!'

'You are alone in thinking so. Indeed, rumour has it that his fall was personally assisted by the king my brother.'

Anne's carefully plucked brows rose almost to the linen fillet that bound her coif in place. 'Oh, *dear*! Was it?'

'I have no idea, but the world is a better place without him. As for the success of the campaign, Louis is proposing to pay John Howard and Tom Montgomery an annuity of two hundred pounds a year each, the Bishop of Ely one hundred pounds, and Hastings three hundred and thirty pounds. They have also received lump sums and expensive toys, so you may imagine that they consider the campaign to have been entirely successful.'

Her eyes full of mischief, she exclaimed, 'Nothing for you?'

'Think shame on yourself! Very well, some horses and a gift of plate which I was unable to refuse without discourtesy.'

'*Good* plate?'

And so they were back to the conversational sparring that kept their relationship on a safe and undemanding footing.

Anne was determined that Richard should not see how things had changed for her during his absence, how missing him had brought the realisation that she loved him deeply and intensely and could not imagine going on living without him. She had always taken the greatest care in her dealings with him, instinctively aware that he had to come to her like a child to his mother, that he had to make the moves and there should be no pressure upon him. Pressure would only drive him away. And that had not changed.

She couldn't welcome him home with some great dramatic scene, when he was busy breaking up his force, and paying the men off and sending them home. She couldn't burden him with the knowledge of her love.

It was the classic dilemma, she knew, of all intimate relationships — where there is one who loves, and one who is loved.

10

THE BABY arrived without a struggle in the middle of February 1476, when there was snow all around and the fires had to be built high indoors.

There had been the formal ceremony of leavetaking before Anne's confinement, when everyone gathered in the Great Chamber to partake of spices and wine. And after that she had retired to the birthing chamber, richly decorated and full of comforts, where no men were permitted to enter during the days of waiting.

Afterwards, Anne lay torn and exhausted in her big curtained bed, rejecting the sweetmeats her women offered her and watching the midwife sit by the hearth to wash the baby, working his little limbs to chase away evil humours and anointing them with salt and honey. Then, taking him in her lap, the midwife rubbed his gums with honey and dripped a few drops of warm wine into his mouth before wrapping him in silk and laying him on a bed of furs by the fire.

He was alive, and seemed healthy. But he was very small. He would need all the care Anne could give him.

Richard decreed that he was to be called Edward, which came as no surprise. He even picked him up and looked as if he were about to toss him in the air. Anne shrieked, 'No!' and then tried to pretend, when she saw the look in his eye, that she had known he was only teasing her.

So he smiled at her, and looked down into the little swaddled face and said, 'Our son. Well done, my lady.'

Chapter Five

1476

1

THE COURTYARD was a sea of white mud and Anne was becoming very tired of the builders. The master mason had set up his lodge in a corner and there was much coming and going of men with hods and barrows and scaffold poles and plumb lines, much noise of sawing wood and chipping away at stone brought from the quarry and piled inside the walls. That much was bearable. It was the lime dust that Anne detested, and the white footprints left by everyone who came indoors. She was beginning to understand why the master mason wore a white leather apron.

'But Master Attwoode,' she asked, 'why could you not have the lime kiln set up *outside* the walls?' It was deeply irritating when he explained to her – patronisingly, because she was a woman – that once the lime had matured it had to be mixed with sand and water to make mortar, which then had to be taken to where it was needed with all speed, in case it set too quickly. The mortar mixer was an expert who did not like having his arrangements disrupted.

'No one likes having their arrangements disrupted,' she said, 'and I would not complain if the arrangements were more sensible in the first place.'

'Aye well, there's reason in it. He was working on a church, back end of last year, and three times, in the night, fairies stole away the lime and sand. The stone, too. Don't like churches, they don't. They know churches means bells and bells disturbs them, so they try an' stop the building. That's why he likes the kiln inside the walls. Safer.'

It scarcely seemed worth mentioning that Middleham was a castle, not a church, and that fairies were almost unheard-of in the vicinity.

Francis told her for the dozenth time, 'It will be worth it in the end,' and she breathed heavily and went off to see that the baby was all right. It was lucky that he wasn't old enough to be crawling around. She had contemplated moving the entire household to Barnard Castle or Sheriff Hutton until the work at Middleham was finished, but Richard was having work done there, too.

He, of course, barely noticed the inconveniences. He was too absorbed in selling, releasing or exchanging his estates in Wales and the West country in order to add Scarborough, Cottingham, Skipton and Helmsley to his northern lordships. He was extending his religious patronage, too, paying lavishly for the founding of chantries. And, called on to dispense justice, he took care to uphold the law even against his own followers, which was unusual to say the least. With amazing speed, he was becoming a 'good and just lord' to almost everyone.

2

BUT THEN came a major distraction.

Edward had decided that their father and brother, killed at

Wakefield in 1460, should be disinterred from their humble resting place at the priory of Pontefract and taken in procession to Fotheringhay, there to be ceremonially re-interred in the family mausoleum as a symbolic affirmation of the Yorkists' right to rule.

It took an enormous amount of organisation, much of which fell to Richard's charge. Although Edward's household officers were to see to the chapel and monuments at Fotheringhay, Richard was responsible for mapping the route and laying down the timetable, for arranging receptions, resting places and catafalques at every stop, and for the Office of the Dead to be recited each night and a requiem Mass sung each morning. The journey, he calculated, would take ten days.

Anne could scarcely bear to contemplate it – ten days at a funereal pace, in company with six great nobles and their retainers, looking solemn all the way, the hearse surmounted by an effigy clad in purple velvet and ermine, preceded by heralds and the chapel royal, and followed by sixty professional mourners bearing lighted torches.

Fortunately, there was no place for women in such a cortège, so Anne made her own way to Fotheringhay escorted by Francis and her ladies. It was the first time she had left the baby, and she spent the whole journey worrying about him although she had arranged for Nurse Idley to send regular messages to her. The old nurse, who had been Richard's nurse when he was a baby, was illiterate, so had to dictate to someone who could write, or give word-of-mouth reports to one of the messengers who went flying back and forth between Richard and Middleham. It wasn't an ideal arrangement, but it was better than nothing.

The king, the royal family, visiting ambassadors, every lord and lady of note in the kingdom was gathered to meet the cortège, and there were nine bishops to share in the obsequies. Edward was grave-faced in purple velvet and ermine, dressed just like his father's effigy – which Anne thought was in rather poor taste – and although Richard had become increasingly disinclined in the last year or two to show his feelings in public, she could tell that he was deeply moved by the three High Masses sung at the service. His attitude towards his dead father had always approached the mystical.

Afterwards came the funeral banquet in tents and pavilions in the meadows outside the castle. There were fifteen hundred guests with their servants and households, as well as five thousand poor folk to be fed from the royal bounty. It was reported that the king had supplied four thousand gallons of wine and almost twice that amount of ale so, as Francis later said, perhaps it wasn't surprising that it turned into something like a Scots' funeral wake when everyone shed their doleful looks and had an uproarious time.

Tongues were loosened even in the pavilion assigned to the ladies. Anne had hoped that Isabel might be there, but George, his behaviour exemplary for once, said that she was seven months gone with child and not feeling very well. He was worried about her.

Everyone seemed to know who Anne was – she was grateful that she was wearing her best mulberry-coloured velvet with the gold brocade sleeves, though it was far too heavy for July – and everyone enquired most kindly, perhaps too kindly, after the wellbeing of little Ned. She was astute enough to know why, but it made her uncomfortable. Everyone also said how clever her husband was, and what good work he was doing in bringing order to the north. She had the distinct impression that everyone hoped he would stay there.

One of the queen's off-duty ladies asked, gigglingly, whether she had heard the latest about Mistress Shore. Anne had barely even heard of Mistress Shore, so she said politely, 'No.'

'Well, you know she has been trying to have her marriage

annulled for years and years? We all laughed so much when we first learned about it. Really! For such a lovely woman to be seeking annulment on the grounds of her husband's impotence! It's unheard of. And now she has gone to Rome over the head of the Dean of Arches, and His Holiness has intervened and her petition has been granted. The cost must have been enormous and *someone* must have paid. And my mistress the queen suspects it may have been the king. And she is absolutely furious.'

'I can imagine,' Anne said weakly, glancing towards the end of the pavilion where the queen was dining in solitary splendour, as usual, and looking very bad-tempered about it. No one was ever permitted to come close to her, except presumably the king. Certainly, the headdress she was wearing – a veil draped over a wire frame roughly the size and shape of an archer's shield – was enough to keep even the most presumptuous at bay.

And then it was Lady Margaret Beaufort, Anne's aunt by marriage, small, neat and controlled, her enunciation just a little too careful, saying, 'I have myself recently been in communication with Rome and have been granted a papal indulgence in recognition of my contribution towards raising a fleet against the Saracens.'

Anne said, 'How – er – ah – virtuous of you.'

The Lady Margaret inclined her head graciously. 'It is time for a new Crusade on the part of Holy Church. I would willingly go myself and wash the Crusaders' clothes, for the love of Jesus. Does your husband, the lord duke, not favour such a venture?'

'Possibly, but he is much engaged on other matters.' She could just imagine Richard dashing off on a Crusade. He would need no encouragement, because it would be a perfect enterprise for him, one that would satisfy two of the deepest-ingrained elements in his character: his love of a fight and his piety. Internally, she shuddered.

Firmly changing the subject, she said, 'I wonder where on earth all these people are going to sleep tonight.'

3

THREE MONTHS later, as if to round off his reaffirmation of the Yorkists' right to rule, Edward made a determined attempt to lay hands on the exiled Henry Tudor.

Now conveniently allied to Louis of France, Edward hoped to bring more pressure to bear on a nervous Brittany, and therefore despatched an embassy to the duke asking to have young Henry back. All he wanted to do, he claimed, was marry the boy off to one of his daughters, and thus settle the dynastic question once and for all.

But Henry, nineteen years old, tall, slender, with small bright eyes and bad teeth, knew better. His mother had warned him often enough. Despatched to the coast, vainly protesting, in the care of the English embassy, he was overcome by a convincing fever, moaning, 'Let me rest. Let me rest. I am no use to your master dead.'

Both he and they knew this to be untrue, but they had to keep up the fiction. In the meantime, one of the duke of Brittany's counsellors persuaded the duke of Henry's danger, and the upshot was that he sent his treasurer to distract the ambassadors while a servant spirited the young man away into sanctuary at St Malo.

'I am now become so suspicious by nature,' Henry wrote to his mother afterwards, 'that however safe I may be now or in the future, I will never be able to feel truly secure. Had it not been for your warnings, I am sure that my life would have been forfeit.'

4

AT CHRISTMAS 1476, Louis of France sent seven hundred thousand casks of the best French wine to Edward, as a gift.

It was a year's supply for the court, but much of it disappeared down appreciative throats during the twelve days that were celebrated with the splendour that Edward so much liked to affect. Edward was in his element now, fully established after the French war, and Anne could see Richard assessing the value of ostentatious display as a statement of sovereignty. It was impressive, certainly. So were the music and the entertainment. Edward looked every inch a king, and behaved as one while at the same time being entirely approachable by his subjects. He had a phenomenal memory, and recognised everyone – and charmed them.

What was less appealing to anyone of sensibility was the special charm he exercised on women, and the way it affected other members of his court. There was a shocking laxity about it all. The court reeked of sexuality and Anne, too much a child of the grimmer and less flexible north, felt uncomfortable. So, too, she could tell, did Richard, but that was perhaps due to the stern morality that had been bred into him by his mother, who had had a much closer hand in his upbringing than in Edward's. Or perhaps it was just that Richard had been temperamentally more susceptible.

In the meantime, it was the ostentation that influenced him, and Anne found herself caught up in a whirl of spending. Velvets and furs and jewels for herself and Richard. Hangings and illuminated manuscripts and gold plate for Middleham. And vestments and statues and service books for the northern religious foundations that Richard so devotedly patronised.

Anne worried about him. In the almost five years of their

marriage, she had never known him rest or relax, except for an occasional day's hawking. He drove himself too hard, and once or twice she had risked taxing him with it. But all he said was, 'It is necessary. I am young and strong, and there is a great deal to do.' He was paying for it now. She could see that he was tired and harassed, though pretending not to be.

And then she herself, for whom it had become an article of faith always to remain calm and never to make scenes, made things worse for him by giving way to an outburst of ungovernable emotion when a brief, impersonal note came from George's secretary conveying the news that Isabel was dead.

Isabel, her sister, who was just twenty-five years old, to whom she had been so close during their growing up but who had become almost a stranger in these last years when Isabel's husband, and hers, had become enemies. Isabel had borne her baby in October, a boy, a second son. But then her limbs had begun shaking and she had been struck by pains worse and more prolonged than those of labour, and had faded slowly away, to die three days before Christmas.

It sounded like childbed fever, a commonplace tragedy, the lethal end that stalked the creation of every new life. Anne should not have been so desperately shocked, but she was.

'I must go to her,' she said, when the first torrent of tears began to ease, and Richard understood, though she hadn't expected him to. Nor had she expected him to be moved by her own distress. But he took her in his arms and held her, without impatience, and she was grateful while at the same time, deep down, concerned that she was making demands, preying on him, on his natural human kindness. That there might have been more to his response than that did not occur to her for many months.

He said only, 'There is a terrible ache of the heart, of the spirit. I know. But I cannot come with you.'

110

'No. George would not welcome you. It isn't a time for reconciliation.'

He sighed, and shook his head.

5

ISABEL'S BODY was laid out in state in the middle of the choir at Tewkesbury abbey, and Masses were being celebrated daily for her soul. George, tall and handsome, stood vigil. It was awesome and heartbreaking.

Outdoors, the rain was battering against the windows and bitter draughts swept in from every direction, so that the candles fluttered wildly.

'The children?' Anne murmured. Little Edward, not yet two, and Margaret, not yet four. The baby boy who had killed Isabel had died himself, ten days after his mother.

'They are too young to know,' George said. 'They are with their nurse.'

'Yes.' She hesitated. 'George, I cannot believe that this has happened.'

He looked down at her from his splendid height. 'Nor can I.'

Her heart surged inside her, and she could have wept for him as well as for Isabel. He was hurt, and miserable, and lost. An abandoned child. It was so unlike him that it was hard to credit.

'I never loved anyone else,' he muttered. 'I have been faithful to her always.'

She drew in a sobbing breath and wondered if there was anything in the world she could say to give him comfort.

And then he went on, 'They will pay. I will make them pay.'

She thought at first that she had misheard him. 'What?'

'They poisoned her. I will make them pay.'

The candles burned as brightly as ever, but darkness suddenly filled the air. Anne shivered violently.

'*They* poisoned her? *Who* poisoned her?'

George looked down at her. 'Who? The Woodvilles, of course. The queen. My brother's wife.'

Chapter Six

1477-78

1

RUMOURS, HINTS, WHISPERINGS. 'He says ... he claims ... he wants ... he swears ... he is summoning his retainers ... he will no longer obey the king his brother, who was born out of wedlock and is thus no brother and should be no king ...'

Anthony Woodville, Earl Rivers, drawled, 'I am afraid, sire, that the duke of Clarence is uttering treason wherever he goes. I have news even from France that he is viewed there as the natural leader of any rebellion against yourself, and there is no doubt in my mind that he sees himself as such. I have heard it from too many sources.'

The queen said, 'I told you so, sire.' As always, she admired her brother's genius for playing the seemingly reluctant bringer of bad tidings. She knew that he would have taken care to ensure that other busy talebearers would reinforce what he had said.

Edward, as always, was selective as to what he chose to be annoyed about. 'That bastardy nonsense again! It all goes back to my mother being angry with me and saying that I was no son of

113

hers. She didn't mean it, and in any case she only said that I was not *her* son. And since my right to rule comes through my father . . .'

Neither his wife nor his brother-in-law pointed out that this hardly resolved the bastardy issue. Anthony merely gave one of his sympathetic sighs and remarked, 'Quite so. But I felt you should be made aware of what is being talked about.'

'Yes. And you don't have to tell me that the whole problem has arisen because I have refused to countenance the idea of George's marriage to Mary of Burgundy or Margaret of Scotland? God's life! That poor girl Isabel only died a few weeks ago. It's indecent to be looking for a new wife so soon.'

Elizabeth exchanged a glance with Anthony, who in her view – as, indeed, in his – was far more deserving of the exceedingly rich Mary's hand than George was. She had been trying to persuade Edward of it, and Edward had said he would see what could be done.

She said, 'Mary of Burgundy will not be available for long. Her father's death makes her the most desirable match in Europe.'

'And politically the most dangerous. Louis of France has sent to tell me that her stepmother, the dowager duchess – my own sister! – has been boasting of what George would do in regard to England if he became master of Burgundy. So much for family feeling! There is also an implication that Hastings has a finger in the pie . . .'

Lord Rivers pursed his lips and looked judicious.

'. . . but I don't believe that,' Edward concluded.

'I have noticed,' said Elizabeth, who preferred to target one enemy at a time, 'that on the rare occasions when George now comes to court, he seems reluctant either to eat or drink. Almost as if he feared poison.'

Edward snorted. 'He is incorrigible. I am becoming very tired of him and I shall have to do something about it.'

Calmly, Lord Rivers gathered his cloak around him. 'It is indeed becoming necessary, sire. But now, if I have your permission, I must leave for Wales. My duties in the prince's household have been neglected for too long. If you wish it, however, I will continue to report on what I hear of the duke of Clarence. His own connections in Wales mean that I hear a good deal.'

'Yes.' Edward gave vent to a puff of frustration. ' I rely on you to tell me the truth. Everyone else is too much afraid that I might take steps against George that will force him into *doing* something instead of just talking about it. And no one wants another civil war.'

2

UNUSUALLY for early June, there was almost no wind, so the processional candles flickered only from the slow movement of the acolytes who bore them. It was Corpus Christi and Richard and Anne were in York for the performance of the Mystery Plays that were the chief event in the city's calendar.

As stately and splendid as figures from a Book of Hours, they paced behind the Host in its silver and beryl pyx as it was borne towards the Minster, the air filled with summer warmth, and incense, and the murmur of prayers from the artisans, tradesmen and merchants who crowded the narrow streets.

The plays were to come later. Anne had seen them before, many times, but they never failed to move and enthral her. There were forty-eight in all, each enacted under the auspices of one of the merchant guilds and designed to present the essential truths of Christianity in the form of a story. The audience waited at ordained stations, and the elaborately decorated pageant carts came to them in sequence, each cart devoted to a particular episode – all the way through from the Garden of Eden to the Judgement Day.

Some carts had two levels to accommodate hell below and heaven above. The devils all wore masks, while the boys who played the angels had blond wigs and, in some cases, sprouting beards; they had, after all, been up and dressed since four in the morning. Prudently, the Guild of Makers of Tapestry and Couch Covers had provided a partially roofed cart for their 'Dream of Pilate's Wife'. Pilate's exceedingly expensive costume would have been ruined by being rained on.

Although Richard had a strong sense of pageantry, it was Anne who enjoyed the spectacle and Richard who became engrossed in the spiritual message, delivered in strong Yorkshire accents and earthily human terms. The people of the scriptures were represented as real, recognisable personalities. Everyone in the audience knew a nagging woman like Mrs Noah, or brothers like Cain and Abel who did not get on, or loud-mouthed bullies like Herod. And rather than obscuring the significance of the cycle as a whole, this gave it realism, a sense of purpose and coherence. Here were jealousy, pride, wrath, ambition. Here too were humour, pathos, suffering and magnificence of spirit.

It was all very different from worshipping in church, Anne reflected. Reason as an element of faith, meaning conjoined with the instinct for salvation. It was thought-provoking for anyone like Richard who had an analytical cast of mind.

3

HE SCARCELY spoke for days afterwards. There was a frown of concentration in his eyes and all his nervous habits came into play.

Anne said, 'If you continue chewing your lip like that, you will make a hole in it.'

It was something she teased him about, frequently, but he did not respond with a laugh and a shrug, as he usually did.

With unusual asperity, he said, 'I am your grownup husband, not your infant son,' and she bit her own lip, annoyed with herself.

After a moment, he went on, 'Never mind. It is natural enough, I suppose, when you see so much more of little Ned than you do of me. No, I was merely meditating on the unity, the inclusiveness of the plays. The natural logic that you only see afterwards. Is logic something we should also be able to find in the pattern of secular life?'

And then a messenger arrived from George, with a letter for Anne that was to give both her and her husband's thoughts another direction.

Anne opened the letter with some trepidation, hoping that George had abandoned his extraordinary idea that Isabel had been poisoned on the queen's orders. But, without preliminary, he began, 'You will wish to know that Isabel has been avenged. The woman who poisoned her, and the man who poisoned our baby son, have both been tried, convicted and hanged. The man was a yeoman of mine, John Thursby, and the woman a servant of Isabel's, Angharad Twynho . . .'

She could not believe it. 'Angharad? Never!' Tears of shock leapt to her eyes at the memory of the plain, gentle, kindly woman who had served Isabel so faithfully.

It seemed that George had ordered Angharad to be taken from her home in Somerset to Warwick, the seat of his own power where both jurors and justices could be expected to do his bidding. All the stages of the trial had been completed in a single day. 'It was necessary to be swift, in case the queen heard of it and chose to interfere. The Twynho woman's kinsman, John, is in the Woodville camp and I know that things I have said in private have been reported to the king. But I have my own sources. I also know what he has said of *me* – I am incorrigible and he is very tired of me. Well, we shall see.'

Anne took the letter to Richard. 'I think George has taken leave of his senses!'

'You don't surprise me.' But what caused Richard to exclaim was not the sad fate of Angharad Twynho. It was the manner in which it had been determined. 'God's bones, but George takes too much upon himself. To try, convict and execute people on his own authority is to take on royal power. How can he be so foolish as to continue angering Edward in this way? Does he not realise that he is inviting retribution?'

Anne murmured, 'Perhaps he doesn't care. Everything always seems to go wrong for him . . .'

'And whose fault is that?'

'His own, I suppose. But it is a flaw in his nature, and others should make allowances.'

'Perhaps, now, when he is no longer a danger to the throne. Even so, a man must either mend his own flaws or take responsibility for the consequences of them.'

4

A FEW DAYS later, there arrived another missive borne by an urgent messenger from Lord Hastings. This time it was Richard who turned pale with shock.

George had been sent to the Tower.

It seemed that, in May, three men had been brought to trial at Westminster on the not altogether uncommon charge of attempting to encompass the death of the king and his sons by sorcery. But these were not ordinary men. One, 'a notorious necromancer', who had confessed under torture, was a fellow of Merton College, Oxford. The second was a chaplain, also of Merton. And the third was a certain Thomas Burdett, a violent and litigious man with many enemies, who was a close personal friend of the duke of Clarence.

All three had been found guilty by the king's court, and two of them – the chaplain having been pardoned, as men of the cloth usually were – had been hanged, loudly protesting their innocence.

George had then committed the crowning folly of marching in to a meeting of the royal council at Westminster – the king himself being at Windsor – and having the two dead men's protestations of innocence read aloud to it. He had then stalked out again.

'What can he have been thinking of? Has he no sense at all?' Richard raged.

Francis, just back from Minster Lovell, where he had been pleasurably engaged on planning his building improvements – with the assistance of the lady whose identity Anne had not yet manoeuvred him into divulging – suggested, 'Perhaps he wanted to register a belief that they had been wrongly condemned?'

'Instead of which he threw doubt on the competence of the royal courts and identified himself directly with the guilty parties as a man prepared to poison the king!'

In the early days of June, Edward had returned to Westminster and summoned George to present himself. 'Whereupon,' wrote Lord Hastings, 'the king, my master, upbraided him for his misconduct, arrested him, and consigned him to the Tower. It is, I think, his hope that a period in custody might persuade the duke to embrace discretion. The king, my master, has instructed me to inform you of the situation. Rest assured, my lord, of my warmest duty to yourself and your lady wife.'

Richard's lady wife said, 'Poor George! Don't you feel even a little sorry for him?'

'Yes, of course I do. He's a fool, but he's my brother. I feel sorry for Edward, too, to have been driven to this. The Tower! For how long? A few weeks will not suffice to bring George to heel.'

5

THE WEEKS PASSED, and the months, and George remained in the Tower.

No one was permitted to visit him. It was necessary, Edward said, that he should know himself to be isolated. He was being kept a close prisoner in the Bowyer tower, where his movements could be monitored.

Elsewhere, ordinary life went on, the tension at court held below the surface. Meetings of the royal council took place at which there was much discussion about the problem of George, duke of Clarence, but no decision. Richard attended the meetings later in the year, sitting quietly and observing.

Most members of the council were conducting themselves warily, in view of the fact that George was the king's brother, but Richard was soon confirmed in his suspicion that at least three were dedicated enemies. One was Lord Stanley, perennial trimmer and husband of Margaret Beaufort, adept as always at foreseeing on which side his bread was likely to be buttered. Another was little John Morton, Bishop of Ely and Master of the Rolls, for whom humanity meant nothing and legality everything. And a third was the superficially fair-minded Anthony Woodville, Earl Rivers, who saw George as a direct threat to the throne from whose bounty he drew all his own power and possessions.

Rivers was perhaps the most dangerous, not only because he was the queen's brother, governor of the prince of Wales, and wholeheartedly trusted by the king, but because he was a cultured man and thus generally – if wrongly – assumed to be above such feuds as shaped the dealings of other men of rank.

As if to demonstrate his cultural quality, in November he formally presented the king, an ardent book collector, with a copy of *The Dictes or Sayengis of the Philosophres*, which he had himself translated from the French and which had been printed by Master Caxton at his new press in the precinct of Westminster Abbey. In a velvet-voiced speech, Lord Rivers mentioned that he had acquired the original French manuscript when he had been on a pilgrimage to St James of Compostela and had unwittingly distressed the king by being absent from court when he was needed. This book, he gracefully hoped, would serve as both apology and compensation.

Edward, equally gracefully, accepted and admired the book, saying – as if he had never seen a printed book before – how interesting it was that the artificial writing should be so legible, considering that it was all carried out by mechanical means with no human scribe involved. He must visit Master Caxton and see how it was done.

George remained in the Tower.

Also in November, a grand official banquet was given by Edward, prince of Wales, to celebrate his seventh birthday. His younger brother Richard, duke of York, aged four-and-a-quarter, was perched on a bed-seat beside the cloth of state, sitting up stiffly to receive homage from members of the court after they had paid homage to his brother.

George was still in the Tower in mid-January, when the little duke of York was married to a five-year-old bride in St Stephen's Chapel, Westminster. The royal family was out in formidable force. The king's and queen's immediate kin amounted to well over a score, a figure almost doubled by husbands and wives, and more than trebled when close cousins were added. The intricacies of marriage alliances multiplied the total almost beyond counting.

The gold and jewels were blinding, the furs and velvets suffocating, the fires and candles sweltering, and the conversation clamorous. Anne, herself spectacular in crimson cloth-of-gold edged with fur and embroidered with rubies and pearls, could have wept for the little bride and groom, who looked pale and terrified. Would they live long enough, she wondered, for their marriage to be confirmed and consummated? Children often didn't. She thought of her own little Ned, with his delicate constitution, far away at Middleham, and wanted desperately to be back with him. Although Richard had been at Westminster for Christmas, she had stayed determinedly at home, and was here now only because a direct royal command was not to be disobeyed.

Richard, she saw, was moving systematically among the guests, tossing a few words here, a pleasant smile there, but to her perceptive eye ill at ease.

She had barely been able to snatch a word with him since she arrived, and when she had said, 'You are worried. Is it to do with George?' he had replied, 'Worried? Why should you think so?'

Once, she would have held her tongue, but now, loving him, she was not to be so easily put off. Smiling, she laid a light finger on his forehead between his eyebrows and said, 'Those two little vertical lines are deeper than they were when last I saw you. Is there any news of George?'

He smiled back ruefully. 'He is to be put on trial before Parliament. For treason.'

'Oh, no! I know the king wants to teach him a salutary lesson, but surely this is going too far?'

Richard sighed. 'We shall see.' And then, 'Elizabeth and the Woodvilles are determined on it.'

That had been yesterday. And tomorrow, many of those present at the little duke of York's wedding feast would be assembling in parliamentary session in St Stephen's Chapel, the selfsame place where the child had just been married, to decide whether his uncle, the duke of Clarence, was to live or die.

Anne shivered.

6

THE CHAPEL, which lay adjoining and at right angles to the Great Hall of the Palace of Westminster, served a religious purpose only irregularly, since the king and queen had separate chapels of their own for daily worship. It had become predominantly a place of ceremony, painted and panelled and gilded accordingly, and smelling on the day of George's trial almost as strongly of freshly carved wood and beeswax candles as of stale robes and sweaty humanity. The low January sun was too weak to struggle through the high lancet windows, and the stained glass cast only the dimmest coloured shadows on the scene.

The Lords spiritual and temporal sat on hard wooden benches while the Commons, when they were summoned in from their meeting place in the Chapter House of the abbey, either stood, or sat on the floor. There were almost three hundred of them in all, and most were already committed. The Lords had been bought, in one way or another, and they in turn had bought the Commons. It was hard to be elected to Parliament without patronage.

George – brought by river from the Tower under the escort of the Gentleman Gaoler – knelt before the marble altar steps until the king entered to a flourish of trumpets and took his seat beneath the canopy of state.

He scrutinised George closely for a few moments and then waved him to his feet. Not for years had the resemblance between the two brothers been so pronounced. Whereas Edward, now thirty-five and addicted to the pleasures of the table, had steadily become more fair of flesh, George at twenty-eight had always led an active outdoor life and kept his splendid physique. But after six months in close confinement, with nothing to do other than think, sleep, eat and plot, he too had put on weight.

Both men looked tired about the eyes, and Edward's face, stripped of its customary faint smile, was slack-muscled and strained. George, on the other hand, looked as if he had not a care in the world. Only those sitting within a few feet of him – Richard among them – could feel the waves of tension radiating from him.

Bishop Rotherham's opening sermon fell on deaf ears. All those present were too busy thinking what a fool George was and wondering how far the king would go in pressing the Bill of Attainder against him. Everything was up to the king.

'As all my people know,' Edward began, and then stopped and cleared his throat. 'In the sometimes disturbed years of my reign I have been noted for a clemency far surpassing that of my predecessors or of my contemporaries on the thrones of Europe.' He cleared his throat again. 'There are many men living who, had it not been so, would have paid on the block for their treason.'

Then, as if aware that he was sounding self-justifying, not to say ingratiating, he took a deep breath and, his voice strengthening, went on, 'But now I have learned of further treason, more offensive than any I have before encountered because it displays all the signs of a most extreme and deliberate malice, and because it originates from one who before all others should be true. Namely from George, duke of Clarence, who should be loyal not only as a brother but as one whose king has endowed him with livelihood, wealth and power exceeding anyone else in the land.'

George's long, uncompromising mouth — the only one of his features in which he resembled Richard rather than Edward — twisted insolently as he sighed, folded his arms, and raised his eyes to scan the magnificent hammerbeam roof.

'And all this,' Edward continued, his jaw muscles visibly tightening, 'after and in despite of his treasonable rebellions of sixty-nine to seventy-one, when he wished to claim the throne for himself. We now know that in 1470, when I myself, his brother and anointed king, was in exile, there was an Act passed by the illegitimate Parliament then sitting that gave him the entail to the throne if the House of Lancaster, with which he was then allied, should fail or otherwise be destroyed. And since then, deviously, he has devoted himself to making good that false title to the crown.'

With an almost audible snap, George dropped his pose of nonchalance and exclaimed, 'No. That is not true. You cannot prove it to be true. Show me a copy of that Act. For, if it was passed, a copy must exist, even if only in the Patent Rolls.'

Edward ignored him. 'It is my royal duty, therefore, to proceed against a brother who has been reported as claiming that I intend to consume him like a candle and be quit of him, and that it is my purpose to deprive him of everything that in my generosity I have given him. Nothing, it seems, will placate him.

'He seeks the throne not just as supposed heir of Lancaster, but also of York. For this, it is necessary to set aside the titles of myself his elder brother, and of the princes, my sons. His servants have gone about the countryside claiming that "the king our sovereign lord is a bastard and not begotten to reign over us". Placards have been posted. Disturbances have been fomented. He last year planned to send his son abroad to the care of our sister, the Dowager Duchess Margaret of Burgundy, whose stepdaughter Mary he was anxious to wed, she having her own Lancastrian claim to the throne.

'He has claimed also that Thomas Burdett, who was found guilty of trying to procure my own and my sons' death by sorcery, was wrongfully condemned, thus impugning my royal justice. He has taken upon himself the king's prerogatives in arresting, trying and hanging the woman known as Angharad Twynho, claiming her to be a poisoner. We have seen the documents, and there appears to be no vestige of truth in the charge. He has caused numbers of his retainers to swear upon the Blessed Sacrament to be true to him and his heirs alone, overriding their allegiance to the crown . . .'

George, his attention caught, lowered his eyes from the ceiling again to stare into his brother's. 'I have done no such thing,' he proclaimed hotly. 'And if I had done, those who swore would have been as guilty as I and should be standing here beside me.'

As before, Edward ignored him. 'Despite all his past sins,' he said heavily, 'for the love I bear him as a brother I could have found it in my heart to forgive him. But he has proved himself incorrigible and the safety of the realm requires that he be punished.'

Silence fell as he scanned his Parliament.

He had been impressive, the more so for having made his indictment entirely without notes. His memory had always been excellent. He had not appeared angry, but regretful and resigned. Nothing he had said had come as news to the Members of Parliament. His accusations of necromancy, poisoning and plotting had been common currency among the gossiping classes for months. But they had been put together in such a way that, although no single charge was treasonable, the combined effect was to make George appear as if treason was second nature to him.

Richard knew it was necessary. If George were to be frightened into behaving himself, the case had to be strong and the threatened punishment rigorous. The law did not require that he be given proper opportunity to defend himself, or to examine witnesses, if they were called. The king's word was, by definition, taken to be the truth. It would have been permissible for any of the lords to rise and defend George, but none did. He had made too many enemies, and his few friends were disinclined to commit themselves to a lost cause when they might suffer for it later.

Among the Commons, Richard estimated that fifty-six of those attending were royal servants; another twenty-five belonged to the Woodville connection; a further dozen to the Mowbrays, now linked by the marriage of Anne Mowbray to the little duke of York; and ten to Lord Hastings, the king's most devoted friend. This meant that well over one third of the members were already committed to finding George guilty.

George. His brother. Who had been his closest companion during the first seven years of his life. Who was now standing there in his dark blue cloth-of-gold looking as if the proceedings were of no possible interest to him.

Richard wondered whether Anne was right about him being tired of living, tired of fighting for the honour and respect to which he considered he was entitled but which had never been granted him. If only he had behaved more sensibly . . .

Edward opened his mouth again, and the shifting and shuffling that had marked his brief pause for effect promptly ceased. There was noise and shouting from outside on the river, probably one of the quarrels between bargees that punctuated life on the Thames, but no one noticed.

'Everything of importance having now been put before this sitting of Parliament,' Edward said, 'I require that George, duke of Clarence, be found guilty of high treason, and that he be deprived of all his titles and of all estates and other properties granted to him by the crown.'

High treason meant hanging, drawing and quartering. A terrible, terrifying death.

A faint sigh, like a ripple over a cornfield, passed through the chapel.

And then the trumpets sounded and Edward rose to his feet without another glance at his brother, and stalked out of the chamber, leaving George standing alone before the empty chair.

George straightened his shoulders and for the first time turned his head to scan the benches around him. Most of the peers were carefully looking elsewhere, but not Richard.

Catching his eye, George smiled scornfully, and said, 'Well, little brother? I suppose you will have *all* the Warwick inheritance now.'

7

EDWARD HAD decided how he wanted things done, and Richard knew he was right. The game had to be played out to the bitter end. The due forms of law had to be observed, the sentence of death formally pronounced. And then it would take about ten days, Edward estimated, for George to come to the full realisation that his end was in sight and that there was going to be no royal pardon.

'If we pass sentence on February 7th,' Edward had said, 'but set no date for the execution, I can begin to feel merciful on, say, the 17th, when he's given up hope.' Then, morosely, 'Though I don't suppose I shall get any thanks for pardoning him. I doubt if George will ever see the error of his ways.'

'Probably not,' Richard had agreed, 'but he is no longer dangerous. You are too firmly established on the throne. George may be a focus for discontent over taxes and the like, but not for rebellion.'

'That's all very well for you, young Diccon. Myself, I never know where one of George's small riots is going to pop up next, and very annoying it is. Oh well, let's forget it.' He gave Richard an invigorating buffet on the shoulder. 'Let us go and watch the jousting. Who will win, do you think? In my own view, Anthony Rivers is getting a little past his prime.'

8

ON FEBRUARY 7TH, according to plan, the death sentence was pronounced by the specially appointed Steward of England, the twenty-two-year-old duke of Buckingham. He did it very well.

A familiar figure at court, Harry Buckingham was a hand-some young man, save for his slightly rabbity front teeth and projecting ears. He was also arrogant, greedy and ambitious, and all too ready to remind people that he, too, had a claim to the throne. To no one's surprise but his, this had led Edward to mistrust him and hold back the political honours that young Harry considered his due. So now he was in his element, given the undivided attention of everyone in the kingdom who mattered. The only flaw was that he found himself on the same side as the Woodvilles, whom he detested and who had worked so hard to have George condemned. But he was able to shrug that off since he had always detested George, too.

After that, increasingly as the days passed, George's impending execution elbowed out all other subjects of conversation. When would it take place? Where would it take place? Why had it not already taken place?

Richard – the words, 'I have no idea' rarely off his tongue – became reluctant even to venture outdoors. He had in any case a great deal to do at his new London home at Crosby Hall, being engrossed in the final stages of planning the establishment and endowment of two chantry colleges, one at Middleham and one at Barnard Castle, for which he needed not only royal licence but the consent of Parliament to enable him to appoint clerks, chaplains, scholars and choristers. He wanted it all settled before this Parliament rose.

Only on February 17th, therefore, did he ask for an audience with Edward.

He found him at the Palace of Westminster, quite alone in the great Painted Chamber with its carved ceiling and walls adorned with bands of paintings showing scenes from the Bible. He was sitting on a chest at the foot of the great fourposter bed, close by the fire, and looked exhausted.

Before Richard could speak, he said, 'George will die tomorrow.'

He spread his fingers over his eyes, and so did not see the change in Richard's expression as disbelief, shock and finally rage surged through him. It took him several moments to control his voice sufficiently to say, 'But . . .'

'Yes, I know! I know I said I would grant George a pardon, but I cannot do it. I have thought about it further, and it is too dangerous.'

Richard crossed to one of the windows with the paintings of Virtues and Vices on the reveals, and stared out at the jumble of buildings that filled the palace courtyards. In his nostrils, he could smell nothing but the great logs burning in the fireplace, but in his mind he could smell the outdoors, the brown, swift-flowing Thames with its burden of sewage, and the tainted streets, and the sweaty, itching palms of London's inhabitants. How he disliked the place!

Turning, he said in a tone that dismissed the myth of danger and went to the root of things, 'Why?'

Edward, ten years his senior, met his gaze, thinking that Diccon had always been a clever little brat but had no real idea of the pressures of kingship. Slowly, he said, 'I left things too late. Today, the Speaker of the Commons came to the Lords to ask that the sentence be carried out.'

The Speaker was a certain Sir William Allington, who held the post of chancellor to the prince of Wales. A dependant of the Woodvilles. Richard felt no surprise.

'And the Lords carried his request by acclamation.'

Led, no doubt, by the queen's brother Anthony Rivers and Margaret Beaufort's husband Lord Stanley, and perhaps by Hastings, and followed by all the others who hated George or hoped to profit from his death by acquiring the estates and titles he had held by royal grant.

Richard said, 'But you are the king. You can still issue a pardon.'

'I might have done, before that. But not after. By then I was committed.'

Inside his head, Richard heard a childish voice crying, 'But you *promised*!'

'You do understand?' Edward asked, his fleshy forehead creasing in his earnestness.

At that moment, the door opened and Richard turned to see the queen and her brother enter smiling and slightly breathless.

He said drily, 'Oh, yes. I understand.'

Their surprise and pleasure at seeing him were as false as a golden groat. He guessed that they had rushed here the moment they heard of his arrival, fearing that he might undermine their success with the king.

The queen was already wearing black, which made Richard feel queasy. She said, 'Has the king your brother told you that the Duchess Cicely had an audience of him earlier today?'

'No.' He looked at Edward.

'Our lady mother hoped to persuade me that George should not die. Or not by my order.'

'Really.' Richard's voice was flat.

At her coolest, the queen intervened. 'But she understood, I think, when I reminded her of the calumnies that George has uttered against both the king and myself, and that our sons could never be safe, might never come to the throne, while the duke of Clarence was at liberty.'

Richard said, 'You don't mean "at liberty". You mean "alive".'

The intolerant eyes surveyed him. 'Perhaps.'

Anthony Rivers was looking sympathetic and regretful, and Richard longed to hit him. Instead, he controlled his anger and turned again questioningly to Edward.

'All I could do,' Edward said, 'was agree to our mother's demand that George should be spared the pain and indignity of a public hanging, drawing and quartering.'

It was a relief, of sorts. 'So?'

'So I have sent to ask him how he would prefer to die.'

9

'STAY WITH ME,' Richard said. 'Please. I need you.'

Anne could scarcely believe her ears. In six years of marriage, he had never before said such a thing. She had been supervising the packing of her boxes in preparation for going back to Middleham and the baby, assuming that Richard would stay on in London until the parliamentary session was over.

She couldn't tease him about it, because it was obvious that he was deadly serious. 'What is wrong?'

When he told her, she took him in her arms, and he wept.

All the night through, he talked incessantly and often incon-sequently. 'Once, he gave his word and never wavered. But now . . . He is *king* but he has allowed himself to be overridden by Lords and Commons who have their own axes to grind. The Woodvilles! Why does he allow himself to be swayed by them? Why, why? How can he kill our very own brother?'

Helplessly, Anne said, 'I don't know. My dear, you mustn't . . .'

'*Could* I have saved him? Should I have spent these last ten days always at Edward's side, keeping him up to the mark? I didn't think I needed to. I *trusted* him.'

'Edward has an iron will. If his mind was made up, you could have done nothing.'

He did not even hear her. 'I know George has been a nuisance, and sometimes a dangerous nuisance, but nothing justifies this. If George had been killed in battle when he rebelled in sixty-nine, that would have been forgivable. There would have been honour, of a kind. But not this. Not this!'

Anne held him, and was horrified. Horrified that George should have to pay the ultimate penalty for his weaknesses, and at his brother's hands. Even more horrified to discover how little she knew of her own husband. Cool, controlled, sardonic Richard, who had passion in him after all.

Just after six in the morning, he withdrew from her arms and made an effort to be himself again, his neck muscles cording with the strain of it. 'Thank you,' he said. 'Now I must dress and go to Baynard's Castle, to my mother.'

'Yes,' she said, and when he had left lay down in her bed again, and wept for Richard, for George, and for herself.

10

AS HE had expected, he found the Duchess Cicely, enviably calm, saying Matins with her chaplain. After that, he knelt with her to hear Low Mass in her chamber. And then came a glass of honeyed ale and a piece of bread and the opportunity to talk.

She had never spoken to him freely before of her early life, or marriage, or the father he had scarcely known. He had almost forgotten that he himself was his parents' seventh son rather than their fourth, because three others had died in infancy. Two sisters had also died as babies. 'Twelve children in all and, of my seven sons, after today there will only be you and Edward left.' Meditatively, she went on, 'Your father was an exciting man, and a hard man. I have been paying the penalty ever since for having loved him. Strange that you, the youngest, should be the only one who is the image of him. You are so like him in every way, but cleverer and cooler and not so rash. You are *not* rash, are you? I scarcely know you since you have grown up.'

Richard said, 'No. I try not to be rash.'

She sipped her drink. 'I cannot believe that one of my sons is proposing to murder another. I pray to God for the peace of his soul.'

'Not murder,' Richard lied. 'There has been a process of justice.'

She had been a great beauty in her day, known as the Rose of Raby, and her eyes were still lovely as they flicked up at him.

'Perhaps. Why is Edward so susceptible to the influence of that vulgar, pretentious wife of his? And of her family? Is there a weakness in him? Is there something I have missed? I was proud of him and of his achievements – until yesterday.'

'I don't know. I have loved and admired him for as long as I can remember. I had not expected this.'

'As long as you can remember?' She gave a tiny laugh. 'Do you remember, just before the battle that gained him the throne, I was so fearful for you and – and – George that I shipped the three of us off to the Low Countries for safety?'

He smiled faintly in response. 'Our first dazzling experience of the court of Burgundy. And we had barely arrived when we heard that Edward had won the battle and had been proclaimed king.'

'Yes.' She rose to her feet. 'But now it is time for me to go to chapel for divine service. To pray for all three of my sons. Bring Anne to see me some time, and the baby.'

He knelt to her, and then left, oddly soothed. Her quiet, unswerving piety had brought back the sweet days of his early childhood and he was moved to find that it possessed her still.

He envied her.

11

IT WAS all over by the time he reached the Painted Chamber again, with the bells still ringing for *tierce*.

He found the Constable of the Tower reporting to Edward, who was looking even more haggard than on the day before.

George, it seemed, had declared that he had always thought drowning the best kind of death, though not in the filthy waters of the Thames.

135

In a cask of fresh spring water, perhaps? And then he had said, no, he did not believe that any city water was fit even for swallowing, far less drowning in. It must be ale or wine. He remembered that, in the cellars of the Tower, there were some butts of Malmsey. One of those would do very well. Since he was a big fellow, he should fit in quite neatly.

It was bravado so characteristic of George that Richard felt his own lungs go into spasm.

Edward also gasped, then said, 'And did he?'

'Yes, sire, though the men lowered him in head first and only as far as the chest. Otherwise, he would have displaced most of the contents of the cask and there would not have been enough for him to drown in.'

Edward shuddered. 'I understand.'

Richard, who had closed his eyes briefly, opened them again to ask, with distaste, 'Was it quick?'

'Oh yes, my lord duke. Quicker even than it would have been in water. A few bubbles, a jerk or two, and it was over. I don't suppose it took more than the length of a *Paternoster* from start to finish.'

Edward said, 'You will report to Parliament this afternoon, in due form, that the death sentence has been carried out under your supervision and witnessed by the Lieutenant of the Tower, the Chaplain, the Surgeon, the Gentleman Gaoler, and so on.' He gestured limply. 'Thank you, you may go.'

As the Constable bowed and backed his way out, Edward murmured, '*Requiescat in pace*, George. Rest in peace.'

Richard thought, 'You, too, Edward. And all of us.'

Chapter Seven

1478-80

1

THE RAIN WAS coming down as if all the cherubim and seraphim were baling out the vaults of heaven, while the brown and churning surface of the Thames suggested that the legions of the damned were equally hard at work below. The courtyard of Windsor castle was one huge, muddy puddle and the noise was indescribable.

The king was occupied, as so often, on one of the building projects for which he was renowned; after five years of preparation, the choir and the aisles of his new chapel of St George were at last beginning to rise.

With a satisfied smile he said, 'I have conscripted so many stonecutters into my service that the university of Oxford cannot find anyone to work on their new divinity school. Perhaps that will encourage them to mend their manners in dealings with their king. I am sending one of my purveyors to Cambridge, too, to press masons for work on Fotheringhay.'

Richard, concentrating on where to put his feet, remarked, 'Useful to be a king and able to draft in workmen when you need them.'

An apprentice scuttled forward and laid a board for the king to walk on. Edward nodded to him. 'Thank you, Billy.' His memory for names and faces never failed him. It was one of the keys to his charm.

'Useful, yes,' he rejoined, 'but the cost, the cost! It's not only the labourers. It's the craftsmen for the panelling, the carving, and the stained glass. I am determined that the vestments and hangings, the statues and the service books shall all be of the finest. And I have my eye on that great jewel of John of Suffolk's – you know it, the one with the gold and enamel image of Our Lady with the Holy Infant in her arms and seven angels around – but he wants a knight's ransom for it.'

'You're the king,' Richard said. 'Beat him down.'

Four sodden servants were holding a canopy over the brothers' heads, but Richard, edged sideways by Edward's bulk, was aware of a steady drip of rainwater from the golden fringe finding its way down one side of his neck under his winter furs. King's brother or not, he was forbidden by protocol to complain.

Repressively, Edward said, 'It is not so easy, being the king. You cannot always do what you want to do, and often you have to do what you do *not* want to do.' He gave a practised groan. 'Think of George. He was condemned by the envy of the lords, but it is I who have to bear the blame.'

'Yes.'

It was tactlessly blunt and Edward's eyelids flickered. 'Let us go indoors. I want to show you my new gallery.'

Regardless of new chapels and galleries, it was George they had to talk about. Edward had given Richard back the post of Great Chamberlain which he had been forced to relinquish to George six years earlier, and Parliament had granted him additional portions of the Warwick inheritance as well as permission for certain exchanges of land. Also, one of George's titles — forfeit whether he had lived or died — had been bestowed on Richard and Anne's two-year-old son Ned, who was now a diminutive earl of Salisbury.

There was some resultant gossip, Richard knew, about the profit he had made from George's death, but the profit in fact was not great — certainly not great enough to have influenced him — and he had a shrewd idea of the source of the gossip. As the king's only surviving brother, he had naturally fallen heir to some of the suspicions that had dogged George for so much of his life. He would, he knew, simply have to resign himself to it — and demonstrate his detachment from the succession question by staying away from court. It would be a relief to get away from the southerners, the courtiers, whom he increasingly disliked, and get back to the cleaner north and Middleham. And Anne.

Edward said, 'By the by, I've had George's body escorted to Tewkesbury for burial beside his wife. There'll be a monument, of course, incorporating their effigies. George owed the abbot almost four hundred pounds for some work already done on the tomb, so I've paid some of that. I've authorised payment of his household servants, too. His debts have to be paid for the good of his soul.' Then, tartly, he added, 'And I should be grateful, young Diccon, if you would contrive not to look so disapproving. It is not your place to disapprove of your king.'

'I was not aware of looking disapproving.'

'Humph! You have looked nothing else for these past four months, ever since I decided that George must stand trial. As I have told you before, there are some things that a king *must* do, like it or not, and being strong and decisive is one of them. You're too young to remember, but at Towton in sixty-one I ordered the beheading of every Lancastrian nobleman and gentleman we captured, including no fewer than forty-two knights. I didn't like it, but it was needful and I don't regret it. And in seventy I had twenty of Warwick's men publicly impaled at Southampton. Again, it was needful. Mercy, in this world of ours, is usually seen as a sign of weakness – and no king can afford to be seen as weak. Look at Henry VI!'

Richard would have preferred not to. The unworldly Henry had died, as far as he knew, of a seizure when he heard that his son had been killed at Tewkesbury, but his death had been so convenient for Edward that gossip had been rife. Richard and George and others of Edward's followers had been in the royal lodging in the Tower that night and had fallen under suspicion. When he himself had gone to pay tribute to the body lying in state at the Black Friars a few days later, it had seemed to begin to bleed again, which had been unfortunate in view of the popular belief that corpses always bled afresh in the presence of their murderer. It had not, of course, been bleeding. It had been leaking embalming fluid as a result of slovenly workmanship. The spices and perfumes for embalming cost more than the surgeons' fees, and the surgeons made no secret of resenting it. It was an unpleasant memory nonetheless.

Edward said, 'When retribution is needful, it should be carried out swiftly. And a fundamental law of power is, once committed, never retreat. People forget very quickly and the dispensing of a few favours helps to speed forgetfulness along and ensure goodwill of a sort and, more importantly, obedience. I was not born a king, but I have learned. And I am a successful one.'

Richard was silenced. He had always believed that Edward, no deep thinker, had achieved his success by instinct. Now it appeared that cold calculation had also been at work.

His admiration for his brother had faltered because of George, but he could now see Edward's justification. Whether he could accept it was a matter that only the days, weeks, months, perhaps years would decide, but in the meantime there was considerable food for thought in what Edward had said.

2

ARRIVING HOME at last after his six-months' absence, Richard found that, under a sky of palest blue, the snow still lay thick around Middleham, fresh and pure, marked here and there by human presence but not marred by it. A prison in its way, but a prison of choice, as bustling with people and activity inside its walls as a small town, and free from intrusion.

A world under control. A life under control.

The thaw changed little at first, the melt-waters pouring down from the hillsides to fill the rivers and becks to overflowing so that travellers stayed at home for fear of drowning.

And then came frosts, and skies full of stars, and the crying of the new lambs that arrived every April, with admirable promptitude, just in time for the last brief snowfall of winter. The lambing snow, everybody called it. Impervious to the cold – indeed, seeming to revel in it – they went running, skipping and jumping around the meadows, tails twirling madly as they dived under their mothers to feed.

Ned was just old enough to want to play with them and help to look after the orphans. When he decided to adopt one of them, Anne had to say, 'No', very firmly.

'But I'm a n'earl,' he objected. 'You're not 'llowed to say no to a n'earl.'

Smothering a smile, Anne picked him up and told him, 'An earl you may be, my pet, but I'm a duchess and that's better than being an earl and it means I *am* allowed to say no to you. And I can tell you that it may be fun to have a dear little hand-reared lamb cuddle up in your lap, but when the lamb grows up into a great big sheep it will still want to cuddle up in your lap. And then you'll be *squau-au-au-au-shed*!'

She tickled him and he gurgled and tried to wrap his tongue round the word 'squashed', unsuccessfully at first but improving with practice.

Some little time later, Richard came in, pursuing some piece of paper he had mislaid. Raising his brows at Anne, he asked, 'Why are you looking so glassy-eyed?'

She said, 'Ned, tell your father what you are doing.'

'Learning a new word!' he informed Richard proudly. 'I have to say it over and over, so I remember it.'

'Oh? What is it?'

'Squa . . . Squa . . . Squashed!'

Richard looked admiring.

Ned repeated, 'Squashed!' And then again, 'Squashed!'

Anne murmured, 'Three hundred and forty-three . . .'

'Squashed!'

'Three hundred and forty-four . . .'

'Squashed!'

'Three hundred and forty-five . . .'

Richard threw back his head and laughed. 'Yes, I understand!'

So he put an end to the litany by picking Ned up, putting him on his shoulders and bouncing him up and down, much to the child's delight. Anne found herself sniffling with pure happiness.

She said, 'How nice to feel like a *family*, even if only for five minutes. When are you leaving for London again?'

'Never. Or not from choice.'

3

HE WAS as good as his word for almost three years. Twice in 1478 the king and court came north – to Nottingham in August, and to Pontefract and York in September before returning to Greenwich for the hunting in October. Richard and Anne attended him as required, but the atmosphere was slightly strained.

Otherwise, Richard was away from Middleham often, sometimes at Barnard Castle, sometimes at Sheriff Hutton, sometimes as far north as Harry Percy's lair at Alnwick, but most often at York. As his reputation spread, he and his staff began to take on the colour of a travelling court of law, a 'justice eyre', offering unbiased justice to all who sought it, rich or poor, gentleman or cottar.

Sometimes Anne accompanied him, sometimes not. She disliked leaving little Ned, who was prone to chest complaints. After an agonising miscarriage, she showed no sign of conceiving again, which was a sadness to her, but she was still only in her early twenties, so there was time enough. The queen, who was over forty, was said to be pregnant yet again – for the eleventh time.

Richard seemed now to be very little interested in what was going on at court, although every time he returned to Middleham Anne had further news for him. Her auntbymarriage, Margaret Beaufort, had begun writing to her conscientiously, and she occasionally also heard from the queen, but far more entertaining were the wonderfully indiscreet letters she received from two of the queen's ladiesinwaiting.

The king's amorous appetites, it seemed, were diminishing as his appetite at table increased, although Lord Hastings and the marquess of Dorset continued to compete with each other as his panders. Happily, seduction or near-rape was no longer the automatic fate of any pretty woman who smiled at him. Even so, Mistress Shore was still his favourite companion. A delightful person, according to the ladies-in-waiting, who clearly found her more congenial than they did their employer. It said much about the queen, Anne reflected, that she could not even rely on her ladies to be loyal to her.

Herself in need of a new lady-in-waiting – her favourite, Mary, having recently married and departed for Cornwall – she found herself mentally running through a list of those she had known in the past, and when Francis arrived on a visit from Minster Lovell, was inspired to ask him, 'Do you recollect Constantia? A dark-haired girl, handsome rather than pretty, but with lovely smiling hazel eyes? She was at Middleham when we were children and then she was one of Isabel's ladies for a while. She helped you and Richard track me down when I was a "kitchen maid". Remember? Have you ever heard anything more of her? I was wondering where to find her.'

It had been a casual enough enquiry and she was startled by his reaction. The expression on his face was . . . What was it? There was embarrassment in it, certainly, and – guilt?

It couldn't mean what she thought it meant. Her eyes like saucers, she said accusingly, '*Francis!*'

'Yes, well . . .'

'I don't believe it! Is *Constantia* the "charming lady" you have an arrangement with?'

He gulped. 'Yes.'

'Well, why in the world didn't you say so? She's a splendid girl! Why have you been so secretive about her?'

'I didn't know what you would think.'

'Oh, Francis! I always liked her when we were children and she's *perfectly* respectable – I know her mother was Italian, but it doesn't show. Her father is a Northamptonshire gentleman, isn't he?'

Gratefully, he smiled. 'Yes. But I wasn't sure that Richard would be so understanding. I do have a wife, and you know what he's like about moral laxity.'

Anne could only laugh. 'My dear, you're the last man in the world he would accuse of moral laxity. It's the shameless promiscuity of Edward's court that Richard can't abide, and if you and Constantia have had your arrangement for — what? — three years . . .'

'Four. Almost five.'

'Well, then, you can hardly be called promiscuous. But you *must* divorce Nan, you know.'

'Yes, I'd like to, but . . .' As always when the question arose, he looked slightly hunted. 'If I went to the Dean of Arches to have our marriage annulled, it might frighten her into changing her mind and offering to come and live with me after all. Which would completely undermine my case if I had to take it to Rome in the end. It could ruin my life. I love Constantia so much.'

She said doubtfully, 'Perhaps Richard could do something to help.'

'What, for example?'

'I don't know.'

4

FRANCIS made it a rule never to presume on his friendship with Richard by asking favours, so he presented himself before his friend a day or two later, looking very much like a nervous supplicant at one of Richard's ducal courts. His thin, fair-complexioned, sensitive face wore a worried frown, his voice was deprecating, his light brown hair ruffled, and he seemed unsure of what to do with his lanky limbs, as he said, 'I wonder if I might impose on your good nature . . .'

Richard gave a splutter of laughter. 'Pray do,' he said cordially, 'but have the decency to sit down so that I don't have to crick my neck by staring up at you. Though you may kneel, if you'd rather.'

Francis grinned back at him. 'Well, I'm embarrassed, but there's something Anne says I should talk to you about and I'm not sure how you're going to take it.'

'You'll never find out until you try.'

Richard couldn't imagine Francis ever doing anything he himself would dislike or disapprove of and, indeed, when the story of Francis's romance with Constantia came tumbling out, his friend's good fortune gave him nothing but pleasure tinged with a mild surprise. Richard distantly remembered Constantia as a striking dark little girl with an occasionally sarcastic tongue who might have been expected to dominate the gentle Francis, but there was no hint of the relationship being other than loving and equal. Constantia, Richard deduced, must have developed into a warm and wise young woman.

He gripped Francis's hands and said, 'I am truly delighted for you. The question is, what can we do to iron out your difficulties? I'm not sure that I am the right man to ask. I have not yet succeeded in extracting a dispensation from Rome for my own marriage to Anne! But you, at least, don't have to contend with the tables of affinity. What I could do, I suppose, is talk to your wife's brother FitzHugh and discover whether it would be acceptable for you to buy your way out of the existing marriage to his sister. He's a sensible fellow and might well be cooperative if you went to the Court of Arches for an annulment. Shall I try it? It's easier for me to talk to him, than for you.'

Francis would have preferred no one to talk to anyone. His difficulties were not acute, and he feared that talking about them might make them so. But whereas his own instincts were to let sleeping dogs lie, he knew that, for Richard, this would not be an option. So he smiled, and said, 'Would you? But don't make too much of an issue of it.'

'I'll be careful. In the dreary world of today, I can't tell you how tempting it is to be offered an opportunity to help a friend towards happiness.'

5

NEXT YEAR there was plague in the south and the king's third and youngest son died of it, aged one-and-a-half. His baptismal name had been George.

Richard was silent at first when Anne told him. Then he said bleakly, 'The sins of the fathers' – and went off to the mews to see to his hawks.

Anne was left standing with her hand out to stop him and shock in her heart, murmuring, 'What if it had been Ned?'

Richard's response had been orthodox enough but quite unlike him. He refused to talk about it and she could not bear to pursue it.

He reacted uncharacteristically, too, when Lord Hastings glee-fully reported to him later in the year an item of news which Anne found improperly but deliciously funny.

The king had been unsuccessful in persuading the duchy of Burgundy that Anthony Woodville, Earl Rivers, minor noble-man that he was, would be a suitable husband for the country's new ruler, the lovely young Duchess Mary. The queen had been highly offended and insisted that another wife 'of suitable rank' must be found for her brother. The only candidate – who had also been the alternative object of George, duke of Clarence's marital ambitions – was Margaret, sister of James III, king of Scots.

Mistress Margaret had just emerged from a nunnery to make her début at the Scots court and, since James was anxious for an alliance with England, in due course all was arranged. A safe conduct was duly issued for Margaret to enter and travel through England with three hundred attendants for her marriage to Lord Rivers on or about May 16th, but she did not set out. The Scots explained that King James was too busy besieging his annoying brother, the duke of Albany, in Dunbar castle to give full attention to his sister's affairs.

In August another safe conduct was issued for a marriage date in November. But again, she did not set out.

In the end, it emerged that the young lady's affections had been secretly engaged elsewhere, and that she was pregnant as a result.

It was a truly shocking insult, and one which gave great pleasure to all those who detested the Woodvilles.

The queen was scandalised and the king sent furious messages to James, talking of deceit and betrayal and generally conveying that he held James to have dishonoured himself by trying to introduce a wanton into the royal family of England. It was outrageous and not to be borne.

Anne laughed, but Richard was not entertained. 'For Edward to talk of wantons! In any case, it was an ill-conceived match from the start. Anthony Rivers is already the virtual ruler of Wales through his control of the prince's person and household, and to arrange a royal marriage for him was madness. He has more than enough power already. I thought Edward had learned from experience not to encourage the rise of over-mighty subjects.'

Anne looked demurely down at her hands. When Richard spoke of encouraging over-mighty subjects, he meant her father but, although it had been Richard who had inherited most of Warwick's power and influence, he never thought of *himself* as an 'over-mighty subject'. It was a strange blind spot. Or perhaps it was simply that he knew himself devoted to strengthening Edward's rule rather than weakening or contesting it.

Even so, she was uneasy. What drove him had not changed since George's execution, but where once he had accepted Edward's policies with a cheerful, if occasionally argumentative readiness, he had now become colder and more critical. It was not that his devotion to Edward had diminished. It was more that he suspected Edward, increasingly lazy as the years passed, of being too much under the influence of bad advisers – notably the Woodvilles. Anne knew he thought that Edward was not being true to himself.

He said, 'One good thing. If Edward has indeed written to the king of Scots in the terms Hastings reports, we should see some action soon. Even that weakling James will not tolerate being spoken to in such a way.'

6

HE WAS proved right within weeks. One of his constant preoc-cupations over the previous eight years had been dealing with the wild men and the blood feuds of the Anglo-Scottish border, and in particular with four Liddesdale families – the Nixons, Arm-strongs, Elliots and Croziers – who terrorised their neighbours on both sides of the border, raiding, reiving, murdering, burning, blackmailing and kidnapping. Between them, they had been known to raise more than two thousand armed men for maraud-ing expeditions into the northern counties of England, but Richard and Harry Percy had succeeded in holding them in check, so that forays under cover of dark by no more than a handful of them had become the norm.

But now, abruptly, they reverted to their traditional ways, and the barbaric Liddesdale valley just north of the border rang to the equally barbaric sound of war axes and knife blades being honed.

With grim pleasure, Richard sent out a summons to the local gentry to meet him at Barnard Castle with their archers and men-at-arms for a punitive expedition and then, gathering three hundred of his own men around him, set off from Middleham for the Border.

It was a morning of swirling fog as they took the familiar track in their steel helmets and leather jacks, so that sometimes the head of the cavalcade faded into the murk and Richard's white boar standard seemed to flutter unsupported above the mist. And then the fog would break and re-form and this time it would be the tail of the cavalcade that vanished. Richard had instructed the trumpeter to save his breath, but his scouts – his 'scurriers' – had little difficulty in finding and reporting back to him. A large body of horsemen, no matter how well disciplined, could never travel in silence.

It did not matter greatly. They were still too far south of the Border to stumble on any stray bands of reivers ripe for pouncing on, and Richard's object, in any case, was to surround their known hideouts and attack in full force.

He gave a signal to swing round slightly to the east, where he had agreed to pick up Francis and his dozen men on the way to Barnard Castle. Francis had at last made up his mind to embark on the work that needed to be done at Killerby, though it was rather too close to the estates of the FitzHughs, his wife's family, for Francis's emotional comfort. He had long ago received from Edward a licence to crenellate the castle, enabling him to strengthen its fortifications, but architecture had become an obsession with him and, as a result, he was also full of such modern delights as solars, bay windows and water piped up to the top of the towers. Richard smiled briefly to himself, wondering what was the point. Francis would certainly not be able to live at Killerby or bring Constantia there without provoking a nasty clash with his FitzHugh in-laws. When Richard had put out feelers, Lord FitzHugh had not responded well to the suggestion that he might agree to his sister and Francis being divorced. Poor Francis. He didn't deserve such a hard time.

The fog was becoming thicker as they reached the low-lying pastures, smothering sounds and distorting their direction. Even so – Richard frowned – it was unnaturally quiet. And then came the muffled tattoo of horsemen riding fast; one or two, no more. His scouts? He signalled a halt.

'Reivers, my lord!' the scouts gasped. 'They've sacked the next hamlet. No sign of them now, though.'

They had indeed sacked the next hamlet. Its dozen houses lay black and smoking, with men's bodies scattered around and a few empty-eyed women and infants wandering among them or sitting weeping by the side of the track. The only other sign of life was the hoodie crows perched waiting on the fallen roof beams.

One of the widows held out a beseeching hand to Richard. 'Help us, my lord! Help us!'

'When did this happen?'

'This very morn, my lord, at break of day. Help us, my lord!'

'How many of them? Where else have they been? Where have they gone?'

'I dinna knaw, my lord. A score of them, mebbe. They drove our cows and sheep off Easby way.'

He flung a handful of coins at her. 'You must fend for yourselves until I can send help. Or make your way to Middleham and tell the Duchess Anne what has happened. She will see to your needs.'

If they were driving cattle and sheep with them, they would make poor speed. Richard urged his troop to a gallop.

'Easby way' was also Killerby way.

7

HE HAD seen battlefields enough in his twenty-seven years, but it was like a hammer blow to the heart when he cast his eyes on Killerby.

Will Kent, one of Francis's retainers, was hanging from a tree, a great knife slash splitting him from breastbone to belly and his guts hanging out. Another man, whom Richard did not know, had been hanged by the feet and shot full of arrows. A third had been tossed, wounded, into the courtyard fire, and logs piled on top of him; he was moaning still when Richard's men dragged him clear. And bright little Jemmy, one of Francis's pages, had had his adolescent balls cut off and then been tied down head first in the midden to suffocate. In his mind, Richard could hear the reivers joking about wee cocks and their own dunghills. He pulled the boy out, but it was too late.

They had fought hard, and had paid for it. There were another dozen hacked bodies strewn around on the grass, among them three, perhaps four, of the attackers.

Keeping fifty men with him, Richard sent the rest off in pursuit of the reivers. 'I want their heads,' he said.

And then began searching for Francis.

The stone castle had not burned, of course, but all its contents, its floor and roof timbers, were still smouldering from the burning brands that had been flung inside, and occasional bursts of flame shot out from the arrow-slit windows. Part of the parapet had collapsed.

It was under the rubble that Richard, beginning to despair, found Francis at last, covered in dust and blood, a great slice of flesh and muscle off his shoulder and an axe wound to his skull. Miraculously, he was still alive.

Just.

8

RICHARD'S MEN brought back a small flock of sheep, three cows, a dozen ponies, and fifteen human heads in a couple of makeshift sacks. They had caught up with the reivers no more than a mile away.

He said, 'Tom Scroby, see that the cattle and sheep are returned to the hamlet they came from. Reeth, take charge of the heads; we will deliver them personally to their families when we reach Liddesdale. Tyrell, ride on to Barnard Castle and say I have been delayed. Surgeon John, see what you can do for Lord Lovell while Ratcliffe and I make a stretcher to carry him back to Middleham. A horse litter would throw him about too much, so we will need relays of four men to carry the stretcher – men who can take equal lengths of stride and move fast and without stumbling. Fifteen minutes on, fifteen off. Take as many men as you need, Ratcliffe, and Surgeon John will go with you. Take one of the scurriers, too, so that I can be kept informed.'

Then, the anger still foaming in his veins, he turned to his chaplain. 'No, father. Do not presume to reproach me for retaliating against these wild men in the only way they under-stand. Occupy yourself with praying for the dead who lie around you and arranging for their burial. I will leave you twenty men to help. Then ride on and join us on our way to Liddesdale. There will be many there in need of the last rites before this expedition is over.'

9

THE LOOKOUT in the Middleham watch tower sounded the series of calls on his horn that signified friends approaching, but Anne came close to fainting when she looked out and saw the far-off little procession.

Richard.

Then she observed that the face of the figure on the stretcher was not covered, which meant that he was not dead, and steadied herself sufficiently to summon everyone in the castle whose services might be needed. By the time the procession entered the gatehouse, beds were being warmed, cauldrons were on the fires, the parish clerk was on his way with his aspersion and holy water, and the apothecary was gathering together his self-heal, yarrow and shepherd's purse to control any bleeding as well as fresh moss for the poultices to hold them in place. She found her key to the painted wooden chest where spices and other expensive household ingredients were kept, and took out the little box of dried mandrake root from the Mediterranean, the most effective pain-killer there was.

Only then did she discover that the patient was not Richard after all, but Francis — kindly, peaceable, humorous Francis, quite undeserving of terrible injuries and imminent death.

Unlike Richard, who regularly went out looking for just such a fate but rarely suffered more than minor flesh wounds.

She dashed the tears from her eyes and saw that everything was being done that could be done. Then she sat down and wrote a hurried letter to Constantia at Minster Lovell and sent off a messenger with instructions to ride like the wind.

10

FOR EIGHT long days, Francis hovered on the edge of death, limp and motionless at first, and then dangerously restless so that it was necessary to watch over him every hour of the twenty-four in case he disturbed his healing wounds. After that, he floated in and out of consciousness for days on end, but when he opened his bruised eyes one bright spring morning to see Constantia beside his bed, a Constantia ready to drop with exhaustion from her panic-stricken two-hundred-mile gallop but her smile alight with love and mockery, he knew everything was all right and his return to the world began.

By that time, Richard was back, full of vigour and baleful cheer at having wiped out the nest of vipers – or most of them. It had been a highly satisfactory expedition, he said, and only the first of many.

Francis said, 'Good. I'll come with you next time,' and recoiled slightly as Richard showed signs of being about to give him an approving clap on the back.

Anne and Constantia exchanged despairing glances. Men had no sense, even the best of them.

Belatedly, Richard noticed Constantia. 'Ah, you've arrived, have you? Welcome. I wondered why Francis was looking so much better.' But before Constantia could reply, he had turned back to Francis. 'It is high time that the Scots are taught a lesson they will not forget. We need to make a clean cut through the tangle that has developed. Edward has been plotting with Louis of France against Burgundy. He has also been plotting with

Burgundy against Louis of France. That old spider Louis has therefore sent a certain Dr Ireland to James of Scotland – are you following me? – to stir him up against England.'

'Does he need stirring up?'

Richard chuckled. 'Not after Edward's messages to him com‚ plaining not only about the Lady Margaret but about his raiding and pillaging over the border. Charming though my brother is in person, he can be odious on paper.'

Constantia laid a soothing hand on Francis's forehead and Anne said, 'Richard, will you go away? Francis needs rest.'

'Oh, very well. Have you told him that Edward has appointed me lieutenant‚general of the north?'

'And that you are now entitled to call the whole of the north to arms? No. He has had enough excitement for one day. Go away.'

11

THAT JAMES resented Edward's hectoring tone very soon became apparent. One of his barons, Archie Douglas, earl of Angus, marched twenty miles down the east coast of England and not only sacked the great clifftop fortress of Bamburgh Castle but had the impertinence to stay there for three nights and three days instead of scuttling off home again.

Joyfully, Richard and Harry Percy mounted a retaliatory raid into Scotland, killing, burning and laying waste as custom required.

Insults continued to ricochet back and forth between Edinburgh and Westminster until, at the end of the year, Edward and his council decided that an invasion of Scotland was inevitable and that Edward himself should lead it.

Edward's instructions to his ambassador were duly copied to

Richard, who told Francis, now out of the sickroom, 'Unless we have reparation for the Scots' breaches of our existing truce . . .'

Constantia said, 'Truce? I didn't know we had a truce with Scotland.'

For weeks, Constantia had cared devotedly for Francis, but it was her presence more than her nursing that had brought him back to himself. He was uneasy when she was away from him and they had become so close that they thought and spoke as one, their alternating voices driving Richard to complain that holding a conversation with Francis was like watching a game of tennis, very hard on the neck muscles. 'I wish the pair of you would sit closer together,' he said. 'I'm tired of having to wag my head all the time.'

12

ANNE HAD asked Constantia whether it had always been like this. She was a little wary of asking questions at first, because it was more than ten years since she and Constantia had been on the easy terms of childhood, and people could change a great deal during their growing up. She knew Constantia couldn't have changed for the worse, otherwise Francis would not have loved her, but having written to summon Constantia to his side she had found herself worrying dreadfully over it. The situation, she recognised, would be difficult for both of them. She herself had come to regard Francis as if he were a dearly loved brother, and was terrified of Constantia seeing her as possessive. And Constantia, of course, would know herself to be an intruder, though an invited one.

But there had not been a single clashing moment. For both of them, Francis's wellbeing had been their sole concern.

'Have we always thought alike?' Constantia repeated. 'Yes, but the last few weeks have brought us beyond that.' She smiled. 'I suppose it's not to be wondered at in such a situation.'

'No. Not for two people who truly love each other. As you do.' Anne thought she saw uncertainty in Constantia's eyes, and said, 'Don't look so doubtful! How many times a day does he tell you he loves you?'

Constantia laughed. 'Dozens.'

'Without prompting?'

'Of course.'

'Is that something new?'

Constantia, who as an unmarried young woman – as she took pleasure in pointing out – was not expected to wear her hair tightly bound up under a cap or hennin, cocked her curly dark head. 'The frequency is new, but I don't think a day has passed since we have been together when he has failed to tell me at least once that he loves me.'

'How delightful,' Anne said, quite unaware of how wistful she sounded.

'Some men are more demonstrative than others.' Constantia, annoyed with herself, hurried on, 'But if I was looking doubtful it was only because I was wondering whether this closeness can survive into ordinary life, without such crises to feed on.'

Anne gave a little puff of amusement. 'Closeness or crises. What a choice!'

'Not a difficult one.' Constantia smiled back at her. 'We will contrive perfectly well without the crises.'

13

NOW, RICHARD replied, 'Yes, we *do* have a truce with the Scots, even if it doesn't show. Anyway, Master Leigh is required to tell

James that Edward is determined to make "rigorous and cruel war". He is also – if he sees fit! – to remind James that the Scots are unlawfully in occupation of Berwick, Roxburgh, Coldingham and other English towns, and that James has failed to pay due homage to Edward.' He laughed. 'The Scots really will *not* like that. They have never acknowledged England's overlordship.'

Francis asked, 'No "but ifs" to offer a way out?'

'Well, only if strictly necessary and "to avoid the effusion of Christian blood" – though I myself would put a pretty low estimate on the Christian content of Scots blood. The idea is that James could simply give back Berwick and send us that seven-year-old boy of his who is supposedly betrothed to little Princess Cicely, to be brought up in England and thus prove that he is committed to the marriage alliance. And then all would be sweetness and light again.'

'Will James do it?'

'*He* might, but his barons would never permit it.' Richard looked from Francis to Constantia reflectively. 'And talking of marriage . . .'

He had taken care that the FitzHughs should know of Francis's life-threatening injuries but there had been no response beyond a polite note of commiseration from Francis's brother-in-law Richard, Lord FitzHugh, a pleasant man. From Nan there had been nothing.

'And talking of marriage,' he repeated, 'I am prepared, if you wish, to speak to FitzHugh again about you buying your way out of your marriage to Nan. His initial response was negative, but he may by now have had second thoughts. Even he must see that the present situation is untenable, and if you were to offer to make not just a satisfactory but a generous settlement on his sister, Constantia's name need not enter into it. You could afford it. What do you think?'

Francis shrugged — and winced. Save for a few scars and a lingering weakness in his left shoulder, he had recovered well, so well that he occasionally forgot that there were movements it was wiser not to make.

What was interesting to others was the way his illness had changed him, had made him not weaker but stronger. Francis, who had always been self-deprecating, was so no more. He knew he had proved himself.

'I appreciate the offer,' Francis said, 'but I'm not sure that it's worth your while.' He took Constantia's hand in his, and they smiled into each other's eyes. 'Constantia and I are perfectly content with things as they are.'

Constantia chuckled. 'Besides,' she said, 'if everyone at court can have a dozen mistresses without it causing problems, I don't see why Francis should be criticised for having just one.'

Anne teased Richard afterwards. 'You are as pleased with their love affair as if you had masterminded it yourself.'

Richard said, 'Ha!'

Chapter Eight

1480-83

1

'EIGHTY BUTTS of Malmsey for the use of the king and his army against the Scots! Has Edward *no* sense of propriety?'

All Richard's rage and resentment over George's death had revived. Anne had never seen him so coldly angry.

Between February and April, a stream of royal mandates concerning victuals and transport for the invasion of Scotland had been issuing from Westminster, Edward having confirmed that he would lead the invasion himself and therefore taking a very personal interest in the arrangements. This time, his campaigning luxuries did not extend to a portable house such as he had taken to France in 1475; just some strikingly lavish tents and fittings. And the Malmsey.

Richard and Harry Percy had spent the winter inspecting the Border garrisons, repairing the fortifications of Carlisle, and conducting a census of men who could be called to arms. Then Richard had paid a swift visit to London to discuss tactics with Edward.

Naval operations on the east coast were to be entrusted to Lord

Howard, with a fleet crewed by three thousand men, and there was to be an independent squadron to patrol off the west coast of Scotland, commanded by Sir Thomas Fulford. The land force Edward proposed to bring north with him was to include three thousand men supplied by Lord Rivers, the same number of archers from Lord Stanley, and a further six hundred men from the queen's elder son by her first marriage, the marquess of Dorset. Edward also had an idea of stirring up disaffection in Scotland by issuing a commission empowering Richard to promise lands, lordships and gifts to all Scots prepared to collaborate with England.

'I will come north as soon as I conveniently can, although I may be delayed by my negotiations with Burgundy and difficulties with Louis of France,' Edward said. But the months passed, and Jocky Howard's fleet inflicted a spectacular defeat on the Scots navy in the Firth of Forth, and Richard and Harry Percy gathered their forces in the north and raided into Scotland and fought off Scots incursions into England – and still Edward did not come, or tell them when he was likely to.

Not until September did he leave London for Woodstock and nearby Oxford, where he was entertained at the new college of Magdalen and attended a public disputation at the university. At the end of October, he moved on to Nottingham, there to enjoy three weeks in the sumptuous new privy lodging he had built there. By then it was too late in the season for war in the north, so he went back to London, throwing out hints about a new idea for setting the Scots by the heels.

'Why're you so grumpy?' five-year-old Ned demanded of his father.

Richard treated him to the annihilating stare that reduced his military subordinates to gibbering idiocy but troubled his small son not at all.

'There has been a bad harvest this year,' he said — speaking to the child, as he always did, as if he were a grownup — 'and it is going to be a hard winter, and, unless we succeed in storming Berwick, which I think unlikely, I am probably going to spend most of it sitting outside the walls of the castle with the earl of Northumberland and Lord Stanley and a great many others, hoping it will surrender.'

'Can I come and watch?'

'No.'

'I want to!'

'No.'

'But I *want* to!'

Richard said, 'Anne . . .'

She took the child by the hand. 'Come along. You'd get all cold and wet and catch that horrid cough, and then you'd be in bed for weeks and not be able to play with the new puppies.'

'Don't care, I *want* to go and . . .'

He was very like his father.

But when she had handed Ned over to his nurse, she went back to Richard, who was now deep in discussion with Sir James Tyrell and the lawyer William Catesby, and said, 'I would like to come and watch, too.'

'What?'

'I said I would like to come and watch, too.'

'I heard that. Watch what?'

'The siege, of course.'

'The answer is the same. No.'

'Why not? It would be interesting, and it would make a change.'

'No.'

'Other men allow their wives to watch them fight. From a distance.'

163

'Only men who do not love their wives. I have better things to do than spend my time worrying about your safety. Now, Catesby, the king has granted me ten thousand pounds to pay my men. Is it enough, and how do we allocate it?'

Anne stared at him. 'Only men who do not love their wives.' It was the most extraordinary thing for him to have said, and what made it even more extraordinary was that he did not seem to realise that he had said it.

Her eyebrows somewhere up in her hairline and her eyes impossibly wide, she decided she had better go away and think about it.

2

JAMES OF SCOTLAND had had sufficient foresight to provision his coastal fortresses, including Berwick, against the possibility of siege. He had also spent money on bombards and serpentines, as well as two galleys capable of outrunning and outmanoeuvring Jocky Howard's 'great ships' and thus well suited to supplying or reinforcing coastal fortresses when the need arose.

Berwick's defenders, unfortunately, knew what they were doing. By March, after a long, long winter, Richard's besieging force had succeeded only in bringing down part of the recently built outer wall of the town, while the castle remained virtually untouched. England needed siege artillery.

With his troops increasingly cold, bored and sickly, Richard decided to leave the siege to Lord Stanley while he himself went off with Harry Percy to repel James's Border raids in the west and put down the disorder affecting the northern counties as a result of the bad harvest and Edward's demands for taxes to finance the Scottish war.

Francis went, too.

Anne and Constantia knew better than to protest, but Richard understood. Giving Constantia a brief embrace as he and his men prepared to ride out again, he murmured, 'I will see that no harm comes to him.'

Afterwards, her lovely amber eyes gleaming with tears, she said to Anne, 'He is a good man. His manner is so hard and single-minded – he is such an elemental force – that it is easy to forget.'

Anne sighed. 'It comes and goes. He wasn't always a stranger to . . .' She stopped. Stranger to what? Gentleness, kindness, humour, tolerance? They were all still there beneath the surface for the small number of people he liked or loved, but not for those he had reason to mistrust. She had thought about it a good deal, and had come to see that there were, indeed, very few people worthy of being liked or trusted. Everyone knew that the world was in terminal decline and rushing towards judgement, which was perhaps why there was now so little humanity, so little that was disinterested, so much of selfishness, so little care for others.

But life had to be lived. It was not a *good* world and her own instinct was to stay withdrawn from it, but Richard could not. Would not. There was a streak of responsibility, a sense of destiny in him that forbade him to stand aside. She did not know what would come of it.

3

IN THE first days of June, Lord Stanley abandoned Berwick to one of his lieutenants and went off irritably to answer a summons from his wife to attend her at Westminster. He habitually added a leer when he told anyone that his wife needed him, but he knew from experience that she never needed him for anything more interesting than to sign documents. What would it turn out to be this time?

Her son. Of course.

After their marriage, it had not taken him long to discover just how obsessed she was with young Henry and his rights. She hadn't even seen the boy for a dozen years, and only rarely before that, when he had been a ward of the Herberts in Wales. But they corresponded endlessly, Henry demanding funds and moaning about his 'incarceration' at the court of Brittany, when in fact – as far as Stanley had been able to discover – he was leading the usual comfortable life of a valued hostage, all his needs paid for, and taken along with the court whenever it went on its travels. He was probably hunting and hawking and dancing and feasting with the best of them.

But whenever he said as much to Margaret, she replied that the boy was not *free*, was deprived through no fault of his own of his hereditary rights, and that it was her intention that they should be restored to him. He was, after all, of royal blood, and the last surviving heir to the claims of the House of Lancaster. She had been trying for years to manipulate Edward into giving him at least some of his due.

When Stanley arrived at the Palace of Westminster, the Great Hall was full of people. He knew most of them, or most of those who proclaimed their rank by the number of flatterers who surrounded them. There was only one stranger, a skinny dark fellow in extravagant clothes who seemed to be laying down the law with great conviction and whom no one offered to introduce.

Margaret was seated, with her receiver-general Reginald Bray in attendance, in the partitioned-off corner of the Great Hall which served as the Court of Chancery. The massive figure of the king was standing over her, looking as if he proposed giving her not a minute more of his time and attention than was absolutely necessary. Stanley knew how he felt. When Margaret got the bit between her teeth, there was no stopping her. The bishops of Ely and Worcester were there, too, and a cardinal legate, all so heavy-eyed and lethargic that it was obvious Margaret's monologue had been going on for some time.

Small, neat and erect, she gestured to Stanley to join them. 'Ah, husband, we are drawing up a document concerning certain appointments and agreements. Your signature is required.'

'And what am I to sign?'

The king said wearily, 'Your lady wife is anxious to attract her son back home to England, which requires not only my consent but his. I have no particular views on the subject . . .'

Changed days, Stanley thought.

'. . . but the honour of Richmond, which she claims for him, has reverted to the crown and there are also trusts and Wills involved which require my approval of their terms. Lady Margaret appears to believe that her son might refuse to return to her maternal bosom unless financial incentives – and my goodwill – are guaranteed to him.'

It was clear to Stanley, as to everyone else, that the king was sick to death of the last imp of the Lancastrian brood, who no longer posed even the most distant threat to his throne, and anxious only to hear the last of Margaret's interminable pleas.

Margaret smiled sweetly at her husband. 'So, if you would please sign this undertaking not to interfere with the arrangements I made some years ago to assure my son of my estates in the West country . . .'

Stanley took the quill and scratched out his signature.

She said, 'He will also receive an increased proportion of my late mother's estates if he agrees to return from exile.'

From a quick glimpse as he handed the document back over the table to her, he saw that the boy was to be induced to return from exile not only by money but 'to be in the grace and favour of the king's highness'.

Good for him!

There was more talk, and then one of the royal clerks appended the king's seal to the indenture and that was the end of the matter.

The king said, 'By the way, Stanley, I require you and Hastings to come with me to Fotheringhay tomorrow. Richard will be there. We have important matters to discuss.'

Stanley was aggrieved. Fotheringhay was only four leagues from Collyweston, one of Margaret's favourite residences. If today's business had been conducted at Fotheringhay instead of at Westminster, it would have saved him a ride twenty leagues longer than it need have been.

However, he dutifully congratulated his wife on her perseverance and she replied in a low tone, 'I have warned my son so often against the king that I fear it will not be easy to convince him now of Edward's good faith.'

'I am sure you will manage it.' He said it with absent sarcasm, before he went on, 'Who is that fellow by the fireplace, the one who's doing all the talking?'

'Him? Oh, some Scotsman, I believe.'

4

RICHARD ARRIVED at Fotheringhay feeling uncharacteristically weary, although nothing would have induced him to admit it, from his recent incursion into southern Scotland, in the course of which he had given Dumfries and several other towns to the flames. He had had no opportunity to rest before setting out in response to Edward's summons.

The flat, treeless cornfields and pastures leading towards the bridge across the Nene were today an armed camp full of men and horses and gaily coloured, conically roofed tents with pennants flying from their summits. As Richard and his riding household negotiated a path through them towards the single street of good stone buildings and collegiate church that constituted the settlement of Fotheringhay, Richard glanced up at the castle and admired the work his brother had done on restoring it. Inside, he already knew, there were recently built chambers, kitchens and latrines but, Edward being Edward, that was unlikely to be the end of it.

Devoutly he hoped that Edward was not proposing to stay here and oversee further works instead of leading his army on the invasion of Scotland. Though if he did decide to stay here while investing Richard with the sole command, that would be a good solution. As long as he made a firm decision to do *something*. His procrastinating over the last eighteen months had got on everybody's nerves.

The new arrivals were formally welcomed by the steward of the royal household. Richard said cordially, 'Tired of sitting outside Berwick?'

Stanley's small lopsided mouth under the big nose twisted slightly. 'I was summoned.'

'Ah.'

Richard knelt before Edward and was jovially ordered to, 'Get up! Get up!' Then, surveying him, Edward remarked, 'God's teeth, but you're dusty. Never mind. There's someone I want to introduce you to.' The man who had been standing behind him moved into view and Edward said to him, 'This is my little brother . . .'

Richard detested being referred to as 'little brother', and Francis saw his face tighten just as the stranger said, 'Aye, weel. He's bound to be wee by comparison wi' you, is he no'? And he isnae *that* wee!'

It was so unexpected that Richard gave a spurt of laughter.

Majestically ignoring the Scotsman's reference to his girth, Edward resumed, '. . . Richard, duke of Gloucester. *And*, Diccon my boy, this is . . .' He paused dramatically.

Richard said, 'Alexander Stewart, duke of Albany, brother to the king of Scots. Yes, we've met.'

'Oh.'

'During the truce, when as wardens of the West Marches we foregathered to discuss the possibility of controlling the border reivers.'

'Aye,' agreed Albany. 'We didnae get very far wi' it, though.'

'That, of course,' Richard said politely, 'was partly because you were declared a traitor and had to flee your country.'

Edward intervened. 'Well, well, we're not here to talk about the past. Let us find peace and quiet in my closet and discuss what we *are* here to talk about. Stanley, you had better come with us. I wish Hastings were here, but he is in Calais. You may join us, Lovell, if you wish.'

'Thank you, sire.'

Richard, his brows raised in false innocence, ushered Albany courteously before him, and Albany, who was perhaps two years younger, took it as his due. Francis smiled to himself. Men who were too full of themselves, or not very clever, usually failed to observe Richard's sardonic edge.

When they were settled in Edward's closet, the plot began to emerge.

The background was already familiar. The king of Scots had been anxious for years to stay at peace with England, but in this he had been at odds with his nobles, for whom England was the traditional enemy. His nobles opposed him on other counts, too.

James III was something of a dilettante, with a fondness for music and culture that failed to accord with the cruder instincts of his subjects. There was much criticism of his low-born favourites and of his laxity in administration. He was generally dismissed as being a weak king – this, by nobles whose ancestors had not hesitated to assassinate his grandfather, James I, for precisely the opposite failing. Perhaps it had been good, rather than bad luck that had enabled the second of the Jameses to escape the animus of his barons by standing too close to a faulty cannon and blowing himself up.

The present James's inclination towards peace at any price had given his younger brother, Albany, the opportunity to endear himself to those of the belligerent tendency – those who consid-ered it their God-given right to do as they damned well pleased, king or no king – which he had accordingly done by urging on the wild men of the Borders and loudly declaring in favour of war against England.

James had finally been driven to act against him when a witch prophesied that the king would be slain by one of his nearest kin.

From gaol in Edinburgh Castle, Albany had escaped to France, looking for military support. But now, Louis having provided him with a wife and not much else, he had turned to Edward to reinstate him in his Scottish estates and titles.

'It's wicked being cut aff frae yer hameland,' he said. 'Ye've been an exile yerself, and ye ken it's a right scunner.'

Edward looked at Richard, who obligingly translated, 'You know how disagreeable it is to be exiled.'

'Indeed I do.' Edward was at his most stately, and very convincing, too. 'But human sympathy is hardly a sufficient reason for me to help you regain your estates, especially when you have always been such a troublesome neighbour to England. I believe your possessions in Annandale adjoin the Debatable Land and are locally known as a den of thieves?'

Albany glowered at Richard. 'They're jist folks who love their country.'

'I see,' Edward responded blandly. 'However, as you will appreciate, you cannot expect aid from England save in return for a substantial *quid pro quo.*'

'A substantial whit?'

'Spare us, Albany!' Richard snapped. 'You're among – for want of a better word – friends. You don't have to pretend to be an illiterate peasant. And we won't hold it against you if you speak plain English.'

Albany's thin, long-nosed Stewart face, with its small mouth and pouched eyes, did not change, but he said, 'And what kind of *quid pro quo* did you have in mind?'

Edward let out a puff of relief. 'That's better. I hear you've been describing yourself as the king of Scots. I wouldn't object to helping turn that into a fact rather than a fancy by helping you depose your brother and place yourself on his throne. With guarantees, of course.'

'Such as?'

'You'd have to do homage and fealty to me, declare yourself my vassal. Break the old Scots alliance with France. And – er . . .'

'Surrender Berwick,' Stanley suggested.

Edward nodded. 'Yes.'

'And all the Scots Border lands,' Richard contributed.

'Yes. And you should divorce your new French wife and marry my daughter Cicely.'

'But,' said Albany, managing to get a word in edgeways, 'I thought she was betrothed to my brother's wee boy?'

172

Edward waved it away. 'That can be arranged. Ye-e-es, I think that will do for the moment. We'll have a treaty drawn up . . .'

'In the Scots tongue,' suggested Richard helpfully.

'. . . and then we'll all be committed. That do you, Albany?'

The young man was looking rather pale – understandably, Francis thought.

'You can get off as soon as you like,' Edward said. 'I've decided not to lead the expedition myself. I've other things to do, so I'm putting Diccon in charge.'

Richard said, 'Thank you, sire. But may I raise one problem? Apart, that is, from the duke of Albany's unexpected *volte face* in his view of relations between Scotland and England, which, may, one suspects, lose him some of his traditional allies among the Scots barons.'

Albany didn't turn a hair.

'Defeating and deposing James,' Richard went on, 'might well meet with the approval of the majority of the Scots people. How they will feel about Lord Albany carrying this out with the aid of an *English* army may be another matter. Also, James has three small sons, every one of whom has a better claim to replace him than my lord of Albany.'

Edward, however, had lost interest. 'Even the Scots must see that desperate situations require desperate remedies. And as for James's sons, they're Albany's problem. They'll just have to take their chances.'

His face lit up as a gentleman usher made his appearance, bowing low, to announce that the king's meat was on the board in the Great Chamber.

'Aha! Supper. A fish day for all of you,' Edward said jovially, 'but not for me. I have a papal dispensation to eat meat. Fish and I do not agree.'

5

PRIVATELY, Richard said, 'What am I supposed to be doing? Prosecuting a war against the Scots, or installing that charlatan Albany as king? Which is the priority?'

Edward stuffed another pastry in his mouth. 'Albany.'

'Why?'

'It will cost less. There's nothing more annoying than always having to watch my back whenever I turn my attention to France, so I want the Scots permanently under my control. Defeating them in battle is the kind of victory that doesn't last. We've done it often enough before – the first of my namesakes spent half his life hammering at them and two hundred years later we're no further forward. No, once we defeated them we'd have to garrison the whole country, and an occupying army costs a fortune. But with a strong Scots king paying me formal homage, it could be very different.'

Richard refrained from remarking, 'Scots kings never live long,' but said, eyebrows raised, 'Well, if you think you can trust Albany . . .'

'We'll find out.'

'We will, won't we?'

Edward glared at him. 'Behave yourself, young Diccon. You'll have Stanley and Harry Percy with you, so make sure you discuss things with them.' He bit his lip. 'I trust you but, on the whole, I'd feel safer being consulted about what's going on. We can set up a courier system. If we have riders stationed every seven leagues, they can relay letters at a rate of – what? – thirty to thirty-five leagues a day. So let's call it three days from you in Scotland to me at Westminster.'

'And six days for the round trip. Well, I don't suppose anything is likely to be more urgent than that.'

6

WITHIN A WEEK, Richard and Albany were being most graciously received at York by the mayor, aldermen and guilds, men of the city, Albany not as a king-in-waiting but, as had been agreed, as no more than the ducal brother of the king of Scots. And by mid-July, they were back outside Berwick with an army of twenty thousand men. The town's citizens took one look and opened the gates. Berwick had had its nationality forcibly changed from Scots to English and back again twelve times in the last three hundred years, and was getting tired of it. The citadel, however, still held out.

Just a few days later, the situation began to degenerate into farce.

An excited Albany erupted unannounced into Richard's tent, dragging an unwashed ruffian by the ear.

'One of my men,' he explained. 'James summoned the host — that's what we call the army, you know? — to relieve Berwick, and Donny here was caught up in it. He's brought me news. Wait till you hear it!'

Richard sat and waited, unmoved. Alexander of Albany was a man easily excited.

'When James and the host reached Lauder, about ten leagues to the west of here,' Albany went on, 'some of the lords gathered together in the kirk and decided to get rid of James's favourites. I told you they've been James's undoing, did I not? So they arrested them and hanged them from the Lauder bridge. And now — *and now!* — they've taken James back to Edinburgh and imprisoned him in the castle.'

'How interesting. And where is the — er — host now?' enquired Richard after a moment.

It didn't seem to have occurred to Albany to wonder where the

Scots army had got to, but Donny said, 'Och, they've a' went hame.' Given half a chance, amateur armies always did tend to disappear in the direction of home, but usually at harvest time, not in July.

'Well, that's helpful,' Richard said.

He despatched a courier to Edward, consulted his captains, and marched his force off to Edinburgh, leaving Stanley to sit things out at Berwick.

7

'AS IF I did not have enough on my mind,' Edward complained, smiling and nodding graciously across the clearing in his deer park of Waltham-in-the-Forest towards the lodge built of leafy boughs where the mayor and aldermen of London and their wives, dressed in their considerable best, were feasting on the royal venison. 'Go and make sure that they are enjoying themselves, Hastings, will you?'

Hastings who, as Edward's lieutenant-general in Calais, had been back and forth across the Channel so often of late that he had begun to develop a nautical roll, leapt obligingly to his feet and went off to have a word with the merchants.

Edward's complaints about the trials that beset him were so frequently rehearsed that the queen barely troubled to ask, 'More problems? Richard?'

'No, he's managing. He's all right. I can trust him. It's Hastings, as a matter of fact. I've been hearing gossip that I don't like.'

Elizabeth thought, 'Good,' but said, 'Oh, dear.'

'God's teeth, but it's hot.' Edward pushed back the ribboned and jewelled bonnet, leaving a red ring round his perspiring and slightly swollen forehead. 'I've heard, and I've no idea where the story came from, that he's had copies made of the town keys to Calais. Now, why should he, I ask you? There are two factors I have to take into account. Or perhaps they're the same. Louis of France wants Calais back, and Hastings has been accepting an annuity from him ever since Picquigny.'

She knew exactly where the story came from, and had to explain away her smile by saying, 'So have you.'

'That's different. I'm the king. There's no danger of *me* selling England out.'

Picking reflectively at a small, roasted songbird, she remarked, 'Lord Hastings must be over fifty by now. Perhaps he is tired of always being at your beck and call and wants to retire.'

'Do you think so?' Edward was startled. Hastings showed no signs of his age, and no one was more adept than he at finding the latest good whorehouse. And he certainly didn't need the money. 'No. Hastings is the most loyal servant I have. He'll outlive me, I have no doubt. But I wish he and that boy Dorset of yours would settle their differences. They spend all their time slandering each other. It's a pity, because I'm fond of them both. But I don't like having my court divided into warring factions.'

'That boy Dorset' was not only Elizabeth's son but Hastings's son-in-law, and she knew that there was not the remotest likelihood of the two men settling their differences, most of which came down to competition over mistresses. Hastings, she had discovered, was already retaliating for the rumours about himself and the keys of Calais by finding – and paying – witnesses to swear that Dorset was the one who had had the keys cut.

Elizabeth knew how unpopular her family was with most of the nobility, and while it would make no appreciable difference on that front, it was going to give her great personal satisfaction to see Hastings's perjured 'witnesses' swing for slandering the

Woodvilles. Between them, she and Anthony would make sure that they did.

She said, with her most opulent smile, 'When my son Dorset returns from the Scottish campaign, I am sure everything will resolve itself. I look foward to hearing what he has to say about young Richard's conduct of that affair.' Nothing complimentary, if she had anything to do with it. If Richard were too successful, he could become over-ambitious. She feared his turning into a second George.

Hastings, cheerful and pink-faced as always, everybody's friend – except the Woodvilles' – rejoined his master and blithely reported, 'All's well, sire. They are overwhelmed by your benevolence towards them.' Since the queen was present, he was careful not to say, 'Especially the ladies.'

'Excellent.'

8

'NEGOTIATE?' Richard erupted. 'If only I could find someone to negotiate *with*!'

The English army was camped below the hog's-back ridge on which Edinburgh was perched, and nobody was paying it any attention – which was insulting, to say the least.

'I cannot afford to pay the army for more than another ten days, and Edward writes that there are no more funds available.'

'As bad as that?' said Francis.

'Yes. And James is inaccessible in that damned castle up there, and so are his gaolers. The queen is miles away in Stirling Castle with the little princes, and as for Albany – well, he seems to have forgotten about wanting the throne. Having his estates and offices back seems to be all that now concerns him . . .'

In the end, three of James's counsellors emerged from the woodwork, including an archbishop, which at least lent respectability to the proceedings. When they mentioned a truce, Richard said he had no authority to negotiate anything of the sort. When he in turn mentioned Albany, they assured him that, as far as they were concerned, Albany could have his estates back and welcome, provided that he observed his allegiance to King James III. He could even be lieutenant-general of the realm, if he liked.

Unfortunately, they could *guarantee* nothing, since the royal seals, like the king, were locked up in Edinburgh Castle.

Richard sighed.

The provost and burgesses of Edinburgh also offered – if the English king no longer wished to pursue the marriage between his daughter Cicely and the Scots king's son and heir – to refund all the instalments of Cicely's dowry which England had already paid, something over £16,000 Scots or £5,000 English. Richard very much disliked the assumption that England could be bought off but, since there was real money involved, knew that Edward would feel differently.

Publicly, Albany said all the right things. Privately, 'I'm not sure,' he said. 'I don't know. I can't make up my mind.' He consented to Richard's demand that he sign a bond reiterating his adherence to the treaty he had made with Edward at Fotheringhay, but, otherwise, said he thought it would be too risky at present to pursue, or even mention, his designs on the throne. So if Richard would just leave things to him . . .

Richard sighed again.

Finally, tempted though he was to teach everyone a lesson by letting his men loose to sack and burn the self-satisfied little city of Edinburgh, Richard broke camp and marched back to Berwick to see how Stanley was getting on with the siege.

If his capacity for disbelief had not by now been suspended, he would have found himself gasping when he heard of the leisurely approach of a Scots army whose purpose was to relieve Berwick, an army commanded by – Alexander, duke of Albany. Fortunately, the defenders of the citadel had already lost interest in the whole affair and, casting a jaundiced eye on Richard's new siege train of artillery, decided to capitulate.

With relief, Richard dismissed all but the seventeen hundred of his men whom he could still afford to pay, and sent a courier to Edward to say that Berwick had been taken and was English again.

9

HE WAS SURPRISED, though not displeased, to have his investment of Edinburgh and capture of Berwick greeted in London as if he had won a second Agincourt.

Francis said, 'How does it feel to be the hero of the hour?'

Anne said, 'Ooooh, what a fraud!'

To Francis, Richard replied, 'Very pleasant,' and to Anne, 'Am I to blame if the south has no sense of proportion about anything to do with the north?'

'You didn't even fight a single battle, as far as I can tell,' said his wife sorrowfully.

'One does not fight pitched battles against the Scots. They don't like it.'

Constantia, who had been keeping Anne company at Middleham during the campaign, murmured, 'Well, that's a relief.'

'We had some quite good skirmishes on the way to and from Edinburgh, though,' Francis told her innocently. 'Good enough to justify Richard creating about twenty knights banneret for valour in the field. Including me.'

'How charming for you!'

180

Ignoring this exchange, 'The truth, I suppose,' Richard said reflectively, 'is that Edward is embarrassed by the way Louis of France and Maximilian of Burgundy are playing games to which England is not invited. Edward needed a diversion, a famous victory of some kind, and most people hate the Scots more than they hate the French. Hence the rejoicing. I wish I had been allowed to have my way and fight a proper war, instead of trying to satisfy Albany's political ambitions. Then we would really have had something to rejoice about.'

Francis said, 'It could have been very different if Albany had been a less erratic personality.'

'Yes. I like that word "erratic". If only he could have made up his mind which he really wanted – reinstatement, or the crown. Unless he now pulls off some miracle, which I doubt, it will all have been an object lesson in how *not* to seize a throne.'

10

RICHARD AND Anne spent Christmas at court, and were much fêted. The envy was almost palpable.

Anne said, 'How long must we stay? My flesh creeps every time one of the Woodvilles so much as looks at me. I wish Constantia were here, so that I could feel I had at least *one* friend.'

'Francis will have to be here in January. Edward intends to raise him to a viscountcy.'

'How lovely!'

'Yes, but I don't know whether Constantia's presence would be politic. One of Francis's sponsors is – believe it or not – Richard, Lord FitzHugh.'

'You mean he's prepared to help Francis to a more distinguished title . . .'

'. . . but not to help him to a divorce. Precisely. Francis's elevation makes it even less likely that the FitzHughs will be prepared to sever connections with him.'

'Oh, dear. Poor Francis! Though it doesn't seem to trouble him much. Or Constantia. It's very odd, but I don't think she even wants to be a married lady.'

'Maybe not. But he can't bring her to court with him.'

'We will just have to pretend that she's one of my ladies-in-waiting.'

'Well, if you think you can sustain the pretence . . . In any case, we ourselves will have to be here until February, I'm afraid. Edward intends asking Parliament . . .'

'You mean *telling* Parliament!'

There was a gleam of humour in his eye. '*Asking* Parliament to grant me the wardenship of the West Marches towards Scotland on a permanent and hereditary basis.'

'Goodness!'

'And I am to have the castle and city of Carlisle and all the king's manors and revenues in the county of Cumberland, outright. *And* any future conquests I win from the Scots. So I will have undisputed possession of my own principality.'

'Oh, well. It's worth staying for, I suppose.' A thought occurred to her. 'What fun! If you nibbled away long enough at Scots territory you might end up with a whole kingdom as well.'

Richard laughed. 'Well, I might, though I have no fancy to be the king of Scots. But you must admit that it's gratifying to have my services to the crown formally acknowledged.'

So they stayed until February, with Anne fretting constantly about little Ned and his health. Whenever Richard sent a messenger home to Middleham, the man carried a letter to Nurse Idley and Anne waited anxiously for her reply, brief and unsatisfactory though it usually was. To be told that young Master Ned had caught a cold but was recovering well sometimes caused Anne more worry than silence would have done. But she could not resign herself to silence. And although Ned's own laboriously penned missives filled her with maternal pride, they told her more about puppies and ponies and how chilly the schoolroom was than about his own health and wellbeing.

The court was at its most gorgeous, and Edward, disturbed though he was by the recent Treaty of Arras between France and Burgundy – which had played havoc with his foreign policy – was at his most spectacular and charming best. Always a devotee of splendour, he seemed to be setting a new fashion with robes whose full sleeves were lined with the most sumptuous furs; the coincidental effect, as Constantia remarked, was to disguise his girth. And just to ensure that royal splendour was not subject to competition, he intended telling – no, asking! – Parliament to pass a sumptuary law reserving the right to wear silken cloth-of-gold to the immediate royal family. No one beneath the rank of duke was to wear tissue-based cloth-of-gold, and no one below the rank of peer was to wear cloth-of-gold at all.

Edward's statuesque magnificence was enhanced by the presence of his five lovely daughters, from sixteen-year-old Princess Bess down to two-year-old Bridget. For years, it had been accepted that the Princess Elizabeth would become bride to the dauphin of France, but although the Treaty of Arras had put an end to that plan, Bess seemed perfectly cheerful about it. 'The king my father will soon find me another husband,' she told Anne gaily, 'and one whom I will like better!'

Week after week, the members of the court ate, danced and flirted, hunted and hawked, smiled into one another's faces and stabbed one another in the back. It was all thoroughly exhausting.

Anne also found, as she had done before, that she was made uncomfortable by the courtiers' lascivious eyes and wandering hands. When some gentleman kissed her hand, it was not unusual for him to hold it for far longer than was necessary. When another was wending his way past some gossiping group of which she formed part, she felt herself waiting with gritted teeth for the inevitable hand laid casually on her waist or hip. Eyes ostensibly admiring her jewelled collar all too readily strayed down into her décolletage.

She hated it, and so, she knew, did Richard.

The only truly likeable person there, Anne decided, was Edward's long-standing mistress, the delectable Elizabeth Shore, commonly known as Jane. She was about thirty, small, shapely and fair, pleasant, witty, and obviously kind-hearted and considerate. Anne was amused to note, on the occasions when she made an appearance at court, that she was not publicly acknowledged by the king, and certainly not by the queen, and that everyone else pretended she was merely the daughter of John Lambert, an important city merchant and civic dignitary.

Anne also discovered that it was not only the king who found the lady attractive.

'Lovely woman,' sighed Lord Hastings, doggy-eyed.

His son-in-law, the marquess of Dorset, twenty-five years his junior, merely looked lecherous; a handsome, arrogant young man who allowed no one to forget that he was the queen's son. Anne found it odd for a young man to lust after his mother's husband's mistress.

As far as it was possible to judge, they both had enough sense to keep their desires under control. Stealing the king's mistress was no passport to the king's continuing favour.

Anne found herself wondering if Hastings, after his last visit to Middleham, had found the whorehouses he had asked about in York. She had been mildly shocked to discover that Richard knew there were 'several'; had sometimes wondered whether he frequented them himself when he was away from home. She thought not, and told herself strongmindedly that, even if he did, it had nothing to do with her. He loved *her*, even if he had let that fact slip by accident, and she was content. Bed, after all, was not everything.

She sighed and then shrugged, daily more obsessed by the desire to get back to Middleham and Ned.

In the end, Richard told her, 'We have Edward's permission to leave.'

She threw her arms round his neck, regardless of the scandalised presence of her ladies-in-waiting. '*What* a relief!'

He put his hands on her waist, kissed her lightly on the tip of her nose, and said, 'My feelings exactly.'

Despite the snow, and sleet, and cold, the journey was pure pleasure. Anne was consumed by visions of settling down again into a comfortable, reassuring routine, where there was warmth of spirit and no envy or hatred. Even Richard, she thought, could be relaxed and secure at last, presiding over his own principality.

Her happiness lasted for just over a month.

And then the news came that Edward was dying.

And then that he was dead.

Chapter Nine

1483

1

'GOD'S TEETH! Why is everything so dark and dismal? Bring more candles! More, more! I can't see what I am doing.' And then, when every candle in the castle was burning, 'Why is everything so bright? How can I be expected to work when my head is aching from the glare?'

Anne, almost as distracted as her husband, spoke to the steward. 'My lord duke is very much upset over the death of the king his brother. We must have patience, and he will be himself again.'

But they had patience and the days passed and he was not himself again.

At first he could not bear to be indoors, because he felt as if the great high stone walls of Middleham were coming down on him, crushing him. From dawn until dark, he was out riding for the sake of riding, either alone or accompanied by his falconer and two or three hawks, or by the huntsman and his greyhounds, whom he set to chase anything that moved. But although he returned from these outings physically exhausted, and then sat until bedtime listening to messengers from the south, or surrounded by papers and staring blankly into infinity, he could not sleep at night.

Anne tried to talk to him but he had retreated into himself, blocking her out. It hurt.

'Why won't he play with me?' little Ned demanded. 'Have I annoyed him? He looks at me as if I'm not here.'

Ned, at seven and two months, was past the age of being picked up and cuddled, but Anne took his hands in hers and, trying to explain to him what was wrong, found that she was trying to explain it to herself, too.

'Your father is very sad because his brother has died . . .'

'He hasn't any brothers left any more. Wish *I* had some brothers.'

'Yes. But . . .'

'He was sad when my uncle of Clarence died, too, but he wasn't nasty to me then.'

'You were very little and, anyway, that was different.'

'Why?'

'Oh, because – because – he and your uncle of Clarence had been boys together, so he was sad remembering how they had been friends, but much more sad because your other uncle, King Edward, had had to order your uncle of Clarence to be executed.'

'Uncle Clarence must have been *awfully* wicked.'

'No, but very foolish. Oh dear, how can I explain this to you? You're too young to understand.'

'I'm not. I'm *not*.'

'Don't stamp your foot at me. Well, your uncle of Clarence had been asking for trouble for years, so when he died it was an ending that everyone, except himself, had foreseen . . .'

'Like when I'm reading a story and can guess what's going to happen?'

188

'Something like that. But your Uncle Edward's death has come as a dreadful shock to everyone. He caught a chill, and then he had an apoplexy. But in his case, though it's the end of one story it's also the beginning of a new one. That's what happens when a king dies. Your father is sad for his brother's death, because he loved and admired him, but he's also thinking, "What happens next? What next?" His feelings and his brain are all muddled up. When he's trying to think, his sadness interrupts his thoughts, and when he's just *feeling*, his brain keeps telling him there are things he should be doing.'

'It sounds awfully com⁓compul⁓compulicated.'

'Complicated. It is. That's why he doesn't have time to spare for us.'

'Well, I don't like it.'

'Neither do I, but we must try and understand. Now, come along. It's time for bed.'

2

SHE SUCCEEDED at last in forcing Richard to talk to her, something she had never thought she would dare to do.

She said, 'I can't bear to watch you going through all this alone. I know there is nothing I can say to – to ease your feelings about Edward, but if my love can help . . .'

Miserably, she ran out of words, so she held her hand out to him and, after a moment, he took it and gave it a gentle squeeze. 'Your love *can* help,' he said sombrely, 'just by existing. I should be very alone without you.' Love was not a word that they had ever bandied about between them, and she could not tell what it meant to him beyond warmth and friendship and loyalty. For her it had become an obsession, but she had taken care that he should not know it, for fear of driving him away. It could be harder to receive than to give.

He said, 'But you cannot help in what concerns me at this moment. What should I do? What should I do?' His grey eyes were dark as the North Sea and their focus was suddenly far away.

Determined not to lose him again, she said, '*Must* you do something?'

'Yes. I have had a letter from Hastings. He is very uneasy over how the succession is being handled. We had all thought that Edward would live to see his sons grown, but Eddie, the prince of Wales, is only twelve. Just in case such a situation arose, Edward said years ago that he wanted me to be Protector during the boy's minority, but now it seems that important decisions are being taken without consulting me. Hastings says the Woodvilles are behaving just as one would expect, determined to take control of the boy and ensure a permanent increase in their own power and influence. They have an advantage in that Anthony Rivers has been young Eddie's mentor since he was two years old. It means I have to decide what to do.'

'Why?' she asked sharply. 'Why do you have to do anything? Why can't you take life as it comes, sometimes good, sometimes bad? Why not wait and see what happens?'

'I can't afford to. If the Woodvilles are allowed to grab control, anyone who subsequently opposes them will end on the executioner's block. I don't intend that to happen to me. They must be forestalled.'

She sighed. Oddly, she found herself worrying less about him, herself and Ned, than about the Duchess Cicely, who had borne seven sons, of whom only the seventh still lived – the mystic, sacred seventh. If only one could believe in the power of numbers . . .

FRANCIS, having set out from Minster Lovell for Middleham as soon as he heard the news of Edward's death, arrived to a barely coherent welcome from Anne.

'Oh, thank goodness. I don't know what's the matter with him – well, I *do* know what's the matter with him – but although at the beginning he didn't seem to be thinking at all, now his mind is either racing or jigging about like a pea on a drum, and he keeps muttering, "What next? What next?" '

'Yes, that's what I was wondering,' Francis said.

'And you know how carefully he always plans things. Well, now he says there is no time to plan intelligently. I don't know what to do with him. It was a letter from Lord Hastings that set him off. He's closeted with Master Catesby and Sir Richard Ratcliffe. Go in. And Francis – be the good friend you have always been. Try and make him see things in a more balanced way!'

'I'll do my best.'

There was the merest hint of drowning men and straws in Richard's greeting, but then all was impersonal again and Francis found himself being formally introduced to Catesby and Ratcliffe, with both of whom he had been acquainted, though not closely, for years.

William Catesby was a clever lawyer, thought by some to be too clever by half and said to be as slender in his morals as in his figure. He was a lugubrious-looking little man, with a dashing taste in clothes, a small, down-turned mouth, and large enough pouches under his eyes to make the purse at his waist seem almost superfluous. One of a new breed of professionals who worked for gain rather than out of traditional duty, Catesby had built up a large and lucrative practice as counsel, estates steward, and trustee to some of the greatest men in the land, among them the duke of

Buckingham and Lord Hastings. Those who bought his services received excellent value for their money, although some of them were apt to take offence when they discovered that his loyalty to their interests ended with his contract.

Francis, who had usefully employed him on more than one occasion, had no such reservations. Buying a man's skills for a particular purpose did not, in his view, equate with buying the man's heart and mind for all time. If it had, he would have found it worrying.

He respected Catesby's opinions, neither liking nor disliking the man himself, and felt much the same about Sir Richard Ratcliffe, whose training was not in the law but in worldly wisdom. That he was a bold tactician had emerged in the course of the Albany expedition, but it was less apparent that his northerner's military bluffness – which southern aristocrats saw as lack of breeding, although there were some among them who far surpassed him in vulgarity – covered unusually shrewd judgement of men and affairs.

Richard said, 'Let us take a moment to bring Lord Lovell up to date with the present situation.'

'Thank you, that would be helpful.'

Visibly, Richard gathered his thoughts together. 'I recently received a letter from Hastings, from which it is clear that the Woodvilles are trying to take over the whole matter of the succession without reference to me, as Protector.'

'Can they do that?'

'It's possible. They are reported to have seized the royal treasure in the Tower, and Sir Edward Woodville is about to put to sea with a fleet, supposedly to protect our coasts against Louis XI's admiral, Crèvecoeur. But, more to the point, they propose that young Eddie should be crowned on May 4th, just over two weeks from now . . .'

'But he's only twelve years old!' Francis exclaimed. 'He's far too young!'

'Too young to rule, but old enough to "choose" his advisers.'

Ratcliffe shifted, stretched, and raised both hands to scratch his red head vigorously. 'Not hard to guess who they'll be, either.'

Richard said, 'When he takes his coronation vows, he will become king in fact as well as in name. And my rôle as Protector could end almost before it has begun instead of, as Edward intended, lasting until the boy reaches his formal maturity at fifteen.'

It was said coolly enough, but Francis saw that Richard was twisting the rings on his fingers, a sure sign of tension. Francis could understand it. Richard's life would be worth very little if the Woodvilles, who feared him, succeeded in gaining control of both king and government.

'B-b-but,' Francis essayed, and stopped short. He hadn't stuttered for years.

A faint and, in the circumstances, unexpected gleam of amusement lit Richard's hard grey eyes, though only for a moment. '*But* my late brother named me Protector for the entire period of the boy's minority? Tell him, Catesby.'

The lawyer ran his quill thoughtfully through his bony fingers. 'The wishes of a dead king have no binding force in law. In the case of previous royal minorities, in 1377 and 1422, the appropriate lords — the forerunners of today's royal council — assumed that the royal authority devolved upon *them* by reason of the death of the king and the minority of his heir. Even if the Woodvilles succeed in dominating today's council, precedent will have been observed.'

'They are proposing,' Richard resumed, 'to enforce their domination by summoning the boy to London from Ludlow, where he has been brought up, at the head of an army. His governor, Anthony Rivers, the queen's brother, will of course be in command.'

Francis's brows rose almost to his hair. 'They *are* nervous, aren't they?'

'They are right to be,' Ratcliffe muttered, but Richard said nothing.

Spring came late to Middleham. Riding up from Minster Lovell, Francis had felt that he was riding back through the seasons. But now, standing by the window, seeing the white-capped hills outlined against the bright blueness of the sky, he remembered how he and Richard had revelled in such days when they were boys. In crispness, freshness, and promise.

Promise.

And now it had come to this.

He turned, sharply. 'There must be *something* you can do.'

Wearily, Richard said, 'The question is, what?'

4

WHEN Catesby and Ratcliffe had been dismissed, Richard sat with splayed fingers pressed hard against his temples. 'It is a nightmare,' he said. 'I feel as if I am being controlled by the forces that always control nightmares, utterly senseless but weirdly rational. Half of me is mourning Edward and the other half is furiously aware that I have to take action if I am to survive.'

Francis said, 'I would not have expected you to be quite so disturbed by Edward's death. You have not been uncritical of him in the past.'

Richard sighed. 'That was my brain speaking. But now I have been overtaken by emotions I didn't know I possessed. Strange, isn't it? These last days, I have tried – God knows I have tried – to discipline my mind, but it goes round and round like a roast on the spit.' He looked up. 'I cannot trust my own judgement, and that frightens me.'

'But you must have made some response to the situation, surely?'

'Oh, yes. I have sent reassuring letters to the queen and the council, reminding them that I was always loyal to my brother and will be equally so to his son. We held a requiem mass for Edward at York – two days before he died, as it happens, because the news of his death arrived prematurely. And I have summoned the nobility and gentry of Yorkshire to assemble and swear a solemn oath of fealty to the boy.'

'You should be in London.'

'Yes. That is what Hastings says. But I think it is his own terror speaking. He knows the Woodvilles will ruin and probably execute him. The queen has always hated him, as have Rivers and Dorset. He says I should bring an army, take forcible possession of the boy, and arrest any Woodvilles who stand in my way.'

'That seems a trifle provocative.'

'It does, doesn't it? On the other hand, he is in touch with the situation, which I am not, and he may well be right about the course of action I should follow. Buckingham takes much the same view. He has offered to help "with a thousand good fellows, if need be".'

Francis said doubtfully, 'Do you trust him?'

'No. But I would rather have his support than his opposition. However little he may be liked on a personal basis, he is the greatest peer of the realm after myself and little Richard of York, and his name carries immense weight with the old nobility. He always resented Edward's neglect of him and failure to give him the honours he feels are his due. I will undoubtedly have to pay for his support in the end. The question is, how much?'

Francis, whose stomach was clapping against his ribs with

hunger, heard with gratitude the fanfare announcing supper. A moment later, there was a ceremonious knock on the door and the steward entered to announce that my lord duke's board was laid.

'Thank you. We will come.'

Rising, Richard said heavily, 'God's bones, how can I plan when my brain will not settle to the problem, and all my information is out of date before I even receive it!'

'You will just have to feel your way.'

Richard's eyebrows rose sardonically. 'Thank you. I wonder why I was so pleased to see you when you arrived?'

Francis grinned. 'A friend? And a friend with no axes to grind?' Then, hearing his own words, smothered a grimace.

'Quite,' Richard said. 'Let us refrain from talk of axes. There is something too apposite about them in the present situation.'

5

THE BODY of the late king had been formally viewed by those of the lords spiritual and temporal who happened to be within reach of London at the time, and also by the mayor and aldermen of the city. Then, embalmed with care, wrapped in waxed linen, clothed in royal finery, with a cap of estate on its head and red leather shoes on its feet, it lay in state in St Stephen's Chapel at Westminster for eight days. During those days, the chapel was filled with the sound of requiem masses, and if any of the nobles or royal servants who stood watch over it were aware of the irony of Edward lying in state at the very spot where he had condemned his own brother to death just five years before, no one was so tactless as to mention it.

And, all the time, the funeral bells tolled.

Then, on April 17th, the body began its journey from

Westminster to Windsor, carried on a bier and covered with yellow-gold velvet. A life-sized image of the king, clothed, crowned and bearing the orb and sceptre, stood beside the bier when it rested overnight on the three-day journey. After the body had been laid in its tomb in St George's Chapel, with a pomp and ceremony the living man would have approved, the great officers of the household – Hastings weeping unashamedly the while – cast their staffs of office into the grave.

The funeral bells continued to toll.

Death had come too soon. No one had been prepared. Even the tomb Edward had designed for himself was not yet complete, the effigy lacking and also the stone slab carved with the figure of death. But the splendour was there nonetheless. When Hastings returned later to kneel and pray privately for the man who had been his friend and indulgent benefactor as well as his king for twenty-two eventful years, the accoutrements laid out on the tomb set him weeping afresh over the memories conjured up by the royal coat of gilt mail, its crimson velvet cover embroidered with Edward's arms in pearls, gold and rubies.

It was not armour for fighting in, unless at the kind of battle Hastings expected to face the next day – against the Woodvilles.

6

SINCE most members of the royal council had taken part in the obsequies, the problems attending the succession had been well rehearsed before the meeting began. On one point all were agreed, that the young king should succeed his father as smoothly as possible. But there the concord ended.

It was not apparent at first. No one objected to the proposed coronation date of May 4th, although Bishop Russell wondered whether it might be too soon to permit all the requisite ceremonial to be arranged.

As fair and arrogant as the queen his mother, the marquess of Dorset said, 'Let us have no such evasions. If something *must* be done, it *can* be done. The city merchants have money enough to pay for the processional arrangements and have them hurried along. It will do no harm to squeeze them a little. I believe my uncle, Lord Rivers, should be appointed Steward of England for the coronation ceremonies.'

'An excellent suggestion,' agreed Archbishop Rotherham, but the young Lord Maltravers — present as representative of his aged father, the earl of Arundel — observed the sour expression on the face of Lord Stanley, who had been the late king's steward, and gently demurred.

And so it went on.

Hastings, his pink, perpetual half-smile a cover, as always, for his calculating mind, sat and planned his intervention. He was irritated that the council as a whole was permitting the Woodvilles to dominate the meeting as if their wishes were paramount, as if no one else mattered. The name of Richard of Gloucester had not even been mentioned. It was as if he did not exist. Hastings glanced towards Stanley, but Stanley's head was bent and he appeared to be absorbed in a study of his fingernails. Black-rimmed and chewed down to the quick, they were not a pretty sight. Hastings averted his eyes again.

It was time to say something. He cleared his throat. 'If I may speak? I do not feel that important arrangements should be made so hurriedly, and without consulting the Protector.'

It was his son-in-law and devoted enemy who replied. 'Indeed?' said the marquess of Dorset in his most patronising tone. 'Yet I believe that we on the council are sufficiently important, even without the king's uncle' — he made the relationship sound dismissively distant — 'to entitle us to make and enforce our decisions.' By 'us' he meant the Woodvilles, and everyone knew it.

An increased chill descended on the monks' refectory of Westminster Abbey, where the council was meeting. It was a chill enough place at the best of times, since monks were not supposed to be pampered.

The more prudent members of the council had no wish for the young king to be controlled by the Woodvilles, to whom his father had given too much latitude. Indeed, many believed that Edward had latterly governed more for the financial benefit of his family and friends than for that of the country. If this had been so with a grown man, it would be even more true of a twelve-year-old boy who had been brought up under the governance of Anthony Rivers and entirely under the Woodville influence.

Unfortunately, those same prudent members of the council also felt the need to be prudent on their own behalf. If, as seemed likely, the Woodvilles won the day, those who had opposed them would be made to suffer. Only Hastings, their acknowledged enemy, had nothing to lose.

'Furthermore,' Dorset went on, 'the king's uncle of Gloucester is not Protector until and unless we confer that office upon him.'

'Then I formally propose,' Hastings said, glancing round the table and gathering everyone's eyes toward him, 'that the late king's brother Richard Plantagenet, duke of Gloucester, should be appointed Protector until our new king, Edward V, comes of age at fifteen.'

The queen was too quick for him. Before anyone had time to agree or disagree, she said, 'But my son is barely acquainted with Duke Richard. I believe it would be unjust to tear him away from Lord Rivers, to whom he has been attached for all of his childhood and to whose wise and gentle guidance he is accustomed. I do not believe that a boy of his tender years should be entrusted to the governance of such a hard and warlike man as Duke Richard.'

Her maternal concern aroused no more than a mechanical response in her hearers, who had no interest in the boy's emotional wellbeing, but just as Hastings was about to repeat his proposal, the lawyerly little Bishop Morton intervened. 'I believe we must consult precedent here,' he said.

Hastings knew that the bishop's beady little eyes must have observed his own angry tightening of the lips, but there was nothing he could do about it other than amend his expression to one of polite interest. 'Yes?' he said.

Undeceived, the bishop continued, 'In 1429 a previous duke of Gloucester, Duke Humphrey, had his Protectorate brought to an end when King Henry VI was crowned at the age of nine. Authority then passed to a regency council which ruled in the king's name until he was declared of age. This might, I believe, be an appropriate solution in our present case.'

It was a solution with general appeal. Hastings could see – and so, he thought, could everyone else – young Dorset and the queen's brother Lionel calculating that the Woodvilles would have little trouble dominating such a council, which would be almost as satisfactory as having sole charge of the boy. So, spitefully, he waited until general consent had been signified, before saying, 'And Duke Richard should, of course, be appointed chief member of the council.'

'Aye,' said the dean of Wells. 'That would seem to be fair and just, besides being in accordance with the late king's wishes.'

Everyone nodded except the Woodvilles. Young Dorset cast a poisonous glare at his father-in-law, who beamed back at him, pleasingly aware that Dorset's hatred of him owed something to the fact that he had forestalled the young man, with what some might have thought indecent haste, by taking up residence with the delectable Mistress Shore within days of the king's death.

The queen changed the subject, or appeared to do so. 'It is my wish,' she announced, 'that my son should enter on his reign in a fitting manner, at the head of a magnificent retinue.'

The air in the refectory stirred slightly. An outsider might have put it down to a slight draught from the kitchens, but in fact it was an indrawing of breath on the part of all the uncommitted members of the council. A twelve-year-old boy at the head of an army meant an army under the command of Anthony Rivers, its purpose not to declare the new king's sovereignty but to overawe any who might choose to dispute Woodville supremacy.

'Never!' Hastings exploded. 'We have had enough of armies. The king needs only a moderate retinue. If the council agrees to anything greater, I myself shall have no recourse but to retire to Calais.' He tried to sound as if he meant it. As governor of Calais, he had been lyingly accused by Anthony Rivers not so very long before of plotting to sell it back to the French, and had spent several nerve-racking weeks in the Tower as a result. Now, he *could* sell the damned place back to the French.

It was risky, but he was rewarded. The council hastily decreed that the king should travel to London with a retinue of no more than two thousand. Hastings could barely conceal his glee. If Richard took his advice, he and Buckingham would arrive on the scene with a far larger force than that.

7

RICHARD had not, as it happened, taken his advice, which he considered too provocative.

Francis said, 'But Hastings is at Westminster, and knows what is likely to be needed.'

'Yes. His primary purpose, however, is to save his own skin.'

'That is the case with most people.'

'Most people do not incite civil war to serve their own ends.'

Francis stared at him. 'When has civil war ever developed out of anything other than personal ambition?'

'You are becoming unpleasantly cynical.'

'Realistic.'

'Cynical.'

There was a tiny, intimate jingling from the rowels as, impatient at the stately rate of progress imposed on them by their mourning garb, Richard lightly set spurs to his charger. 'We must be at Northampton by the 29th.'

'To meet Buckingham? Would it matter if we were a day late?'

Drily, Richard said, 'I do not propose to put it to the test. We are also to meet Rivers and the prince of Wales – the king! – there, so that we may proceed to London together. It's essential for the sake of appearances that I ride in at the king's side.'

It was the first Francis had heard about this part of Richard's plan, and he had no fault to find with it save for its unexpectedness.

He hadn't needed Anne's whispered injunction, when they left Middleham, to, 'See that he doesn't do anything outrageous!' although he wasn't sure why she should have thought that Richard might. Woman's instinct? He had learned from Constantia that women *did* have an instinct about some things, that they were better at reading people's minds than men were.

Now, he wondered what else Richard had chosen not to reveal. Not that he *would* be likely to do anything outrageous, even in his present disturbed state of mind, but Francis would have been happier to feel that Richard was being open with him.

Suddenly, his heart lightened at the sight of a small cavalcade of riders coming towards them from the south, with a slender, dark-haired woman in its midst. It was Constantia and her bodyguard, en route for Middleham. He had left her at Minster Lovell before dashing off for Yorkshire, instructing her to follow as soon as she could. He had guessed that Anne would need her, and was pleased that she was making such good time.

Richard greeted her amiably but absently, reluctant to call a halt, and Francis only had time for a brief word or two before spurring his horse to catch up with Richard again. The extraordinary thing was that Constantia, her eyes large and fearful, said virtually the same as Anne had said. 'Don't let him do anything foolish. Remind him that whatever he does now will echo down the months and the years. There is danger everywhere. Take care, my dearest.'

Woman's instinct? Or, as with Anne, terror of losing her man? He didn't know. How could he strike a balance between his love for Constantia and his friendship for Richard? He could, and would, die for either of them.

Richard resumed what he had been saying as if there had been no interruption. 'Furthermore, if we were to find ourselves bringing up the rear I am prepared to wager that we would arrive to discover Anthony Rivers's men already standing guard over the Tower, the Treasury, the Palace of Westminster and every other centre of administration. In effect, there would be a Woodville *coup d'état*.'

'Would two thousand Welshmen suffice for that?'

'Perhaps not alone, but I would guess that Dorset is busy raising a supplementary army of supporters in the city.'

8

ALL THE WAY from York, men stopped working in the fields to watch Richard and his six-hundred-strong retinue riding past. As they clattered through the towns, floury-armed women and inquisitive urchins flocked to the roadside to gaze at them. Everyone had known, or learned from his banners, who Richard was. In the north, they had cheered him, but further south the response became more subdued. There was cap-doffing and curtseying for Richard himself, but his followers were greeted by a wary silence. Country people had long memories and had not forgotten the depredations of the northern army that had been let loose on the countryside a generation before.

Reaching Northampton, Richard halted outside the walls and sent two of his serjeants and a handful of men in through the North Gate to discover whether the young king and his followers had arrived and, if so, where they were lodged. The town was not large, no more than eight hundred paces from end to end, and the men were soon back. The king, it seemed, had passed through earlier with his retinue, which was too numerous to be accommodated in the town. It was likely, the innkeeper had suggested, that they had decided to go on to the south, to Stony Stratford.

Still sitting his horse, Richard said, 'Go and see.' If his gauntlets had not prevented it, Francis knew that his fingers would have been rattling an irritable tattoo on his armoured thigh. 'Ratcliffe, go with them,' Richard added. 'And when you find Lord Rivers, tell him I am here and waiting for him.'

'Yes, my lord.'

As the little party galloped off, Richard said, 'That should put an end to any idea he has of going straight on to London with me chasing after him. We will stay here for the moment. Buckingham should arrive soon, and we need to confer.'

Leaving most of the retinue outside the walls, Richard and a handful of his attendants rode in and along the Sheep Market to receive an effusive welcome from the innkeeper, with whom Richard had long been acquainted, Northampton being on the posting route from Fotheringhay to London.

A pleasure to see my lord duke, or should he say 'my lord Protector'? Yes, he had rooms, and yes, supper would be ready in the twinkling of an eye.

The twinkling of an eye had extended to well over an hour and it was growing dark when Richard, taking only two men as bodyguard, decided to stroll back to the North Gate and assure himself that everything was well in his camp. Since the Sheep Market was all too redolent of that morning's occupants, he chose to hook round past the Benedictine house of St Andrew, forgetting that the quiet street on which it stood was the site of the weekly horse market. No one had swept up. He was therefore staying close to the houses that bordered it and placing his feet with care when there was a faint scuffling sound behind and to his left, over by the abbey wall. It might have been a girl and her lover hidden in the shadows. It might have been a tethered pony. It might have been a stray pig snuffling in the rubbish.

But it was none of these. It was a pack of armed ruffians.

'To me!' Richard snapped, and his bodyguard closed in beside him, backed against a doorway, drawing their swords as he had done, engaging steel with steel in a shower of sparks. One of his men stabbed at their attackers with the flaring torch he carried, but then he dropped it and it went out. Half-blinded by the sudden dark, ducking and weaving, stabbing and slicing, they fought in a clashing silence, with no breath to shout for help, no moment's respite to hammer on the door behind them.

The attackers' clothing was anonymous, and their weapons were not beggars' weapons, nor peasants' weapons, nor battle weapons. Not axes or pikes, but the long daggers known as hangers.

Richard, having discarded his armour at the inn and wearing only a mailed jack and sallet helmet, lunged and drew back, lunged again and ducked to escape a head-high whirling blade. Then he drove at a big unshaven lout whose vile-smelling breath was extinguished by the blood bubbling from his mouth as he fell to the filthy ground. Shifting his grip, Richard raised his sword again, two-handed, and brought it down with all his strength on the head of the man who was aiming for his unprotected throat. In the periphery of his vision he could see two other men staggering away from their encounter with his bodyguard.

It seemed to go on for ever, although he thought afterwards that it had lasted no more than a few minutes. No one came to their aid. The Black Friars were perhaps too far away to hear, and as men of God would in any case have been unlikely to intervene. The local householders, too, were prudently deaf.

There was no help for it. With the attackers beginning to waver in face of the damage being done to them, it was time to take the initiative. Gathering himself together, Richard shouted an order and moved foward, his men breathing hard at his side. It was enough. The remaining attackers broke and ran, except for one who, relying on his own unusual height and reach, made one last attempt on Richard's life, prancing around as if taking part in some parody of a duel. But almost at once, skipping backwards to escape Richard's blade, he backed hard against the edge of a horse trough and toppled over into it, arms flailing and legs kicking madly. One of the bodyguard, before Richard could stop him, plunged his sword into the man's heart.

Richard – breathless, bleeding from a slash to his upper arm and another to his forearm – was annoyed. It would have been useful to question the man.

As the innkeeper's wife, a few minutes later, bound up his wounds and those of his bodyguard – a severed finger in one case and a sliced jaw in the other – she maintained, 'We've never had no vagabonds here, my lord, not even when the end of the French wars loosed all them bands of unemployed soldiers on the countryside. I don't understand it.'

To Francis, Richard said, 'Nor do I. No casually roving band would show their faces with my six hundred men so close, and the royal entourage of two thousand a mere dozen miles away. They were not, I am sure, ordinary robbers. They were far too purpose/ful. They were there to kill, and to kill *me*.'

'They weren't very well prepared, were they? Daggers are no match for swords, and they must have known you would be armed.'

'True. Which makes me think that whoever set them on had no fighting experience of his own. Numbers, however, do make a difference. Even for three swords, warding off a dozen daggers is no easy task. If they had caught us in the open, without a wall at our backs, the ending could have been very different.'

'But who would want to kill you?'

Richard was surprised into a gust of laughter. 'My dear sweet innocent Francis! Can you not guess, or are you too dedicated to your belief in human goodness to confront the obvious?' Then his laughter died as abruptly as it had begun, and he said, 'Well – now, at least, I know where I am, and what stakes we are all playing for.'

Francis still thought he was leaping to conclusions about the whole affair.

9

ROAST MUTTON was by no means a noble dish, but it smelled sublimely appetising as the innkeeper came bustling in with the platter and the news that my Lord Rivers had just arrived and was wishful to know if the lord Protector would receive him.

'What excellent timing,' Richard murmured. Then, 'Say to him that I will be pleased if he will join us for supper.'

Apart from a slight pallor, Richard looked his normal self, his bandages hidden by the ample sleeves of a fresh shirt and tunic. Francis told himself he was imagining the closeness of Rivers's scrutiny as the newcomer said by way of greeting, 'I trust I see you well, Richard?'

'I am in my usual health, Anthony, thank you. And you?'

'I am well. The king asks me to present his compliments to you and tell you that we are quartered at Stony Stratford.'

'So I understand.'

'It seemed to us that Northampton was too small to accommo-date both the king's retinue and yours.'

'And my lord of Buckingham's,' Richard intervened amiably. 'I expect him hourly.'

'Indeed?' Rivers's tone was cool.

Francis waited with interest to discover what they were going to talk about over supper, since it seemed likely that the only subject that interested them all – the accession of the young king – would be banned.

It began with the weather, of course, and its effect on farming, and rents, and the income of the landowning classes. Then it was the stern landscape of Wales and its effect on the character of its people.

Idly, Richard asked, 'So our new young king is hardy, as his father was in youth?'

'He is that, of course, but has a more scholarly disposition. He reads and speaks Latin as if it were his native tongue, can understand almost any work of verse or prose that comes into his hand, and is of a maturity beyond his years. He also has his father's charm. He is a dear boy.'

For a man as low-born as Rivers to speak so familiarly of his soon-to-be-anointed king was not acceptable. The temperature in the room dropped several degrees.

Aware of it, Rivers said, 'But let us talk of you, my lord Protector. We have met so rarely in recent years that I feel as if I scarcely know you. The Duchess Anne is well? And your son? What news of the north? And of the Scots and that mad pretender of theirs — what was his name?'

'The duke of Albany.' Richard could be very entertaining when he chose, and tonight he chose. The tale of Albany's efforts to unseat his brother lost nothing in the telling.

Anthony Rivers never did anything as human as laugh. When he felt the need to appear amused, he resorted to a curling of one corner of his mouth. He did so now. 'So what next?' he asked.

Richard carved himself another slice of mutton. 'My most recent information is that Albany has made his peace with James and, in return for James's promise to "love him heartily", has agreed to behave himself for all time to come and have no more treacherous dealings with the English.'

'Will he hold to that?'

Carelessly, Richard said, 'Oh, no. I would guess that he will be back with us, asking for help, within the month.'

Just then, the duke of Buckingham came strolling in, unannounced. In his mid-twenties, tall, handsome and smiling, he was vaingloriously sure of himself. It was amusing to watch him and Rivers patronising each other. Francis decided that, although Rivers had had fifteen years' more practice, Buckingham was innately better at it.

'Ah, food and warmth!' he exclaimed as rapturously as if he had not expected to find such luxuries in an inn at suppertime. 'Diccon, I have left my fellows with yours, encamped outside the walls. I may add that it is an unpleasantly cold, dark evening and it is trying to rain.'

Rivers stirred himself. 'Then I fear I should set out back to Stony Stratford as soon as may be.'

Almost in unison, Richard and Buckingham exclaimed, 'No.'

Buckingham said, 'The evening has scarcely begun,' and Richard added, waving Rivers back to his seat, 'Stay. Indeed, why not stay for the night? I am sure the landlord will be able to find you a chamber. I should be uneasy at the thought of you returning to Stony Stratford with only your riding escort in the cold and the dark, especially when you might encounter the thieves and murderers who are on the prowl in the vicinity.'

Rivers's surprise was well done but not, perhaps, quite well enough. 'Thieves and murderers? Here? I thought such ruffians had all been hanged long before now.'

'I would have thought so, too,' Richard responded blandly. 'But I had an exchange with them myself earlier this evening.'

'I am happy that you emerged unscathed.'

Richard inclined his head graciously. 'I feel strongly that you should remain here tonight – you may send a messenger to reassure them at Stony Stratford – and then Buckingham and I can ride out with you to make our obeisance to the king in the morning. You have left him in safe hands, I take it?'

'Yes, of course. He has his household, and also his half-brother, my nephew Richard Grey, who met us here earlier with despatches from London.'

Richard Grey, full brother and close ally of the marquess of Dorset. A young man with no personal experience of fighting. Who had been here in Northampton earlier in the day. Francis wondered if it would be possible to find out whether he had left Northampton with a dozen fewer attendants than he had arrived with. Surely not. The Woodvilles might hate and fear Richard, but Francis still did not think they would try to murder him.

They passed a convivial evening, assisted by the landlord's excellent ale. It transpired that there was plenty to gossip about, without touching on what really mattered, although Anthony Rivers waxed sarcastic about the tears Lord Hastings had shed at the royal obsequies.

'Well might he weep, considering what profit he has made over the years from the late king's friendship for him. Chamberlain of the Household, Knight of the Garter, Master of the Mint, Lieutenant of Calais, Constable of Nottingham, receiver-general for the duchy of Cornwall, keeper of the Lord knows how many royal castles and forests, owner of endless manors and lands of his own, a household as extravagant as any court, virtual ruler of the Midlands ... A more acquisitive man never lived.'

All of which was a bit rich, Francis thought, coming from a man whose family was a byword for avarice.

'The future may not prove to be so rosy for him,' Buckingham remarked in the end with his special friendly smile, the slack-muscled and rabbity one that displayed the entire battery of his admirably white teeth, upper and lower. There must be some trick to it, Francis thought sleepily. Most people showed only their upper teeth, and not even those if they were black and decaying, as most men's were.

Rivers retired at midnight, but no one else followed his example. Francis would have done so, except that he had no intention of missing any planning that might be afoot. Richard and Buckingham, with Ratcliffe, back from Stony Stratford, and the lawyer Catesby, made up a formidable quartet, and would certainly, with Rivers out of the way, be settling down to discuss what happened next.

Unfortunately, the food, warmth and ale proved too much for him. Even as Buckingham said to Richard, 'I brought only three hundred men, as you suggested,' Francis began drifting off into sleep where he sat.

At some time during the course of the night – he had no idea when – he half woke to hear Richard saying, 'It all depends on the boy. I cannot afford to gamble my whole future and probably my life on the preconceptions and prejudices of a lad who knows nothing of me except what he has heard from his mother's family, none of it flattering, you may be sure. If the Woodvilles have their way, he could be exercising full royal power under their control within the week.'

Buckingham said, 'It must be prevented . . .'

Drowsily, Francis thought, 'Yes, indeed,' and relapsed into sleep.

Later, he heard Buckingham again. 'Once the boy is in his mother's care in London, and crowned, it will take a civil war to unseat the Woodvilles.'

'True, or false?' Francis wondered briefly, and went back to sleep again.

In the days, weeks and months that followed, he was to curse himself for it. At the time, he supposed, he had felt himself an outsider whose opinion would contribute nothing much to any discussion. And he had been wrong. There were times when an outsider's common sense view was needed to counterbalance the intricate reasoning of those for whom politics were inseparable from life.

10

HE WAS brought to full wakefulness by the sounds of unguarded movement and a suppressed jangling of keys.

Buckingham's voice said, 'Excellent. That went well.'

The candles were still burning and the windows showed darkness outside. 'Ah,' said Richard, 'you have rejoined us, Francis, have you? Welcome back.' He looked tired and drawn, the two narrow vertical lines incised between his brows despite the smile. His open right palm was resting lightly over his left upper arm, as if to calm the raging of the wound under the bandages. 'No, don't look so concerned. I will survive.'

'What is happening?'

'We have won the first round. Rivers and his attendants are locked into the wing of the inn containing their chambers. When they awake, they will discover that they are under arrest.'

'*Under arrest?*' It came out as something approaching a squawk.

'What else? They must be neutralised. And at least I have not set a pack of armed ruffians on them.'

Francis dropped his head into his hands. 'Are you sure about this, Richard? Are you *entitled* to do it? Is it wise?'

'Come, have some bread and ale to set you on your feet again.'

'Ale? Thank you, no.' He shuddered violently, the desire to retch intensified by the knowledge that Anne would never forgive him. Clever Richard, careful Richard, Richard in emotional and physical pain. Unstable Richard. Francis groaned.

The dawn light was just beginning to break through the black panes of the windows when there came a thunderous knocking from somewhere above, and a voice shouting.

'He sounds annoyed,' Buckingham said.

Other voices joined in, and sword hilts began battering against solid timber doors. The landlord said worriedly, 'I hope they don't do any damage. This inn is my whole living.'

'You will be recompensed.'

'Thank you, my lord duke. Thank you.'

Everything had been thought of. Rivers's outdoor servants had been manhandled into the stables and left tied up with the horses. There were men on guard outside the windows, and others had been sent to block the road to Stony Stratford. It was unfortunate that the imprisoned men still had their weapons, but that had been unavoidable.

'I don't think he'll come out fighting when we unlock the doors,' said Buckingham airily.

'No,' Richard agreed. 'He has always been a famous jouster, but this is real life. He cannot afford to fight, in case he loses.'

Through the door, Rivers demanded to know what was the meaning of this, and Richard told him courteously that it was by no means proper for such a man as he to turn the young king against the man whom that king's father had appointed as his Protector. 'Which being so,' Richard concluded, 'you must cool your heels here while my lord of Buckingham and I ride to Stony Stratford and hold conference with the king.'

It was to a continuing chorus of angry hammering that they took their armour down from the wooden hooks on the walls and dressed themselves for the possibly momentous day to come. Then they mounted and, with Buckingham's three hundred men in attendance, rode swiftly off for Stony Stratford and their first audience with King Edward V.

11

THE BOY was already in the courtyard with three or four members of his household preparing to set out. It struck Francis that, if Rivers had been with them, they would not simply have sat with their mouths open when they heard the approach of a large body of horse. It was scandalous that the king should be virtually unguarded and surrounded by such incompetents. He was not even wearing armour.

Reining in with a dramatic flourish, Richard and Buckingham leapt from their horses, bared their heads, and bent their knees in the approved fashion.

The king said politely, 'My lords?'

He was a goodlooking lad, tall for his age – almost as tall as Richard – and angelically fair, though there was a touch of ice and arrogance about him that spoke more of his mother than of his father. People had always warmed to the father; they would not do so to the son. Otherwise, his manners were impeccable.

Glancing with something that was half smile, half frown, towards their following, he asked, 'My uncle, Lord Rivers, does not accompany you?'

'No,' Richard said. 'I wonder, sire, if we might speak to you in private?'

The king looked for guidance towards the little group consisting of his half-brother Richard Grey, Sir Richard Haute, another of his Woodville kin, and his chamberlain, Sir Thomas Vaughan, but it seemed they had none to give. So he dismounted and led Richard and Buckingham and their immediate entourage into the inn where he halted, turned, and stood waiting. 'Yes?'

Richard had not expected it to be easy, and it was not. As he expressed his and Buckingham's sympathy over the death of the young king's father, his own emotions came flooding back. This was his brother he was talking about, a man whom he had loved and admired for most of his life, whom he had known far better and been far closer to than had this pretty boy, to whom Edward had been – as Richard's own father had been to his sons – a distant god encountered only on ceremonious terms and ceremonial occasions.

He could not afford to let his weakness show. It was vital that the boy do as he was told, and with at least a semblance of complaisance.

Hardening his voice and his heart, he said, 'Your late father, before his death, named me, his brother, as your Protector during your minority, but it grieves me deeply to say that your mother's family is doing all it can to undermine your father's wishes.'

The boy said, 'I do not . . .'

'Wait. They have behaved, in the royal council, as if they – not you, and certainly not I – have the governance of the country. They believe that, through your natural love for them, they will be able to dominate you and achieve for themselves the power and wealth that they so avidly desire . . .'

His spine stiffening, the boy said, 'I have every confidence in the ability of the queen my mother and the royal council to govern the kingdom in my name.'

'Women!' exclaimed Buckingham contemptuously. 'It is not for women to rule kingdoms!'

Richard cast him a reproving look and resumed, 'The old nobility, the men who have made our country what it is but whom your mother's family dare to despise, go in fear that your Woodville kin will influence you as, alas, they influenced your father, ruining his health and bringing about his death by involving him in their debaucheries.'

It was Sir Richard Grey who, this time, interrupted. 'I cannot stand by and listen to . . .'

'Wait.' Richard, his eyes fixed on those of the young king, did not even glance his way. 'In the meantime, failing to overawe the royal council, they have attempted to put a crude end to my Protectorship by murdering me. I was fortunate, yesterday, to escape with my life from a vicious ambush.'

Now, swiftly, he did cast a glance at Richard Grey, who swallowed and said, 'I am sorry to hear that.'

'Sorry that I was attacked, or sorry that I escaped?'

His sardonic tone had the effect of rousing the king to speech again. His fair eyelashes fluttering nervously, he said, 'I cannot permit you to speak so to my brother. Nor am I prepared to listen to what you say of my mother's family. You must be mistaken in them. I have no anticipation of taking instruction or guidance from you, my lord duke, whom I scarcely know. My present advisers, however, were given to me by my late father, and I have every faith in them. I have never seen in them any sign of the evil you speak of, and it is my firm intention to remain in their care.'

'Their "care"?' Richard scanned the lad's high-buttoned, knee-length purple velvet gown, with its bagpipe sleeves swelling out from the wrists to form hanging pouches or pockets; his long hose of black Milanese fustian; the purple velvet bonnet with its narrow turned-up brim perched on his short fair curls. 'You are wearing no armour.'

Young Eddie's chin rose autocratically. 'I have no need of armour. I am the king, and in my own country. And I have two thousand men to protect me, if the need were to arise.'

'As I understand it, they form an escort, not an army?'

'Well, they — they carry arms, of course, and they wear breastplates and sallet helmets. No more than that.'

'So the carts we saw as we passed, laden with barrels of weapons, are not for them?'

Francis found he could no longer watch the little scene. It was pitiful to see the boy floundering in search of an answer. Richard was being too hard on him.

Richard said, 'Your half-brother, the marquess of Dorset, is known to be trying to raise an army in London. Armies need weapons. They also need money, which may be why he has seized the royal treasury.'

'I do not know what my brother Dorset has done or is doing. But I do know that my uncle, Lord Rivers, and my brother Sir Richard here, are innocent of any such deeds.'

Buckingham broke in again. 'They are traitors who have kept the knowledge of it from your Grace.'

'No. They're not, and they wouldn't.' It came out, for the first time, childishly.

His manner softening slightly, Richard said, 'Sire, you have lived for little more than twelve years, leading a sheltered life at Ludlow with your servants and tutors, and – if your father's instructions were obeyed – no one permitted to come near you who was guilty of, if I remember correctly, "swearing, brawling, backbiting, gambling, ribaldry or adultery". You have been taught Latin and poetry, music and noble bearing.' He paused and then, his voice hardening again, went on, 'No doubt you have also learned to play chess – on a chessboard. But you know nothing of the chess game of life, and you must, I fear, concede the superior wisdom of your elders in worldly affairs. Now that you are king, you must give yourself into the guidance of those whose concern is not for themselves, not even for you, but for the welfare of the realm.'

He extended a hand. 'Come, sire.'

After a moment, the boy stepped forward. Then, aware of not being followed, turned his head and saw Ratcliffe, Catesby and two of Buckingham's entourage interposing themselves between him and Grey, Haute and Vaughan, who showed no sign of resistance. He looked back at Richard, but Richard merely repeated, 'Come, sire.'

The boy's lips quivered, but to his credit he walked erect through the door into the courtyard, where his grooms helped him to mount.

If he had been quick, Francis thought, he could have galloped off to seek the protection of his armed escort, but perhaps dignity forbade, or perhaps he was just afraid.

12

THE NEWS reached the Palace of Westminster just before midnight and was broken to the queen, who had already retired. She threw back the covers with an unqueenly screech which one of her ladies later described as despairing, another as panicky, and a third as sheer bad temper.

'Mistress Cobb! I want my chamberlain, my steward and my secretary this instant! But first, my son Dorset. And send also to have my daughters roused and dressed, and my little son the duke of York. Go now! What are you waiting for? No, no, I can dress myself. Go, I said. *Go!*'

And this, gossiped one of the same ladies a few days later, from a mistress who was in general unable even to hook up the neck of her gown unaided! 'It's just as I have always said. Scratch a Woodville and you find a commoner . . .'

'Gloucester and Buckingham,' she snapped when Dorset finally appeared from the whorehouse to which he had been traced. 'Jesu, but you smell of women! Stand away from me. They have forestalled us. I cannot guess what Anthony was doing to permit it. They have arrested him, *and* your brother Richard, *and* Haute and Vaughan, and are proposing to send them north to imprisonment at Pontefract, of all disagreeable places. And my poor darling Eddie is in their clutches. What will they do to him, the helpless little innocent? I am *so* afraid for him, and for myself.'

Dorset knew enough of his mother to discount her wilder flights. Although not much given to reflection, he had wondered sometimes about her maternal instincts, suspecting that her much vaunted love for her children had more to do with the fact that they were *hers* than that they were human beings in their own right. Not, he supposed, that it made her feelings any less intense. He said, 'Gloucester can't afford to harm the boy. At least, I don't think so. But I wouldn't have expected him to take such an extreme initiative as this. What are you going to do?'

She threw up her hands. 'What am *I* going to do? I summoned you for help, not for stupid questions. What *I* am going to do is seek sanctuary in the abbey with my children. I have sent to Abbot Estney to inform him.'

'Is that necessary?'

'Perhaps not, unless Gloucester is proposing to start a war, of which there seems as yet to be no sign. But if I show myself fearful of him, I will attract public sympathy and make whatever he has in mind more difficult for him. Perhaps impossible.'

'That's clever.'

'Thank you. You may join us, if you wish. Fortunately, after my previous sojourn in the Abbot's Lodging, when Eddie was born during my husband's exile, I know what I need to take with me for my comfort during a possibly prolonged stay.'

'Ah. I wondered, as I came in, where all the beds and chests and coffers were going.'

'Well, now you know,' she said shrewishly. 'And if you want to make yourself useful, you may go and ensure that his foolish tutor has my little York up and dressed. Oh, how I wish Anthony were here!'

She was still in her chamber when, somewhere in the middle of the night, Archbishop Rotherham fought his way through the mob of servants carrying packs and bundles, boxes and chests, and found her sitting alone amid domestic chaos.

220

He was not accustomed to being out of his bed at dead of night, but Lord Hastings had been insistent. He must tell the queen, Hastings had said, that all would be well, although he had failed to explain how he knew, or even what he meant by 'all'.

With loathing, the queen exclaimed, 'Lord Hastings wishes to reassure me? He who has never faltered in his desire to destroy me and my family? I could never be reassured by anything he has to say.'

'Now, now, your Grace . . .'

'Do not, "Now, now" me! If he knows that all will be well, how does he know? It is a conspiracy and one in which he is deeply embroiled. Oh, my poor little son, what are they doing to you?'

'I assure you, madame . . .' Then he hesitated. Could she be right about Hastings? But Hastings's loyalty to the late king had been legendary, and he, of all men, could most be relied on to be true to the son, if not to the mother.

With her long blonde hair curling to her waist and her blue cloak loosely tied at her throat, she was still an astonishingly beautiful woman even to – or perhaps especially to – an elderly prelate.

Soothingly, he said, 'Madame, I have brought you something to calm your fears. I have brought you the symbol of royal power – the Great Seal of the kingdom that permits you to issue orders in the king's name.'

It did not have quite the effect he had hoped for. Indeed, before she remembered her manners, she looked as if she would have preferred a siege train of artillery.

But he gave her the seal, and she accepted it, and he did not foresee that, within days, the council would instruct him to get it back from her. Immediately, if not sooner.

13

AT MIDDLEHAM, Anne was fretting, with no idea what was going on. It was only two weeks since Richard had left and, in the past, far longer than that had elapsed without her having news of him. But, in the past, he had been himself and now he was not.

Constantia was a tower of strength, but as the days passed she, too, became uneasy as no message came even from Francis.

Little Ned had one of his feverish attacks, and Anne spent day after day by his bedside, worrying about him also.

In the end, anxiety overcame the care she had always taken not to make demands on Richard.

She said, 'I *can't* write and ask for news of what is happening, but young George Neville's death gives me an excuse to send him a message. It's something he should know about, and it might extract a response from him.'

Constantia, well aware by now of the strangely guarded relationship between Anne and Richard – so very different from her own relationship with Francis – said merely, 'If you are sending a messenger, perhaps he could also take a note from me to Francis?'

'Of course! Of course! I cannot bear the thought of Richard dragging Francis into a danger Francis would otherwise have the sense to avoid.'

Constantia was silenced. Her own life with the peaceable Francis had blinded her to what it must be like to be married to a man for whom power and danger were the breath of life. At home at Minster Lovell, she never had to fear that, when Francis rode out, he would not return again. Anne, for all her phsyical delicacy, was possessed of a strength of mind that Constantia could only admire. But she did not envy it.

'My dear lord,' Anne wrote, 'I am busy as always with the affairs of Middleham and our people here, but my thoughts and concerns are with you, knowing the difficulties that must face you. I write to you today because I have just received unhappy news of which I believe you will wish to be apprised. It is that young George Neville has died.'

Family feeling was not the issue. The issue was that after the inheritance squabble of ten years before, Parliament had granted to Richard lands that should have passed by entail to young George Neville, duke of Bedford — but with the proviso that Richard should hold them only during the lifetime of George or his direct heirs in the male line. It could not have been foreseen that George would be dead at eighteen, leaving no direct heir. It meant that Richard would have to give up much of what had bolstered his power in the north — including, unthinkably, the lordships of Middleham and Sheriff Hutton — which should now rightfully pass to other members of the Neville family.

If Edward had lived, he would have found some way to circumvent the terms of the grant for Richard's sake, but Anne could not guess what would happen now except that, if the Woodvilles had anything to say in the matter, Richard would be the loser.

She picked up her pen again. 'I do not know the cause of his death, although there is talk of poison. But there is always such talk when young men die unexpectedly in their beds. I send this letter to you by Master Metcalfe, in the hope that he will find you at Crosby Hall, and that you are in good health.' She signed it, as she always did, 'Your dutiful and loving wife, Anne of Gloucester', and went back to waiting until she should be granted some hint of what the future held.

223

14

ON THAT same day another, younger man than George Neville was riding towards London, a lad dressed in purple velvet and attended by two black-clad dukes and an escort of five hundred men. Coming in on the main road from St Albans, they were met at Hornsey, five miles from the city, with the ceremonial welcome to which kings were entitled.

Richard smiled at the boy, who had never seen a royal welcome before. He said, 'It was like this, years ago, when London first welcomed your father, although then it was inside the city and the fountains were flowing with wine. That was twenty-two years since, and I was younger than you are at the time. I can still remember how impressed I was.'

But the boy failed to respond. If he had smiled back, or even nodded, what followed might have been very different.

Instead, ignorant of the human dramas of those twenty-two years, he took it all as his due — haughtily surveying the mayor, sheriffs and aldermen in their scarlet robes and gold chains, and the five hundred members of the great livery companies all clad in violet, and then murmuring, 'Can we ride on, or must we wait for these people?'

'They have come to escort your Highness to London. You must bow and wave to them and accept their company graciously.'

The fair face turned coldly towards him. 'Do not, I pray you, instruct me in how to behave towards my subjects. I have been well taught.'

Buckingham's snort was all too audible. 'Taught by those whose pretensions to royalty far outweigh their entitlement to it.'

In the four days since Richard and Buckingham had detached the boy from the Woodvilles, he had been so much reassured by their deference that he seemed to have lost any fear of them.

Acidly, he replied, 'But I do not recall *you* having had a hand in my upbringing, my lord Buckingham?'

Richard flashed a warning glance at Buckingham, whose healthy complexion had paled with rage, and Francis, close by with Ratcliffe and Catesby, reflected with wry amusement that Buckingham looked like being no more popular with the new king than he had been with his father. But at least Edward IV had always been tactful in his dealings with his subjects. Clever though the boy might be, he still had a great deal to learn.

Black and purple, scarlet and violet, the procession made a striking impression on bystanders as it wound its slow way to the city, where the lords spiritual and temporal, summoned by Richard to swear fealty to the new king, awaited it.

Margaret Beaufort, curtseying at her husband's side, watched everything and everyone with intense interest. It was her son's future that, as always, obsessed her; whether the agreement that she had reached with the late king allowing Henry to return to England would still stand. There was no reason why it should not, if the Woodvilles – or those of them who remained at liberty – gained control of the new king and his advisory council. Stanley, she thought, would still have sufficient influence there to ensure it. But if Richard of Gloucester's protectorship were extended beyond the coronation and until the boy came of age at fifteen, as was being widely suggested, it might be a different matter.

'That's queer,' Stanley muttered.

Following his eyes, she saw four horse-drawn carts in the procession, carts with the high wheels and ridged treads used for transport over rough or muddy ground. The carts were laden with barrels full of weapons and armour, the barrels bearing heraldic devices identifying them as belonging to the Woodvilles.

Rumour travelled with the carts. It was said that the weapons had been intended for use by the Woodvilles in ambushing the dukes of Gloucester and Buckingham on the road from St Albans into London.

Stanley said, 'Nonsense. I know those barrels. They weren't meant for an ambush. Edward had them stored away for use against the Scots.'

'But since they do not seem to have been used against the Scots, they presumably remained available to the Woodvilles for other purposes,' Margaret pointed out absently.

'I suppose so. Richard must know something that I don't, or he would not be spreading such a tale.'

15

TEN DAYS after Anne had written to Richard, ten days during which she and Constantia had worried more, rather than less, a small troop of horse under Sir Thomas Gower arrived at Middle, ham with a prisoner in its midst. The prisoner's feet were tied together under his horse's belly and there was a rope, its end attached to the saddle tree of one of the men,at,arms, binding his upper arms tightly to his body but leaving his hands free for the reins. He was a young man and a sorry,looking sight.

It was the queen's son, Richard Grey.

'Sir Richard!' Anne exclaimed, and turned questioningly and with unease to Thomas Gower, whom she could not think of as 'Sir' Thomas because he had earned his knighthood so recently on Richard's Scots campaign.

Gower said, 'My lord duke required me to bring Sir Richard Grey here to be kept under strict guard until I have further orders.'

'But . . .'

As if repeating something he had learned by heart, Gower

went on, 'Sir Richard has conspired with others, notably the Earl Rivers, Sir Richard Haute and Sir Thomas Vaughan, to assassinate the lord Protector and has therefore been arrested by the lord Protector . . .'

'Is he all right?'

'The lord Protector? I believe so, my lady. He put Lord Rivers and Sir Richard in my charge, and I have left Lord Rivers to be held at Sheriff Hutton until further notice.'

Richard Grey was still capable of managing a sneer. 'You are right to look concerned, my lady. By daring to take such action against my family, your husband has signed his own death warrant.'

She could have wept with fear and frustration, but had too much pride. 'I believe the gatehouse dungeon would be the best place, Sir Thomas,' she said. 'When you have settled the prisoner there, I should be pleased if you will report to me in my chamber.'

She turned away.

To Constantia she said, 'Young Grey has always been an objectionable youth, and is no doubt fully deserving of whatever fate awaits him. But Richard! Oh, Richard! What risks are you taking?'

And then, for the first time, she broke down and wept on Constantia's shoulder.

16

JUST THEN, Richard was taking no risks at all.

Not yet. Though, increasingly, he was confronting the possibility that he might have to.

In the meantime, his primary concern was to counteract the

227

queen's baleful influence and establish his own position in the council and the country. After the first day or two, the nervousness that had overtaken everyone at the news of his seizure of the young king had begun to subside. People remembered that this was Duke Richard, the brother of the late king, who had a reputation for loyalty, justice and effectiveness, and was a far more desirable guide for the new young king during his minority than the selfseeking, arrogant Woodvilles. And if he had the support of the blue-blooded duke of Buckingham and Lord Hastings, the late king's most intimate and trusted adviser, well . . .

'Good,' was all Richard said when Francis reported this back to him, a Francis who, for so long an automatic participant in Richard's life, did not at first recognise that he was now being deliberately excluded.

He was kept too busy being tactful on Richard's behalf to all the people Richard needed on his side, or discussing with the city livery companies the arrangements for the coronation and who was going to pay, or arranging with Hastings the issue of a new coinage to be struck in the name of King Edward V. It occurred to him only when the royal council met first thing in the morning of May 10th and formally appointed Richard as Protector, setting a new date for the coronation which gave Richard several weeks of undisputed sovereignty until a regency council took over. *If* it took over.

Francis, like many others, was moderately sure that it was Richard's purpose to extend his protectorship beyond the coronation, until the boy came of age, giving him far more control than if he were reduced to no more than the leading member of a regency council. But Richard volunteered nothing to confirm or deny the suspicion, merely reporting that the royal council meeting had been unable to see beyond the coronation and had failed to discuss what might happen afterwards.

What it had discussed, to Richard's intense annoyance, had been his demand that Anthony Rivers and his associates be declared traitors and have their possessions forfeited for their attack on his life in Northampton and the proposed ambush on the road to London.

No, no, had said the council politely but firmly, manipulated by the wily little Bishop Morton. Since Duke Richard had not yet been formally appointed as Protector when those events took place, the attacks on him could not be construed as treasonable and his rights in the matter were no more than those of a private citizen. His arrest of the accused, although perhaps understand-able, was not justifiable in law.

'Well,' he snapped at Catesby afterwards. 'Is that good law, or bad law?'

'Can you prove that the Woodvilles were responsible for the attack on you at Northampton?'

'Prove? No. The evidence was circumstantial.'

'Can you prove conspiracy to ambush you on the road to London?'

'Prove? No, but everything pointed to it.'

'Not good enough. You could, I suppose, try what the rack would elicit from some of the Woodvilles' retainers.'

Richard shook his head.

Catesby shrugged. 'Then you will have to accept that the opinion of the council was correct. Indeed, it should have required you to free the Woodvilles from custody.'

'Thus inviting them to attempt further violence against me? It had more sense than that.'

Catesby stroked his quill back and forth across his lips. 'Per-haps it would be best to keep your prisoners where they are. If the council can be discouraged from discussing their fate, if you can divert its attention to other matters, it might forget about them.

After all, they have few admirers.'

'Other than the young king! Well, I can find plenty of diver╱ sions to occupy the council. In the meantime, since I am now officially Protector, I shall start behaving as such and exercise my powers of appointment and patronage.'

'You must, however, ensure that writs and warrants are issued in the king's name. And I would suggest some phrasing such as "by the advice of our dearest uncle, the duke of Gloucester, Protector of this our realm during our young age".'

'Very well. Also, it is high time that a proper register of government grants and warrants was kept. My late brother depended largely on his memory in the matter of what he had given to whom, and under what terms, but a written record is a more satisfactory tool of government. See to it, Catesby. In the meantime, I will rejoice the soul of the duke of Buckingham by telling him what he is to be paid for the support he has given me.'

Francis, who had been doing his best to appear unobtrusive and harmless, said provocatively, 'May I stay? Or have you some errand for me?'

His sarcasm passed Richard by. 'Yes, stay if you want to.'

It proved to be worth staying for. Francis could feel his jaw drop slightly as he listened to Richard endow Buckingham, in the course of a mere ten minutes, with castles, estates and offices giving him unprecedented power in Wales, on the Welsh borders, and in the West country, which the duke accepted with the unexcited smile of one who was much obliged even if he were being granted no more than was his due.

Francis had never before noticed what pointed ears he had or how his eyes showed the faintest tendency to cross when he was trying to convey what a sincere and honest fellow he was.

When he had gone, Francis said, 'You don't trust him, but you have just awarded him the powers of a viceroy. It seems an extravagant reward for the few days' support he has given you.'

Richard sighed. 'Francis, you are being naive. It was partly reward and partly bribery. I still need him. And having removed Anthony Rivers from Wales, which he has virtually ruled for years, I have to install someone else as a replacement. There is no time at present to give considered thought to any diffusion of power in the region, so, for the moment at least, a single transfer seems to me to be the answer. Whether the transfer is temporary or permanent depends on how Buckingham behaves. What is given can as easily be taken away.'

Tempted to say, 'I hope you know what you're doing,' Francis restricted himself to a derisive grimace.

'Oh, go away!' Richard exclaimed. 'Go back to Constantia! Is she well?'

'Yes. But I've sent for her to join me in London. She longs to see the coronation.'

'God's bones! I haven't sent for Anne yet. Thank you for reminding me.'

17

IN THE next few days, Richard made a few minor but carefully calculated changes to the composition of the royal council, in the course of which Bishop Rotherham – whose indiscretion with the Great Seal had not been forgiven – lost the chancellorship to Bishop Russell of Lincoln, but most of the late King Edward IV's household men retained their positions.

He also promised Jocky Howard the dukedom of Norfolk, and made it clear to Harry Percy that his powers on the Scots borders would be increased. He succeeded in so undermining Sir Edward Woodville's illicit command of the English fleet that Sir Edward was forced to flee to Brittany, taking only two ships with him.

He sent Buckingham to persuade the queen to emerge from sanctuary in Westminster Abbey, since her continued refuge there demonstrated all too publicly that she had no trust in her son's Protector – 'Though what she expects me to do to her, I cannot imagine!' he complained exasperatedly.

Buckingham, not altogether surprisingly, had no success. So Richard went himself.

'I am perfectly at home here,' she said with her irritating, tinkling laugh. 'As you can see, I brought my furnishings with me, so I have every comfort, and it is pleasant to have a change of scene. There is much coming and going from the almshouses and the tenements and shops, while it amuses my little son very much to watch the hungry monks trying not to run through the cloister on their way to the refectory.'

It seemed a very juvenile amusement for a nine-year-old, but Richard allowed it to pass. He said, 'However comfortable you may be, my lady, I believe that it would reassure the king your son's subjects greatly were you to leave your sanctuary and take up your public rôle again as the king's mother.'

'But I do not wish to reassure them.'

'No?' He was not surprised.

'I wish everyone to understand that, while you remain Protector, my only safety lies within the precincts of the church. I do not, however, expect to remain here for long.'

Tightly, Richard said, 'Because your son Dorset is here with you, and violating the sanctuary by sending out messengers to try and gather together an army?'

She smiled and said, 'Perhaps.'

'Be sensible, Elizabeth! Everything is running smoothly, and a new date has been set for young Edward's coronation. Do you want to start another war?'

'If necessary. Though I would hope to achieve my ends by other means.'

He did not ask her to elucidate, but said only, 'I never now venture into dark alleys without a bodyguard of at least fifty men.'

'How wise.'

'And I never eat or drink anything without it first having been assayed for poison.'

Almost flirtatiously she said, 'Dear me. I will have to think of something else, will I not? Because I will never leave this place until I have seen the last of you, my dear brother-in-law.'

He bowed and left. Caged she might be, but no less dangerous for that.

The royal council was disappointed by the queen's instransigence. It looked so bad to outsiders. But of more immediate concern was the undesirability of staging the coronation of Edward V while his younger brother and heir apparent was so stubbornly withheld from view. The Protector must see to it, said the council, that the queen release the little duke of York to keep company with his brother, now ensconced in the royal apartments in the Tower.

So negotiations had to be begun all over again.

In Richard's seemingly endless round of activity, there was only one oversight, but one that was to prove disastrous. While making huge and valuable concessions to men such as Buckingham and Jocky Howard, Richard granted Hastings – who had set all the events of the previous weeks in train – no more reward than to confirm him as Master of the Mint.

Hastings felt that he was being taken for granted.

Chapter Ten

1483

1

ON JUNE 5TH, the Duchess Anne arrived in London with her attendants and baggage train to find a great many people rushing around Crosby Hall with papers in their hands, but no Richard.

She had never liked the house, which had been built by an indecently rich and ambitious merchant less than twenty years before and was a monument to the quatrefoil, which appeared on cornices, fireplaces and windows with such frequency that she felt as if her eyes and her brain were also being partitioned in fours – until she went upstairs, where there were cinquefoils instead. But modern though the decorations were, there was still an antiquated central hearth in the Great Hall as well as the wall fireplace. Richard didn't seem to mind. The place was light and sumptuous and therefore appropriate for a royal duke.

Who, when he arrived back and found her there, looked as if the ground had opened under his feet. Or, she swiftly realised, as if she were an intruder from another world which he had forgotten.

But Catesby was beside him, saying, 'Welcome, my lady,' and, almost in the same breath, 'My lord duke, if I might ask you to . . .'

'What? Yes. Oh, yes. I am afraid, my lady, that there are things I must attend to.'

Her voice clear and carrying, she said, 'My lord, I and my ladies-in-waiting are hungry and tired from our journey. Perhaps the clerk of the kitchen could have an all-night brought to my chamber, some bread and wine and a little meat? And then I shall rest.'

It was the right thing to say, the necessary thing to do, and it enabled her to pretend that nothing was amiss.

2

SHE SOON LEARNED from Francis that a great deal was amiss.

Having done his best to hug the life out of Constantia, he stood with his arm round her shoulders and said, 'He never stops to draw breath. I *think* he is trying to plan what is best to do, but he is for ever being diverted by minutiae. Unlike Edward he is constitutionally incapable of leaving things to other people, and he is finding many things that need to be rectified. Well, you know Richard. He is *always* right.'

'He usually is!'

'He knows that, you know that, and I know that, but there are a great many people here in the south who don't know it. He does, within limits, consult men who expect to be consulted but then pays no attention, or very little, to what they say. They are beginning to understand that he trusts only his own judgement and is not to be influenced by others. It is not going down well.'

Defensively, Anne said, 'Edward was the same. He had an iron will and he did what he chose.'

Francis sighed. 'But Edward was the king, and everyone knew him, and everyone was charmed by him and found it easy to forget what they would otherwise have disliked about him. Whereas no one here in the south really knows Richard. He has been too long away.'

'And he is not himself,' she said tonelessly.

'No. His emotions are still disturbed and his judgement is flawed.'

'Can you do nothing?'

'When did you ever know Richard allow himself to be influenced?'

3

A FEW DAYS LATER, Francis wandered into the parlour at Crosby Hall in search of Richard and found, instead, Lord Hastings in conference with Catesby, a man whom Hastings still thought of as being devoted to his interests.

Catesby was saying, '. . . northern supporters to come south in force,' but broke off sharply when he became aware of Francis's presence.

Hastings nodded to the newcomer, a frown on his normally affable brow. 'I don't see the need for that. I'll have to think about it.'

'But you will keep it confidential?'

'Naturally.'

When he had gone, Francis said, 'And what was that about?'

He was in an awkward position in relation to Richard's staff, having no formal appointment but being known as Duke

Richard's closest intimate. Luckily, he and Catesby were on reasonably easy terms, so Catesby, who could be as communicative as an oyster, revealed that, 'My lord duke is just about to send Ratcliffe off to the north with letters for the mayor of York, Percy of Northumberland and others, requiring them to come to his aid.'

'Why should he need aid?'

'The queen appears to be determined to put a period to his existence. And my lord Buckingham's.'

'What, still at that? I would not have thought her completely lacking in sense. Anyway, what can she do, immured in the Abbot's Lodging, especially with Rivers and Grey safely under lock and key?'

'Dorset is still trying hard to raise an army. Not with any notable success, but if the queen can attract support from even just one of the great lords and persuade him to summon his followers on her or her son's behalf, we could have war again.'

Francis groaned. 'I think I will take the Lady Constantia home to Minster Lovell and pull up the drawbridge! Why were you telling Hastings about Duke Richard's letters to the north? Hastings is not a happy man these days.'

'Testing him. My lord duke needs to know who is loyal and who is not.'

Francis thought it was a risky way of finding out, and would have said so to Richard — if Richard had given him the opportunity.

4

HASTINGS, choosing to interpret 'confidential' in a comparative rather than an absolute sense, had gone straight off to consult another member of the royal council, Bishop Morton, not a man he liked, but the most worldly of the lords spiritual. He found him in conference with Archbishop Rotherham and Lord Stanley.

The bishop advised him to go and see the queen.

'But . . .'

'But you and she have never been on the best of terms? True. Now, however, the time may have come to set that right. You must think of the good of the country. Duke Richard will have no need of his northern army if you can persuade the queen to accept the status quo – and she will have no need of an army, either.'

'I can try, I suppose.'

Filled with rosy visions of becoming saviour of the country, Hastings dropped in again at Crosby Hall to tell his friend Catesby that the queen had agreed to see him – and why – on the afternoon of the next day, the 12th.

In the meanwhile, Bishop Morton sent a private note to the queen with his own recommendations as to what she might say to Hastings. And at much the same time, Catesby told Richard that Hastings had made an appointment to see the queen, but omitted to tell him its purpose.

5

'HE WANTS the throne for himself,' Elizabeth said. 'It is the only reason why he should need an army. He intends using it to overawe the country.'

Hastings wished he had not come. 'No, no. He does not desire the throne! The army is intended to combat your own threats against him, your Grace. He takes them very seriously.'

'*My* threats?' The queen looked helpless and feminine, a trick she had perfected over many years. 'All I told him was that I would not leave sanctuary until I had seen the last of him. No more than that.'

'Oh.' Hastings was disconcerted.

'All the threats are from him! It is my son I fear for. What will happen to him if Richard should decide to take the throne for himself?' Delicately, she dabbed her eyes. 'Oh, William, we have never been friends, but you were loyal to the king my husband for so many years and you *cannot* let his son down now.'

He did not hesitate. 'Of course not. I could not do it. I would lay down my life for him.' Which was true – more or less. He did not expect the question to arise.

But the queen was cleverer than he was, and also had the benefit of Bishop Morton's considered advice. By the time half an hour had passed, Hastings was beginning to wonder whether Richard might indeed have undisclosed ambitions, in which case it was perfectly understandable that the queen should want her son to have an army of his own. Hastings had strongly objected to that idea when it would have had Anthony Rivers in command. But Rivers was now out of the way, and someone more responsible could be appointed.

It seemed like a perfectly natural progression when the queen said, 'If the men my son Dorset is trying to raise could be reinforced by the supporters of one of the more responsible lords – yourself, for example – I would have no more fears for my little Eddie's future.'

The mention of Dorset was a mistake, but Hastings knew he himself could raise enough men to cast Dorset in the shade. He was so busy working out how many that he almost missed the queen's next remark. 'There would, of course, be rewards,' she said meditatively. 'If conflict arose, and Duke Richard were defeated, all his estates and offices would be freed for redistribution.'

He drew in a breath, and tried to cover it with a cough. 'Things will not come to that,' he said with conviction.

But the seed had been planted.

When Catesby arrived at Mistress Shore's house later in the afternoon with a document for Hastings to sign, Hastings could not resist telling him all about the meeting, making a joke of it. 'She must be desperate!'

But when Catesby reported this back to Richard, he failed to report more than the bare facts, omitting the waggish overtones. Hastings might have an eye on Richard's territories and offices, but Catesby had an eye on Hastings's.

6

ANNE, returning from a visit with Constantia to some silk merchants' warehouses, found her husband, grim-faced, telling Catesby, 'You may go now. We will talk again in the morning.'

She had scarcely seen him in the last six days, so she stopped, and smiled, and said in her most dulcet voice, 'Ah, Richard! Remember me? I am your wife.'

For a moment, he stared at her, his eyes full of pain. Then he put his hands on her shoulders and breathed, as he had breathed once before, 'I need you.'

She would have preferred not to hear it, or not in such a tone.

Every bone and muscle in his body seemed to be shuddering when at last they were rid of attendants and were able to lie together.

'Your arm!' she exclaimed, her eyes on the half-healed wound in his arm. He shook his head. 'I was attacked. It will be better soon.'

He kissed her with no passion other than the passion of nervous tension. 'I only want to hold you. Be with me.'

And because she was who she was, and loved him so much, she gave him warmth and comfort and did not ask why he needed it.

7

'HE HAS been like this only once before,' she said to Francis next morning. 'And that was when Edward condemned George to death.'

His face strained, Francis said, 'Yes. And that was after the event, an event for which he had no responsibility.'

'So?' The question was bitter in her throat.

'So this time *he* has to make the decisions. And he is afraid. He is afraid for his soul.'

They stared into each other's eyes, the only two people in the world who loved him.

'No,' Francis said. 'I don't know what those decisions are.'

8

BUT THEY HAD been made, and were already being fulfilled.

After Matins, Richard had tried and failed to stomach the few mouthfuls of bread and ale with which most men broke their fasts. He was late, therefore, in mounting and setting out with Buckingham and Jocky Howard and their combined retinues to ride the half-mile alongside the old Roman wall to the Tower of London, where he had called a meeting of a select few members of the royal council.

As they entered Edward's recently built Bulwark and crossed the causeway, they could hear the roaring and snarling of the lions and leopards and other strange beasts in the royal menagerie by the western wharf. 'The meeting seems to have started without us,' remarked Jocky Howard cheerfully.

Then they passed through the Coldharbour Gate to the inner precinct and began the climb to the old Council Gallery at the top of the White Tower, where Lords Hastings and Stanley, with Archbishop Rotherham, Bishop Morton and the secretary, Oliver King, awaited them.

Richard and Buckingham were by far the youngest of the company, at thirty and twenty-eight respectively, and the churchmen the eldest, Morton with sixty-three devious years of experience behind him, and Rotherham with sixty. They were all, Richard saw, looking as amiable as their natures permitted, Hastings beaming cooperatively, Stanley tight-mouthed and calculating, Rotherham grey and learned and benevolent, and Morton beady-eyed as always. Buckingham had a glitter in his eyes, and Howard's joviality was never more than a thin veneer over his violent temper and domineering nature.

Richard himself was aware of being unnaturally pale, with perhaps a faint tinge of green. If anyone noticed, he would simply say, 'Last night's fish', and everyone would understand; queasy digestions were one of the everyday hazards of life. But he was angry with himself that a friend's betrayal should cause such turmoil in him and drive him to a deed that was personally painful, however necessary politically.

While waiting for him, they had been talking not of matters of state but, of all things, about gardening. Bishop Morton was boasting of strawberries already ripe in his walled garden at Holborn and Richard asked politely, 'Perhaps you might send me some?'

And then it became necessary for him to say, 'Your pardon, but I must leave you for a moment.'

When he returned something over half an hour later, he had wound himself up to do what must be done, and without delay. He had no idea of how angry he looked, his eyes wide and hard, a heavy frown on his brow, and his thin lips narrowed to invisibility. Everyone else was seated, so he remained standing as he surveyed them and demanded brusquely and without preliminary, 'What, tell me, should be the penalty for anyone plotting the destruction of me, who am Protector of the realm and so nearly related to the king?'

His startled audience was silent, except for Hastings, who after a moment helpfully supplied the answer that Richard so obviously expected. 'They should be punished as traitors.'

'Then what about that sorceress the queen, and her associates?' He stripped back his left sleeve to display his wounded arm. 'What about this? And what about Shore's wife, and *her* associates?'

There was nothing new in accusing the queen of sorcery. It was widely held that she and, more particularly, her mother had bewitched the late king into marrying her. But the implied link with Mistress Shore, whose very name was enough to send the queen into a cold fury, mystified everyone.

And then it became clear that Richard was linking the queen not to Mistress Shore but to Mistress Shore's 'associates' – Hastings, who was present, and Dorset, who was not.

Richard slammed his fist down on the table and, in response, doors opened and armed men led by Jocky Howard's son came rushing into the room to find Richard pointing at Hastings and shouting, 'Arrest him!'

Hastings half rose, his fists supporting him on the table, and gasped disbelievingly, 'Me, my lord?'

'Yes, you. You are a traitor! And you others, who have been meeting privately together. What have you been plotting?'

Lord Stanley leapt to his feet, but received a glancing blow from one of the men-at-arms which sent him to the floor, blood gushing from his temple. The prelates Rotherham and Morton made no move.

'Take them away,' Richard ordered. 'And fetch a priest from the chapel below so that Lord Hastings may make confession before he dies.'

Hastings gasped, 'Richard! Diccon, my old friend! Richard!' as he was dragged from the room.

But Richard had turned away, to gaze grimly out at the patch of greensward between the White Tower and the chapel of St Paul ad Vincula, where, after a few moments, some of his men appeared, rolling a log into position. And a few moments after that, Hastings was dragged out and made to kneel with his head over the log.

The priest stood beside him and prayed as the sword fell.

9

IT WAS indicative of Richard's state of mind that he had completely forgotten that the young king was in residence in the old royal apartments below the Council Gallery.

'My lord Protector?'

The voice was tentative, that of a servant, so he did not turn his head. 'Yes?'

'The king's grace is at his lessons in the Great Chamber. He has been distracted by shouting and the noise of many armed men, and wishes to know what the disturbance is. He commands your presence, my lord.'

It brought Richard to his senses. The suppressed rage, the sense of cruel disillusion that had driven him since the previous after-noon when he had heard of Hastings's betrayal, suddenly drained away. For a dozen years he had known nothing but success in the north, because he had always acted immediately and ruthlessly to nip danger in the bud before it had time to develop. But London was a different world, where every act had to be explained and justified to others. It was necessary to take thought before he could face that problem.

The Great Chamber was on the east side of the building, and its windows opened to north and south. So the boy could have seen nothing of what had been happening on Tower Green to the west.

His eyes closed, the bridge of his nose nipped between thumb and forefinger, he said, 'There is nothing that need concern his Grace. Tell him, please, that I am much engaged at present but will come to him at the earliest opportunity.' And if the boy objected to being put off, he would have to learn to suffer it. A twelve-year-old king could not expect to have his twelve-year-old way with the Protector of the realm.

'But, my lord Protector . . .' the servant essayed.

'Go!' Richard said tightly, and the man went.

10

FRANCIS HAD a private chamber at Crosby Hall and, that afternoon, in a snatched moment with Constantia, told her what had happened. It was so bad that it overrode even their need for each other. He kissed her lightly, and held her quivering in his arms, and said, 'He is in deep distress.' There was no need to define who was meant by 'he'.

'Murder?'

'It will be seen as such, although he had reason.'

She murmured, 'Anne . . . Oh, God. What will he do next?'

'I don't know. But he is boxing himself in. Everything he has done in these last days has reduced his options. If he goes back, he is dead. So he must go on.'

'Is it as inevitable as that?'

'I think so.'

'And you?'

'I cannot abandon him.'

'No, I can see that,' she said. 'And neither can Anne. Dear God, what will be the end of it?'

11

'HE CANNOT, he *cannot*, have done such a thing. William Hastings, of all people!'

'He cannot, but he has,' Francis said.

Through the fingers spread over her lips, Anne moaned, 'That lovely, friendly, open-hearted man, who never had an unkind word to say of anyone . . .'

Trying to be politically wise, Francis said, 'We should never speak ill of the dead, but we are not compelled to speak only good of them. Hastings was far from disinterested. Though he stood by Edward through thick and thin, he was lavishly rewarded for it, which enabled him to reward others, to smile and be popular and make friends. Friends are more profitable than enemies.'

'But such a cheerful man, such an open, honest man, who was never deceitful but always said what he truly thought!'

'You should know better than to take men at their own valuation. Try to remember that men who say *what* they think do not necessarily say *all* that they think. Catesby tells me that Hastings was plotting with the queen to raise an army from among his followers to overthrow Richard's protectorship. Let us wait and hear what Richard himself has to say.'

Anne was not in the mood for being soothed. 'If he has *any*thing to say! I sometimes wonder whether his mind and his voice are even connected with each other.'

'Well, he is certainly going to have to say something to explain himself, otherwise the city will be in turmoil. No, don't look at me like that. I have no idea whether he is behaving sensibly or stupidly. We must just trust him.'

'But *Hastings*, of all people!'

12

IT WAS what everyone else was saying, too. Hastings had been much liked and trusted and there was commotion in the city as the news spread, despite official statements — Richard and Buckingham, at a hastily convened meeting, having treated the mayor and aldermen to a carefully edited version of the plot — about his intention to kill the Protector and the duke of Buckingham, and seize the person of the king.

The charges were repeated in a hasty proclamation sent round the city by herald, and not only repeated but amplified, because it was necessary to persuade hearers that Hastings had never been the good and gentle knight he had appeared, but dissolute and corrupt in his personal life, so lacking in judgement as to take counsel in his treason from the loose woman, Mistress Shore, with whom he lay nightly, and above all responsible for leading the late king into debauchery.

Further trying to counter public fear and dismay and an

incipient disorder whose extent he had not foreseen, Richard commanded that Lord Stanley be released and sent home to the care of his wife. Archbishop Rotherham was to be allowed to cool his heels for a few days before also being released and permitted to rejoin the royal council. Bishop Morton, however, preserved by his holy vows – which Richard respected more than the bishop did himself – from the same fate as Hastings, was despatched as a prisoner to Buckingham's Welsh mountain stronghold of Brecon, where he could do no more mischief.

But there was one circumstance that was to have a more pronounced moderating effect than mayoral statements and official proclamations – the burgeoning rumour that a force consisting of twenty thousand of Richard's northerners was now approaching the capital. Its purpose was said to be defensive, but no one who had been alive in 1461 had forgotten Margaret of Anjou's northern army sweeping down on London like a baleful tide, preying on the innocent, laying waste to the land and stripping people of everything they possessed.

No one who remembered it could bear to envisage the same thing happening again. Northmen were, by definition, rough, wild and dangerous, a different breed from the civilised men of the south.

In truth, the northerners – no more than four thousand of them – were still sitting peaceably at Pontefract, waiting for orders, but rumour fled about the streets of London and was not to be denied.

Men put their arms away again, but the calm that ensued was the calm of secret hostility, not of acceptance.

13

RICHARD CONCEDED, 'Yes, I reacted more sharply than was, perhaps, wise. The worst betrayal is that of a friend. But delay could have been dangerous. Talks, discussions, arguments, proofs – and, all the while, bribery, blackmail and deceit, private deals being made . . . You should know by now what court circles are like, unscrupulous to their very roots. Hastings's plot would have blossomed in no time at all and, short of starting a war, I could have done nothing to prevent it.'

'You are sure,' Francis asked uneasily, 'that there *was* a plot?'

'As sure as I can be. Hastings was never able to keep his mouth shut and poured everything out to Catesby. He always deluded himself that Catesby's first loyalty was to him.'

It was clear that Richard was exhausted, but Francis was not prepared to drop the subject. 'Hastings was always a good friend to you. Why should he have become involved in such a plot?'

'Profit, why else? But executing him was the most painful thing I have ever done.'

The door of Richard's sanctum opened to admit Anne, as pale and drawn as her husband. 'Richard, you must come and have something to eat. Starving yourself will achieve nothing.'

His brows drawing together and his voice flat, he said, 'I do not think I have time to eat. Nor do I want anything.'

'Please. Even just some frumenty and a mouthful of wine?'

It was easier to consent than to continue to refuse, so he said, 'Very well.'

As they walked through the gaily painted doorway, Francis asked, 'What happens next?'

'I don't know. I can only try to regain control of the situation and play the game through to the bitter end.'

14

HASTINGS had died on Friday – Friday the thirteenth – and on the following Monday the slightly subdued remainder of the royal council met to discuss, yet again, the vexed question of the king's younger brother's continued residence in the sanctuary of Westminster Abbey. The coronation lay only six days ahead, and it would emphasise rather than minimise divisions if the closest member of the king's family were absent.

Whatever happened, the council felt it might be wise further to postpone the coronation, possibly until November, which would give the lord Protector time to set everything on a satisfactory administrative footing.

'We are agreed, then?' Bishop Russell drawled, contriving to convey that his own agreement, as a man of superior intellect, was a matter more of courtesy than conviction; that he might have reservations too subtle for lesser mortals to comprehend. It was one of his most irritating mannerisms, but so familiar to the council that they had ceased to heed it.

Buckingham said, 'The queen refuses to attend to any requests from the lord Protector. I suggest that Cardinal Bourchier speak to her on the council's behalf.'

Cardinal Bourchier, the archbishop of Canterbury, was seventy-nine years of age, which automatically conferred on him a trustworthiness that might have surprised some who had known him in his younger days, but made him the perfect choice for the task. He also happened to be the boy's great-uncle.

Bishop Russell, Lord Howard, Duke Richard and the duke of Buckingham accompanied him by barge to Westminster and waited at the palace while he vanished through the postern to the abbey. While they waited, Richard quietly dictated letters to his secretary, John Kendall; Bishop Russell went in to St Stephen's Chapel to pray; and Howard and Buckingham took wagers on the outcome of a bargees' race on the river. Their armed retinues stood around looking expressionless.

It was a beautiful day, but the council deputation was too hard-headed to read any symbolism into the way the sun was sparkling on the water when the archbishop reappeared, his arm benevolently round the ten-year-old duke of York's shoulders, and a small procession of servants bearing the boy's bed and hangings and clothing boxes trailing along behind.

Richard, standing in the doorway of the Painted Chamber, stopped dead in the middle of his dictation and went smilingly to embrace the boy.

'How happy we are to see you, my lord duke, and how happy the king your brother will be to have you as a playmate in the Tower.'

The little duke's responding smile was no more than dutiful, since it seemed not to have occurred to his uncle that the brothers were barely acquainted, the elder having spent most of his life at Ludlow in the care of Lord Rivers, while the younger was under his mother's tutelage at Westminster or Windsor or wherever the court happened to be. Nor did the word 'playmate' match with anything the duke of York knew of his brother, who was alarmingly scholarly and seemed unlikely to want to play at ball or with spinning tops. But at least it might be more amusing than being cooped up in the abbey.

'Her Grace perfectly understood the council's desire to reunite her sons,' said the archbishop, 'and I have promised her that the duke of York will be restored to her after the coronation, although by that time I hope she herself will have agreed to emerge from sanctuary.'

'Excellent, excellent!' Richard said. 'Now, let us be on our way.'

15

THE KING'S pleasure at seeing his younger brother was less immediately apparent than his anger at the sight of his uncle.

'Three days, I believe, have elapsed since I commanded you to attend me?'

Richard inclined his head, as did Buckingham beside him. The duke of York, standing in front of them with Richard's hands resting lightly on his shoulders, smiled nervously, any instinct to run towards his brother suffocated at birth.

Richard said, 'Will you not greet your brother of York, sire?'

The king, seated at a table in the Great Chamber with his tutor, held his eyes for a moment before waving his brother to come and sit beside him. Then, 'I am still waiting for an answer, my lord Protector.'

'I fear I have been much taken up with the affairs of the realm.'

'Including, I discover, the murder of my late father's closest friend and the chamberlain of his household, Lord Hastings.'

Richard opened his mouth to reply but was forestalled. 'Oh, no. Tell me no tales of his treachery!' the boy said pettishly. 'Or of his plotting against you and my lord Buckingham, or his intention to abduct me. I will not believe you.'

'*Will* not?'

'Will not.'

'In that case, I will spare my breath.'

Briefly, the boy was silenced, but only briefly. 'And I will not have you taking the law into your own hands and executing a loyal servant of the Crown out of hand, without even the pretence of a trial.'

Since Richard was still showing no inclination to speak, Buckingham volunteered, 'No trial was necessary. His guilt had been proven out of his own mouth.'

Edward ignored him. 'It is an act for which I will never forgive you, and you will pay for it when I cease to be king only in name and become your anointed sovereign.'

Buckingham intervened again, 'That will not be as soon as you think,' tacking on a belated and unconvincing, 'sire'.

This time Edward did deign to look at him. 'Your meaning?'

'The royal council – *your* council – has agreed that your coronation should be postponed until November.'

The shock was apparent, but the boy rallied quickly enough. In theory, even a twelve-year-old king could override his Protector, but only if he had powerful support within his council. Or support of a different kind outside it.

'No. My half-brother Dorset will persuade the council otherwise.'

Richard raised an eyebrow. 'How? By force?'

'I am entitled to have an army!'

'Certainly. But I take leave to doubt whether the marquess will have much success in raising an army from his refuge in sanctuary. Men tend to prefer leaders who come out in the open.'

The boy could not hide his triumph. Tossing down his quill, he said with juvenile contempt, 'So my lord Protector does not know everything, after all! As it happens, Dorset has escaped from sanctuary and is busy about my affairs. You will see. And if necessary we will fight to ensure that in future you, my lord Protector, will have no say in the governing of my realm.'

Almost absently, Richard asked, 'Have you ever witnessed a battle, sire?'

'No, of course not. I do not approve of fighting. But battles are sometimes necessary for the public good, and to cleanse the country of evil.'

'I used to think so, too.'

'And what has caused you to change your mind?'

Richard shrugged. 'As one becomes older and wiser and perhaps more humane, especially in a country where there has been peace for many years, battles begin to seem a wasteful means of resolving conflicts. So many innocent men killed or maimed just to settle a dispute originating amongst no more than a handful of people.'

The boy had been trained in logic as well as Latin. 'I believe I see the direction of your reasoning. You would argue that it is preferable simply to dispose of those around whom the dispute revolves. Such as Lord Hastings and my uncle, Lord Rivers?'

'Possibly.'

'But then it is necessary to assess which disputants are in the right and which in the wrong. So it becomes a matter of personal opinion.'

Richard shook his head. 'A matter of experience and judgement.'

Buckingham shifted impatiently. 'Sire . . .'

The king said, 'You are in a hurry? You have other men to murder? Then perhaps you had better leave us. Good day, my lords.'

16

MASTER Oliver King, secretary to the royal council, was no great admirer of Richard, duke of Gloucester, a man whose insistence on efficiency and the keeping of accurate records was, in Master King's easygoing view, entirely unwarrantable. He had, in the course of less than three weeks, succeeded in disrupting all Master King's customary arrangements.

And now, with the coronation postponed at less than a week's notice, the secretary's office was filling with men who had requested to be knighted on that occasion and were presenting themselves, as required, four days before the event. He had to delegate staff to explain the situation to them, staff who should have been more usefully engaged in sending out messengers to members of the Parliament which had been summoned for June 25th and was now also to be cancelled. Many of them would already have left home, and would be in a thoroughly bad temper – with Secretary King – when they discovered their journeys had been in vain.

Wistfully, he remembered how courteous and obliging the late king had been – 'Do it when it is convenient to yourself, Master Oliver.' Quite unlike the lord Protector.

17

THE LORD Protector said, 'Ratcliffe, before you set off for the north, arrange for someone to make a search for the marquess of Dorset, who appears to have escaped from sanctuary and may still be in London.'

'Yes, my lord. He's probably at Mistress Shore's house. He's always been sweet on her and she's so soft-hearted that she would probably take him in – now she hasn't got Hastings in her bed. I'll send young Howard.'

'Well, if she is, or has been, sheltering him, she is to be arrested.'

'Yes, my lord.'

Richard turned his attention to matters of greater portent. 'Now, you know what you have to say to Harry Percy? There are things I prefer not to put in writing. With the weather as it is, you should have a swift run to Northumberland. Oh, and I believe the Lady Anne may have a message for our son when she knows you are going to Middleham. What else? No, I think that's all.'

'Very well, my lord.'

Two hours later, trapping her husband by the undignified expedient of stationing herself close to the main door of Crosby

Hall and stepping out to block his path when he appeared, she demanded, 'Why is Sir Richard Ratcliffe going to Middleham?'

He was startled. He was also displeased, as if she had no right to question him. 'It is to do with Richard Grey.'

Her stomach turning over at the note of rejection, she persevered. 'To do with?'

'That is none of your concern. But I am having him transferred to Pontefract.'

'So Middleham will cease to be a prison? Well, that's a relief. And while you are here, perhaps you will tell me whether the king has indeed been reunited with his brother in the White Tower, as rumour has it?'

'Rumour, rumour! Yes, he has.'

'Thank you. When one is the wife of the lord Protector, one is expected to know these things.'

He almost smiled, which was an improvement, and then spoiled it by saying, 'But he will have to be moved from the White Tower. The Constable of the Tower tells me that ensuring his safety and wellbeing in the royal apartments for months, rather than just a few days, will be virtually impossible . . .'

'Months?'

'The coronation date has been postponed. He and his brother will be safer in one of the lesser towers.'

'Won't he take that as an affront to his dignity?'

They had reached the courtyard by now, and servants were running to help him mount, and his retinue was converging on him. 'Probably. And he will be offended at having his staff replaced, too, but I cannot – the country cannot – afford to have his views coloured by the gossip of the streets fed to him by ignorant country servants.'

'Poor boy.'

Austerely, Richard said, 'He is not a "boy", poor or otherwise.

He is the king. And he reads Latin and admires Caesar and believes himself entitled to be as omnipotent as Caesar ever was. Anne, my dear, I must go now. Forgive me.'

The 'my dear', mechanical though it was, restored her a little. If only he were open with her, she would have forgiven him most things. But she had the frightening feeling that Francis was right and that he was running out of control. Out of his *own* control, because no one else in his adult years, other than, occasionally, Edward, had ever tried or needed to exercise control over him.

18

ON THE DAY when the young king should have been crowned, the great bell of St Paul's cathedral rang out summoning London's citizens to St Paul's Cross, where, outside the cathedral walls in the angle between nave and transept, was a public space with a wooden pulpit erected in it from which meetings of the folkmoot were conducted and important proclamations made.

There was a large audience of ordinary citizens as well as lords spiritual and temporal, and the occasion was graced by the presence of the dukes of Gloucester and Buckingham, with their households in attendance, and their armed guard, which did not intrude on the space but, ranged around it with swords and pikes, seemed to enclose it.

It made the audience uneasy, but their unease was soon transformed as the lord mayor's brother, the Cambridge divine Dr Ralph Shaw, embarked on the most startling public sermon of his career.

'My text for today,' he began, 'will be "Bastard slips shall not take deep root".'

It sounded innocuous enough, so much so that Francis, in

attendance on Richard, found himself wondering why Richard was here at all and came to the conclusion that he must recognise the necessity of making himself known to a London which had seen little of him in recent years.

So, like many others, Francis shrugged and settled down in the comfortable expectation of a soporific theological discourse leavened with horticultural metaphor.

But it was not like that.

It very soon transpired that the 'bastard slips' in question were not the side shoots of carnations but the children of the late King Edward IV and his so-called queen, Dame Elizabeth Grey, née Woodville.

The normal small sounds – the rustlings and shufflings and coughings – of a large number of people on their Sunday-best behaviour were drowned by a huge, single indrawn breath.

Francis turned sharply towards Richard, and found him looking cool and enigmatic. Certainly not surprised or shocked. Oh God, Francis thought, let this not be what I fear it is.

'Proof there is,' declared Dr Shaw, 'that when the late King Edward without the knowledge or permission of his people clandestinely married Dame Elizabeth Grey, he was already betrothed to the Lady Eleanor Butler, the daughter of the earl of Shrewsbury, and was therefore in the eyes of the church already married. The children of his bigamous union with Dame Elizabeth, including the boy who is being hailed as the new king, are therefore "bastard slips".'

No, Francis thought. This is madness, Richard! Enough, enough.

But it was not enough for Dr Shaw. His voice rising over the excited babble of his congregation, he went on to besmirch the reputation of that most saintly of ladies, the Duchess Cicely of York, by resurrecting the tale that had been circulated years earlier by the earl of Warwick – that the magnificently golden Edward himself had been a bastard, having been born in France, and bearing no physical resemblance at all to his supposed father, the short, dark, wiry duke of York.

Duke Richard of Gloucester, however, was every inch the son of his father. He it was who should rule England.

The preacher ended on a high note, a note that invited cries of, 'King Richard! King Richard!' from his audience. But the cries did not materialise.

19

'TESTING the waters,' Richard said.

'You mean you *were* behind it?' Francis demanded.

'As a matter of fact, no. If I had been behind it, there would have been no slanders directed at my mother.'

'So – who?'

Richard scratched the tip of his ear thoughtfully. 'I am not entirely sure where the idea originated. In the city, perhaps. The merchants detest royal minorities, which are always unstable and bad for business. And Buckingham certainly had a hand in it for his own reasons – better to have a king beholden to him than a mere Protector, perhaps. Beyond that, I cannot guess. But I am not displeased. It is, after all, a sensible notion . . .'

'You don't think you might be prejudiced in that?' Francis heard his own voice, uncharacteristically sharp, and cursed himself, because this was not the way to make Richard stop and think, to bring him to his senses.

Richard merely smiled limpidly. 'Perhaps,' he said. 'But I would be less than honest if I underrated my own talents. Consider. I have experience, and a strong hand, and a talent for administration. The country could go straight into a new period of firm and effective government, whereas with that self-satisfied boy, who knows nothing of how the world functions, years of instability would lie ahead.'

'But . . .'

'But what? He is my brother's son? Yet more than once I have heard Edward himself say that the interests of even close family must sometimes, necessarily, be sacrificed for the good of the country. He said it about George. He also said it about the small sons of James III of Scotland, during the Albany affair. And young Eddie is also a son without true claim. I didn't know about the marriage pre-contract until the bishop of Bath and Wells came to me and confessed that he had acted as go-between in the troth-plighting with Shrewsbury's daughter. I was shocked but not altogether surprised. Much though I loved my brother, there is no denying that he was – how shall I put it? – addicted to women, and troth-plight is a tried and tested way of coaxing reluctant young women into bed.'

'None of us is perfect.'

Richard was in an odd mood. Secretive, satisfied, apprehensive, guilty – Francis couldn't tell which emotion predominated. But Richard did not snap his nose off, merely flashed a sardonic grin at him.

'I was wondering,' Francis went on slowly, 'why the bishop should have conjured up such a revelation at this particular moment?'

'He claimed that it had been on his conscience for years, but while Edward lived he had felt it advisable to remain silent.'

'Mmmm.'

'I thought,' Richard responded, suddenly irritable, 'that you had broken yourself of the habit of saying "Mmmm" in that exasperating way.'

261

Aware that he was risking a great deal, Francis asked, 'Do you really think you can get away with it? I don't, though that's only my own, untutored opinion. What happens next?'

Richard subjected him to a penetrating gaze, his closest and most transparent friend. 'Francis, you of all people do not need to be afraid of me.'

Then, after a vibrating moment, 'What happens next? More testing of the waters. The Members of Parliament whom Master King failed to stop before they left home will begin arriving in London tomorrow. Then we shall see.'

20

FOR ANNE, her wifely feelings at war with her maternal instincts, each hour seemed to become more nightmarish. Every time she thought of the young king immured in one of the towers, deprived of the attendants he had known all through his short life and with only strangers and his dependent younger brother for company, she found herself imagining Ned in the same situation. It was unbearable.

With some vague idea of comforting the boys, she rode with her ladies to the Tower and demanded admittance. But the Porter said he couldn't take the responsibility. 'I'll send word to the Constable, my lady.'

So, within the new red brick Bulwark, they waited, and waited, and waited, their horses tossing and blowing at the dangerous and unsavoury smells of wild animals from the royal menagerie on the wharf. There was a vicious screaming and snarling from the lions and leopards caged there, the sad trumpeting of an elephant, and visible in the moat was the long snout of an alligator.

Constantia was just saying, with a shudder, 'This is horrible,' when the Constable appeared on the drawbridge with a retinue of yeomen warders.

Although Anne recognised the man's face, she had completely forgotten his name, so, when she had responded to his bow with a graceful inclination of the head, she said merely, 'My lord, I wish to pay a visit to my nephews, the young king and the duke of York. Be so good as to conduct me to them.'

The Constable's eyes were cold. After a moment, he said, 'Much as it grieves me to refuse, my lady, I have the strictest orders from the lord Protector that, without written permission from him, visitors are not to be admitted.'

Without pausing to think, Anne exclaimed, 'But I am the lord Protector's wife!' and then felt more foolish than she had ever felt in her life before when the Constable nodded, 'Yes, my lady. I am aware of that.'

The hot colour flooded to her cheeks. Soon, no doubt, the whole court would be aware that the lord Protector's wife had not dared to ask her husband's permission to visit the princes.

Constantia saved her, saying with aplomb, 'I fear that her ladyship charged me with the task of asking the lord Protector for written permission, but it slipped my memory. My deepest apologies, madame.'

Anne succeeded in looking reproachful and then, taking her leave of the Constable, gathered her palfrey's reins and led her little group of expressionless ladies out through the Bulwark gate and back into the city.

Next day, they rode down to Westminster, Anne's purpose to discuss the situation with Elizabeth in her sanctuary. But there were guards over the gates. Constantia said, 'You don't want to meet with another such rebuff as yesterday. Let me go and ask?' Anne weakly agreed, and was not much surprised when

Constantia met with a refusal couched in even blunter terms than on the day before and for the same reason.

Richard was elusive, by day and by night. The second was worse. A solitary bed was nothing new to his wife; it had been solitary far more often than shared during the eleven years of their marriage, but she had become accustomed. And now, without rhyme or reason, she found herself lying awake listening to the suddenly urgent demands of her body and the desperate desire for Richard's arms around her. More than that – for another child. She knew that, in times of danger, it was natural for women to want to bear more children than in peacetime, to replace those who would be lost. But, dangerous though life had unexpectedly become, it was not that.

It was a need of the heart.

21

CROSBY HALL, always thronged with servants and secretaries and retainers, became fuller by the minute as the lords and commons arriving for the Parliament that had been cancelled were maliciously redirected by Master Oliver King – who had been dismissed, but was taking his time about going – to the Protector's residence.

His malice failed in its purpose, because the Protector was happy to see them. Abandoning his mourning black for royal purple velvet, he devoted himself, with the ardent assistance of the duke of Buckingham, to sounding visitors out and canvassing their support.

Richard himself was careful what he said, but Buckingham had no inhibitions. Two days after Dr Shaw's much-discussed sermon, he gave an address to the mayor and leading citizens at the Guildhall, one specifically adapted to their business interests, in which he not only repeated Dr Shaw's arguments in favour of Richard's right to rule, but enlarged on the abuses which had marred the government and the court during the years of Woodville ascendancy and could be expected to continue under a Woodville-guided boy king. 'Woe is that realm, that has a child as its king.'

Under the mature Richard's rule, by contrast, there would be no more unjustified taxation, no more legalised theft, no more abuses of government. Lechery was one of the greatest sins in the eyes of society. There would be no more of that, either.

Buckingham prided himself on his oratory, and indeed he was unusually impressive, though not in the grand manner. Seldom did he close his mouth completely between sentences, lest his hearers might think he had concluded, and his eyebrows shot up towards his jewelled velvet cap at calculated intervals, the same intervals at which he put stress on the particular points he wished to make. Arrogant though he was, he appeared as an honest man, who had not polished his periods too carefully and who spoke from the heart.

Since he was handsome as well as eloquent, he was accustomed to having his speeches met with enthusiastic applause, but on this occasion the applause was lacking.

He had, in fact, made a fundamental error which he failed to recognise – he had not appreciated how difficult it was to target the Woodvilles while leaving the late king free of stain. Having himself detested the king, he failed to see that this was a problem at all. But Edward had been a man liked by everyone despite his faults, and for an arrogant young sprig like Buckingham to denigrate him was not considered seemly.

He therefore met with a cool reception when he concluded in a rallying tone that, though the Protector was reluctant to assume the crown, he might be persuaded if the citizens of London would join with the peers of the realm in petitioning him to do so.

At the back of the hall, a few of his servants threw their caps in the air, shouting, 'King Richard, King Richard!' but their voices rang hollow in the great chamber.

Even so, when Buckingham declared that it was quite plain that his hearers wanted this noble, upright and devout prince for their king, there were no dissenting voices. It was not only that men were cowed by Richard's reputation; it was also that there was no party or single leader strong enough – or strong-minded enough – to contest his claim, and if anyone did so a return to civil war would be inevitable. Which Richard, widely known as a capable man and experienced warrior, would probably win. So where was the point in arguing?

22

ANNE SAID, 'Richard, you *cannot* mean to take the throne?'

'Why not, if peers and people require it of me?'

'You know perfectly well why not!'

Pleasantly, he said, 'You have the advantage of me.'

Torn between tears over what he proposed to do and exasperation at his manner, she wailed, 'Because it's *wrong*!'

'In what sense?' It was a question he frequently asked when confronted by what he considered as irrational arguments, and one which invariably threw his opponents into disarray. 'Perhaps we should define our terms.'

'Do we need to define the word, "wrong"? I mean *morally* wrong. Right and wrong are absolute terms, surely?'

He gave it a moment's thought. Then, 'Is it morally wrong to condemn the country to years of misgovernment under an arrogant boy and self-interested advisers? Or morally right to save the country by deposing the boy?'

She couldn't answer, because she didn't think they were the appropriate questions. She said, 'I don't know all your arguments, of course . . .'

'Really? I would have thought that Francis and Constantia would have kept you informed, even though I have been too busy.'

She bit her lip. '. . . but the arguments I have heard are irrelevant. It *cannot* be right for you to depose and imprison your brother's son, in order to take power for yourself.'

'You are, of course, entitled to your opinion, my dear. But now, if you will forgive me, I must go.'

'Very well, go!' She drew a deep, quivering breath. 'But, oh, Richard! Do think what you are doing before it is too late. You can still draw back.'

23

TWO DAYS AFTER Buckingham's address at the Guildhall, Richard rode from Crosby Hall to Baynard's Castle – from one corner of the city to the corner diagonally opposite – with a restless and vaguely hostile murmur rising from the people going about their business in the streets, and his wife's anguished plea of, 'You can still draw back!' echoing in his ears.

He remembered Edward, after George's execution, telling him it was a fundamental law of power that, 'Once committed, never retreat.' He had added, 'People forget very quickly.'

It resolved his own private doubts.

Draw back? And look like a fool or a coward? And open the way to years of negotiating and compromising to give the country the responsible government it needed? And lose most of the possessions on which his northern power depended? And always at personal risk from the Woodvilles and their adherents. Although if Ratcliffe had made good time to the north, he and Harry Percy ought by now to have tried and executed the most dangerous of them – Anthony Rivers, Richard Grey, Vaughan and Haute. Dorset, however, had succeeded in vanishing, with the aid of the wanton Mistress Shore, who was now locked up in Ludgate gaol. Richard couldn't make up his mind what to do about her.

Baynard's Castle was almost as old as the Tower, and like the Tower had been a fort in its early days but, since it had become the London home of the Yorkist royal family, Richard's mother, the Duchess Cicely, had done much to improve it – not throughout, since it was vast, but at least in parts. To Richard's relief, she was not at present in residence, so there would be no pious reprimands over the path he had chosen to take. Or not yet.

Buckingham, he knew, had on the previous day followed up his dissertation to the leading lights of the city by gathering together the lords spiritual and temporal who had come to London for the cancelled Parliament and drawing up a lengthy petition which they, and the mayor and aldermen, were to present to him today at Baynard's Castle. A petition begging him to assume the throne.

Uncomfortable though he was about the emphases in the petition, there was little radical that he had been able to do about them – short of completely redrafting them himself, which time and circumstances did not allow – and he was hardly in a position to amend them now. With a chuckle of dark humour, he imagined himself replying, 'Yes, I will take the throne, but only if your petition refrains from slandering my brother. Go away and rewrite it.'

So Buckingham had his way, and when Richard appeared at a window of the castle and enquired politely as to why all the lords and commons were assembled there, he had to listen to a harangue that exaggeratedly described his late brother as 'delighting in adulation and flattery, led by sensuality and concupiscence' and counselled by 'persons insolent, vicious and of inordinate avarice'. Hence the prosperity of the land had daily decreased, ruled by 'self-will and pleasure, fear and dread'. The laws of the church had been broken and justice set aside, with a consequent growth of 'murders, extortions and oppressions', so that 'no man was sure of his life, land nor livelihood, nor of his wife, daughter or servant, every good maiden and woman standing in dread to be ravished and befouled'.

Edward's bigamous marriage to Dame Elizabeth Grey had been brought about through the sorcery of the said Dame Elizabeth and her mother, and all the issue and children of the marriage were bastards and unable to inherit by the law and custom of England.

Because of this, the assembled lords and commons now acclaimed Richard as 'the very inheritor of the said crown and dignity royal, and as in right king of England', and begged him to ascend the throne in recognition of 'the great wit, prudence, justice, princely courage, and the memorable and laudable acts in divers battles which ye heretofore have done for the salvation and defence of the same realm, and also the great nobility and excellence of your birth and blood'.

Richard was not immune to flattery, even when he had edited the wording himself, so he allowed his expression to run the gamut of surprise, appreciation, reluctance, and finally consent. If this was what the lords and commons required of him, then he was at their disposal.

The assembly was too numerous to take the customary route by river from Baynard's Castle to Westminster, so they rode by Fleet Street and The Strand, past the wide stretch of gardens north of

Charing Cross which supplied the city's fruit and vegetables, and then on by King Street to the town and palace of Westminster. There, partitioned off in the corner of the Great Hall adjoining St Stephen's Chapel, were the Court of King's Bench and the marble throne which gave the court its name.

Courteously interrupting the business of the court, Richard seated himself on the marble bench while the petition was read aloud once more.

Then, calmly and clearly, he told his new audience of lawyers that this was the place at which he should assume the crown, because he believed it to be a ruler's chief duty to administer the law. Today would be the day on which he began to reign.

And so the victory was won.

Chapter Eleven

1483

1

RICHARD'S coronation date was set for July 6th and his queen spent most of the intervening ten days in tears.

Constantia said, 'But my sweet, you have no choice in the matter.'

'Yes, I have. I don't need to stay. I can go back home to Middleham and leave Richard to ruin his life in his own way.'

'Can you?'

'He doesn't even notice I'm here.'

'He would notice if you weren't.'

The silence seemed to last for ever.

More gently, Constantia said, 'It would be the worst of betrayals for him. *Can* you go?'

Anne's, 'No', was barely audible. Then, almost violently, 'If only I knew how his mind was working. If only I thought *he* knew! But he tells me nothing. He appears as he always does on the surface, but he has withdrawn right into himself.'

'Francis says the same. Did you know that Richard has asked him to be chamberlain of the household?'

'As poor Hastings was to Edward? *No,* he hasn't told me. How could he do it? That's horrible!'

Constantia stared at her. 'I'm not surprised he hasn't told you, if this is how you behave. What is the matter with you?'

'*Everything!*'

'Oh, is that all?'

Anne was surprised into a watery giggle. 'Dear Constantia. What a good friend you are.'

With difficulty, she went on, 'I suppose the real problem is that Richard thrives on trouble, and I don't. I spend my time worrying about what might go wrong, whereas Richard *knows* that if he follows his instincts and experience, everything will go right. My father was just the same, and look what happened to him!'

'Yes. But Richard's model isn't the earl of Warwick. It's Edward, who took what he wanted from life and got away with it. A man full of charm, but also a man full of sin. Avarice, pride, gluttony, lechery . . .'

'Well, Richard doesn't suffer from any of those,' said his wife almost disconsolately. 'Except pride, I suppose. But I'm never sure whether irredeemable stubbornness and singlemindedness don't count as sins in the Lord's sight, as they do in mine. I asked him, when Edward died, could he not just sit back and let things take their course? Did he have to force the pace? Did he always have to win?'

'And what did he say?'

'You can guess perfectly well what he said. He said, "No, yes, and yes".'

'It's the way he's made. Francis hopes that, in his own new rôle of chamberlain, he might be able to influence Richard towards being less headstrong, but I doubt it myself. He says Richard has been listening too much to Buckingham and Catesby and Ratcliffe.'

'Listening to them, perhaps,' Anne rejoined gloomily, 'but probably not heeding what they say. His own judgement is all that matters to him, and that judgement has, I think, been distorted since Edward died. You cannot believe how upset he was, and I'm not convinced that he has recovered the balance of his mind even yet.'

Constantia thought, but did not say, that Richard's distress over Edward's death was not preventing him from blackening his brother's name by association with the Woodvilles, in order to prove that he himself would be a more virtuous and upright king and that the country would benefit accordingly. It was, she supposed, a question of priorities. Richard had landed himself, voluntarily or involuntarily, in a situation where he could not afford to be other than hard. Weakness would be the death of him.

So she said, 'Let us look at these cloths-of-gold and see which will be the most becoming for you at your coronation.'

She knew, as Anne did not, that the ermines, velvets and cloths-of-gold strewn across Anne's bed had originally been ordered by the Master of the Wardrobe for the enthronement of young Edward, not of Richard.

What would happen to the princes now? Francis said they could not be permitted to go free; certainly not until Richard was firmly and incontestably established on the throne.

Poor lads, unhappy pawns of their royal destiny.

2

AT THE beginning of July the northern army, the threat of which had paralysed the minds of so many Londoners for weeks, finally arrived — four thousand men rather than the rumoured twenty thousand, and all of them bedraggled from their march, their arms and armour battered and rusty in the eyes of observers who were more accustomed to seeing their warriors beautifully scrubbed and polished for ceremonial processions through the streets.

King Richard, however, held a review of them at Moor Fields, just outside the city wall, and was resoundingly cheered, which, as Francis Lovell said afterwards, made a pleasant change.

Margaret Beaufort, watching the review with her husband, his injury from the Hastings fracas now healed, murmured, 'Might you and the lords have chosen to resist Richard if you had known this was all he could call on for support?'

Stanley twitched slightly and glanced round to be sure they were not overheard. 'They may not look much, but don't be deceived. In any case, by the time we knew we might have to resist him, it was too late. He's taken the initiative right from the start – waylaying young Edward, arresting Rivers, executing Hastings, claiming the throne – and we foresaw none of it.'

'Why not?'

Stanley, always sensitive to criticism, was tempted to snap, 'Because we are not as clever as you are,' but restrained himself. After a moment's reflection, he said, 'The essential difficulty, I suppose, is that the royal council is an administrative body whose main business is civil affairs, and its mind works accordingly. But Richard has approached the last two months as if he were on a military campaign, and has carried everything through with an efficiency I can only admire. He has won the throne at a cost of only five lives.'

Margaret knew her husband well. Richard had not only demonstrated a talent for success, but had confirmed Stanley as steward of the household and implied other favours to come. 'So you will give him your support?'

'Yes. For the time being.'

His next words were almost lost in a blaring of trumpets, but

Margaret thought he said, 'Anyway, it's safer.'

She had already decided, on her own account, to establish good relations with Richard in the hope that he would endorse the agreement she had reached with Edward in the previous year, permitting her son Henry to return to England from his long exile.

She also hoped he might agree to a marriage between Henry and Edward's eldest daughter, Elizabeth, but knew he would be suspicious of the idea. And rightly so. Because *if* anything should happen to seventeen-year-old Princess Elizabeth's brothers — which was highly probable, since no king could tolerate the continued existence of rivals for his throne — the princess would become their legitimate successor; Margaret, like many others, dismissed as pure invention the bastardy story that was being spread about. And *if* Yorkist Princess Elizabeth were married to Henry Tudor, with his Lancastrian claim, then Richard's own position could become — with a little assistance from interested parties — highly insecure. All the residual Lancastrian loyalty to Henry VI, as well as the Yorkists' personal loyalty to Edward IV and his children, could be marshalled against him, and Margaret's years of intriguing on her son's behalf might at last bear fruit.

She had already instructed her receiver-general, the invaluable Reginald Bray, quietly to sound out her tenants and other gentlemen in the Midlands and south.

Margaret had no sense of irony, otherwise she might have smiled when the command came for her to carry Queen Anne's train in the coronation procession.

3

IT TOOK an immense effort of will for Anne to go and visit Richard's mother but, leaving Crosby Hall soon after dawn, she covered the seven leagues to Berkhamsted in something under five hours, arriving as she intended at eleven o'clock, which was dinnertime. It meant that she did not immediately have to embark on conversation, because it was the Duchess Cicely's habit to have the work of her favourite mystics, such as St Matilda, St Catherine of Siena, and St Bridget of Sweden, read aloud and discussed over meals. Today, it was the visions of St Matilda.

By the time the meal was over, Anne, whose religion was more practical than mystical, found her brain in a daze, but the duchess had a shrewd idea of why she had come and was kindly enough to give her an opening.

It did not mean that she was not angry.

To her women she said, 'You may leave us,' and then, 'I have heard about Dr Shaw's sermon. Slanders can always be relied on to wing their way across the miles at extraordinary speed. It was not, I hope, Richard who authorised the resurrection of that evil gossip to the effect that Edward and George were not their father's sons?'

'No! Oh, no! That is why I came. I have no idea how the gossip arose in the first place, but Dr Shaw is completely in disgrace with Richard. He has forbidden that it should ever be mentioned again.'

Coolly, the duchess said, 'I know how it arose, and it was my own foolish temper that was at fault. I was not always as calm as you see me now. When Edward married that appalling wife of his – in secrecy, in privacy, without even the banns being read – I said in the hearing of others, "He is no son of mine!" It was taken up, of course, by Edward's enemies, including your own father, the earl of Warwick.'

Anne was puzzled. 'But it makes no sense. You may have said he was not *your* son but you didn't say he was not his *father's* son, so it's all nonsense, isn't it? By any standards.'

The duchess nodded. 'The only remotely logical version would have been that I had been unfaithful to my husband — which I never would have been — and my husband had agreed to bring up my illegitimate children as his own — which he never would have done.'

'It sounds very farfetched! In any case, I can assure you that it will not be repeated if Richard has anything to do with it. That is what I came to tell you.'

The duchess smiled at her. 'It was thoughtful of you, my dear. But you look pale. Are you quite well?'

'Tired. These last few weeks have been difficult.'

'I can imagine that. I am not sure that Richard is behaving as virtuously as I would have expected of him.'

'O⌃h⌃h⌃h!' It came out as a wail. How could she defend Richard when she herself was convinced that he was doing wrong? 'You mean the throne?'

'Partly. I can understand his motives, and I trust he will not harm the boys, but I am concerned that he should be permitting, even encouraging, the blackening of Edward's good name. He was always devoted to Edward when he was alive. And now it appears there is nothing good to be said of him.'

Anne could not explain that Richard's spiritual beliefs strongly resembled his mother's, that he believed — as many people did — that the deadly sins of worldliness of which Edward had undoubtedly been guilty were not, in a prince, a private matter between the sinner and God, but of wider importance, setting an evil example and, perhaps, prompting God to punish all of that prince's subjects. Anne could not believe that God could be so unjust, but few people did not fear His wrath. There were examples enough in the Bible of His destroying whole peoples.

She said, 'He is still devoted to Edward's memory, and still mourns him deeply. But he is determined that the Woodvilles will not take power for themselves, and therefore blames them publicly for leading Edward into depravity. You know how people fear and detest moral laxity. The trouble is that . . .'

'Some mud sticks? Well, I have lived long enough to know how the world's tongue wags. Does Richard know you have come to see me?'

She was a very astute lady. Anne shook her head.

'Then I will not ask you to give him my love and duty.' She smiled with youthful mischief. 'Now it is time for my nap. Fifteen minutes precisely, and then prayers until Evensong. Stay if you wish.'

'Thank you, no. There is no moon, so I need to be back in London before dark.'

'What an exhausting day for you! Take care of yourself, my dear. And of Richard.'

4

BY TRADITION, kings of England set out for their coronation from the Tower of London, so on July 4th Richard and Anne proceeded there by river in the state barge, brightly painted and propelled by gilded oars, to spend the night in the royal apartments. Anne couldn't sleep for the thought of young Eddie and the little duke of York locked up only a few yards away in one of the towers.

Next day came the ceremonial procession to the Palace of Westminster. Much of the English peerage took part in it – three dukes, nine earls, twenty-three barons and almost eighty knights – and very magnificent they looked, the duke of Buckingham being particularly eye-catching in a robe of blue velvet embroidered with golden cartwheels.

But Richard outshone them all. As he had earlier remarked to Francis, one of the things he had learned from Edward was that the money spent on personal splendour was a necessary investment in the business of kingship. In his doublet of blue cloth-of-gold under a purple velvet gown trimmed with ermine, and mounted on a white horse intricately trapped in gold and plumed in purple and white, he was the epitome of royal magnificence as he bowed and smiled to right and left along the way.

A nervous Anne, borne behind him in a horse litter supported by two beautiful white coursers and escorted by five mounted ladies-in-waiting, including Constantia, was so relieved by the cheers of the Londoners lining the route that she forgot their willingness to cheer almost any colourful happening that broke up the monotony of their days. All that mattered was that Richard was not greeted by an inimical silence or shouts of reproach or vilification.

Reaching Westminster, Richard divested himself of his ermine and velvet and went back to work with his chief justice, William Hussey, while Anne stood patiently in her chamber, submitting to the final pinnings and tuckings of the gowns she was to wear next day.

5

RICHARD HAD decreed that this was to be the most magnificent coronation that had ever been seen, and did no more than look innocently enquiring when Francis pointed out that the competition was not great.

'Ever been *seen*?' Francis exclaimed. 'Edward's coronation was twenty-two years ago, and some people will remember it. But it's fifty-four years since Henry VI was crowned, and very few men alive today will remember *that*!' Then, observing the telltale quirk appearing at the corner of Richard's mouth, 'Oh, yes, I know! If you say something loudly enough and often enough, people will believe you. Very well, then, this *is* going to be the most magnificent coronation that has ever been seen. Which being so, I will go and make sure that those thirteen thousand white boar devices of yours are properly displayed around Westminster.' As he marched irritably out of the chamber, he heard Richard laugh and call, 'Thank you, Francis.'

Next day, preceded by heralds and trumpeters and escorted by the prelates and clergy who had come to meet them from the abbey, Richard and Anne emerged from the palace to walk barefoot over a cloth laid on a thick carpet of sand and rushes that had considerately been laid for them.

'Mortifying the flesh is all very well in its place,' Richard had told Buckingham, who had put himself in charge of the event, 'but it will hardly add to the dignity of the occasion if the royal participants look as if they are walking on eggshells – or grit, or pebbles, or broken glass, or any of the other litter which no amount of sweeping up can ever entirely sweep away.'

'There is a precedent,' Buckingham had replied grandly. 'A carpet was laid for the coronation of Henry Bolingbroke in ninety-nine.'

'Excellent!' Richard's response was so extravagantly cordial that Francis found himself swallowing a grin. 'Then we have no problem, have we?'

Beside Richard, in his blue cloth-of-gold doublet with its pattern of nets and pineapples and his purple velvet over-gown with its ermine trim and three thousand tufts of lamb fur, stalked Francis and the earl of Kent bearing the Swords of Justice, and behind were Buckingham, carrying Richard's train, followed by the bishops, then Harry Percy bearing the Sword of Mercy, Stanley with the Constable of England's mace, the duke of Suffolk with the sceptre and his son with the orb. Jocky Howard, newly created duke of Norfolk, had the honour of carrying the crown. Fortunately, he and Buckingham had enough sense to hide the fact that they were not on speaking terms, Buckingham having insisted on acting not only as organiser but as master of ceremonies, when it was Norfolk who had been officially appointed steward for the great occasion.

After the king's procession came the queen's, her regalia borne by two earls and a viscount, and her ridiculously long train carried by four of her ladies, with Margaret Beaufort in charge, small but splendid in crimson velvet trimmed with white cloth-of-gold. Anne's own gown was white, under a white mantle trimmed with ermine, and her hair flowed virginally loose almost to her waist, as was traditionally required of queens at their coronation. It was wonderfully comfortable, for a change, not to have it pinned up and hidden under a headdress. Making a valiant snatch after her vanishing sense of humour, she had said to Constantia, 'Perhaps I should be crowned more often.'

But it was different when she found herself at the high altar inside the cold stone abbey, her bodice removed so that, like Richard, she was stripped to the waist for the sacramental anointing with the oil and balsam of the chrism. Her hands crossed modestly over her breasts, she cast a swift glance at Richard and saw that he was spiritually warmed and uplifted by the ceremony, while she herself shivered both mentally and physically. How had all this come about, and what would be the end of it? It *could* not be right.

Afterwards, they retired briefly to change into purple cloth-of-gold lined with white damask before having the crowns set upon their heads by a sour-faced Cardinal Bourchier – who did not approve of Richard's usurpation – and hearing High Mass and taking communion. Then, after another brief respite, it was time to return, under their canopy of state, to the Great Hall of the palace for the banquet.

Anne had no idea how many guests there were, but there appeared to be thousands, and all of them talking at the pitch of their voices. The noise, and the heat generated by so many people and by the sun beating in through the high windows, swept up to the royal daïs in waves, so that she found it increasingly difficult to smile regally at the peers and city dignitaries who honoured the royal couple by acting as table attendants, arriving in succession to offer dish after dish, from crab and trout to roast swan and peacocks in all their plumage.

As one course followed another, the tables were successively adorned with marvellously wrought subtleties sculpted out of fruit pastes or marzipan and decked with real gold or silver leaf – among them St George slaying the dragon, King Richard slaying a Scot, a Chessboard of Life and Death whose symbolism was perhaps a little too pointed, and a romantic representation of Middleham with a pretty little sugar lady, complete with crown, leaning out of a window.

There were musicians and mummers and acrobats to entertain the company between courses, and then everyone backed away hurriedly as Buckingham escorted into the hall a horseman in white armour mounted on a huge charger caparisoned in white and scarlet. It was Sir Robert Dymmock, whose family had the traditional honour of acting as King's Champion at coronation ceremonies. That the present Sir Robert's father had ultimately annoyed Edward IV into executing him was something that all concerned chivalrously agreed to ignore as Sir Robert dramatically threw down his white steel gauntlet in challenge to anyone who might dispute Richard's right to the throne. Fortunately, no one did. Indeed, most of the guests rose nobly to the occasion, crying, 'King Richard! God save King Richard!' as the champion drank the king's health from a silver-gilt bowl which he then carried away with him as a gift.

Anne, watching in a daze of weariness, suddenly realised that the mayor was kneeling beside her, offering yet more spiced wine. Smilingly, she accepted because to decline would have been ungracious, but nothing in the world would have persuaded her to drink it. Was the banquet never going to end? Above the din, she could just hear the bells for Compline, which meant that it had already been going on for five hours.

At last, huge torches were brought in against the growing dark and the guests began to make their way to the daïs to pay homage to the king and queen and take their leave. But it was almost midnight before Richard and Anne and their attendants were themselves free to go.

6

IT WAS the most exhausting day Anne had ever spent and she collapsed into her vast, soft, curtained bed with a sense of infinite gratitude and barely enough energy to turn over on her side. She had thought she might be too tired to sleep, but was already hovering on the blessed, dizzy threshold when she became aware of a new presence and a voice instructing her attendants to remove themselves from the room.

Richard.

Tonight, of all nights, after the weeks of waiting for him to come to her.

He was bursting with vigour and self-congratulation and desire. She should have known.

Full of cheer, he urged her, 'Wake up, my dear. Wake up! This is the greatest day of my life, and of yours. It's time to celebrate.'

She knew that some men were quick, too quick, in their love-making, but Richard had never been like that. He had always wanted to savour it, to discover how long he could spin out his own pleasure and, she supposed, hers. But tonight everything was wrong. She could have accepted a swift penetration and swift collapse, but Richard would not and could not. Instead, he talked and teased and massaged her until she thought she would scream.

She tried, God knew how she tried, but it was too much. She felt no response inside her, no warmth, no speeding of her heart, no springing of her breasts, no melting of the muscles at the base of her spine. Nothing.

Even as she forced herself to kiss and caress and stroke him in return, inside her head she was begging, 'Leave me alone, leave me alone!' It had nothing to do with loving or not loving, but he wouldn't understand that. And in the maze of her mind, she knew that he needed, really *needed*, to know that he was loved.

She could not bear to disappoint him. But she did.

After half an hour, he made to leave her and she murmured, 'No, stay. It's just that I am so tired. Let me sleep a little and then it will be all right.'

But he did not stay, and it was not all right.

7

SHE COULD have made it up to him on the following night, but he did not come to her. Indeed, even by day she did not see him for a week. He was busy, Francis said, constructing his new council

284

and household, which was a delicate balancing act because he did not want to lose the men who had served Edward so well – except the wilfully awkward ones like Secretary Oliver King, and Sir John Cheyney, Edward's Master of the Horse – but still wanted to reward men who had been loyal to him personally.

In the end, she sent him a message by Catesby saying that, as Richard knew, she was always concerned about the welfare of little Ned when she had to be away from Middleham for long. She was a little concerned by the last message she had received from Nurse Idley saying that Ned had caught some minor ailment from the children in the village. Might she therefore have permission to leave London for the north?

Never before, in their life together, had it been necessary for her to ask Richard's formal permission for anything.

And now she received a formal reply. Yes, she might visit Middleham, but the king was soon to set out on a royal progress through the Midlands and the West country, so that his subjects might become acquainted with him, and he with them. He would expect the queen to join him on his progress as soon as convenient. At least he had the grace to add that he trusted she would find their son in good health.

Constantia, concerned about her, said, 'Shall I come with you?' Anne had never been strong, but a contented mind had always kept her in health. Now she was worried and depressed and troubled about Richard, and it was having an effect. She needed comfort and support.

Anne hesitated. 'I don't know what I would have done without you during these last weeks. You have been so good and kind and understanding. But I have been asking too much of you. I would love you to come with me, but I have taken you away from your life with Francis, and you are entitled to have *some* time together . . .'

Constantia smiled ruefully. 'If I had been at Minster Lovell, I would not have had much time with him recently.'

Somehow, Anne achieved a small ripple of laughter. 'Well, now is your opportunity. For a while, at least, we can abandon the pretence of your being my lady-in-waiting and behave normally, as the friends we are. Oh, how I *wish* you could be accepted as Francis's wife and take up your proper position as Lady Lovell!'

'Don't concern yourself,' Constantia said, as she always did when the subject arose. 'Francis and I love each other, and that is all that matters.'

'Yes,' Anne said. 'It is, isn't it?'

8

SOON AFTER the coronation and in preparation for his departure on progress, Richard occupied himself with tidying up some outstanding details.

Mistress Shore was one of them.

It had been impossible to prove that she had been guilty of sorcery or that she had collaborated with Hastings in the plot against Richard, so those charges had to be dropped. But her loose living was notorious – with Edward, and Hastings, and Dorset – and to punish her publicly would be to emphasise that there was no place for whores and their like in the new reign.

It was not a matter for civil law but for the church, and the bishop of London therefore imposed a penance on her, that on the forthcoming Sunday she should walk barefoot and clad only in her undergown through the streets of the city, bearing a lighted taper. She was a very pretty woman, and even prettier when she blushed, as she did under the eyes of the populace.

Afterwards, she was released from prison.

Afterwards, too, Richard visited Lady Hastings and swore to her on oath that Hastings's possessions would not, as she must have expected, be attainted, that neither her son nor Hastings's brothers would suffer from his fall, that all she had lost from her husband's death was his person and the occasional pleasure of his company.

She took it as an admission, although it was not so intended, that Richard had executed her husband unjustly, and accorded him her most grateful thanks.

9

WITH A magnificent entourage including five bishops, Lord Stanley, Lord Lovell, and many others of the principal officers of the kingdom, Richard set out from Windsor for his royal progress on July 20th. All too aware of the rumours buzzing about the countryside, he was anxious to show that he ruled not by force but by consent, and therefore dispensed with the armed escort that would normally have been expected of him. Much of the preceding two weeks had been spent by his secretary on organising pageants and ceremonial entries designed to delight and impress the inhabitants of every centre along the route of the progress.

Many of the nobles and most of the gentry in the southern half of England knew Richard only by repute and by gossip. Now, he needed their support and set about attracting their loyalty by showing himself sympathetic to their needs. At Oxford, he attended and apparently enjoyed two scholarly debates on theology and moral philosophy. At Woodstock, he gave back to the inhabitants some lands which Edward had annexed to the royal forest of Wychwood. At Gloucester, he proposed granting a new charter of liberties. To the abbot of Tewkesbury, he was intending to pay the remainder of the sum George had left outstanding when he had ordered his tomb.

But before he reached Gloucester, he had news of a plot which had erupted in London within days of his departure.

10

REGINALD BRAY, Margaret Beaufort's receiver-general, was well equipped to sound out the landholders and tenants known as the lesser gentry, men who might be knights by rank but in most cases were rarely seen at court, preferring to remain big fish in their own small countryside ponds. Since Margaret Beaufort was one of the great landowners, Bray not only collected rents from her tenants but gave them friendly advice on how to improve the value of their holdings. Few of them foresaw that this would lead, in due course, to their being required to pay higher rents.

Margaret was a martinet where estate management was concerned, and did not hesitate to reprimand her tenants personally if, as she rode about the land, she saw unsymmetrically harrowed fields or raggedly shorn sheep or badly stooked corn. As a result, and despite her charming manner, they were terrified of her and Reginald Bray had little difficulty in confirming that, in politics as in farming, their instinct was to do as she bade them.

He was therefore able to report back to her that, almost to a man, they thought it shocking that the new king – who, as Bray had taken care to remind them, would do anything for power – should have usurped the throne and imprisoned the real little king. Something should be done about it.

'Yes,' Margaret said, her mouth turning down thoughtfully. She was a bony little person and the slanting sun caught her triangular face in such a way as to make it skull-like under the white linen 'barbe' headdress that framed it. She spent a scandalous amount of money on clothes but, well aware that a sumptuously dressed and ornamented woman subverted God's will by valuing appearances above her precious inner spirit, was successful in convincing herself that the unflattering linen barbe amply compensated for her extravagance in the matter of silks, velvets and furs.

It made her seem almost human.

'Yes,' she said again in her light, sweet voice. 'Something should certainly be done, but who is to do it? And what do we mean by "something"?'

Bray had been considering the matter. It would be convenient for his mistress and especially for her son Henry Tudor, earl of Richmond, if the real little king and his brother were to be eliminated from the succession. Then it would become a simple matter of Richard versus Henry. But it was vital that neither Lady Margaret nor her son should be publicly perceived as being guiltily involved in any of the preliminary manoeuvres.

Carefully, he said, 'I believe the best method would be to precipitate events that will then take their own course.'

'A favourable course?'

'Naturally.'

'Snowballing.'

'Yes.'

'And how do we set the snowball in motion?'

'The simplest way would be to stage an attempt to rescue the little princes from the Tower.'

Her thin, arched brows shot up over the hooded eyes. 'Elucidate, please.'

He could not, of course, say all that he was thinking, but he did not need to. If the princes were rescued, it could bring about the end of Richard's tenure of the throne, so the Lady Margaret and her son would be no worse off than before. If, on the other hand, the enterprise failed, the attempt itself would be enough to force Richard to take steps to ensure that there was no recurrence. The natural thing for him to do would be to have them quietly killed; no usurper could tolerate the continued existence of other aspirants to his crown. And if Richard didn't do it, then for Henry's sake someone else would have to.

He said, 'If the rescue were to succeed, I have no doubt that Richard could very soon be overthrown. If it were to fail, at the very least it would provoke Richard into a reaction which might in itself suffice to raise the country against him.'

She was a clever woman, and it was instructive that she did not ask what kind of reaction he had in mind. She said only, 'I could not condone a war.'

What did she expect Richard to do? Abdicate? Saintly women could be very irksome to deal with. 'Indeed not,' he responded soothingly.

She caressed her arthritic knuckles frowningly. 'A rescue attempt would be acceptable. I will fund it, but my name must not appear. Whom will you approach?'

'I had thought of John Cheyney. As former Master of the Horse, he should be acquainted with strong-armed men in plenty. He is also devoted to the Woodville interest and to the young princes.'

'I know him. The tallest man I have ever seen. And somewhat naive, perhaps?'

'Yes.'

11

ONE OF Cheyney's strong-armed men was a minor groom of the wardrobe in the Tower itself, which should have made access easy.

But sneaking around the precincts was not, he maintained, the way to go about things.

The rescuers' final plan, therefore, was to set fire to a number of buildings in the city close by the Tower – fire being a guaranteed distraction in a city built largely of wood – and then, with the air full of smoke and fire bells, and every able-bodied man occupied with buckets of water, to storm the citadel in force.

It was a mistake. With so much rushing around going on, a solid body of fifty bucket-less men heading for the Tower merely drew attention to itself. In no time at all, the rescuers found themselves collared and clapped in gaol, charged with arson as well as treasonable intent.

Richard, spending a few pleasant days at the graceful manor house of Minster Lovell as the guest of Francis and Constantia, was promptly notified and equally promptly instructed that the ringleaders be put on trial.

He said, 'I am mystified. We have a wardrober, a groom of the stirrup, a serjeant of London and a pardoner of Hounslow. Ordinary men. *Very* ordinary men. I think we have mislaid the leader somewhere.'

'Not a very intelligent leader, by the sound of things,' Francis said.

'No. There must have been someone else behind them. I wonder who? I have written to Chancellor Russell to take matters in hand. I have also written to John Nesfield with instructions to strengthen the guard around the sanctuary at Westminster. There is another rumour, of a plot to "rescue" the princesses and spirit them abroad.'

Constantia said, 'Do they need rescuing? If Elizabeth simply agreed to resign herself to the status quo and emerge from sanctuary, she could be honoured as queen dowager and there would be no necessity for such dramas. What a tiresome woman she is!'

Richard turned his head to smile at her. His peripheral vision had never been good, and people tended to interpret his frequent head-turning as a sign of edginess or unease, which irritated him. However, there was nothing he could do about that. He said, 'If only others had as much sense as Constantia. I could force Elizabeth and the girls out of sanctuary easily enough. It would only take a few men-at-arms, but think what a fuss she would raise.'

Francis said, 'Edward violated sanctuary often enough. I can think of quite a few villains he ordered dragged out to their deaths.'

'True. But I am not thinking of dragging Elizabeth and her five pretty daughters out to their deaths, although Elizabeth behaves as if I am. I have no ambition to be a mass murderer.'

Francis said, 'If the attempt to rescue the princes had succeeded, what do you suppose the plotters intended to do with them? March Eddie into a meeting of the council and demand that the council vote between you and him?'

Richard grinned back at him. 'Oh, very comical! I would guess the intention was to hide the boys somewhere while they scraped an army together from those who feel I should not have denied the boy the throne.'

There was a question that still needed to be asked.

The trees were in full leaf, not yet tired of their summer colours, and the grass was wonderfully green. There was a soothing rustle of water from the river. High in the clear blue sky, small chubby white clouds were frivolling about aimlessly, with no wind to direct them. The city of tents that always accompanied a royal progress was out of sight and out of hearing.

Francis said, 'What will you do about the boys?'

'What *can* I do? The obvious answer is to keep them under closer watch in the Tower, or alternatively send them up to Sheriff

Hutton, well out of the way of any more rescue attempts.'

Constantia said, 'Could you not set them up in a manor of their own, where they would at least have some freedom?'

Richard's eyes were on the clouds. 'Anything is possible, but not yet. When things have settled down, perhaps. When Elizabeth and the Woodvilles acknowledge defeat. When it is safe to do so.'

But he and Constantia and Francis knew that it would never be safe.

12

THE PROGRESS continued on its spectacular way towards York, with minor hints of trouble following it. A certain John Welles was discovered to be organising a conspiracy at the manor of Maxey in Northamptonshire; John Welles happened to be Margaret Beaufort's half brother, and Richard did not fail to note the fact. There were others in London who were behaving suspiciously and obviously needed watching, among them Peter Curtis, Keeper of the Great Wardrobe, and Robert Morton, Master of the Rolls, who also happened to be the nephew of Bishop Morton, now languishing in prison at Buckingham's castle of Brecon. The queen dowager's brother, Bishop Woodville, also appeared to be indulging in activities more secular than sacred.

Richard had expected small conspiracies to break out as soon as his back was turned, and the identity of the conspirators came as no surprise. However, when Buckingham, who had briefly honoured the progress with his company, left it at Gloucester, Richard instructed him, as soon as he returned to London from Brecon, where he was bound, to head commissions into treason in the Home Counties and in London itself.

Buckingham said loftily, 'As you command, sire.'

As he rode away, Francis remarked, 'Well, that's a relief. Even two or three days of his company constitutes a surfeit. The squires, in case you are not aware of it, refer to him as His High and Mightiness.'

Richard said thoughtfully, 'He has felt very important for the last three months, arranging and directing and commanding, being seen to be the most important man in the realm.'

'After the king!'

'Yes. I gave him his head in London because it was convenient to do so, but now he is feeling left out. He is all too aware of coming second, when he believes he should be first. He has his own claim to the throne.'

Francis was dismissive. 'But a very distant one.'

'Indeed. It would only carry conviction if I and my son and all Edward's brood and my brother George's son and that damned boy of Margaret Beaufort's were removed from the scene. Even allowing for the bastardy of Edward's children . . .'

'Of which you are not wholly convinced.'

Richard ignored it. 'And allowing also for the fact that George was declared forfeit, which invalidates *his* son's claim unless an Act were to be passed reversing the forfeiture, there are still several obstacles in the way of Buckingham's ambitions.'

'Well, I hope he encounters a good solid one on his way to Brecon and trips over it.'

Richard's lean, increasingly gaunt features crumpled and he gave a shout of laughter that sent Francis's spirits soaring. It seemed a very long time since he had heard Richard laugh in such an open and uninhibited way.

Richard gasped, 'I wish you would speak your mind more often. You have been tiptoeing around like some damnable puss-cat for far too long. I was beginning to think I had lost you.'

'Were you? Have I? Well, you haven't been exactly encouraging, yourself.'

'I suppose not. But I don't know what I would have done without Anne and you and Constantia . . .'

Riskily, Francis said, 'It hasn't been easy for us, you know. Especially Anne. You give us no hint of how you are thinking.'

'You would like me to rule by private committee, would you?'

'No, but . . .'

'If I had consulted the three of you, lily-livered as you are, where would we be now? I would certainly be dead at the Woodvilles' hands, and you, too, probably. And our estates would be forfeit and our wives homeless and penniless. Whereas by playing the political game according to the rules of this rough century of ours, I have brought everything to a satisfactory conclusion.' He paused. 'Go on, say it! How long will it remain satisfactory? Is it, in fact, a conclusion? The answer is that I don't know. But we'll find out.'

Chapter Twelve

1483

1

THERE WAS no moon and, with a cool night following a hot and sticky day, a faint mist was wafting from the Thames into the precincts of the Tower of London.

It suited the two men creeping noiselessly along the roofs of the royal apartments towards the Wakefield Tower, clinging to the river face of the pitched roofs and slithering barefoot over the flat. The tide lapped gently against the shore. When they heard the occasional splash of oars, they froze. But at two in the morning, no bargee was likely to be studying the skyline of the curtain wall against which the royal halls and chambers were built.

They were taking the long route to their objective, because the more direct one would have been dangerously exposed. By day, the Tower environs were clamorous with armed guards, with priests and moneyers, craftsmen, builders and labourers, but even by night the garrison remained alert. Or supposedly so. The new Constable was a northerner, who had only taken up his post a couple of weeks earlier, and the members of the garrison were still in the process of establishing what they could get away with. The two men knew all about that, because they were part of it.

When they drew level with St Thomas's Tower, the water gate, they took extra care even though any of the guards who happened still to be awake would be looking outwards rather than in.

And then they reached the Wakefield Tower and could duck behind its crenellations before dropping down, lightly as thistle-down but sweating with exertion and fear, on to the roof of the adjoining Garden Tower. They had a copy of the key to the door that opened on to the spiral staircase inside, and though they hadn't yet handed over the scandalous price the ironmonger was asking, it was in truth very little in comparison with what they were being given for their night's work. They had smothered the key with grease, but it still had to be forced.

They slipped down the staircase, built of stone and cold on their feet, the torches in the wall sockets throwing their shadows huge and black and wavering against the curving walls. Halfway down they came to the door that opened into the first-floor chamber. They had a key for that, too, but didn't need it because the door gave access from the chamber to the garderobe and had been left unlocked in case the chamber's inhabitants needed to relieve themselves during the night. If you weren't royal, you had to make do with a thunderjar.

So they eased themselves inside, wary at first but then reassured. It was a handsome room, with a big fireplace, a brightly tiled and patterned floor, a pleasant window seat and, at either end, incon-gruously, the huge bits of machinery that operated the portcullises guarding the gates below. The vigil candle also showed a hand-somely carved fourposter bed, with the curtains open and two blond young sleepers wrapped in each other's arms on top of the coverlet, lost to the world.

There was a truckle bed on which a servant should have been resting, except that the servant had been paid to absent himself.

The bigger of the two men went over to the truckle bed and tested the thin, lumpy mattress. 'Rag-filled,' he muttered disgustedly.

'Pretty boys,' grunted the other man.

Just then, the older boy shifted and moaned and the younger one murmured drowsily, 'Does your tooth ache?'

The intruders didn't dare risk their coming fully awake, because there was a guardroom below and they couldn't afford cries and screams and thrashing about. They had been instructed to leave no signs of violence, so that the deaths would be a mystery – which ruled out the knives they would have used from choice, and left them with only one option.

The second man gestured urgently at his companion who, with a shrug, picked up the despised mattress and bore it over to the bed. Then, taking one end each, they dropped it over the boys' heads and leaned on it, feeling through the stuffing for the noses and mouths that were to be stopped for ever. If the boys had not been lying on the coverlet, they would have used that, because its soft feather filling would have settled lightly and moulded itself naturally, suffocatingly, into position. As it was, they had to force and tuck the rag-filled mattress round their victims' heads and hold it down tight as the children fought, chokingly, against it, their arms waving, hands clawing, and legs kicking out wildly.

The two men continued to hold the mattress down for what seemed like an eternity after all movement ceased. Then they took it away and gave a hiccup of fright to see the dead eyes staring at them.

Hastily, the smaller, cleverer man closed the lids.

Then, hands shaking, they tidied the bodies into a more natural position, restored the mattress to the truckle bed, and began rummaging through the clothes chests and picking out a few trinkets to take with them. But their leisureliness was a cover for the terror that had suddenly overcome them, and all they wanted to do was run. If they were caught, they knew that hanging, drawing and quartering would be their fate.

After a few moments, the bigger of the two murmured, 'Let's get out of here.'

So they pattered softly back up to the roof, locked the door, anchored a rope to the parapet and shinned down hand-over-hand in the shadowed junction of the Garden and the Wakefield Towers. Then, with a skilful twitch, they brought the rope down after them and went back to their beds. As they went, they laughed hectically with relief. The bigger man even tried to mask his loss of nerve by pointing out that the duty serjeant was going to have a nasty shock when he went to wind up the portcullises in the morning.

2

'WHAT IN God's name . . . ?' Francis demanded.

Stanley shrugged. 'Messenger,' he said succinctly. 'He's annoyed about something.'

'Out! Everybody!' Richard's voice was so rough the cooks could have grated cheese on it.

Francis spent an hour wondering what could have put him into such a mood, and finally ventured to put his head round the door, saying, 'Errr . . .'

'Oh, come in, come in. You, but no one else. Close the door.'

Since remaining silent seemed to be the only alternative to asking something brainless like, 'Is there anything wrong?' Francis remained silent.

After a moment, Richard said, 'Someone has murdered the princes.'

Francis stared at him dumbly.

Richard's colour was high and his voice savage. 'That fool Brackenbury! I can scarcely believe it! After that attempt to get to them ten days ago, he thought it would be safer to move them into the Garden Tower as being closest to his own lodging. So he did, without properly checking the security of the place. "I hadn't time." And then someone – God's bones, *who?* – contrived to get in and smother them. No signs of entry or exit. They were discovered when the duty serjeant went in to wind up the portcullises at first light. And as if that was not enough, Brackenbury panicked. Instead of screaming, "Murder," and starting a hue and cry, he hid the bodies. He *buried* them!'

'Oh, Jesu!'

'Well may you say so. If he had wanted to make me look guilty, he could not have done better. It was *I* who appointed him to the post of Constable. It is *I* who will be seen to benefit from their deaths. It is *I* who will be thought responsible for trying to conceal the deed.'

Francis said, 'But how could he think it possible to keep it secret? I take it he didn't dig the grave himself?'

'No. He used two of his own men and has at least had the sense to send them back to Barnard Castle with money and dire threats of retribution to their families if they ever breathe a word.'

'Well, that's something. Oh, poor lads!'

Richard's anger was beginning to abate. 'Yes, poor lads. But who had them killed, and why? I have been worrying away at the problem for the last hour. Why, why, why? They can hardly have been murdered for themselves, though Eddie may have made others than myself feel like throttling him. There seem to be only two alternatives. They were killed either to embarrass me or – which I can hardly bear to consider – in a misguided attempt to help me.'

Francis said, after a moment, 'Buckingham? Or Jocky Howard?'

'Not Jocky, I think. Not his style. But Harry Buckingham is just a possibility. I will have to put a watch on him.'

'As for enemies . . .'

'Yes. My worst enemy, I suppose, is Dorset. If he were not the boys' brother, he would be my first choice. There are any number of lesser men, but most were close supporters of my brother and their main objection to me is that I did not permit Edward's son to succeed to the throne. That being so, it seems unlikely that they would be involved in murdering him. More than that, I don't believe that any of them has sufficient gumption to have taken the initiative.'

'Bishop Morton has.'

Richard stared at him. 'He's a ruthless little man, certainly, but however lightly he wears his religious vows, I don't think . . .'

Francis said suddenly, 'All this casts a new light on last month's attempt to rescue the boys from the Tower, doesn't it?'

'Does it?'

'Don't you remember? We were talking about what the plotters intended to do with the boys after they were rescued. What if their real object was for the boys to be "accidentally" killed *during* the rescue?'

'It's possible, I suppose,' Richard said doubtfully.

'And though we don't yet know who was responsible for the murders, we do know who was involved in the rescue attempt. If the originator was the same both times, finding out who was *behind* the rescue attempt could lead us to the murderers!'

'Don't get too excited, Francis. Remember, the rescuers have already been executed.'

Only momentarily downcast, Francis exclaimed, 'But at least we know who they were. They have families and associates who could be questioned. Someone must know something.'

'Well, I can try throwing money at them. It's preferable to putting them to the rack. In the meantime, I shall send – who? – Tyrell, I think – to see what he can discover at the Tower itself.'

Richard had been striding round the room, fidgeting with the dagger at his belt, but now he stopped short. 'Appropriating the throne was one thing. It made political sense. But to be held responsible for the killing of my brother's sons . . .'

Francis said, 'It *must* be kept quiet. No one must be allowed to find out that they're dead.'

'Do you think that's possible? I don't. But Brackenbury has ensured that I am left with no alternative other than to try. Jesu! If I had wanted them disposed of, I could have arranged things better than this!'

3

NO ONE KNEW where the rumour started. To begin with, it was more assumption than rumour, the assumption of men who, if they had been in Richard's position, *would* have murdered the princes and therefore supposed that he had done so. It was standard practice for usurpers to kill off the kings they had replaced. Henry IV had had Richard II assassinated; Edward IV had done the same for Henry VI, even if he had taken ten years about it and was popularly held to have delegated the task to his younger brother – Richard.

But the whispers which had begun even before the bungled attempt at rescue gained strength as it became apparent that the boys had disappeared, and that it was not simply a matter of their no longer being seen playing in the garden or sitting on the window seat watching what was going on outdoors. Their confessor, who had visited them daily, had been told he was no longer required. And their physician, Dr Argentine, who had been treating young Eddie for toothache, had been told the same.

The two men should not have gossiped about it, but they did.

That Richard did not come hurrying back to London was thought to be conclusive. If they were still alive, he could have settled the rumours by letting the princes be seen in public. As it was, the one or two councillors who had sufficient courage to go to the Tower and ask to see the princes were politely turned away – and went, without a murmur. Their shame at their own weakness was later to make them vindictive.

4

THE ROYAL PROGRESS had reached Warwick, and Richard and Francis were up on the castle battlements discussing the possibility of adding a new tower with gun emplacements, and the amount and cost of the building work that would be necessary. Since they had left Gloucester, Richard had not mentioned the princes again, although he was looking careworn and had frequent moments of frowning abstraction.

Hearing trumpets, they glanced down and saw a smart little procession heading towards the gate tower. It was the third such procession in the two days since they had arrived. The first had been that of an ambassador from Ferdinand and Isabella of Spain, welcoming Richard to the fellowship of European sovereigns. Richard had said, 'How kind.' The second procession, less well turned out, had been that of Archibald, duke of Albany, who had yet again fallen foul of his brother, King James of

Scotland. Richard had said, 'What a surprise!'

This time it was Anne.

Unemotionally, Richard remarked, 'Ah, the queen,' which Francis found annoying. Admittedly, there were men with set-squares, levels and plumb-lines standing around with their ears waving in the breeze, but even kings were entitled to be pleased to see their wives.

Had her weeks at Middleham given Anne back some of her strength, as Constantia had hoped? She looked calm and controlled as she rode in between the twin towers of the gatehouse.

'Let us go down,' Richard said.

In the courtyard, Anne curtseyed to him, 'Sire,' and he bowed in response. 'My lady.'

It was all very correct and formal, but Francis was relieved to see that Richard was studying her carefully, his eyes concerned but the hint of a questioning smile around his mouth, as if asking whether she had recovered the even tenor of her mind.

He received no perceptible answer. Anne simply looked back, pale and solemn and a little strained. She did not recoil when Richard took her by the arm and said, 'Let us go indoors. You must be tired.'

Briefly, Richard wondered where all the pleasure of their relationship had gone. In these last months, secure in the knowledge that he had done only what it was necessary to do, he had reassured himself that, as a sensible woman, Anne would eventually come to accept it. He could see that it had not happened yet. He would just have to wait, and not force her. Not even – especially not – in bed. The night of his coronation had taught him a lesson he would never forget.

Neither of them foresaw how long the tension between them was to last; she waiting for him to come to her, and he waiting for her to come to him.

BUCKINGHAM had decided not to go rushing home to Brecon but to pass a few days at his mansion of Thornbury on the way. Richard's instruction to hold commissions into treason could wait; there had been quite enough rushing about over the last three or four months. Now, he would go on his own stately and unhurried progress, exposing himself and his retinue to the admiration of all who saw them as they passed. He knew that, tall and handsome in the saddle, he was everything anyone could expect of England's premier nobleman, ruler of Wales, and confidant of kings.

He was just about to leave the Worcester road for the track to the west when he became irritably aware of competition. There was another expensive-looking cavalcade in the distance, not quite as grand as his but quite grand enough. Long before they met, the marguerite daisies on the banners told him it was his aunt by marriage, Margaret Beaufort, Lady Stanley, Countess of Richmond.

She was more pleased to see him, than he her. 'Ah, nephew! Are you well? And Katherine your wife? What a happy accident that we should meet.'

In truth, it was not quite as accidental as it appeared.

Buckingham made the appropriate replies although he guessed Margaret must be aware that he had no idea how his wife was, or even where she was. However, since Margaret and Stanley were equally rarely together, he tried to retaliate by mentioning that he had left her husband at Gloucester just a few days before.

'Yes, I know. On progress with Richard. Does the progress go well?'

'Yes.'

'How fortunate that he is going north, rather than south.'

306

'Fortunate?'

She looked down at her finely gauntletted hands, flexing the knuckles that so tormented her – although there were some among her acquaintance who had noticed that they tormented her most often when she wanted time to think – and then raised the hooded eyes to meet Buckingham's again. 'I have been in London more lately than you. There are strong rumours that he has had those sweet children, the little king and his brother, murdered. In just a few days, he has lost all the support he has been at such pains to attract.'

She was, of course, heartbroken by the death of the sweet children, and had prayed ardently for their souls, but their pruning from the royal family tree had opened vistas for her own son that she had never dared to contemplate. She could not think of it without a thrill going through her.

Buckingham shrugged dismissively and said, 'Rumours!'

'They are so strong that they must be more than rumours. It puts you, Harry, in a very awkward position, since you have been his closest associate.' Watching him, she was reminded of why the late king had never given him any of the positions of responsibility to which, by birth, he should have been entitled. He was clever enough in a cunning way, but anything unexpected threw him off balance. And he failed to realise that it showed.

She went on with a kindliness that was wholly deceptive, 'If I were you, I would give the matter careful thought. Why not go straight on to Brecon, where there are fewer distractions than at Thornbury?'

And where wily Bishop Morton, with whom she had been in communication, was a not altogether reluctant prisoner.

Buckingham's face wore the slightly glazed half smile that meant he was about to evade the issue if he could – probably by asserting his integrity, his innocence of deception, his ignorance of wrongdoing.

She was not in the mood to listen to the silly man, so she fanned herself and said, 'Pooh! It is hot. We will have to pay for this later in the year. But today it is getting late and I have still some way to go. Goodbye, Harry. Take my advice and consider your position.'

'Yes, aunt. God go with you.'

6

IT WAS Francis who, in the end, told Anne about the rumours concerning the princes, rumours that had reached Warwick with a rapidity that suggested wilful intent rather than mere idle gossip.

With all the conviction at his command, he said, 'Richard is furious. I have never seen him in such a rage.'

She had always been quick. 'In a rage about the rumours? Or in a rage about their deaths?'

Francis at twenty-eight was by no means as transparent as he had been at sixteen, but his face gave it all away. She said, 'They *are* dead, aren't they? What happened?'

She had known since the beginning that the boys were doomed, had known they were bound to be victims of the events Richard had set in train, whether or not direct responsibility for their deaths would end by being laid at his door. She had thought endlessly, 'What if it were Ned?'

So Francis told her what had happened. With an almost icy detachment that Francis could not understand, but which Constantia could have told him was self-protection, an armour against fate, she said, 'Even if Richard had nothing to do with it, the responsibility is still his. He was their guardian, their Protector. And he let them die.'

She was unrelenting, and in the end, Francis gave up trying to persuade her. Despairingly, he said, 'But you love him. You have loved him always. Will you stop loving him because of this?'

She thought for a long, long moment. 'No. Love isn't about feeling warmth and passion for someone who never puts a foot wrong. Love isn't a matter of "because of". It's a matter of "in spite of". That is the test.' She paused. 'That is why I have come back to him, against my better judgement. For good or ill, that is why I have come back to him.'

'Tell him so! Explain to him!'

She raised a delicately plucked fair brow, almost amused. 'He wouldn't understand. I would be criticising him, and he has never been one to tolerate criticism. You know that as well as I do. I will just have to wait and see how things turn out. Jesu! If only we could laugh together again. Laughter heals. But all that has gone.'

There was nothing Francis could find to say.

7

SIR JAMES TYRELL had a brother, Thomas, whom Richard had appointed Master of the Horse. But Thomas was sickly and James, hoping to succeed to his post and having a forward-looking turn of mind, had been keeping a close eye on the serjeants and grooms of the royal stables, with a view to discovering which of them would be worthy of his trust when he achieved his ambition.

All were rough men, who cared more for horses than for people, but some were quick-witted enough, and all spoke the language of the common man. It was what Sir James needed in the present situation, because it seemed to him that the princes' assassins must have had more knowledge of the routines of the Tower than could be expected of any outsider, and that therefore his first enquiries should be directed at the insiders, the staff and the garrison. The king had said firmly, 'No torture. Torture does not elicit truth.' He had also been forbidden to disclose the reason for his enquiries. It was as if the king was deliberately making things difficult for him.

But if he were successful, it would certainly advance his career.

'Strange 'appenings?' John Dighton repeated. 'What's that mean, sir? What sort o' strange 'appenings?'

'Any sort. People creeping round at dead of night. People vanishing. People suddenly flush with money.'

Dighton, a big, broad, square horsekeeper, glanced question-ingly at the shifty-eyed fellow he had brought in with him, then back at Sir James. His mouth turning down, he shook his head and said, 'We 'aven't 'eard nuffing.'

'Well, ask around. Quietly. Don't rouse suspicion. I'll make it worth your while.'

He knew very well that, the moment the pair of them were out of the room, they would be speculating – no doubt knowledge-ably – as to what it was all about. But there was nothing he could do about that. They were in a position to gossip naturally with their equals in the garrison; he wasn't.

Dighton brought him results sooner than he had expected.

'Fellow name o' Miles Forest, nasty piece 'o work,' he reported. 'Came into money the day after the Feast of St Peter's Chains. Bought everyone a drink, then disappeared no one knows where.'

'Associates?' Tyrell snapped.

Dighton's solid face broke into a malicious grin. 'You'll like this, sir. There were one man 'e were close with, but 'e's dead.'

Tyrell swore. 'How?'

'Got in a fight with an ironmonger on Thames Street about

being overcharged for summat, an' the ironmonger clouted 'im with a 'ammer.'

'Ah!'

Dighton grinned again. 'No good, sir. The ironmonger's disappeared, too.'

Sir James closed his eyes. Fingers drumming on the table, he said, 'Any hint of where – or *who* – the money came from?'

'Uh, uh.' A negative grunt was the only reply.

Sir James opened the purse at his belt. 'Keep asking,' he said.

8

FROM WARWICK the royal party had gone on to Coventry. And then to Leicester. And then to Nottingham.

Nottingham was at the very centre of England, strategically placed for a monarch who might fear himself open to military or naval attack from an unpredicted quarter. Edward had considered it sufficiently important to begin on the transformation of the castle on its rocky hill from an old-fashioned fortress into a civilised royal residence. He had completed one magnificently ornate tower to its full height and another was half built. Richard had every intention of finishing it.

In the meantime, the privy lodgings in the new tower were comfortable and convenient. There was even a privy kitchen in the basement.

Anne, struggling for normality, showed it to Constantia, saying gaily, 'Just like old times, being back in the kitchen. I sometimes wonder, when we are being so marvellously formal, whether Richard even remembers rescuing me from my fate as a temporary kitchen maid before we were married. It was so funny! But oh dear, it all seems so very long ago.'

'Francis told me about it. But this is wonderful. Everything the cooks could possibly need.'

'The great advantage, of course, is that the timetable in the great kitchen is so rigid – work on dinner begins at half past five in the morning, and with so many people to feed there is no flexibility. The whole household revolves around the kitchen timetable. But the privy kitchen means that Richard and I need not be bound by set mealtimes and can eat when we choose.'

Constantia giggled. 'How very housewifely you sound!'

Anne grimaced at her. 'We also expect to be better fed. With only two or three chickens on the spit, rather than two or three sheep, the cooks can watch over things more carefully. And there's less danger of poisoners, too. The only difficulty, and I don't really mind it, is that my chamber is directly above – and rather full of cooking smells!'

'It's an unusual arrangement.'

'Yes. In past times, the king's and queen's apartments were always on the same floor, but when Edward began improving the castle, he remembered what he had seen in Burgundy during his exile. So the queen has the ground floor and the king the floor above. It gives us both more space. My only complaint, apart from the cooking smells, is of the constant traffic on the spiral stair up to Richard's chamber – messengers, secretaries, officials, courtiers. It's never-ending.'

'Oh, well. Whatever is cooking at the moment smells very appetising,' Constantia remarked encouragingly. It was a delight to find Anne talking freely about domestic matters, rather than brooding about her and Richard's troubles.

But her slightly forced cheerfulness was not proof against the life she now had to lead.

She took to disappearing, retreating from the castle down the stone staircase leading to the river bank, there to sit gazing

312

blank-eyed over the marshy ground across the Leen with a mind deliberately but not always successfully empty.

Francis came upon her one day when he, too, was in search of quiet, and tried to amuse her by telling her that Secretary Kendall was engaged on writing to the Corporation of York, asking them to 'receive his Highness and the queen as laudably as their wisdom can imagine.'

He said, 'Rather a good turn of phrase, I think. And in case their wisdom lets them down, he takes the liberty of suggesting decorations in the streets and so on. All the usual kind of thing. This, he hints, would impress the southerners in Richard's retinue – most of whom, as *we* know, are approaching the uncouth north in a spirit of craven trepidation. Heigh ho. What strange animals people can be. You would sometimes think northerners and southerners came from different planets.'

But Anne only smiled faintly, and said, 'When do we move on to Pontefract? I have arranged for Ned to be brought by horse litter to join us there. Richard wants to have him with us when we enter York, so that he can be formally invested as prince of Wales. I am worried. Although he is full of spirit he is still physically delicate. And he's only seven. I hope the ceremonial will not be too much for him.'

Francis said, 'If he has inherited both your spirit and Richard's, he should be able to survive anything!'

9

AT BRECON, Buckingham glanced down superciliously at Bishop Morton and thought what an odd little man he was. If he had not been a cleric, he would have been deprived of his head when Hastings was, and deservedly so. Yet here he was, bright and predatory as a fox with his eye on the hen run, trying to talk his gaoler into a course of action that Buckingham could only regard as dishonourable. He wanted Buckingham to betray the king he himself had set on the throne.

'No,' Buckingham said austerely.

'That, of course, is up to you, your Grace. I am merely setting out the courses of action that you might care to consider.'

The bishop sighed to himself, wondering how, or if, Lady Margaret's highly secret negotiations with the queen dowager were progressing. He could not afford to reveal the full extent of the plot to Buckingham until he was sure that that gentleman would not feel compelled to pass the details on to 'King' Richard. So – to appeal to vanity, fear, or ambition? The duke was lavishly supplied with the first and last, and the fear could be utilised on both counts.

Fear first, therefore.

'It is a matter of concern to those who honour and admire your Grace, among whom I humbly count myself one, that you should be endangered by your association with a usurper and murderer.'

'Murderer?' After careful thought, Buckingham had dismissed what his aunt had told him about the rumoured death of the princes, and now supposed the little man to be referring to Hastings. Which had not been murder but a necessary execution.

'Yes,' said the bishop. 'Murderer of Lord Rivers and Lord Hastings, of Sir Richard Grey, of Vaughan and Haute. But far more culpably, infinitely more heinously, murderer of those innocent babes, our true king, Edward V, and his brother and heir the duke of York.'

Buckingham said indifferently, 'Well, hardly babes. And I have yet to meet a twelve-year-old who could be considered innocent.'

Bishop Morton looked shocked, as was appropriate for a distinguished cleric, even one who was a lawyer in his very bones and

314

had taken holy orders only to further his legal career. Buckingham was right, of course, but 'innocent babes' was a much more telling courtroom phrase than 'worldly-wise adolescents'. He said, 'Your Grace may have the right of it, but for them to be cruelly cut off in the flower of their youth by their uncle, their Protector, is something that will not be forgiven by men of Christian heart. Or,' he remembered, 'by God.'

'I do not believe that Richard has murdered them. It is mere rumour.'

'No, it is God's truth. There can be no doubt.'

'I would have known. Richard does nothing without my advice.'

Bishop Morton's eyes under their tufted brows were like slits, guarding his thoughts, but a more observant man than Buckingham might have seen a gleam in them. As it was, Buckingham went on, 'If he had been considering it, I would of course have discouraged him.' Then, with perhaps a little less conviction, 'I would have known.'

The bishop, with forty years' experience in reading men's minds, watched Buckingham thinking, 'If the princes *are* dead . . . Richard did not tell me. He *should* have told me. It means he doesn't trust me, despite everything I have done for him. So why should I sacrifice myself for him?'

So far, so good.

'It would be wise, I believe – if your Grace will deign to hear my view – for your Grace to protect yourself by placing some distance between yourself and the usurper. Make it clear that the murder of the princes has destroyed all your faith in him and goodwill towards him.'

'Yes. If you are *quite* sure of what has happened. Perhaps I should issue a proclamation.'

And that would not do at all. The bishop thought rapidly.

'That might, I believe, place your Grace in personal danger. It will enrage the usurper greatly, and you know how rapidly and ruthlessly he moves. If your Grace permits, we should consider further in a day or two, when I have the most recent news from London.'

Belatedly remembering their respective rôles, Buckingham snapped, 'You are supposed to be my prisoner. How dare you be in communication with London?'

10

ON THE last Friday of August the royal entourage made its ceremonial entry into York, a York whose narrow streets had been swept clear of booths and stalls, its houses splendidly draped with tapestries, hangings and silver and gold bunting, its mayor and corporation in their fur-trimmed scarlet velvet, its leading citizens also clad in scarlet, and everyone else dressed in their best. Three striking street pageants had been arranged, and Richard and Anne were presented with a small fortune in gold coins.

Plays, tournaments and sports followed, and for three weeks not a day passed without some magnificent banquet or other enter-tainment given by the city or by the king and queen.

The high point of the three weeks was the investiture of the prince of Wales. Under the soaring limestone pillars and rib-vaulted roof of York Minster, with the great stained glass windows casting a dazzling kaleidoscope of colours over the scene, Richard placed a golden circlet on his son's head and then, smiling but solemn, put a sceptre in his hand.

Ned's eyes were enormous in his small face, and Anne felt the tears spring to her own as the music swelled and filled the cathedral with wonderful, soaring sound. Then it was necessary for the three of them to walk in procession through the streets, still wearing their crowns, and preceded by forty trumpeters whose flourishes echoed back and forth from the buildings, while the people cheered as if they would never stop. Anne held Ned's trembling small hand throughout.

She tried to ignore her blinding headache, but Richard revelled in it all.

Richard had been the city's 'good lord' for a dozen years, and that he should now also be king delighted everyone. The little prince's investiture had been so spectacular that it seemed almost like a second coronation, and the boy's composure and the king's glittering crown were the subject of much admiring comment.

The mayor, aware from the city records that York had in past times taken precedence over London as the centre of government, airily mentioned the fact to the king, who nodded judiciously and conceded that it was a point worthy of consideration. He had every intention of establishing a permanent royal household at Sheriff Hutton. In the meantime, he proposed relieving York of the need to pay taxes for the next half year.

It was all highly satisfactory to everyone except Harry Percy, who had been hoping to regain dominance of the north now that Richard was fated to be out of the way in London for most of the time.

11

BISHOP MORTON'S careful tutoring had brought Buckingham round to the desired way of thinking with gratifying rapidity, and so decisively that the bishop felt justified in mentioning the names of some of the men in the southern and western counties who could be relied on to rise in rebellion – *if* there was a rebellion and *if* his Grace would take the lead. Lewkenor and Fogge, Poynings and Gaynesford, Beauchamp and Tocotes, St Lo and Daubenay. Not to mention the marquess of Dorset, Bishop Lionel Woodville, and Sir Richard Woodville. All of them loyal to the memory of King Edward IV, and enraged by the treatment of his children.

The treatment of Edward's children interested Buckingham not at all, now that the two boys were out of the way. 'And if – when – Richard is overthrown, who will take the crown?'

The bishop thought, 'Oh, no, you don't, my friend!' but said with a hint of hesitation, 'The Princess Elizabeth has, naturally, the best claim.'

'A woman to rule England in her own name? Never.'

'It would be necessary for her to marry.'

The duke of Buckingham looked thoughtful and Bishop Morton almost felt sorry for the duchess of Buckingham, although to feel sorry for Katherine Woodville was not easy. Swiftly, in his lawyer's mind, he ran through possible grounds for divorce. Affinity? No. Lack of consummation? No, there were children. The court might always question the identity of the father, but then it could become nasty.

His reflections were interrupted. 'She would have to marry an English nobleman,' Buckingham said.

'Of course.'

'And possibly one with his own claim to the throne.'

'That would be advantageous.'

'This needs to be thought about.'

12

MARGARET BEAUFORT said, 'That seems to have gone well.'
Reginald Bray nodded, then resignedly discovered that

Margaret had been going through her accounts.

She said, 'You seem to have spent a great deal of money on arranging that unsuccessful attempt to rescue the little princes?'

He could not say that three-quarters of the sum involved had been expended on the second attempt – the successful, the lethal one that had rescued them from all the pains of life. So he shrugged. 'It was expensive. These things always are.'

'I suppose so. Anyway, now that Buckingham has agreed to take a public rôle in the rising, we may proceed to the next stage. I will send Hugh Conway to my son in Brittany. Henry has had much more freedom of movement since Edward died, because Duke Francis has taken a dislike to our new king and sees no reason to please him by keeping Henry "safe". It appears that Richard has been slow to respond to Brittany's demands for help against France.'

'Which is no longer needed, with Louis so recently dead.'

'True. However, I believe that if I send Henry as much money as I can spare, Duke Francis might be prepared to support him in gathering an army and an invasion fleet to reinforce the rebellion against Richard.'

'Which ought to be enough to convince the waverers.'

'Yes. And I require you, Master Bray, to devote most of your energies to them for the next few weeks. Though Morton suggests you go to Brecon first, to confer with Harry Buckingham.'

'As your ladyship desires. And – er – in the meantime you will begin negotiating with Queen Elizabeth, will you? Using Lewis Caerleon?'

'Yes. He has agreed to act as go-between; one of the unforeseen benefits of my having the same physician as the queen. Despite the heavy guard round her sanctuary, he will be permitted access to her.'

'So – we need her support and that of all her adherents. And you will pursue her agreement to a marriage between your son Henry and her daughter Bess . . .'

'Master Bray, is this my plot or yours?'

He did his best to look embarrassed. If she only knew! Then, being a realist first and last, he gave a mental shrug. She probably *did* know.

Her high aristocratic brow became impossibly higher. 'And when the rebellion succeeds and the marriage is celebrated, my son will take up his rightful place as' – she drew in a deep breath – 'as king of England!'

Chapter Thirteen

1483

1

OBSERVERS, informers, spies, scouts, scurriers – there were many names for those whose task it was to keep their master informed of what was going on in the world beyond his immediate vicinity. Some did no more than act as an advance guard when he was on the move; others found their way into private households and, more particularly, foreign embassies, to sniff out plots that might be forming at home and abroad.

Richard had learned the value of spies during his adolescence in the household of the earl of Warwick and, later, from Edward during the crisis years of 1469-71. Now, his own agents were coming in with nebulous but disturbing reports of messengers flying back and forth in the south of England. Most of the communication appeared to be between members of the richer gentry based in the area spanning the country from Kent to Cornwall. The names were instructive. Richard knew some to be Woodville supporters; some were tenants of Margaret Beaufort; others had been loyal members of Edward's household who might be presumed to resent the dispossession and rumoured

321

death of his sons; and the West country was traditionally Lancastrian, although there was one name mentioned that had nothing Lancastrian about it, one that sounded immediate alarm bells – that of the marquess of Dorset. So that was where he had vanished to!

Even Richard's decision to have Buckingham watched in connection with the murder of the princes was producing results, though not the kind of results Richard had expected. The duke, summoned politely to rejoin Richard at court, stayed away, pleading infirmity of the stomach. But Richard, issuing orders for Bishop Morton's nephew Robert to be dismissed as Master of the Rolls, and for the seizure of Bishop Woodville's worldly goods, noted with interest that Buckingham's infirmity had not prevented him from travelling the many miles from Brecon to Thornbury, or from taking Bishop Morton with him or, when he arrived at Thornbury, from entertaining Bishop Woodville there.

Francis said, 'Whatever's afoot, surely Buckingham can't be involved? You have endowed him with everything he wanted. In fact, you have grossly overpaid him for the support he gave you when you needed it. He could only lose by becoming involved in any rising against you. If there *is* such a thing being plotted.'

'Unless he fancies the throne for himself,' Richard replied meditatively. 'He has quite a fair claim, now that the princes are dead. Perhaps he may have taken the initiative in their murder for his own reasons and not, as I previously thought, in a misguided attempt to help me.'

With a wry grin, Francis said, 'Well, you never trusted him, did you?'

'Looking at the princes' death from that point of view, something else has recently occurred to me. Margaret Beaufort's son Henry has also become a more viable claimant.'

'Lady Margaret?' It was a startling thought. 'You can't be suggesting that *she* had anything to do with it? And surely, if she were in any way involved, Stanley would not still be here at your side?'

'Perhaps not, though if he suddenly develops a desire to be elsewhere, I will scrutinise his explanations with the greatest interest.'

The door opened and Anne came in with Ned, beaming all over his handsome little face at the sight of his two favourite grownups. It was impossible not to respond, and Richard laughingly picked the boy up, hugging him and saying, 'Well, my little prince?'

His little prince chortled. Then, 'My mother the queen and I . . .'

Francis gave a splutter of laughter, and the child looked at him reproachfully. 'My mother the queen and I would like to go back to Middleham, if your Highness pleases. If you could come, too, it would be lovely. I could show you my new hunting puppies, and the cygnets the corporation of York brought me when you were made king, and . . .'

Richard planted a resounding kiss on the boy's forehead – an unprecedented token of affection – and said, 'No, little one. My Highness has to go back to London. There are important matters to be attended to.' Over their son's head, he smiled at Anne, 'I would prefer to have you with me, but there is a possibility of trouble, and I would be reassured to know you safe at Middleham.'

She smiled back, but there was more of duty in it than warmth. 'As you wish, Richard.' Then, with a sudden hint of the old mischief, 'Though my son the prince of Wales and his mother the queen will always be happy to welcome you there, if you can find the time.'

2

DR CAERLEON, a grave and learned man, was displeased to find his patient, the queen dowager, in the lowest of low spirits. She had, of course, heard the rumours of her sons' deaths and was convinced of their truth.

'I have been expecting it. In these last months I have lost everyone I cared for. My husband the king. My dearest brother Anthony, Earl Rivers. My second son, Sir Richard Grey. And now my two little princes. And all except my husband at the violent hands of that monster, his brother. I only have my dear daughters left to me, and I fear for them, too. We cannot stay here in sanctuary for much longer. It is like being in prison.'

Caerleon glanced round and thought what a comfortable prison it was. He suspected that Abbot Estney would be pleased to have his Lodging returned to him, instead of having to trail back and forth daily to his house in Pimlico.

He said, 'Where will you go when you leave, your Highness?'

'I have no idea.' Suddenly, tears were welling from her eyes, which surprised him. The queen dowager had never permitted herself to express emotion, which he guessed was why her face remained so unlined, despite her forty-six years. 'That evil man,' she went on, 'will no doubt take away, if he has not already done so, all the houses and estates with which my husband endowed me. Where *can* I go?'

It was a better opening than the doctor had hoped for. The Lady Margaret had told him he must present her plan to the queen dowager as if it were his own spur-of-the-moment idea. Then the queen would not suspect the Lady Margaret of attempting to manipulate her. The queen did not like being manipulated.

He drew a sharp breath. 'I wonder . . . Something occurs to me. I do not know whether you are aware, but there is a plan to overthrow Richard. If it succeeds, a different king would certainly behave more kindly towards you.'

'Kings, kings!' she shrugged pettishly. 'My eldest daughter should be queen in her own right.'

The doctor was an elderly man, and set in his ways. He was shocked. 'I believe there is no precedent in England for a woman to rule alone – except for the regrettable Matilda, of course, and I don't know whether she counts.'

The tears vanished, but the pettishness remained. 'What is so important about precedent? It only needs to happen once, and then there *will* be a precedent. Anyway, when you say, "a different king", who do you mean? Not Harry Buckingham, I hope? He would be every bit as bad as Richard.'

'No. I was thinking more of Henry Tudor, the true heir to the lamented Henry VI. He is a young man of good repute, and unmarried. It occurs to me that, if Richard were to be overthrown in favour of Henry Tudor, and if Henry Tudor were to marry the Princess Elizabeth, your daughter would be queen after all. Also, the houses of York and Lancaster would be united, to the benefit of the country.'

The benefit of the country was an alien concept to the queen dowager, for whom the benefit of her family had always taken priority. Caerleon could see her mentally reviewing the pros and cons. After a moment, she said, 'Henry Tudor is not the only candidate, or even the most likely. Surely George of Clarence's son must have a better claim?'

'No. He lost his claim through the attainder of his father. Furthermore, he is only nine years old and said to be backward for his age, so we would be faced again with the prospect of a long minority such as precipitated the events of these last tragic months. Henry Tudor, on the other hand, is fully adult and competent to rule.'

She nodded and then said slowly, 'I would need a guarantee, and I would need it now. Henry would have to swear on oath that, if he came to the throne, he would marry my daughter Bess. Or, if anything should happen to her – which I pray God it may not – my second daughter, Cicely.'

'I am sure that could be arranged.'

The fair face under the pearl-sewn headdress smiled at him. 'What a clever man you are, Master Caerleon. In a single moment of inspiration, you have solved all our problems. Now let me think. What must I do?' She was not a stupid woman. 'The Lady Margaret must have made some suggestions?'

He felt himself colouring, but did not make the mistake of denying Margaret Beaufort's interest. 'It would clearly help if your Highness would consent to procuring all your friends and associates to take part in the rising against Richard.'

She smiled again, lavishly. 'It would, wouldn't it. You may tell the Lady Margaret that I agree to her terms – my whole-hearted support for her son, in return for his promise to marry my daughter.'

3

DUKE FRANCIS of Brittany was a thin, pale, middle-aged man with flat cheeks and a nose that merged straight into his forehead, with no bridge. He was unworldly in the sense that he disliked and detached himself from everyday reality whenever possible, but very worldly indeed in his devotion to beauty and display. Jewels were his passion.

Henry Tudor, on his knees begging favours, found himself watching distractedly as the duke set to work with the beautiful new toothpick that hung round his neck, a bittern's claw superbly mounted in gold and diamonds. Henry estimated that he could have fitted out a ship for what it had cost.

He tried to concentrate on what he was saying. '. . . a rebellion against Richard of Gloucester, who calls himself king of England. I have been invited by the duke of Buckingham, who is the first peer of the realm and is leading the rebellion, to raise an invasion force and join those who wish to overturn the usurper.'

'Why should you be involved?'

Henry hesitated, trusting Duke Francis no further than the duke trusted him. They both knew that Henry Tudor, earl of Richmond, had long been a pawn in Brittany's campaign to persuade England to give the dukedom military support against France, which was perennially anxious to bring it to heel. Louis XI's recent death had taken the pressure off, but only temporarily.

'My gratitude to Brittany,' Henry said tentatively, 'which has given me succour and protection for so many years, could at long last be repaid if I were to become king of England, which is the proposal that has been put to me.' He did not mention that Buckingham's letters had invited him only to join in the fray, not to become king. That suggestion had come from others. 'It would need . . .'

Briefly, the duke's toothpick was still. 'Yes?'

'I have some funds, but not enough. Furthermore, unknown and untried as I am, I cannot raise troops or hire ships without your Grace's sponsorship of the venture.' It cost him a good deal to admit his inexperience, but the duke already knew about that.

'You have never commanded an army.' It was not a question.

'No.'

'Or a fleet.'

'No, your Grace. But I am acquainted with the theory.'

The duke returned to investigating his cavities. 'Well, that will not see you far. Speak to Landois and tell him I have no objection to the venture, that I will lend you ten thousand golden crowns, and that he should supply you with a sailor who knows something about the sea, and a soldier who has some experience of soldiering.'

'Thank you, your Grace. Thank . . .'

'You may go.' The duke had never cared for his reluctant guest, anxious and sulky by turns, his skin sallow and his teeth an offence to the eye.

The duke dismissed him from his mind as well as from his presence and went dreamily back to remembering his lovely mistress, Antoinette de Maignelais, whose taste in jewels had been so much superior to that of his wife Marguerite, who had never risen above enamelled pansies. Delicately, he shuddered.

4

AS HE PROGRESSED from Pontefract to Lincoln, and Lincoln to Leicester, Richard daily learned more about the rising. By the beginning of October, he knew from Jocky Howard that the men of Kent were about to break into rebellion – seemingly ahead of the appointed day, but Kentishmen were notorious for making a nuisance of themselves at a time most convenient to them.

He also knew that Buckingham was deeply committed. As he fumed for days waiting for Bishop Russell, who was indisposed, to send him the Great Seal that was needed to endorse his written commands, it was Buckingham's defection that enraged him most. 'The man who had best cause to be true to me!'

Francis said for what felt like the hundredth time, 'But you *knew* you couldn't trust him!'

'That is very different from expecting to be betrayed by him. However, one benefit of his taking the lead in this stupid affair is that it virtually guarantees me Stanley's continuing support. His hatred of Buckingham far outweighs his love, if any, for his wife and stepson.'

Stanley, indeed, made no bones about it. 'Harry Buckingham has no military experience, and he's no leader. And everybody knows it. If he manages to raise an army at all – and he's so unpopular in Wales that that in itself would be a miracle – it'll be a reluctant one. We won't have much trouble with him.'

Richard said, 'I am sure you will prove to be right, Thomas, but I have a personal preference for overestimating rather than underestimating the opposition. Jocky Howard assures me that he has the defence of London in hand, so that need not concern us now. The rebels' plan appears to be for Buckingham to cross the Severn with his Welshmen and join up with the body from the West country. Our first move should therefore be to prevent this by driving a wedge between them.'

'And you,' he told Francis afterwards, 'may have the privilege of acting as the thin end of the wedge until I am able to follow with the northern levies. I am formally issuing you with a commission of array to enable you to raise troops.'

Francis had never before held an independent military command and hoped, a little nervously, that he knew enough to justify the appointment. That Richard was prepared to invest such faith in him was, he supposed, one of the reasons why Richard had always been able to command his friendship and loyalty. Richard was unfailingly true to those whom he liked and trusted.

'I have also instructed Secretary Kendall,' Richard went on, 'to draft an order requiring proclamations against the rebels to be issued by the sheriffs of Devon, Cornwall, Shropshire, Wiltshire . . .'

'. . . Somerset, Dorset, Staffordshire and all the rest. Yes, I know. I've seen the draft. I'm not sure that leading off with a lecture on morals is the best idea.'

Richard let out an exaggerated sigh. 'Is he at that again? Well, it will just have to do. I have a great many other things to attend to, and there is little point in employing a secretary if I have to do his work myself.'

Francis shrugged. Kendall was inclined to reflect Richard's personal views rather too closely when he was drafting public pronouncements, and dragging Dorset's affaire with Mistress Shore into a proclamation against rebellion, Francis thought, verged on the farcical. Richard's detestation of Mistress Shore was a continuing mystery to him.

Constantia had said once, 'I wonder whether Richard is attracted to her? That might explain it.' But Francis had been dismissive. 'No, first she led Edward astray' – a phrase which had induced a cynical giggle from Constantia – 'and then went straight to bed with Hastings, and then with Dorset! Two dangerous men, and you must admit that the speed with which she moved from bed to bed after, first, Edward's and then Hastings's death was, at best, tasteless. Also, she has certainly been sheltering Dorset. She is a thoroughly undesirable character.'

'Anne says she is a delightful woman.'

'Anne always thinks the best of people.'

5

BUCKINGHAM raised his standard at Brecon on October 18th, according to plan.

And then the rains came.

They had begun two or three days earlier, but the Welsh were used to being rained on and no one would have thought much about it if the downpour had kept to its usual pattern. But instead of easing and becoming sporadic, it became ever heavier and more relentless. Every trickle of water on the slopes of the Black Mountains became a waterfall, every stream became a river and every river a torrent. Fords disappeared and valleys turned into lakes. Although Buckingham and his men – a much smaller force than he had hoped – did not know it, the Severn had burst its banks. The likelihood of the sodden little army linking up with the West country rebels became increasingly remote.

It was a steadily diminishing army, too. Squelching along muddy tracks that were unsuitable for armies even in fine weather, Buckingham's ramshackle levies became ever more aware that they would be better employed elsewhere, gathering fuel for their homes and bedding for their cattle, storing the beans and grain their families needed to keep them alive over the winter. In twos and threes, then tens and twenties, they began to vanish into the soaking night.

Behind them, around them and ahead of them, smaller and more mobile groups who were Buckingham's enemies and therefore Richard's allies, demolished the already swamped bridges over the upper Severn and blockaded the roads into England, and even captured Brecon castle itself.

By the time Buckingham reached Weobley in Herefordshire, where he had originally intended to declare himself king of England, he was almost alone. Soaked, exhausted, and terrified, his only thought was to hide. Bishop Morton helped him divest himself of his dripping furs and disguise himself as a farm worker, then saw him on his way to the home of an old servant at Wem in Shropshire.

Morton himself, who had fled the country once before in his Lancastrian days – in snow and ice rather than rain – prepared to make his own unobtrusive way across country to his diocese in the

Fens, where he would find shelter until he could cross the sea to Flanders and safety.

It was the wiser course.

6

AS RICHARD moved swiftly south and west, able to use the established roads which the rebels took care to avoid, the rumour of his coming ran ahead of him. The rebels who had waded through the floods and quagmires of the West country to their appointed meeting places already knew that Buckingham had failed them. Depressed and demoralised, they set watches on the coast for the arrival of Henry Tudor's fleet. But it did not come.

When Richard reached Salisbury, it was to be told that Buckingham's host, tempted by Richard's £1,000 reward for the duke's capture, had betrayed him to the sheriff and that he had been duly tried and sentenced to death.

'Before the sentence is carried out,' Catesby reported, 'the duke is most anxious that he should have an audience with you.'

'I imagine he is, but the answer is no.'

'He might have something interesting to say,' Catesby tempted him.

'If so, it would be for the first time in his life.'

Stanley weighed in. 'It'll be pleas for mercy. Why waste effort listening to him? Have his head off and be done with it.'

It almost changed Richard's mind. Was Stanley afraid that Buckingham might say something that would implicate the Lady Margaret? That *would* be interesting. It would, however, make relations with Stanley, powerful nobleman that he was, very difficult.

So he said slowly, 'No,' again. 'Let the sentence be carried out here in the market place of Salisbury. And then we must march on to Exeter.'

After that, shedding small companies of men to guard the coast along the way, they marched on to Bridport and from there to Exeter, and the rebels scattered before them with not a battle fought.

7

HENRY TUDOR had succeeded in gathering fifteen ships and five thousand men and had set sail from Brittany with a high heart. The Breton pilot had warned him, 'All will depend on the winds and tides. The Atlantic rollers that arrive from the west between the Île d'Ouessant – or Ushant, as you English call it – and your Isles of Scilly, become compressed, shorter and steeper, as they enter La Manche . . .'

'The English Channel,' Henry corrected him.

'Évidemment! But you understand what I say? Plymouth lies to the nor'-nor'-west of us here at Paimpol, so we must tack into and across these powerful, choppy waves, which we cannot do without the aid of the wind. If we are blown to leeward, as is most likely, then it will be needful to run up the Channel to the easier harbour of Poole.'

Which was well over thirty leagues to the east of where Henry wanted to be. Sea travel appeared to him to be a sadly hit-or-miss affair.

The storm broke when they were barely into open water, so that they had no choice but to heave to and pray that the ships would survive the pounding of the sea, the battering of the wind, the climbing and swooping and corkscrewing in the swells, the staggering under rogue waves. Endlessly through the wild black nights and dreary grey days that followed they could hear the creaking and groaning of the ships' fabric, as the gales blew and blew with unrelenting ferocity. The rain came down in such torrents that visibility was close to nil and it was only when the hateful wind calmed into an ordinary full gale that Henry and the pilot discovered that most of their fleet had disappeared.

'Some will have dragged their anchors,' the pilot said with a shrug. 'Some of the old two-masters may have been blown aground on the Cherbourg peninsula. The three-masters may have sought safety in more open water. What do you wish to do?'

Henry thought of Duke Francis's ten thousand golden crowns. He thought of the funds his mother had sent him. He thought of the duke of Buckingham and the others waiting for him in the West country. He thought of the throne. He knew that, if he abandoned this enterprise, it would be the end of him. Suddenly, the storm became the lesser evil.

He said, 'We still have two ships and six hundred hungry, bruised and seasick soldiers. Why are we loitering here?'

They reached the south coast of England after an eternity of thrashing along through boiling seas, to find an eventual haven in Poole harbour in the dawn.

'Let us wait to disembark,' Henry said, 'in case any others of our ships have survived to join us. In the meantime, the men can take it in turns to sleep for an hour.'

He slept himself, with gratitude, until he was awakened with the information that armed men had appeared in groups along the shore. 'Do we know who they are? Are they wearing livery, showing banners?'

'No.'

Everything about Henry Tudor's life had conspired to make

him careful and suspicious. 'Send a boat inshore,' he said, 'just close enough for the crew to converse with the men. Put my English coxswain in charge.'

From where his two battered four-masters were anchored, he could hear much shouting back and forth, the crew questioning, the armed groups talking all at once with many signs of the cross and much passionate gesticulation.

'Well?' he demanded when the boat returned.

'They *say* they're the duke of Buckingham's men,' the coxswain replied. 'They *say* the duke is on his way with the main body of his army.'

'They *say*? But you're not convinced. Why not?'

The coxswain scratched his head. 'They could be anybody's men. They were too tidy and disciplined for a rebel company. I asked where the king's army was and they said it was still in the Midlands. I asked why they were guarding the coast and they said they weren't. They said they were keeping an eye out for us — to welcome us, like.'

Henry pursed his lips. It was not very helpful.

But then the coxswain added, 'Oh, and the duke's army was supposed to be Welsh, wasn't it? Well, there isn't a Welshman among them. They all sounded like northerners to me.'

Which was decisive.

Without delay, Henry hoisted sail and set off again for Brittany.

8

'SATISFACTORY,' Richard said, as he rode back into London towards the end of November, welcomed at Kennington by the mayor and aldermen in their scarlet robes and further escorted by a troop of horsemen clothed in violet.

Superficially, the situation did seem satisfactory. The rebellion had gained no support from members of the nobility other than Buckingham and Dorset, and it had been swiftly and almost bloodlessly crushed by Richard's own swift and effective action. He could afford to be pleased with himself, even if a few pockets of rebellion still remained.

The only thing that caused him to chew abstractedly on his lip as the weeks passed was the continuing lack of news concerning the leaders of the rebels. Richard had left agents behind to track them down so that they could be brought to justice, but only one of the West country leaders had allowed himself to be caught. Richard sent out a few proclamations about succouring or harbouring rebels, but even the threat of the king's grievous displeasure was unproductive.

'God's bones! Where are they all hiding?' he demanded.

Catesby, drawing his quill through his fingers, murmured, 'Lord Stanley mentioned Brittany, sire.'

'Oh, did he? And what makes him think that?'

'I have no idea, sire.'

'Well, come back to me when you do.'

It was unnecessary, of course. Stanley was husband to Margaret Beaufort, who was mother to Henry Tudor, who had been implicated in the rebellion. And who was now back at the court of Brittany.

Margaret Beaufort was not going to escape unpunished. Neither, if Richard had any say in the matter, was Henry Tudor.

Something occurred to him. 'The bills of attainder for January's Parliament,' he said, and Catesby glanced up. 'When you are drafting them, do not give Henry Tudor's name any particular prominence. We should not imply that he is of importance in the scheme of things.'

'Indeed not.'

9

RICHARD'S STAFF worked hard at the best of times, harder than ever under the additional burdens of the rebellion and its aftermath.

The latter brought the matter of Mistress Shore once more to Richard's attention. She had been living, it transpired, with the marquess of Dorset when he was in hiding in the West country and, as a sequel, found herself once more in Ludgate gaol.

Richard sent his official solicitor, the property and tax expert Thomas Lynom, to interrogate the lady – with the most shocking result. Mr Lynom fell in love with Mistress Shore and declared his intention of marrying her. Her colourful past, he said, meant nothing to him.

Richard was deprived of speech. When he recovered, he wrote to Chancellor Russell asking him to discourage Master Lynom from his fell intent; if he failed, however, the king would make no objection, provided there was some security for the lady's future good behaviour.

As Francis said to Constantia, Richard was prepared to put up with a good deal from people he liked and trusted. Then, in response to the teasing look in his mistress's eyes, 'I mean *Lynom*, not Mistress Shore!'

10

AS KINGS were expected to do, Richard celebrated Christmas in spectacular style. There were balls and masques and carols, tourneys, endless feasting, a Lord of Misrule and a King of the Bean, travelling players, exchanges of gifts on New Year's day, hunting and hawking expeditions, and daily High Mass with the magnificent music of the chapel royal, which under Edward had acquired renown both at home and abroad. Richard, too, had always had a great love for music. And also for splendour.

Wearily, Anne said to Constantia, '*More* clothes and jewels! *More* fittings! *More* of having to change three or four times a day! I begin to feel less like a human being than a walking handbill for the mercers and goldsmiths. I dare not even contemplate what Richard, who used to be so careful about money, must be spending on all this.'

'It's necessary,' Constantia said. 'You know it's necessary. A display of wealth and luxury is essential for a king. No one believes he is powerful unless he looks it. Remember how everyone complained about what a dismal show Henry VI used to make, and how it diminished him? And, you know, Francis brought a Genoese goldsmith to show me some trinkets the other day and he was not at all impressed by the gems we wear in England. He said that, if I wanted to see *real* jewels, I should see what they wear at the courts of Burgundy and Brittany. Philip of Burgundy had a hat — just a hat! — valued at sixty thousand crowns, and Duke Francis of Brittany has so many wonderful chains and brooches and collars and belts that my goldsmith became quite incoherent. By their standards, it seems that Richard is only a beginner.'

'Oh,' Anne said, 'is he? Don't, for goodness' sake, say so to him.'

'I wouldn't dream of it.'

Afterwards, Constantia told Francis that he was going to have to speak to Richard about Anne and the state of her health.

Francis was horrified. 'Speak to him? *I* can't speak to him about that kind of thing!'

Witheringly, his mistress said, 'Well, I will.'

Richard listened patiently, although the endless interruptions by clerks, secretaries and officials did not make Constantia's task easier. In the end, he said with no great expression, 'Anne is my wife and the mother of my son, and I am much attached to her . . .'

Attached!

Constantia seethed.

Seeing the spark in her big, lustrous eyes, Richard sighed. 'You would rather I said that I loved her? Well, I do, even if I am not altogether sure what love is. If I say that there is no other woman with whom I could possibly imagine sharing my life . . . ?'

His smile could be abominably charming. Constantia said, 'Yes, that would do. But you must remember that she is not strong.'

'The physicians . . .'

'It is not a matter for physicians. You may not know what love is, but she does. And she loves *you*, and only you.'

'She loves Ned more.'

'Perhaps. But that is because he is a part of you. And also because he needs her. Do *you*?'

The silence was long. His dark grey eyes were piercing and yet curiously blank as he stared into hers. In the end, he said, 'Yes,' and meant it.

'You must tell her so.'

He pursed his lips. 'Since I took the throne, I have found it difficult to tell her anything. I don't think the fault is entirely mine. I had hoped that she would thaw, but it hasn't happened yet.'

'It won't, unless you explain!'

'Have you ever tried explaining something to someone who *will not* listen?'

He was Richard but he was also the king, so she hesitated for a moment about how much she dared to say. 'Have you really tried?

Or have you simply given up in face of her resistance? Have you been too busy to be human?'

His brows came together, and she prayed that she had not destroyed far more than she had hoped to achieve.

Then the frown lifted, and he said, 'You are a remarkable young woman, Constantia. Francis is very fortunate.'

She felt the blood rush to her face, and bent her head.

'You are right, of course,' he went on. 'It is just that' — suddenly he, too, looked exhausted, as if all the vitality were draining out of him — 'it never, ever stops. There is always so much to do. So many decisions to make. So little time.'

He signed something without looking at it, and nodded to the clerk to take it away. 'I will try,' he said again. 'Thank you, Constantia.'

11

ON CHRISTMAS DAY 1483, a small group of men rode under the Mordelaise gate into Rennes, capital of Brittany, and made for the cathedral. They were by no means as well dressed as they used to be, and some of their mounts were no more than broken-down nags, but that was because they had escaped from England with little more than the clothes they stood up in. They would have been even worse off if their number had not included several customs officers, who had had the foresight to bring their collected customs duties with them on their flight.

Among the better-known figures gathering in the side chapel were the marquess of Dorset, Sir Edward Woodville, Sir John Cheyney, and Bishop Courtenay of Exeter, who had reached Brittany even before Henry Tudor on his return voyage. But in addition to these, there was an almost more valuable group of

gentry who could boast not only extensive administrative experience in their own localities, but also close connections among
those who had been left behind. Missing was Bishop Morton of
Ely, who had landed in Flanders and declared his intention of
staying there. It was regrettable, because Henry knew from his
mother what a valuable ally Bishop Morton was.

Even so, Henry, who for almost half of his twenty-six years had
been isolated in a foreign country with no English-speaking
friends or advisers, gazed wonderingly at the able and knowledge-
able new acquaintances who were to become his court-in-exile.
Clever enough to be aware of his own ignorance of the country
he hoped to rule, Henry sent up a private prayer of thanks as, in
the cathedral, the refugees swore loyalty to one another and
declared their intention of returning to England to overthrow the
usurper.

It was excellent that they were prepared to swear loyalty to one
another, but Henry wanted more than that from them.

He did as his mother had advised. Drawing himself up to his
slender height and scanning their faces with his small blue eyes, he
declared, 'I, too, have an oath to take. Some of you have long held
faith with the House of Lancaster, of which I am the true and
sole descendant.' That was not strictly accurate, but there seemed
no need to wander off into the intricate realms of genealogy.
'Others of you were loyal servants of the House of York until the
usurper Richard murdered the infant heirs of Edward IV.

'For too long England has been scarred by the discord between
the two houses. The time, I believe, has come to put an end to it. If
anyone here would wish to rekindle the civil war between them,
let him leave now.'

No one moved.

'You will ask how unity may be achieved. I will tell you. When
we have swept away the usurper, when I become king . . .'

Turning, he knelt before the richly carved and ornamented altar, crossing his hands over his breast and raising his eyes to the crucifix surmounting it. 'When I am king of England, I swear by this holy rood that I will take the Princess Elizabeth of York to wife as my queen.'

Despite the ambient sounds of the great cathedral – the padding of feet coming and going, the preparations for Mass, the delicate tinkling of the priests' vestment bells, the jingling of the censer chains – he was still able to hear the satisfied indrawing of breath from his companions.

And then, led by Sir Edward Woodville, they were all on their knees to him, swearing homage as if he were king already.

His heart pounding against his ribs, he wished that madame his mother could have been present. She would have been proud of him.

Chapter Fourteen

1483-84

1

THE EXODUS of so many rebels from the south of the country had left Richard in a quandary he could scarcely have foreseen. The men who had gone were the natural leaders in their districts, the men who had officiated as sheriffs, stewards, constables, and crown assessors. If society were to continue to function, they had to be replaced, but too many of those who remained were related to the rebels by blood or other ties, and had to be considered politically unreliable. So Richard had to import outsiders to replace, according to Catesby's calculations, forty per cent of the principal officials in the south. The permutations of who should go where were endlessly consuming of time and parchment and effort.

But outsiders — 'strangers' — were anathema to the tightly linked traditional circles of the shires. Jocky Howard, better acquainted with the area than Richard, told him, 'Be careful. The community of the shire matters hugely to them. A Surrey man is a foreigner even in Hampshire. I remember what trouble I had myself, years ago, as a Suffolk man and a handsome young lad, being accepted as Member of Parliament for Norfolk.'

'So what are you suggesting? That I appoint no one? That I appoint men who are politically suspect? That I spend months trying to find local men who *might* be satisfactory? Or what?'

Howard shrugged his broad shoulders. 'Don't ask me. You're the clever one. I'm only saying you can expect trouble, not necessarily active, maybe no more than a rumbling of discontent. But you'll need to take it into account.'

'Thank you,' Richard said, 'though I'm not sure I'd call it helpful. Unless the administration is to grind to a halt, they'll just have to put up with outsiders, like it or not. I will have to think of some tactful way of reminding them that it's all their own fault.'

Howard's sense of humour didn't stretch to irony, and his long moustaches twitched worriedly. 'Oh, I wouldn't do that.'

Obligingly, Richard said, 'Very well. I won't.'

So, after days — in some cases weeks — of consultation with Catesby, Ratcliffe, Stanley and occasionally Francis, he imported reliable men from the north, men he could trust, and paid them lavishly with the rebels' castles and manors, even though these had not yet formally been declared forfeit by Parliament. It was to appear to the men of the south as an invasion by the northerners whom they had for so long disliked and feared.

Furthermore, pre-empting Parliament's decisions on forfeiture was to prove unpopular in many quarters, and although most people saw the sense in Richard's argument that the country could not afford the delays made inevitable by parliamentary procedure, there was still an instinctive resistance to his arbitrary way of going about it.

'They want firm and consistent government,' Richard growled to Francis at one point, 'but not as much as they want to be listened to and made to feel important.'

It was true enough. The trouble was that Richard, always

irritated by indecisiveness and exaggerated sensitivity, had now become openly contemptuous of them. Impatient to stabilise his rule and to get the country back on an even keel, with justice being done and being seen to be done, he had no time for petty-minded opposition.

Richard knew best. He always had done and, Francis thought resignedly, he always would do. It was the duty of a friend to cushion the impact.

2

RICHARD KNEW HIMSELF to be unpopular for his usurpation and his supposed murder of the princes, but he had expected resistance on those scores to have begun to die down. Six months was a long time for people to continue harbouring resentment over the crimes of their betters, especially crimes that, even in a bloodsoaked age, might offend them but had no direct impact on their lives. Richard was convinced that, when he introduced even-handed justice for all, rich and poor, the situation would improve.

In the meantime, he was gradually being brought to realise that there was an orchestrated attempt afoot to vilify him. Libellous proclamations, manifestos and placards were reported as appearing all over the country, and there was a vicious whispering campaign, a campaign of rumour and innuendo that was almost impossible to counteract since it was human nature always to believe the *first* news, and to scorn subsequent denials.

It was like fighting marsh gas.

Until he discovered who was orchestrating the campaign, and why, there was little he could do. Once, he would instinctively have put it all down to the Woodville account, but the Woodvilles had now been virtually destroyed. So – who? And why?

3

REGINALD BRAY, collecting rents at Curry Rivel, supped his host's soup with appreciation and said, 'He's brought in a Yorkshireman, I hear, to be your local sheriff. That will make life difficult for everybody; no more give and take, no more friendly concessions. They're harsh, dour men, these northerners, and their justice is harsh, too. You will have to tread warily.'

At Queen Camel, over the roast pike, he said much the same. And again, over the mutton tripe at Corfe Castle.

Meanwhile, Hugh Conway was equally busy, though less well fed, in Lincolnshire and Norfolk.

Wherever Margaret Beaufort's servants went, they emphasised the discomforts that were bound to accrue from this new northern invasion, instilling fear and unease even into those who had always stood apart from the centres of power.

4

WHEN PARLIAMENT met at the end of January, besides reiterating Richard's right to the throne and passing some useful and sensible general acts, it duly endorsed Richard's four bills of attainder against a grand total of one hundred and three rebels – noblemen, churchmen, gentlemen, yeomen, merchants, and a stray necromancer who had paid insufficient attention to what the spirits had foretold for him.

And Margaret Beaufort.

Save for the churchmen, attainder meant dispossession and the death sentence, so Margaret had been waiting with ruthlessly controlled impatience and frequent prayer to discover her fate. It was not customary in England to execute women, but with Richard one could never tell, and he had been careful to exclude her husband from the sessions that had drafted the bills of attainder.

It was, however, her husband who had saved her, as she discovered when at last she saw the attainder and was relieved of the worst of her fears.

With scornful amusement, she read the terms aloud. 'Sweet Jesu! Hear what I was accused of! *What* a mishmash.'

Reginald Bray said, 'Satisfactorily vague, however.'

'Vague? There is nothing vague about being "mother to the king's great rebel and traitor, Henry, earl of Richmond, and stirring him to come into the realm to make war".'

'Lacking the originals of your letters, it would be hard to prove anything of that in a court of law, though I am not so sure about this part concerning your dispensing "great sums of money in the city of London and elsewhere to be employed in treason". Money does not always buy silence, and men can sometimes be persuaded to talk.'

'Not, I hope, the men you employed on my behalf?'

He thought about it, his close-set eyes seeming nearly to converge as they always did when he was concentrating. After a moment, he said, 'I think not.' He wondered, however, just how much Richard knew. He must have had specific information, or he would not have proceeded with the attainder. To have Richard investigating Lady Margaret's spending was not a happy thought, when Bray had heard confidentially that he was still pursuing enquiries into the deaths of the princes.

'Good,' said Lady Margaret crisply. 'Oh, and I see I have also "conspired and imagined the destruction of the king" – which is true enough – besides "asserting and assisting Henry, duke of Buckingham, in treason". Well, "assisting" is one way of putting it, I suppose, though personally I find it insulting that I should be thought to have fulfilled a rôle inferior to that of my foolish nephew.'

Bray smiled dutifully. 'No one who knows you, my lady, could possibly believe you guilty of what you are accused of.'

Another woman might have laughed, but laughter was not Lady Margaret's style. Judiciously, she said, 'Probably not. Now, what is all this about my husband?'

'All this' was Richard guarding his back. 'The king, of his especial grace, remembering the good and faithful services that Thomas, Lord Stanley, has done and intends to do to him, and for the good love and trust that the king has in him, and for his sake, remits and forbears the great punishment of attainder of the said countess that she deserves.'

Privately, Reginald Bray knew the king to be sadly mistaken about Lord Stanley's loyalty. Stanley would almost certainly have thrown his weight on the side of the rebels if Buckingham, whom he had detested, had not taken the nominal lead. And that might have brought about a very different result. In some ways it was a pity that the Lady Margaret did not consult with her husband more often.

'However,' Lady Margaret observed, 'I see that I am not to go unpunished. All my titles and estates are to be transferred to my husband for his lifetime, and to revert thereafter to the king.'

'The Act does not specify *which* king, of course,' Bray remarked slyly, his short nose wrinkling in a smile.

Lady Margaret stared at him. 'How true! How very true! I wonder how Richard let that slip past him?'

All in all, Margaret's fate had been surprisingly lenient; a paper punishment. Even the royal council's separate ruling that her husband was to remove all her servants and to ensure that she was kept under watch so that she could not communicate with her son or plot against the king caused her no particular concern. She would continue to administer her estates as usual, and Reginald Bray and all the other upper servants on whom she relied could be nominally transferred to her husband's household.

As for communicating with her son, Stanley could try to prevent her at his peril. She did not think he would be so foolish.

5

FOR TEN long months, Elizabeth Woodville and her five daughters — ranging in age from eighteen down to three — had been cooped up in sanctuary in the Abbot's Lodging at Westminster Abbey. It had been a difficult time, claustrophobic above all, but also nerve-racking, because sanctuary was not inviolable. She did not need the increasingly sharp reminders of it from Richard, to the effect that Edward himself had violated another sanctuary years before by having a number of Lancastrian rebels dragged out from Tewkesbury Abbey and executed.

Not that Richard had any such designs in her own case, of course; he merely wished, he wrote, to impress upon her that the present situation could not continue indefinitely.

She knew it. After the failure of Buckingham's rebellion and Henry Tudor's hasty retreat to Brittany, she could see no prospect of rescue by any outside agency. The girls were becoming increasingly fretful, especially Bess, just turned eighteen, and Cis, soon to be fifteen, who should by rights have been enjoying themselves at banquets and balls but were instead condemned to sit at their stitchery or practising the lute or reading aloud from improving works. Bess had been unenthusiastic about the suggested marriage to Henry Tudor – 'What if he takes after his mother!' – but in the absence of any other young men, apart from a few servants, even Margaret Beaufort's son began to seem attractive to her.

Elizabeth herself was weary to the point of exhaustion, her days indistinguishably tedious, her nights a wakeful testament to loss and isolation.

It could not go on.

6

RICHARD STRUCK his forehead a triumphant blow with the flat of his palm.

'I cannot believe it! She is prepared to give in!'

'She?' Francis echoed, his eyes running down the paper in his own hand, the list of men who were asking for an audience with the king, a list that never seemed to grow shorter.

'The Woodville woman. Elizabeth. Dame Elizabeth Grey. Who calls herself queen dowager. My brother's unwed wife.'

'Oh, *that* "she"?'

'Yes, my boy. *That* she. It's not entirely clear from what she says whether she herself is prepared to emerge from sanctuary, but she agrees to let her daughters out into my safe keeping.' He gave a crack of laughter. 'That's a change of tone, if you like. She makes all sorts of provisos, of course. I will have to swear an undertaking before the most elevated of witnesses that I will allow no harm to come to them . . .'

'Does she specify what kind of harm she has in mind?'

Richard grinned. 'Ravishment, what else? No! No, I stand corrected. "Ravishment contrary to their wills".'

'That's quite a different matter!'

'It is, isn't it? So, if they prove to be natural wantons, I should be exempt from blame. How interesting.'

Catesby, who had been listening to this frivolous exchange with a faint air of disapproval, intervened. 'Since Dame Elizabeth's estates have been confiscated, perhaps you might ensure her own emergence by endowing her with enough money to live on.'

'What an excellent idea! If we calculate it carefully, she might be induced to take herself off to some distant part of the country where living is cheap, and cease to make a nuisance of herself here.'

Catesby sniffed. 'And you should, I believe, provide the prin-cesses with dowries and arrange suitable marriages for them.'

'Oh, I shall certainly do that. If I can marry Bess off, it will wreak havoc with Henry Tudor's plans. It will be the end of all his talk about reuniting the houses of York and Lancaster, and he will stand exposed as merely a Lancastrian claimant to a Yorkist throne. Without Bess, he will lose most of his support.'

Francis sighed blissfully. 'What a pleasant thought! Now all we have to do is find a suitable husband. No, don't look at *me*. Constantia wouldn't like it.'

7

IT WAS weeks since Constantia had lectured Richard about the need to explain himself to Anne, and he had been waiting for a propitious moment ever since. With his brain constantly at full stretch dealing with administrative and political problems, it was peculiarly difficult to persuade it to change focus and confront the personal, anxious as he was to do so. And on the all too rare occasions when he had been in the right frame of mind and Anne had looked as if she might be, too, some crisis or other had blown up to forestall him.

When they set out in early March on a progress through the Midlands, however, he made up his mind that an opportunity *must* be found. It failed to present itself at Cambridge, where he bestowed privileges on the university and Anne presented endow, ments to Queen's College. Nor were their next two halts any more productive, since Anne was uncharacteristically worn out by the travelling. The weather was cold, damp and depressing and, since they expected to be moving mainly by established roads, she had chosen to use her carriage whenever possible, a splendid affair with a gaily painted body and a hood consisting of a cloth-of-gold canopy stretched over hoops. Unfortunately, the wheels had iron tyres so that, despite her mountains of cushions, she was bumped about unmercifully. She complained that even her bones were rattling.

But at last they reached Nottingham, where Richard had decided they should spend some weeks. The Scots were being troublesome, and if he had to go to the Borders in person, Nottingham was a reasonably convenient place from which to set out. It was also a pleasant place now that the privy lodging, begun by Edward, had been completed.

Anne brightened up considerably. 'What an improvement since we were here last July! I know that Edward was too fond of comfort, but there is something to be said for it after all. And the light from these big windows makes an immense difference.'

Richard said, 'I am pleased that you are pleased. Let us enjoy ourselves, just for once.'

'Yes.'

He had thought he could afford to allow her time to unwind, and she did indeed begin to. But after two weeks, she was fretting about Ned, who had not written to her as Nurse Idley usually encouraged him to do. 'I am uneasy about him. I think I should pay a quick visit to Middleham.'

'No bad news?' he asked quickly.

She smiled. 'Just a brief message from Nurse. The usual thing. He is perfectly well, but tires easily and is pining for his mother. I should go. I want to go. You don't need me to be stately and queenly for the next few days, do you?'

'No. I just need you to be yourself.'

He said it gently, intimately, and she felt her heart flutter with shock and longing for the times when there had been no reservations between them, the times that had seemed so irrevocably lost.

'Don't go,' he went on. 'Not at once. A day or two more will make no difference.'

8

THAT NIGHT, as she settled down in her elegant fourposter with its hangings of sapphire velvet embroidered with the white roses of York, she heard Richard's footsteps on the spiral staircase descending from his chamber to hers.

Even in his furred bedgown, he was shivering as he entered, and she said lightly, 'I wish there were some way of heating the staircase. Stone stairs are always so cold.' Then, to the two chamberwomen who shared the truckle bed in the corner of her room, 'Leave us, please. I shall not need you.' Curtseying low, they backed decorously out of the chamber, although they would clearly have preferred to turn and scuttle. Anne had almost forgotten that they had been with her for only a few months and had never before encountered the king in his bedgown. The *evil* king in his bedgown.

Anne hated the reputation he had acquired. People were so

uncharitable, so determined to think the worst. So inventive in attributing crimes to him that he had not committed, and inflating minor misjudgements into major iniquities. His own actions in the weeks after Edward's death, when he had behaved with uncharacteristic ruthlessness, had, of course, set the pattern.

She said, 'You're shivering. Come into bed.'

But instead he hitched himself up to sit on its high edge. 'No, I'm not cold.' Reaching out to take her hand, he held it in his. 'Last time I came to your bed, you were not happy. And neither was I.'

It had been the night of his coronation, nine long months ago.

Once, she would have dropped her gaze and said, 'I behaved foolishly. It meant nothing.' Now, she looked straight at him, blue eyes fixed compellingly on grey. 'There was too much wrong between us.'

'You were over-tired.'

'Yes, but it wasn't just tiredness of the body. It was tiredness of the mind and heart. I felt shut out from all that had been going on.'

He turned her hand over and studied the lines on her palm. The life line was frighteningly short, but palmistry, he reassured himself, was no more than a distillation of old wives' tales. 'I should have found the time to explain to you what I was doing, and why.'

'That might have helped. But I would still have objected, and you would not have liked that.'

He gave an odd little laugh, and then said sombrely, 'No. I would not have liked it. But I might have been wise to listen. I would have made fewer enemies.'

There was a long silence, with no sound but the rustle of half-burned logs settling on the hearth. The flames of the vigil

354

candles rose straight and true, and the scent of beeswax soothed the spirit.

'I still don't know what I could have done differently. The Woodvilles wanted my life, and Hastings sold out to them . . .'

'Are you quite sure about that?'

He looked up at her. 'You're as bad as Francis. Yes, I'm sure.'

'Why?'

'The Woodvilles wanted to rule. They wanted all power for themselves.'

'Yes. But Lord Hastings?'

'He was a good friend to Edward, but he was an acquisitive man and made immense profit from that friendship. And now he was being offered all my possessions in the north in exchange for supporting the Woodvilles. The temptation was too great for him.'

'How did you find out?'

'He told Catesby. He thought of Catesby as one of his acolytes, one of his warmest and most dedicated admirers.'

'Warmth and Catesby do not seem to me to go together. I confess that I don't like the man.'

Richard shrugged. 'He is efficient and has an excellent brain.'

'But to betray Hastings, who trusted him!'

'You think he should have betrayed me instead, by remaining silent?'

'I suppose not.' She withdrew her hand and nestled under the coverlet. 'I have heard it said that executing Rivers and Richard Grey and Lord Hastings without trial was no better than murder. Could you not have done things legally, in court?'

'I could not have been sure what a court would decide. Relationships and money and estates have too great an influence on justice. I hope to change that with new laws.' His voice suddenly became intense. 'What you must realise is that I was fighting a war, and war cannot take account of the niceties.

Without decisiveness, there can be no victory.'

'And in war,' she said, 'the element of surprise is important. You cannot afford to let the enemy guess what you are likely to do.'

His expression lightened at her understanding, but she could almost have wept. Certainly, she could not say that she still thought he had been wrong in what he had done.

She turned back the coverlet and said, 'Come to bed.'

Suddenly, he remembered something Constantia had told him. Had told him to say to Anne. So he said it, and he meant it.

'There is no other woman with whom I could possibly imagine sharing my bed or my life. I need you. I really need you.'

It wasn't, perhaps, as much as she might have hoped for, but it was more than he had ever offered her before.

She felt all her muscles go into spasm at his first touch, but it was a spasm of anticipated pleasure. He was gentle with her, and careful, and controlled until the last climactic moments, when the excitement overcame them both with the suddenness and completeness of an avalanche.

As they lay afterwards in peaceful fulfilment, she said dreamily, 'We used to laugh when we made love.' It was a comment rather than a complaint, and Richard took it as such.

'We will laugh tomorrow night,' he said.

And they did. And on the night after that.

But it was to be many weeks before they were able to laugh again.

9

RICHARD returned to his own bed at midnight, as he always did, and woke with reluctance in the small hours to the voice of his personal chaplain.

Father Dukett, always mournful-looking, bore a paper in his hand and, in the candlelight, seemed to a drowsy Richard to look even more mournful than usual.

'*Si bona de manu dei suscipimus,*' he began, but Richard interrupted. 'In English, please. I am not sufficiently awake to think in Latin.'

There was some crisis, obviously, but he could not imagine what crisis among the clergy could justify his confessor's intruding on him before the ceremonial awakening at the hour of prime.

'If we receive good things from the hand of God,' Father Dukett began again, 'why should we not also sustain misfortune?'

Richard sat up sharply. 'What *is* it, Father?'

The shock was unbelievable, intolerable, unsustainable. A messenger had come from Middleham. The prince of Wales, after a brief illness, had gone to God.

Little Ned. The cherished son. The beloved child.

Richard threw back his head and a terrible groan burst from him as Father Dukett pattered on, in Latin again, about the love of God and God's mercy, which Richard had never before doubted.

'Go away!' he gasped. 'Go away! What does a celibate priest know of *human* love? Send someone to bring the queen to me. Go!'

Anne, told only that the king required her presence urgently, ran up the spiral stairs, losing a slipper on the way and having to go back for it. Breathless when she reached his room, she was terrified to find him groaning and beating his fist against his forehead. 'What is it? Are you ill?'

He could not tell her gently through his own misery, though he tried.

The blood drained from her face, but she did not cry out or give way to tears. After a frozen moment, she put her arms round him and said all the things she knew friends would say to *her*, the sensible, spiritual words of comfort that would have no comfort in them.

'You must not. You must not be like this. We were fortunate to have our son with us for so long. Many children die in the first two years of their life, but Ned had eight happy, loving years. He will be spared all the dangers and heartbreak that come with longer life . . .' Her voice choked. 'He *is* in a better place. We should rejoice for him. Richard, you must not grieve so. I cannot bear to see it.'

Trying to calm him kept her own agony at bay until, in the end, she left him and went back to her chamber, where her head whirled and her legs refused to support her and she collapsed on to the hard stone floor in a dead faint.

10

FOR THE better part of a week, Richard refused to see or speak to anyone, but sat staring emptily out of the great windows of the privy lodging searching for omens as the landscape began to burst into spring. Little Ned had died on the very same day as Edward, a year ago. Richard could not tell whether there was any meaning to be read into that.

Several times daily, he walked heavily downstairs, like an old man, to Anne's chamber where she lay in bed seemingly detached from the world. She did not smile when she saw him, but clasped the hand he held out to her, and seemed to welcome his kiss on her forehead.

She said nothing.

She had retreated into herself. Not even to Constantia could she put her thoughts into words. She had sensed that Ned needed her, but had stayed at Nottingham for the sake of her husband's love.

She *could* have been with her son in his last hours. She *should* have been with her son in his last hours.

She thought she would never overcome the guilt of it.

11

IT WAS Francis who went racing off to Middleham to ensure that the embalming was carried out correctly. It was Francis who had to arrange for the funeral and for the tomb. It was Francis who was pursued by messages from Richard requiring him to investi-gate every circumstance of his son's death, because his meditations had led him to suspect that his son might have been poisoned by his father's enemies. But Francis could not doubt Nurse Idley's tearful assurances that the boy, whose chest had always been weak, had had a bad attack brought on by the dreadful weather and had 'coughed his little heart out, poor innocent!'

The world had to go on, and after the first week Richard plunged into a mind-distracting orgy of activity. From Notting-ham by way of Pontefract and York, he and a haunted Anne went to Middleham to bury their child and say Masses for his soul. Anne could not face a great public display in York Minster, and neither, if the truth were told, could Richard, who was just beginning to confront the fact that he had lost not only his son, but his heir.

It was a dangerous thing for a king to be without an heir, appearing to others, as it did, to augur a war of succession when he died. But Richard was still only thirty-one and Anne would celebrate her twenty-eighth birthday in June. It was perfectly possible that she might conceive again if they were able to live more normally as husband and wife without the separations that had always marked their life together.

Whether by good or ill fortune, they found themselves with a distinguished guest during their first days back at Middleham, a short, stout, ambassador from the Holy Roman emperor. Count Nicholas von Poppelau's eccentric conversation was a welcome relief from the ordinary gossip of the court, even if his accent — whether in English, French or Latin — was by no means easy to follow. He was not sufficiently familiar with English affairs to recognise that the king's strongly expressed wish that he might fight the Turk had less to do with crusading instinct than a suspicion that the Turk would be easier to deal with than the nobility and gentry of England. The count went away well satisfied with ten days of royal hospitality. The king had been wonderfully gracious to him and had presented him with a golden chain, the customary gift to foreign ambassadors. And the music of the chapel royal had been superb.

Leaving Anne at Middleham with the staunch and patient Constantia for company, Richard and his retinue soon set off for Durham and then Scarborough, to settle naval matters to do with the continuing war against Scotland. The duke of Albany was still in Richard's retinue and, optimistic as ever, was plotting a new invasion of his homeland. He had handed over the east coast fortress of Dunbar to an English garrison and James III was busily besieging it while at the same time demanding peace talks with Richard.

Then it was back to York, and then Pontefract, and then Sandal, to set up a Council of the North as a subsidiary of the royal council at Westminster — which annoyed Harry Percy, who had thought he was going to have things all his own way — and then York again, and Scarborough, and Pontefract and Nottingham.

During all this scurrying around, which drove several of Richard's older councillors — not to mention the servants responsible for packing and unpacking their baggage — to the brink of revolt, he found time to conclude a well-publicised truce of friendship with Brittany which included an unpublicised clause designed to neutralise Henry Tudor.

Lord Stanley happened to learn about the secret clause, and happened to mention it to his wife, the Lady Margaret Beaufort, Henry Tudor's mother, who happened to be just about to send her confessor and secret agent, Christopher Urswick, to consult with Bishop Morton in Flanders.

12

THE LITTLE COLONY of exiles, attached to the Breton court at Vannes, had been managing not too badly. Duke Francis had been paying monthly allowances to the marquess of Dorset, Edward Woodville and one or two others, and had also contributed a lump sum of over £3,000 to the colony as a whole, which now, taking comings and goings into account, averaged about four hundred. Rebels who had escaped Richard's attainders or been granted pardons had begun slipping unobtrusively away from the south of England to join Henry and, with time to plan their flight, had sensibly come laden with money and jewels. It helped.

And then, one day, a marvellously clean and tidy English priest rode in over the drawbridge, as unruffled as if he had not just ridden almost four hundred miles in haste and a heat wave, and enquired in excellent French where he might find Henri Tudor, comte de Richemond.

He was directed to a house in the centre of the town, a modern, half-timbered house overhanging the street close by the majestic old cathedral of St-Pierre whose many-voiced bells rang out the *sanctus* just as he arrived. Like everyone else in sight, he dismounted and dropped to his knees for a solemn, silent minute until the bells tolled again and secular life could be resumed.

Inside the high-ceilinged room on the first floor he found Henry Tudor holding court, a tall, slender young man with small, widely set blue eyes and thin, shoulder-length fair hair under a velvet skullcap of a blue that came daringly close to royal purple. His short, pleated velvet tunic, also verging on the purple, showed off a fine pair of legs clad in black satin hose. Henry, it seemed, had an eye for fashion and sufficient personal funds to indulge it.

The same could not be said for his companions, most of them older than he and as provincial in their dress as in their outlook. The only exception was Queen Elizabeth's son, the marquess of Dorset, as handsome and arrogant as Dr Urswick remembered him from the court of his stepfather, though not quite as well-furbished as he had been then. There was an ill-mended tear in one of his leg-o'-mutton sleeves.

All present bowed at the entrance of the churchman in his somewhat creased cope, a garment so ill-suited to journeying that Dr Urswick had carried it all the way in his saddlebag and slipped it over his riding dress only outside the walls of Vannes.

'Welcome, father,' said Henry eagerly. 'You come from my lady mother?'

'Not directly, sire. Your lady mother has been forbidden by the king to communicate with you, so she has instead communicated with our revered Bishop Morton in Flanders, with whom I in turn have been in communication. I do, therefore, have loving messages for you which I will give you in private. I have other messages, too, from Bishop Morton.'

Henry was not yet sufficiently royal in his habits to order his courtiers away with a simple wave of the hand. Instead, he smiled at them apologetically and said, 'Will you leave us alone, please?'

362

They moved away, not without reluctance. Messages from Bishop Morton meant news from the outside world, for which they yearned.

Dr Urswick hastened through Lady Margaret's messages to her son – which were of the order of 'my beloved son, all my worldly joy, my own sweet and most dear prince' – with some embarrassment, even disapproval. In his view, her ladyship's attitude to the young man came hazardously close to idolatry.

Henry Tudor, however, appeared to have no objections on that front. 'How kind!' he exclaimed, his eyes sparkling and his smile wide, displaying the black and gappy teeth which he usually tried to keep hidden behind pursed lips. 'What a gracious lady my mother is!'

'Indeed,' Urswick agreed. 'But I have news for you of a different import.'

'From Bishop Morton?'

'Yes. I am instructed to tell you that you are in danger.'

The young man's eyebrows rose and his voice was suddenly haughty as he said, 'I am always in danger.'

'But this danger is specific and must be acted upon. If you do not escape from Brittany very soon – *very* soon – you will find yourself delivered into the hands of Richard of England.'

Henry paled. 'Impossible! Duke Francis would never permit it.'

'You know best, of course. But it seems that, more and more, the duke is temporarily incapacitated, a fact that is better known abroad than it is here in Brittany. Peter Landois rules in his stead and it was he who, tiring of the English navy's privateering against Brittany – Richard's revenge for Duke Francis's assistance to you last autumn – finally agreed to a truce containing a secret clause.'

Resignedly, Henry said, 'Tell me.'

363

'Landois has nothing against you personally, it seems, but Richard's offer was too tempting for him to turn down. There were certain financial inducements for Landois himself plus a thousand English archers to help defend the duchy against French ambitions, and all that Richard required in exchange was for you to be handed over to him.'

Henry was uneasily silent, then, 'You are sure about this? I have seen nothing lately to make me feel threatened.'

'Your first warning is likely to be your last – the arrival of a large body of men-at-arms.'

'Jesu! What should I do?' The young man's eyelashes were fluttering like oriflammes in the wind, and Dr Urswick deduced that making independent decisions in a hurry was not one of his talents.

'Bishop Morton has made some suggestions which he wished me to transmit to you.'

'Has he? Oh, thank God! Tell me.'

'He believes that you should escape to France, where you will be welcomed.'

'Will I? Is he sure? I feel like a perpetual pawn in the chess game of Europe. France wants Brittany. No one else wants France to *have* Brittany, because it would upset the balance of power. England is prepared to support Brittany. Therefore France will grasp at anything – or anyone – that might be used to embarrass or disrupt England and thus weaken Brittany's situation. Though I cannot see what use the French are likely to make of me.'

Quietly, Dr Urswick suggested, 'They might be persuaded to disrupt England by assisting in an invasion, with you to lead it.'

The small blue eyes were startled, and then became calculating. 'They might, I suppose. But how do I escape to France?'

'Send me ahead to prepare them for your arrival and, in the

meantime, construct a plan that will enable you to cross the border without being caught.'

Henry sighed. 'Easier said than done. I cannot go alone. I cannot abandon my friends. They must come too. They are under attainder and Richard wants them almost as much as he wants me. It will be death for *all* of us if we are caught and handed over to him.'

'The means are for you to decide. But whatever you choose to do, it must be done soon. Every day that passes increases the risk.'

13

HENRY was impressed by Dr Urswick, who had the air of authority and probity he would have expected from a priest who was his lady mother's confessor, so he accepted what the good doctor said without argument.

Reflecting on the physical challenges of escaping from Brittany to France, however, he hesitated as to whom he should consult. It was not that he feared his plans leaking out if too many of his followers knew about them, just that he could scarcely make an unobtrusive escape with four hundred men at his back. Choosing who should go with him was bound to be invidious and productive of time-consuming argument, but it would be poor tactics to arrive in France without a sizeable entourage of men of rank.

So he consulted only his uncle, Jasper Tudor, who had been with him off and on for most of his time in Brittany, and the marquess of Dorset, whose astuteness he had come to respect even if he disliked his airs and graces.

'How do we get our friends out of Vannes?' he demanded.

Between them, they worked out a solution. Duke Francis, lucid or not, was currently residing at a château close to the border with

Anjou in the east. No one at Vannes would be surprised if a deputation of Henry's titled followers were to ride out next day to see him, with the declared intention of pleading Henry's cause; Henry and his begging bowl had become tediously familiar to the Vantois in the course of the years. The deputation would be led by Jasper Tudor, who knew the countryside well enough to be able to skirt the duke's residence and lead his charges along byways and bridle paths towards the border and a crossing into Anjou.

To lend conviction to all this, Henry himself would remain behind in Vannes with the rest of his followers for two days, before making his own bid for freedom.

He spent the intervening days pretending to cast his accounts, a favourite occupation for a young man with an analytical turn of mind, but found it impossible to concentrate. He was up and down from his stool every five minutes, marching across to stand gazing out of the window on the lookout for danger, alternately cracking his knuckles and chewing his cuticles until the most obtuse of observers could have guessed that something was afoot. Fortunately, the only witnesses to this display of nerves were his household servants, Bretons all, who even at the best of times thought the English a very peculiar people.

It was a characteristically soft morning, mild but with the air full of a fine misty rain, when he set out, ostensibly to visit an acquaintance at a nearby manor, with only two pages and three grooms for company. There were a good many travellers over the first league or so, who had to be nodded or bowed to, but after that the landscape became more wooded and the road emptier, so that it was not difficult for Henry and his attendants to vanish among the trees.

'Quickly! *Vite, vite!*' said Henry, gesticulating at the tallest of the grooms who obediently began to strip off his sheepskin waistcoat, his grey cloth tunic and baggy grey leggings, while Henry divested himself of his own russet velvet doublet and neatly tailored brown woollen hose. The exchange did not take long, although Henry jibbed at the first feel of warm, sweaty, coarse cloth against his skin.

At the last minute, just as he and the groom who was to guide him were about to ride off towards the border, he remembered to tell the other four that on no account must they return to Vannes before sundown. The appearance of a groom wearing his master's clothes would all too clearly advertise that Henry Tudor had taken flight.

He was later to learn that they had disobeyed his order, but the troops sent after him were an hour behind and by the time they reached the border he was already safe in Anjou and changing back into the more princely garments that his Uncle Jasper had been carrying in his saddlebag. It would never do to turn up at the supercilious court of France looking like a peasant.

14

RICHARD'S years of experience had taught him that there were few people he could trust to do things as he wanted them done, and now that he was king there were even fewer — Francis Lovell, William Catesby, Richard Ratcliffe, Jocky Howard, and a handful of other tough and conscientious men.

It made for hard feelings when, himself overburdened with work, he left things to them rather than to Thomas Stanley or Harry Percy. It meant that, when blame was being apportioned by ill-informed outsiders — as it inevitably was — Richard and his small group of intimate advisers were the ones who took the brunt of it.

Trusting so few people also meant that Richard had no high

REAY TANNAHILL

expectations in his dealings with foreigners, so he was not surprised to learn, as he very soon did, that Henry Tudor and the more distinguished of his supporters had eluded capture by the Bretons and escaped to an enthusiastic welcome at the court of France.

'And as if that were not enough,' he complained, 'it seems that Duke Francis promptly recovered his wits sufficiently to order that the lesser gentry whom Tudor had chosen to leave behind at Vannes should be conducted, at the duke's personal expense and with all consideration for their comfort, to join Tudor at Angers.'

Francis laughed and, responding to Richard's withering glare, said, 'Well, it *is* funny.'

'In other circumstances I might see the humour of it, but at present I do not. French support for Tudor is far more dangerous than continued Breton support would have been. I wonder what precipitated Tudor's flight? Someone, it seems, must have been talking.'

Francis, serious again, said, 'Stanley?' As so often recently, he had only been trying to lighten the atmosphere; clutching at straws. There had been nothing in Richard's private or public life amenable to being laughed at since Ned had died, and Francis considered it banefully unhealthy for Richard and everyone else. But there was danger on every side, and he was learning that there was nothing he could do to alleviate Richard's dark mood.

'In my brother's day,' Richard said, 'Henry Tudor was an isolated figure who posed no real threat. Now he does. Now he has a following, and a following consisting of perhaps three or four hundred very effective men whose flight has been the cause of most of our recent difficulties. Just because they involved them-selves in a stupid rebellion doesn't mean that I am unable to appreciate their worth as administrators. With French money and troops, who knows what they might achieve?'

'They didn't achieve success in the rebellion,' Francis pointed

368

out helpfully, but Richard merely looked at him.

'No,' he said flatly. 'But they might as well have done. We have had nothing but trouble since. However, let us get on with guarding our backs.'

James III of Scotland had sent ambassadors to Nottingham to discuss a truce, and much though it went against the grain for Richard to concede anything to the Scots, he recognised the necessity of it. Fending off the Scots in the north while at the same time having to fend off Henry Tudor in the south was not a prospect that commended itself.

By a happy chance, England had already been relieved of the presence of the duke of Albany, who had attacked the Scots border town of Lochmaben and, being defeated, had fled not to England but, for a change, to France. All that marred the negotiations, therefore, was a grand oration by James's chief secretary, Archibald Whitelaw, who extolled Richard's great mind and remarkable powers in the most elegant Latin, taking care to explain the meaning of an intrusive word in Greek – 'just in case', as Richard remarked afterwards, 'my great mind might be having a day of rest.'

He, having no time to waste, was curt and businesslike, so a three-year truce was soon agreed, and a marriage arranged between James's elder son and heir and the daughter of Richard's sister, Elizabeth. Open war with Scotland could now give way to soothing plotting and counterplotting, while Richard and his council turned their minds to more important matters.

15

SECRETARY WHITELAW had said that Richard's 'most cele-brated reputation for the practice of every form of virtue' had reached into every corner of the world; that, just as remarkable, was the excellent and outstanding humanity of his innate benevolence, his clemency, his liberality, his good faith, his supreme justice, and his incredible greatness of heart.

It was not an assessment of the king that anyone who had spoken to Reginald Bray or any other of the busy members of Margaret Beaufort's household would have recognised. Bray, without a quiver, represented Richard as 'a homicidal and unnatural tyrant', a new King Herod, a murderer of 'innocent babes'. Increasingly, too, he spread doubts about Richard's title to the throne and publicised Henry Tudor's determination to 'recover' the crown.

Word of mouth was the disseminator of most news throughout the countryside, so that the gossip spread, and spread. To justify Henry Tudor, Richard had to be completely discredited.

Chapter Fifteen

1484-85

1

ANNE burst into tears. 'I can't. I cannot go back. I cannot face it all.' The tears subsided into sobs, and the sobs, in turn, into a hard, dry, shallow cough.

Constantia did not say, 'Are you all right?'

All too clearly, Anne was not all right and had not been all right since Ned died. With no weight to lose, she had lost weight. She had no energy. She complained of not sleeping at night. And now Richard said it was time she returned to court and took up her duties again. The court needed its queen – and he needed his wife.

But the court was still at Nottingham. 'Anywhere else!' Anne gasped. 'But I *cannot* be a wife to him there, of all places. How could I share his bed *there*?' Constantia could almost feel the shudder that ran through her, from the top of her pale blonde head to the soles of her small, neat feet.

Patiently, Constantia said, 'Ned would have died, whether you were at his side or not.'

Anne threw a desperate look at her. 'Would he? *Would* he? How can you tell?'

'How can I tell, when I know nothing of being a mother?' It was the only sadness of her life with Francis. 'I can't tell, of course, but it is medical knowledge, not motherly love, that saves lives. If it were otherwise, there are many men now dead who would still be alive today.'

'You are right, I know you are right, but' – Anne's voice rose to a wail – 'it makes no difference. I should have known! I should have known! I should have been with him when he needed me. My child, my child!'

In the end, she was persuaded that she must try to conquer her misery and return to Richard. 'But not at Nottingham! Not until he goes back to Westminster or Windsor. Then I *will* share his bed, because I know' – she tilted her chin valiantly – 'I know we must try to have another son, so that Richard will have the heir he needs.'

Constantia hugged her fearfully. For Anne to conceive another child would probably kill her.

2

RICHARD'S COUNCIL was as anxious as his queen that he should leave Nottingham, but Richard was obsessed by the need to remain at the geographical centre of his kingdom, from which he could move swiftly to meet any invasion by Henry Tudor, wherever it might make its landfall. Only when the beginning of winter put an end to the sailing season was he prepared to go south again.

Time after time, meeting in private conclave, his inner circle of advisers told him the same thing.

'The north,' Catesby pointed out, 'is already faithful to you. You do not need to woo it. You should be concentrating your attention on the south.'

'I am aware of that.'

'But it is almost November and you have been in the south only once since March.'

A beam of chill sunlight burst through the clouds, and Richard blinked slightly. Catesby's taste in clothes was always a sorrow to his associates and today he was wearing a satin tunic in goose-turd green, together with scarlet hose. Averting his eyes, Richard replied, 'Yes, when I moved the hallowed remains of Henry VI from Chertsey to Windsor. He was a saintly man, and it was the right thing to do. It made, I believe, a powerful impression in the south.'

'Possibly, on some people,' Catesby said, his small, down-turned mouth turning down even further, 'but there was another, less favourable view.'

Richard was impatient. 'You mean, I was thought to be salving my conscience over having killed him in the first place? Which, of course, I did not. Evil minds beget evil rumours, and it is the public habit to see denial as merely lending credence to rumour. I find it mystifying. However, I accept your point about giving more attention to the south.'

Ratcliffe said, 'Aye, and to the knights and gentry in particular. They're the ones who play upon the feelings of ordinary folk.'

'True. And those who were the staunchest of Edward's supporters have been conspicuously less favourable towards me than his supporters among the peers.'

'You could,' Francis volunteered, 'buy favour with a more lavish distribution of titles.'

'To whom? I have been cautious about creating new peers because I see very few suitable candidates, and most of those are northerners. If I am to buy friendship, I want it to be dependable.'

Ratcliffe, his red hair standing belligerently on end, said, 'Better to punish enemies than buy friends. It would not do harm to remind folk that lack of friendship can lead to royal retribution. Deterrence, it's called, and making an example wouldn't go amiss.'

'Collingbourne?'

William Collingbourne had been in treasonable correspondence with Henry Tudor, urging him to invade, and claiming that the people of England would rise in arms and help him defeat and displace the unnatural tyrant Richard. For this, he was to be tried at the Guildhall before nine peers and five justices, and would almost certainly be found guilty and condemned to a traitor's death by hanging, drawing and quartering.

Richard had the option of commuting this brutal, traditional punishment into simple death by the axe, but treason was not Collingbourne's only crime. The man had been a member of the Duchess Cicely's household, which made his treachery personal as well as political.

He had also been responsible for a widely circulated lampoon ridiculing Richard and his advisers:

> The Cat, the Rat, and Lovell the Dog
> Rule all England under a Hog.

Everyone knew who was meant – *Cat*esby, *Rat*cliffe, Francis (whose emblem was a dog) and Richard (whose emblem was the white boar). It was neither funny, nor clever; just vulgarly offensive. But ridicule was one of the most potent of weapons.

Richard said, 'Yes, if he is found guilty, he must pay the full penalty. Now let us consider renewal of the commissions of array. It is necessary to remind commissioners, captains and people that the danger is by no means over and that we need to be assured of the number of men committed to the defence of the country and that they will be horsed, harnessed and armed, and ready to stand to at half a day's notice . . .'

3

THE DANGER was not over, but it was far from imminent, since Henry Tudor, now attached to the French court at Montargis, had found himself having to embark all over again on convincing a foreign ruler that he deserved both support and money. Charles VIII, the new king of France, was a sickly thirteen-year-old dominated by his elder sister, Anne de Beaujeu.

'A boy, and a woman years younger than I am!' Henry complained to the marquess of Dorset. 'How can one talk to such people?'

'How *did* you talk to them?'

'I spoke of myself as the rightful king and explained that the nobility of England, who abhor Richard's tyranny, have called on me to return to my kingdom. I said that, with France's aid, I would hope to do so.'

'Mentioning, of course, that French aid *now* would also buy a guarantee of peace with England in years to come?'

'Of course.'

'And?'

'And Charles made vague promises but said that, in France's present state of political uncertainty, he did not believe that his government would see its way to providing me with tangible assistance in the immediate future. His sister, I may add, had the impertinence to remark that France would not be prepared to back any invasion of England likely to be as ineffectual as my Breton-backed expedition of last year. For her to criticise my military competence! What does she know about it?'

Dorset thought, not much perhaps. But she was a *very* good-looking woman. He sighed lustfully.

And then the situation was transformed. The earl of Oxford – he whose mother Richard still remembered as a fount of tears and lapdogs – escaped from the fortress of Hammes, where he had been imprisoned for the previous ten years, and came to join Henry, bringing with him the captain of Hammes castle and, in the end, its garrison as well. Experienced fighting men all, they were just what Henry needed to make his ambitions look convincing even to the king's beautiful but disdainful sister.

4

WHEN ANNE rejoined Richard at Westminster not long before Christmas, her eyes were bright and there was colour in her cheeks, but she stiffened as he leaned forward to embrace her.

Later, when they were no longer surrounded by people, she said she was well enough, thank you, and how was he?

He, too, was well enough, thank you.

Each of them knew the other to be lying, but both shied away from following it up. The truth would emerge, in time.

He said, 'I have decreed – and I hope you approve – that we should celebrate Christmas in the finest style. We have been taking life too seriously, and we need gaiety, frivolity. We need to enjoy ourselves.'

She was standing before the fire massaging her chilled fingers. It had been a long, cold, wearisome journey from Middleham and she thought she would never be warm again. She said, 'We can try.'

Richard's mobile brows rose over the dark grey eyes. The creases in his forehead had deepened perceptibly in the preceding months. 'Is this *my* Anne speaking? I cannot believe it.'

She had been allowing herself to wallow in her misery for too long. She knew it, and that it was time to do her duty again. 'I'm sorry. Yes, let us by all means enjoy ourselves. How shall we go about it?'

He put his arm round her shoulders. 'The banquets are arranged, and the tournaments, the mummers, and the music. So are the displays and entremets. We have a mechanical dragon, with live birds flying from its mouth. And a Noah's Ark on wheels, with the animals singing motets and playing flutes. And silver ships similarly on wheels, that can be steered by the esquires and pages. And other things of the sort.'

'How exciting.'

His mouth twitched. 'You consider them childish?'

'A little.'

'There is a reason. I believe that the court is too middle-aged. We need young people to bring uncomplicated life and vitality to it. I want you to make it your task to find a sufficiency of youthful knights and squires to light everything up. I have already . . .'

'Yes?'

'I have already sent for John and Katherine.'

His bastard children, now fifteen and fourteen, whom he had sired in his salad days, before his marriage to Anne. She had come to know them well, and liked them, although they had always been quartered at Sheriff Hutton, not Middleham. Richard had recently created John – 'my Lord Bastard' – titular Captain of Calais, and Katherine was newly married to the earl of Huntingdon.

Anne said, 'Well, that's a beginning.'

'And I have also sent for the princesses Elizabeth and Cicely.'

'What? Two *more* bastards?'

Her tone was not as light as she had intended it to be, and

Richard frowned. 'They are nice girls and, I would guess, bright and lively when they are out of range of their mother. I expect you to make an effort to be kind to them, and treat them as members of the family.'

'Of course.'

'And, by the way, I have told Francis to take himself and Constantia off to Minster Lovell as soon as possible. I've told him I don't want to see his face again for at least three months.'

'Has he done something wrong?'

'On the contrary. For months, they have had no life of their own and I think, although Francis denies it, that we have been leaning too much on them.'

Almost inaudibly, she said, 'Without Constantia, I think I should have gone mad. But you are right about them needing time together. It is considerate of you.'

He laughed, and took her hand in a sustaining grip. 'Don't sound so surprised. I can do it when I try.'

5

CHRISTMAS DAY was marked by a special Mass and a banquet that began at an earlier hour than usual, to compensate for the fast of the day before. There were carols and masques, with lesser members of the court disguised in lion and elephant and dragon masks. There were performing bears, too – real ones – and acrobats, fools, and jugglers. There was a Nativity play in the chapel. And there was dancing – not only the formal and stately *basse dance* but merry country jigs. Outside the gates every day, a mob of the poor and not-so-poor stood watching the comings and goings while impatiently awaiting distribution of the leftovers from the royal tables.

As the Twelve Days wore on, the company became more relaxed, and on New Year's Day, the day of gift-giving, the younger members ran wild, chasing the trinkets that had been hidden for them in the great rooms of the palace while Richard bestowed hawks and hounds, rings and brooches on his more distinguished guests.

Then came the day when one of Richard's pages was elected Lord of Misrule. It was the duty of the Lord of Misrule to preside in his master's stead at the high table, to mimic his lord, receive homage and issue outrageous orders, and his success depended entirely on how outrageous he dared to be. For this reason, the honour very often fell to one of the youngest and cheekiest members of the household, who had not yet learned discretion.

Young Wattie Jourdain did not even know the meaning of the word. He was the son of a very rich gentry family who had arranged for him, when Richard was still duke of Gloucester, to enter the household at Middleham and learn the knightly arts under Sir James Tyrell, who was Master of the Henchmen. Not even Sir James's notoriously rough discipline had sufficed to quell fourteen-year-old Wattie's exuberant spirits.

He began by requiring the king to abandon his purple and cloth-of-gold and change into plain green livery, then to act as his wine page, kneeling beside him throughout dinner and refilling his wine goblet every time he drank from it. As mock king under the canopy of state, Wattie also dined on plover and crane while everyone else had to make do with ordinary game birds.

Afterwards, when everyone had paid homage to him, he decreed, 'No dicing or cards or draughts this evening. We will play blind man's buff!'

There were squeals of joy from the youngsters and groans from their elders, but the Lord of Misrule refused to exempt anyone.

'The first blind man shall be my wine page!'

So Richard found himself, a kerchief covering his eyes, in the centre of a giggling, laughing circle, darting back and forth as he tried to lay hands on someone. And when he did, the Lord of Misrule demanded, 'Who is it? Who have you caught? You must guess, before you can take off the blindfold.'

Mildly annoyed, Richard allowed his hands to stray over the slender waist he had in his grasp, feeling the unmistakable rough and smooth of gold on silk with the shapes of velvet roses – or was it pomegranates? – woven into it. It made no difference. According to the sumptuary law passed by Edward a few months before he died, only the king, the queen, the king's mother and the closest members of the royal family were permitted to wear silken cloth-of-gold. 'It is the queen,' he declared triumphantly. And so it was.

Anne said naively, 'How did you know?'

'I would have known even without the feel of the cloth-of-gold.'

'Would you?' There was a mischievous look in her eye, but he paid no attention to it.

After that, the Lord of Misrule having declared it improper for ladies to play blind man, it was Stanley who took on the rôle, and then Jocky Howard, and then a reluctant Catesby. Bishop Russell and one or two others austerely refused, declaring it beneath their dignity, so in due course Richard's turn came round again.

It surprised him greatly when, after prolonged darting and lunging, he laid his hands on the very same cloth-of-gold as before, and the same trim waist. Even the scent of rosemary was the same.

'It is the queen,' he declared.

But it was not. It was Bess – his niece the Princess Elizabeth – wearing Anne's gown. She and Anne stood and laughed at him merrily, and so did almost everyone else, amused at their trick.

Almost everyone else. Bishop Russell and one or two others were shocked at the king 'fondling', as they later put it, the virgin princess who was his niece. Lord Stanley also looked sour, though for different reasons.

Unbelievably, although Richard realised afterwards that everyone in the circle was part of the conspiracy, he became blind man for a third time and for a third time found himself clutching a cloth-of-gold waist. He breathed, 'Who is it?' and the whisper came back, 'Anne'. So, by now as merry as anyone, he released the waist and hugged his captive to him, crying, 'The queen,' and tearing off the blindfold.

But it was Bess again.

His face was a study, and the entire company, with the exception of Bishop Russell and his friends, gave itself up to uncontrolled mirth. After a moment, Richard recovered himself and joined in the laughter, one arm round Anne and one round Bess.

None of them had any conception of the disaster to which the whole frivolous episode was ultimately to lead.

6

REGINALD BRAY took great pleasure in passing on – confidentially, of course – an improved version of the gossip next time he visited the Stanley estates in Lancashire, from where he knew it would be swiftly transmitted into Yorkshire.

The king, he reported, needed an heir and the queen could not give him one. It was said that he wished to divorce her and remarry. His attentions to his niece, the Princess Elizabeth, had been very marked at Christmas. Indecently so, in view of the relationship. She and the queen had even exchanged clothes. It was as if she were a second consort.

Yes, it was scandalous, and would be rightly offensive to the men of the north, whose first loyalty had always been to Anne Neville rather than the husband whose power and influence in the area had derived from his marriage to her. If he abandoned her now, he would – it was to be hoped – lose all his support in the north.

7

'RIGHT TRUSTY, worshipful and honourable good friends, and our allies,' Henry dictated, 'I greet you well.'

He paused, searching for the right words to suit a letter intended for wide, if private, circulation in England and Wales, and snatching at resounding phrases as they drifted into his mind. To his secretary he said, 'Then a bit about knowing they will support me in my desire to take the crown from – yes – "that murderer and unnatural tyrant who now unjustly bears dominion over you". Then something about the joy and gladness in the heart of "your poor exiled friend" when they let me know what force they will provide to help me in my campaign. In the Welsh letters – *not* the English – we should say that I will have the Red Dragon of the old Welsh kings on my banner. And finish on my future gratitude and a promise to requite them for their "great and most loving kindness in my just quarrel". That should do it, I think.'

It gave him satisfaction to sign each copy of the final letter with the words, 'Henricus rex.' *King* Henry. More and more he was convinced that it would become true.

Until he discovered that the dowager Queen Elizabeth had written to her son, the marquess of Dorset, requiring him to abandon his association with Henry Tudor and return to

England, where Richard would grant him a pardon and restore his estates. Elizabeth, it seemed, no longer had faith in Henry Tudor and, hard though it was to believe, had become reconciled with the 'murderer and unnatural tyrant'.

Dutiful son that he was, Dorset slipped away from Paris secretly by night and headed for Flanders, where he hoped to make an unobtrusive crossing to England. It did not occur to him that taking all his possessions with him might provoke awkward questions among those he had left behind. Sure enough, the servants noticed it and reported it, and Henry, thrown into a panic by the discovery that a man who knew every detail of his plans had vanished into limbo, hastily sought permission from Charles VIII to send men in all directions in pursuit. Caught near Compiègne, Dorset was brought back like an erring schoolboy, semi-subdued, airily apologetic, and putting everything down to a misunderstanding.

Acidly, Henry told him, 'The misunderstanding was yours if you thought you could walk away from your vows of loyalty to me.'

That episode was worrying enough. Far worse was the news that Richard, by fair means or foul, intended disposing of his wife and marrying Princess Elizabeth of York. The painted ceiling began to spin around Henry's head and the yellow-and-red tiled floor shifted beneath his feet. If he himself could not marry Elizabeth, his bid for the throne would be doomed. What should he do? *What* should he do?

It was only a few days, but it seemed like an eternity before he heard briefly from his lady mother. She said, if he had heard rumours of a projected marriage between Richard and Elizabeth of York, he was not to be concerned. It would not happen, even if he were to divorce the queen, or the queen were to die.

383

THE STRAIN of the Christmas festivities, during which Anne had summoned up every ounce of willpower she possessed to give an illusion of health and vitality, had drained her of what little strength she had. Afterwards, the exhaustion that had dogged her for close on two years returned with the suddenness and completeness of a rockfall. Rising from her bed in the morning became a nightmare of fits and starts, of having to do everything in slow stages, of interrupting the wearisome routine of being buttoned into her gown because of her need to sit down, of having to stop her women in the midst of pinning up her hair because it was giving her a headache, of choosing what jewels to wear and then casting them off because they were so heavy.

Once she was up and dressed and respectable, it wasn't so bad, and she told herself every morning on waking that all that was needed was a little self-discipline. But it wasn't true.

Richard, deep in plans to counter Henry Tudor's anticipated invasion, was nevertheless concerned about her.

'You look feverish. You don't eat. And don't think I can't tell when you are trying to suppress a cough.'

'It's just some infection or other. A few days in bed will cure it.'

'Well, if you think so . . .'

'I do. I am taking borage for the fever and thyme for the cough. I will be all right soon.' Miraculously, she succeeded in sounding convincing.

He kissed her lightly on the cheek. 'If you are sure. But if you are not better after a week or so in bed, you must see the physician.'

It was wonderful at first to be able to lie peacefully in bed, wearing only a loose, light gown and having to make no effort. But then the fever worsened, and the breathlessness, and the burning in her chest, and the cough – the cough that brought no relief, but only blood.

Richard sent frequently to ask how she was, and she sent back lying messages. She did not want to see him, she said, to take him away from his work, although the truth was that she did not want him to see *her*, coughing and wheezing and surrounded by blood-soaked rags. Her women were very good about taking them away, and washing her, and tidying her, but their presence was sometimes unbearable.

One night she woke briefly, drenched in sweat, and saw him, or thought she saw him, standing by the bedpost and staring at her frowningly. Next day, the physician arrived. He was a dislikable man and she shuddered in revulsion even at the touch of his red-gloved hand on her forehead. Vaguely, before she drifted into blessed unconsciousness again, she saw that he was wearing a linen mask over his nose and mouth. It seemed very odd.

Next time she awoke, it was to find a priest saying the *Kyrie* and scattering holy water over her with his aspersion. Then he was repeating the *Quicunque* and examining her as to her faith and asking if she wished to make confession. She could only whisper in reply, and making confession was quite beyond her. She coughed helplessly through the sacrament of unction and was unable to swallow the host, so the priest said, 'Sister, in this case it suffices for thee to have a true faith and good will; believe only, and thou hast eaten.'

He went away, then, and she thought, 'Is this what it is like to die?'

9

RICHARD HAD BEEN waiting in Anne's antechamber for many hours before the physician told him he could go in to her.

But he must wear a mask, and gloves.

'The queen is suffering from the tissic,' the physician said. 'Consumption, some call it, a kind that develops slowly but in the end strikes swiftly. It is very dangerous, very infectious. The miasma is carried in the air. You must protect yourself, sire.'

It was no different, Richard supposed, from wearing armour on the battlefield. But all else was. In his lifetime, he had seen many people in the throes of dying, but only in battle, never in bed. It was a strange, sad commentary on the world he had inhabited since his childhood.

Anne was propped up wraithlike against the pillows, her face cold and waxen, her eyes sunk deep in pools of darkness, her body so thin that it scarcely disturbed the coverlet.

But she was conscious and tried to smile and hold out a hand to him.

He had done his best to prepare himself, but it was unbearable. He stripped off his gloves and mask and took the thin transparent hand with its bloodless nails in his, and said, 'I can't trust you, can I, if this is what happens when we are separated?' And then, the words bursting out of their own accord, 'Don't leave me.'

She gave a strange little sound that might have been a laugh. 'The choice is not mine.'

'Would you stay, if you could?'

It was a long time before she managed to whisper, 'No.'

He closed his eyes, the pain like a dagger in his flesh. 'Why not?' He knew he should not ask, should not force her to talk, but he needed to understand.

'Horrible world, cruel world . . . enough of it . . . long to be with our son . . . at peace.' The words came out each on its own separate breath, every word a struggle.

'And me?'

She essayed another smile. 'Loved you . . . always.'

'And I you. I never knew how much.'

'You will come and join Ned and me soon . . . I believe . . . my dearest love.'

Just then, the tolling of a church bell broke into the silence of the room. Not the great bell of the abbey but one of the small ones in the tower of St Margaret's, a slow and measured bell whose meaning was known to everyone for miles around. The Passing Bell, signalling all within hearing to stop what they were doing and pray for the soul of one who was dying.

Anne whispered, 'Is that the Passing Bell . . . for me?'

Richard knew that his face was stark as, inwardly, he cursed the physician and the priest for their officiousness, their inhuman devotion to duty.

She managed, 'Don't mind. Need people's prayers.'

He could barely hear her now.

'Getting . . . dark . . . cold . . .'

Second by second, the chamber itself was becoming darker and colder, and he thought at first that it was because he felt himself dying with her.

But then shouting began outdoors, screams of terror, gabblings to God, and somehow he succeeded in straightening himself up and making his way to the window.

It was pitch dark. The sun had gone out.

The symbolism was so fearful that he did not at first recognise that this was an eclipse. He could remember the last one, in 1467, when his brother Edward and Warwick the Kingmaker had become estranged and years of bloodshed had followed.

Then there was a flash, and the first sliver of sun reappeared and light and warmth flooded over the landscape once more.

But inside the queen's chamber, darkness remained. When Richard returned to Anne's bedside, her soul had flown with the shadow of the moon.

Chapter Sixteen

1485

1

AFTER RICHARD had knelt and prayed, he opened the door of Anne's chamber and permitted the world to enter and carry out all the harrowing routines associated with death — the prayers and psalms of the *Commendatio animarum*, the royal council's formal inspection of the body, its preparation for embalming, the arrangements for it to lie in state before burial.

And all the time the higher-pitched of the abbey's bells was ringing the Death Knell, its strokes indicating that it was a woman who had died, a woman twenty-eight years old. A queen. The same bell would toll day and night for several minutes in every hour until Anne was buried.

The days passed and Richard, in a nightmare, stood vigil over her lying in state and barely knew who else was present. Everything was as vague to his sight as things seen in a swoon, every sound — even the sounds of voices, bells and Masses — lost in the turmoil that filled his head, a turmoil like the roaring of stormy waters.

2

BY VIRTUE OF his earlier experience in diplomacy, the chancery official, Master Henry Sharp, was adept at collecting gossip and editing the rags of it into a coherent, if not always correct, whole. That, after all, was what diplomacy was about.

Since it was commonly believed that Richard had wished to be rid of his barren queen, Master Sharp had no difficulty in piecing together and disseminating — sufficiently confidentially to ensure the widest possible circulation — the information that the king had spurned his wife's bed ever since the blind man's buff episode at Christmas, and that his rejection of her had hastened, perhaps even caused, the poor lady's demise. He was capable of anything, and the eclipse of the sun had been an expression of God's displeasure. No nation could prosper under a king of whom God disapproved.

Reginald Bray was barely acquainted with Master Sharp, but, having had that gentleman's memorandum reported to him, thanked him from the bottom of what he called his heart.

3

FRANCIS, who had been at Minster Lovell with Constantia since before Christmas, came galloping back hell-for-leather when a messenger from secretary Kendall brought them the news about Anne, and, after a single look at Richard and despite the ceremonial surroundings, took him by the arm and led him unresisting to the secret chamber where he slept more often than he did in the great state bed in the privy chamber.

Richard sat down at his table, his forearms resting on it loosely and his eyes lowered to the space between, on which lay a sheet of paper, half filled with writing.

Neither of them spoke.

After a time, Richard pushed the paper over to Francis.

It was a prayer, much crossed out and overwritten.

'Most sweet lord, Jesus Christ, keep me, your servant King Richard, and defend me from all evil, from the devil and from all peril, present, past and to come, and free me from all the tribula‚ tion, grief and anguish in which I am held, and from all the snares of my enemies . . . Deign always to deliver and help me, and after the journey of this life, deign to bring me before you, the living and true God . . .'

Francis said, 'A prayer for you, not for Anne?'

'Oh, I have prayed for her. All London has prayed for her. But she was so good and sweet that I have no fears for her soul.' He paused. 'With almost her last breath, she said, "You will come and join Ned and me soon, my dearest love". If I am to achieve that, soon or late, I fear that it is I who need praying for.'

4

VISITING the Lady Margaret's estates in the West country, and writing to her tenants in Lancashire, Reginald Bray said, 'He poisoned her, of course. It is well known. Why? Because divorce would have taken too long, and he wants to marry his niece, the Princess Elizabeth. He lusts after her, and incest matters nothing to him. Furthermore, he needs an heir. And finally, by marrying her himself, he will destroy Henry Tudor's desire to reunite the houses of York and Lancaster. He is an evil man.'

5

IN HIS DRY, precise voice, Catesby said, 'You cannot marry the Princess Elizabeth.'

'I have no intention of marrying the Princess Elizabeth. I have no intention, at this point, of marrying anyone. It is only ten days since my wife died. Allow me to mourn her in peace.'

But they would not. Disregarding his empty eyes and exhausted voice, they told him the full extent of the rumours that were circulating.

He was filled with a dull anger, but had to struggle to ask, 'Who is responsible?'

'We don't know, sire.'

'Then make it your business to find out. I want them punished.'

'Yes, sire. But it has gone beyond that. It cannot be ignored. If the gossip reaches the north – which it may already have done – that you caused the death of the queen in order to gratify an incestuous desire for your niece, the Neville connection will feel betrayed. They might raise the north against you.'

'They know me better than that!'

Doubtfully, Francis said, 'But if they hear only one side of the story . . .'

'Are you suggesting that I should go on another progress?'

'No.' Francis glanced round the table, which was covered with a black cloth, and at the black-clad men surrounding it. Catesby, as always, was caressing one of the quill pens from which he was inseparable. Ratcliffe was absently tugging at an ear lobe. And Richard was sliding one of his rings up and down his finger. There was a curiously lethargic air in the room, not just of Lenten gloom but of depression, of defeat. Francis, exchanging glances with secretary Kendall and treasurer Chadderton, resumed more strongly, 'But you should certainly write a great many personal letters.'

Catesby said, 'If you will permit me to say so, Lord Lovell, I cannot think that that would suffice. A public denial is necessary. Perhaps a statement before the mayor and commonalty of the city.'

'Good idea,' agreed Ratcliffe.

Richard said, 'I would prefer to let it all die a natural death. To make a denial of wicked slanders is to extend their life and give them an authority they do not deserve.'

If he had been his normal self, that would have been the end of it, but he was all too aware that the desolation of his spirit was affecting his ability to think clearly. So, eventually, he agreed to submit to the worst humiliation of his life.

Just before Easter, two weeks after Anne's death, he entered, in state, the great hall of the priory of the Knights of St John at Clerkenwell and addressed an assembly consisting of the mayor and corporation of London, a number of lords spiritual and temporal, and a sprinkling of ordinary citizens.

Speaking clearly and with conviction, without reference to notes, he described his grief and displeasure at the uninformed talk spread by evilly disposed persons – who would be imprisoned when caught – to the effect that the queen had been poisoned by the consent and will of the king, so that he might marry the Lady Elizabeth, the eldest daughter of his brother, the late king of England.

Scanning the faces of his audience as he spoke, he saw embarrassment on some, guilt on none, and nothing on most. It made it all the more painful to have to say – although he said it without a tremor – that, 'It never came into my thought or mind to marry in such a manner, nor am I pleased or glad at the death of my queen. I am as sorry and as heavy in heart as a man might be.'

Did they believe him? He thought not. But he thanked them for their attention, and departed with the same ceremony as when he had arrived.

6

WRITING TO her son at Rouen, Margaret Beaufort said, 'I send this to you by the hand of Reginald Bray. He will tell you everything that I do not.'

Not quite everything. Master Bray had been increasingly uncomfortable in England, uneasily aware that too many questions were being asked about him, that even his generosity with the Lady Margaret's money gave no guarantee of silence on the part of the associates and families of the men he had employed in clearing the way for Henry Tudor. He still knew, in his head, that nothing could be proved against him, but in his nerves he was not so sanguine. Henry was going to have to pay him well when he ascended the throne.

In her letter, the Lady Margaret said, 'There is much gossip here about my poor niece Anne's death, and everyone believes that Richard wishes to marry Bess partly to prevent your doing so, and partly to strengthen his own weak claim to the throne. I do not myself think that the latter argument is tenable, since it was he who declared Edward's children bastards in the first place – you will have to reverse that enactment before you yourself marry the girl – in order to enable him to claim the throne. Richard is not so stupid as to be unaware of the inconsistency.

'I do think, however, that Lord Stanley may be correct when he tells me that Richard desires Bess for herself. She is a very goodlooking and charming young woman. You will like her when you meet her. She will make a fine queen for you.

'So, have no fear. Richard will not dare pursue the marriage plan. There is too much opposition. Indeed, his reputation deteriorates by the day – a process in which I confess to having had a hand, assisted by my invaluable Reginald Bray. Unfortunately, Richard and his hounds are in full cry after the "evil slanderers", and Reginald has come under suspicion, which is why I am sending him to you. I hope you will take his advice now, and reward him more fully when you come to the throne. A knighthood of the Bath would be suitable as a beginning, and the Garter, later.

'Hasten your arrangements for invasion, I pray you, so that I will have the joy of seeing my sweet son once more, after all these years of separation.'

7

WHEN WOULD Henry land, and where? In April, Richard sent a flotilla to patrol the coast of Kent, and in May entrusted Francis with the command of a well-equipped naval squadron to be kept in readiness at Southampton. Jocky Howard was to look after the south-east, and Brackenbury was to guard London – and make a better job of it than he had done guarding the princes, for which Richard had not yet forgiven him. The Tudor family connections in Wales suggested a need for extra precautions there, so three of Richard's most able lieutenants were despatched to the Principality and beacons were set up on the hills to transmit warnings.

All that remained to do was wait until firm news arrived from Richard's agents in France.

There was nothing restful about the waiting, certainly not for Richard's staff. Always demanding, always insistent on speed and efficiency, Richard was never an easy master, but now he was impossible, prowling around Nottingham Castle inspecting the work of his clerical and administrative officers, questioning here, instructing there, giving no one a moment's peace.

Secretary Kendall thought it was not concern over Henry Tudor that caused his master's inability to sit down for more than five minutes, or to do anything at all without fidgeting – rattling his fingertips on the table top, or twirling his rings, or playing with his dagger.

'I think,' Kendall wrote privately to Francis, 'that the king's impatience has less to do with practical matters than with an attempt to keep his own mind occupied and his emotions at bay. He gives all the appearance of being overwrought.

'Furthermore, it is my impression that he feels Tudor's invasion cannot come soon enough. The king is preparing to send out further commissions of array requiring our soldiers to stand ready at an hour's notice, and also issuing proclamations against Tudor – his bastardy, his ambitiousness, his insatiable covetousness, his selling out to the old enemy, France, and so on.

'I believe the king wants to see everything over with and settled, so that he can put the past behind him and rule as he has always wished to rule, with generosity and justice. It enrages him that the treasury has been swallowed up by the costs of preparing to meet Tudor, and that he is having to raise money by forced loans – a thing he last year promised Parliament never to do. Well, it is all in God's hands now.'

Francis did not like the sound of any of it. To Constantia he wrote, 'Richard could have been, could still be one of the finest kings England has ever had. But *everything* has gone wrong for him. The things he has done that some of us have disliked – things that Edward, though far more ruthless, could have got away with – have brought him to the brink of disaster. The time of decision is coming. And I dread it.'

8

IT WAS not only Richard who was having money troubles.

Charles of France had lent Henry Tudor a few pieces of artillery and a moderate sum in gold. But even Henry's spiteful pleasure at leaving the marquess of Dorset behind as a hostage in security for the loan was only small compensation for the financial problems involved in recruiting and paying mercenaries in Normandy and then hiring ships to transport them across the Channel. The mercenaries were no less grasping for being members of the criminal classes, and ships' masters did not much care for the dangers inherent in the expedition. King Richard of England was well known to be a fine practitioner of war at sea.

Henry's army was not going to be large. Perhaps two thousand unprepossessing mercenaries, stiffened by between three and four hundred of Henry's fellow exiles; a small but effective force of professionals commanded by the Sieur d'Aubigny of the French king's guard of Scots Archers; and another small force of bellicose Scots under Alexander Bruce of Earlshall. James III might have made a truce of 'love, amity and alliance' with Richard only a few months earlier, but he was a dedicated believer in hedging his bets.

Waiting at Harfleur for favourable winds – and praying that they would be more favourable than they had been almost two years before – Henry looked at his little army and mentally doubled it. If all the promises made by supporters in Wales and England were honoured, he would find himself at the head of quite a respectable force.

His main concern was that, although he had received expressions of goodwill from his stepfather Thomas, Lord Stanley, and his stepfather's brother, Sir William Stanley, their goodwill had so far fallen well short of firm promises.

His Uncle Jasper warned him, 'See 'ere now, boy, they're a slippery pair, always 'ave been. Don't trust them.' But Henry replied, 'Surely I *must* be able to trust my mother's husband! And his brother. They *must* support me.'

Uncle Jasper grumbled something in Welsh and although Henry, who had almost forgotten his childhood tongue, could identify only the word *saeson*, it was perfectly clear that Uncle Jasper was calling down imprecations on the whole shifty race of Englishmen.

Glancing round nervously, Henry murmured, 'Hush, Uncle Jasper!'

9

AT NOTTINGHAM, Lord Stanley was saying, 'While we are waiting, sire, might I have leave to go home for a while? I have not had the freedom to do so for a good many months and there are estate matters that need my attention.' Observing Richard's tight expression, he added, 'I will not be far away. I could be with you, with my men, in a day or two if we are needed.'

'*When* you are needed,' Richard corrected him.

'Yes, all right. *When* we are needed.'

Richard hesitated. Less and less did he trust Stanley, although Stanley had not put a foot wrong in two years. But Henry Tudor was his stepson. And Stanley could call on three thousand fighting men, and Richard wanted them in *his* army, not in Henry Tudor's.

Catesby and Kendall were busy with their papers and pretending not to be listening.

'Might we have the pleasure,' Richard said, 'of the company of your son, Lord Strange, to act as your deputy during your absence?'

Deputy. Another word for hostage.

Almost imperceptibly, Stanley's big face changed. 'My son would be charmed,' he lied. 'He says often how much he would like to be granted more responsibility in your household.'

'Excellent. Then we are agreed.'

Richard was aware that he had not handled the situation as tactfully as he might, but Stanley was no innocent. He was fifty years old and had been politically active during half of those years, and devious throughout. Above all, he was married to Henry Tudor's mother and must know that Richard was justified in having reservations about him. He *should* be realistic enough to accept that the king could reasonably require some earnest for his good behaviour, but men were seldom realistic about other men's views of them.

Richard gave a mental shrug. If Stanley considered himself mortally insulted, it was unfortunate, but he would have to make the choice — between his son's continued wellbeing, and his stepson's ambitions.

It was not long before Stanley's moment of decision came nearer, while Richard was spurred into swift and purposeful action. The message came that Henry Tudor was preparing to embark from Harfleur, and intended to make his landing at Milford.

The waiting was almost over.

10

WITH THE aid of a soft wind from the south, Henry and his army had a pleasant voyage and landed in a picturesque sunset on

August 7th. Unfortunately, they did not land at Milford in Hampshire, where Francis and the fleet were lying in wait for them, but at Milford Haven in Pembrokeshire, well over three hundred sea miles away.

The news of the landing – and that Henry had immediately and ostentatiously knelt down to kiss the sands of Wales – reached Richard two hundred miles away at Nottingham four days later, a tribute to the efficiency of the scurrier, or courier, system he had set up. As soon as he received the news, he sent out messages requiring the immediate presence of his leading captains and their men – Harry Percy from Northumberland, Jocky Howard from Suffolk, Francis from Southampton, Brackenbury from London, and Lord Stanley from Lancashire.

It came as an unpleasant shock to learn, a few days later, that his supporters in Wales were proving less reliable than his courier system, that towns and fortresses that had sworn loyalty to him had opened their gates to Henry as he marched north, even if few of the inhabitants were joining Tudor's company.

'The towns I can understand,' Richard raged. 'Towns always open their gates to armies, to forestall the likelihood of being sacked. But now, it seems, he has been joined by Rhys ap Thomas and his men. Welshman though he is, I gave ap Thomas the benefit of the doubt when he swore to me that Henry Tudor would cross the mountains into England only over his dead body. Well, he is forsworn, and he will pay the penalty. And Gilbert Talbot also, and any others who betray their king.'

Tudor was by now across the border, and reported to be making directly for Nottingham, not, as Richard would have expected, for London.

Richard went hunting in Sherwood forest.

And then he received a message from Stanley, who could not obey the royal summons because he had the sweating sickness.

The sweating sickness was a new kind of plague which either killed its victim within hours, or kept him desperately ill for days. It was also highly infectious and could lay an army low in no time at all. If true, the sweating sickness was the best possible excuse for Stanley's absence from duty.

If true . . .

But young Lord Strange was then caught trying to escape from Nottingham.

When questioned – though not as harshly as he might have been – he confessed that he and his uncle, Sir William Stanley, had been considering joining Henry Tudor, but denied absolutely that his father had any such thought.

Richard issued a proclamation declaring Sir William Stanley a traitor.

Next came a message from the city fathers of York, mentioning that they had not been called upon to send armed aid to the king. Was this an omission? Did he need men from his most loyal city?

Of course he did, and Harry Percy was supposed to be raising them.

'What is Percy up to? Why has he not arrayed them? Does he think the men from his own estates will suffice? What is the use of commanders who use their own judgement when they shouldn't, and never use it when they should! Secretary Kendall, send a scurrier to York at once, though whether their men can arrive in time for when I need them is open to question. And try to find out where Percy and his men are. They should be at Pontefract by now.'

Tentatively, Kendall said, 'His lordship may not be at fault, sire. His followers are so scattered that mustering them can scarcely be achieved in the short time he has had at his disposal. A retainer like Sir Robert Tempest, for example, has his seat sixty miles away from Percy's own.'

'You are daring to reprove me?' Richard snapped. But he knew very well what difficulties Percy faced and, after a moment, said, 'You are right. It was my impatience speaking. This is Thursday, and I would guess that Tudor may already have turned south for Watling Street, hoping to make a swift march on London. Tomorrow, therefore, we must leave to intercept him. Jocky Howard should be at Leicester soon, and also Brackenbury, though it is hard to say whether Lord Lovell will have had time to array his men from the Thames valley when he himself had to start out from Southampton. What, I sometimes wonder, is the purpose of making plans, when everything conspires to disrupt them.'

Kendall lowered his eyes to his papers again. It seemed to him that the king, famously strong-minded and inhumanly efficient, had at last, following the death of his wife, learned what it was to be human.

Chapter Seventeen

1485

1

A FEW MILES away, Henry Tudor was having a very private meeting with Sir William Stanley, a big, coarse-looking man, who might have a title but was clearly no gentleman. Henry did not take to him, and hoped that Stanley's brother Thomas, his stepfather, was more refined. It had been a dozen years since he had seen his mother, but he remembered her as small and saintly and fastidious, and could not imagine her married to anyone bearing any resemblance to this regrettable oaf.

And then he reminded himself – he needed this man. It did not mean he had to like him.

Sir William said, 'I myself have been proclaimed a traitor for being rumoured to be considering giving you my support. But my brother is in a different situation. Richard holds his son as a hostage and, if Thomas declares for you, the boy will undoubtedly lose his head. You must try to imagine a father's feelings.'

Henry, whose own father had died before he was born, tried to think what Uncle Jasper, his substitute father, would have said. Since Jasper was a tough old bird and a confirmed bachelor,

Henry said, 'Lord Stanley has other sons,' which stopped even Sir William in his tracks, though only momentarily.

Recovering himself, he went on glibly, 'I believe our support for you would be very much more effective if it were not made public beforehand. If you march on to the field of battle with – what? – five thousand men, while Richard has twice that number, it will lull him into a sense of false security. If my brother and I *then* come over to your side, the effect will be twice as potent.'

It made sense, although Henry would have preferred to march on to the field of battle with ten thousand men, right from the start. He had never fought a battle before; had never even witnessed one. If the truth were told, he would have preferred to be somewhere else.

He knew the Stanley brothers to be notorious for their slipperiness, and had no desire to face fearful odds only to find that the brothers had changed their minds again and decided that they would make more profit out of supporting Richard, rather than him. So he said, 'You swear?'

Sir William said airily, 'Of course,' and tipped the better part of a cup of ale down his throat.

Not to be outdone, Henry swilled his own. It was an unusually strong local brew and, when he next spoke, his voice was very slightly slurred. 'I have a fancy to meet my stepfather, who is still a stranger to me.'

'Tomorrow,' Sir William said. 'Or perhaps the day after. He has been suffering from the sweating sickness and is not yet recovered.'

2

HENRY ALLOWED himself to be so deeply diverted by worries over the Stanleys that he lost his army.

He had dismounted by the roadside in order to sit and think in peace for a while, with only his twenty-man bodyguard for company, and had become so engrossed in reviewing his failure to attract the reinforcements he had hoped for during his march, and in calculating the likelihood of the Stanleys throwing in their lot with his, that darkness fell before he became aware of it.

And darkness it was. By the time they had covered half a mile in the direction in which the army had disappeared, the night had become as black as pitch. There was no surfaced road to guide them, and they carried no torches to enable them to read the line of the army's passing, insofar as there would have been any identifi-able line. Five thousand barely disciplined men on the march tended to sprawl over the landscape through which they passed.

Henry and his men wandered about in the dark for hours, increasingly fearful. Even the sight of camp fires would have been no reassurance. Henry had no desire to blunder into Richard's camp by mistake.

What they did blunder into was a village, which seemed to be fast asleep. They could not tell in the dark how large the village was, and Henry by now was so terrified that he did not dare wake any of the householders to find out where they were. If they were recognised, which they might well be – especially if his body-guard failed to keep their French mouths shut – there was a very real risk of being betrayed and captured. So they hid themselves in a nearby wood and, after a night of shivering tension, Henry rode into the village and, masking his own Welsh intonation by mimicking the marquess of Dorset's Midlands accent, asked where he was and in which direction lay Tamworth.

He was in the village of Hopwas, it appeared, and Tamworth lay 'bout a league that way, m'lord.

Henry gave the fellow a half-groat and rode off as if he had all the leisure in the world.

He galloped into Tamworth to find Lord Oxford, worried stiff, about to send out a search party. So he said airily – by this time completely in command of himself, even pleased with himself – 'I omitted to tell you that I had to slip away to a private meeting, to receive some good news from friends who do not yet wish their support for me to become known.'

Trenchantly, Oxford said, 'Then perhaps you should hurry them up. Richard has spent this last night at Leicester, which is no more than six or seven leagues from here. The hour of battle is very close.'

Henry's, 'Excellent!' sounded marvellously convincing, even to himself. 'In the meantime,' he went on, 'let someone bring me food and drink. I am famished with hunger.' But his mind was racing. Lord Stanley's force was at Atherstone on Watling Street, but whether Lord Stanley himself was in command was another matter. Sir William would be there, however . . .

Today was Saturday, and there could be no battle fought on a Sunday. But even Monday still left very little time for him to persuade the Stanley brothers to make up their unsavoury minds.

3

ON SUNDAY MORNING, Richard rode out from Leicester towards Atherstone at the head of his army, wearing full armour under a tabard blazoned with the lions of England and lilies of France, and his gleaming satin banner – showing the white boar, allied with the sunburst and white rose of York – flying proudly beside the royal standard over his head.

With him in an emblazoned riot of yellows, reds, whites, blues and blacks were Jocky Howard, duke of Norfolk; Harry Percy, earl of Northumberland; the earls of Lincoln, Nottingham and

Surrey; the lords Scrope of Bolton, Scrope of Masham, Zouche, Greystoke, Dacre, and Ferrers of Chartley; also most of the knights and gentlemen of his personal household.

Francis, who during the previous two years had spent too much time at court and not enough on his estates, was still reeling from the effort it had taken to raise a respectable force from among his affinity in Oxfordshire.

He had managed only one night at Minster Lovell with Constantia, one weary night when to sleep in her arms was all that he wanted. He had woken once or twice, sensing the uneven beat of her heart, and had raised a loving hand to her face only to find that her cheeks were wet with tears.

'Don't.'

But all he had heard her say before he fell heavily into sleep again was, 'War is so stupid. So wasteful . . .'

In the morning she had been heavy-eyed but smiling, and had hugged him fiercely as he left her.

The mad dash up Watling Street had taken its toll of him, and now, comparing his own ill-harnessed troop with everyone else's armoured and badged followers, he felt a terrible sense of inadequacy, not relieved by the knowledge that most of his noble companions had experienced pitched battles before, whereas his own experience amounted to little more than a few impromptu Border skirmishes.

Well aware that he was out of tune with the times, he still found it very odd to think of two armies standing up and battering away at each other until one of them ran out of men or stamina. If the object of a battle was to win it, there must be more intelligent ways of going about it. And there must certainly be more civilised ways of settling an argument. Constantia was right. War *was* stupid.

Glancing at Richard, he saw that he was wearing the thunderous expression that made him appear fierce and warlike to those who did not know him, although to his household it meant only that his thoughts were heavily concentrated elsewhere, whatever his eyes might be doing – glancing, as now, constantly to right and left over the rolling countryside, assessing the lie of the land and watching for his scouts with news of Tudor's whereabouts.

In the late afternoon, Richard decreed that the army should pitch camp for the night near Bosworth, at Sutton Cheney, beyond which the ground sloped up westwards towards an eminence known as Ambien Hill. While the tents were being erected and furbished, he rode out with his captains to survey the rough plateau and judge its value as a battle position.

'High ground. Good thing,' said Jocky Howard, stating the obvious, as always. 'And a plain without cover below.' He peered. 'Is that a patch of marsh over to the left?' It was. 'That'll make it hard for Tudor's line to fan out.'

Francis wondered absently whether Jocky's long moustaches weren't a nuisance in full armour. If they became trapped when he dropped his visor . . .

Jocky went on, 'Do we know how many men he's got?'

'About five thousand,' Richard said grimly. 'Unless the Stanleys join him with their three thousand or so, which is always possible. Then it is we who will be outnumbered.'

The problem with the hilltop was that, at half a league long, its length was five times its width. Later, sharing a supper of bread and cheese and ale with his household, Richard said, 'It is too long and narrow and runs east to west. I suppose Tudor might be foolish enough to march round by the south, exposing himself to our fire all the way, but we have to expect him to appear from the west and must therefore be ready to engage in that direction.'

'With such a narrow front,' Harry Percy remarked languidly, 'you cannot deploy the army in line. It will have to be in column.'

'Yes. And that will be restricting.'

Francis, whose military education was improving by the minute, said, 'But Tudor has never been in a battle before. Perhaps he might do the foolish thing.' As he himself would have done.

Richard's smile was wry. 'He has Jasper Tudor with him, and Oxford, and that traitor Rhys ap Thomas. Would you wager that they will even allow Tudor to express, far less listen to, his opinions — if he has any — about tactics?'

4

NO ONE slept well that night. No commander ever did on the night before a battle. Richard began by wandering alone, cloaked and unrecognisable, through his drowsy camp but, rendered uneasy by the snatches of conversation he overheard — his men were not going to fight cheerfully, it seemed — he soon returned to his tent and lay reliving past battles in his mind.

He remembered Edward's great triumph at Barnet, where he himself, in command of the right wing, had turned Warwick's exposed left flank and contributed substantially to Edward's victory. Barnet had been fought in a thick mist and the Lancastrian earl of Oxford — now one of Henry Tudor's captains — had allowed his men to scatter and, gathering them together again, had lost his way and led them into a shower of arrows from their fellow Lancastrians, who mistook his starred banner for Edward's device of the 'sun in splendour'. Had Oxford learned from his mistake, or might his judgement be equally faulty tomorrow?

And then there had been Tewkesbury, where the Lancastrians had occupied the high ground, and Edward the broken ground of the plain. Edward had begun by firing his bombards at long range and sending flight after flight of arrows into the enemy, until he had harassed the duke of Somerset, who led the Lancastrian right wing, into charging downhill. Unfortunately for the duke, the centre and left wing had not followed him and he had soon been driven back, hotly pursued by Edward's men. He had been so angry that, instead of resisting Edward's charge, he had gone dashing off in search of Lord Wenlock, command/ ing the centre, and after furiously accusing him of treachery, had beaten his brains out with his battleaxe. It was an episode that had not improved the Lancastrians' morale, and Edward's men, already in amongst them, had soon put them to flight.

Unlike Somerset, Richard was no hot/head, but reliving Tewkesbury reminded him that even a seemingly commanding position was no guarantee of victory. Where, tomorrow, should he position the great bombards and the men with the hand/cannons and handguns, bearing in mind that most of the army hated being close to weapons that notoriously blew up of their own accord? And should he station the dismounted men/at/arms in the centre of the vanguard, flanked by ranks of archers, or put the archers in the centre, flanked by the men/at/arms and pikemen? The centre had to be the main strength, with the pikemen to the fore in any charge, their purpose to break up the opposing formations with their eighteen/foot spears into smaller groups for the men/at/arms to deal with. And where should the supply wagons be located so that the arrow boys would be able to keep the archers constantly supplied? The usual position behind the rearguard would be too far away from the main bodies of archers.

So much depended on what Tudor did. The orthodox view was that always, when foot soldiers marched against the enemy, those who marched lost, and those who remained standing still won. But it was not always possible to hold armed men back when they were ripe for action. And if Richard chose to stand still and hold firm while Tudor followed the same policy, what happened then? *Someone* had to break.

Richard's overactive brain scanned and re-scanned all the possible dispositions of his army with such intensity that, when he rose to be armed an hour before dawn, he was as exhausted as if the battle had already been fought. When his arming pages, engaged in the intricate task of buckling and strapping the various sections of his armour into place, daringly commented on his pallor and asked if he were quite well, he shrugged it off. 'Lack of sleep,' he said, and smiled without humour. 'Dreaming of battles.'

There was no morning Mass because the chaplains were too busy running around in search of the chests containing their missals and vestments, their chalices and paxbread, and Richard had no time to waste. A mouthful of bread and ale, as usual on rising, and then he had to make a rousing speech — which was never his forte and for which he was not in the right frame of mind — and see the army deployed on top of Ambien Hill by first light, before Tudor's force appeared on the field.

Jocky Howard, apprenticed in war thirty years before, was Richard's most experienced captain and, despite an overbearing temper, by far the best man to command the vanguard of something like fifteen hundred archers, foot soldiers and gunners who packed the western end of the site — although Richard suspected that, if one of the bombards happened to blow up, Jocky would too. Richard himself was behind with the heavy main force of three thousand men, including a thousand armoured and mounted knights and men-at-arms, while Harry Percy and his three thousand northerners formed the rearguard. There were personal standards and pennons flying everywhere, rallying points for each captain's own followers.

DAYLIGHT BROUGHT Henry Tudor with a long, long column of men, four deep, who marched in disciplined array on to the field until they formed a snake round the western end of Ambien Hill, whereupon each man turned to his left and the snake became an army formed up in two double lines, kneeling archers backed by standing archers in front, and foot soldiers behind. It was a neat manoeuvre, and Richard guessed it to be the earl of Oxford's doing, since his great battle standard with its single star was flying in the centre. Oddly, the pennant of Sir Gilbert Talbot was fluttering on Oxford's right flank, and that of Sir John Savage on his left, with the black raven banner of Rhys ap Thomas close by.

If this was Tudor's vanguard, it was unbelievably large. Where were the main force and the rearguard?

They did not take long to appear, consisting as they did only of Henry Tudor with a single troop of horse and handful of foot soldiers. There was a good deal of raucous mirth on top of Ambien Hill as Tudor took up a position two or three hundred yards behind his unconventionally deployed army, whose vanguard consisted of what should have been the main force, lined up with a right wing which *should* have been the vanguard – and a left wing, which *should* have been the rearguard.

But the laughter died when an entirely different force appeared from a different direction, and halted about eight hundred yards to the south of Ambien Hill.

Lord Stanley's men, well over a thousand of them.

They showed no sign of warlike intent, but simply stood there as if they had just come to watch. There were pennants fluttering over their heads, but Lord Stanley's personal battle standard was not to be seen.

'Absent friends?' Francis said enquiringly.

Richard was looking grim. 'He succeeded in avoiding Towton, Barnet and Tewkesbury. Why should he change a lifetime's habits?'

And then Ratcliffe uttered a sharp exclamation and pointed to the north, to a small eminence about a mile away which had suddenly become peopled with men and horses.

'Sir William Stanley!'

Sir William's personal standard *was* visible, but his men were dismounting as if they too were merely interested spectators.

Francis had the unpleasant feeling of being hemmed in, and knew Richard must be feeling the same. Henry Tudor's force in front of them, Lord Stanley's to their left and Sir William Stanley's to their right. Francis prayed that the loyalty of Harry Percy, commanding Richard's rearguard, was not as doubtful as Richard half suspected.

Everything now was in God's hands.

Jocky Howard, his silver lion banner flying, his head turned towards Richard, sat his big warhorse with his son, the earl of Surrey, and the lords Zouche and Ferrers beside him. Richard closed his eyes for a moment, crossed himself, left-handed, and then raised his sword high and brought it down in a sweeping arc.

It was the signal Jocky had been waiting for. His trumpeter blew the piercing note that commanded archers and gunners to fire, and the battle began.

The longbowmen were big and powerful men with big and powerful bows, and they fitted, drew and sighted their arrows, tipped with four-inch long steel spikes, with the utmost assurance. The twang of the six-foot bowstrings and the hiss of grey goose feathers as the arrows sped through the air at a rate of five score miles an hour was sweet to Richard's ears, but the effect fell short of the promise. Men accustomed to peaceful target practice could not, in the first moments, be relied on to achieve a range of two

413

hundred yards accurately and reach their expected rate of ten arrows a minute under battle conditions.

It would not have mattered too much if the enemy had been formed up in column; even poor archery could inflict serious damage on solid blocks of men. But against the four tenuous lines of Tudor's army the arrows were wasted, falling harmlessly to the ground. Some of Tudor's bowmen, tauntingly, picked them up and tucked them in their belts for their own future use.

And then Tudor's bowmen responded, with fast-fired flights that did not fall short and struck lethally into the massed ranks of Jocky's vanguard. There were flurries of movement here and there as men fell to the ground, and screams began to contaminate the air.

Through gritted teeth, Richard said, 'Observe. The most damaging flights are coming from Tudor's left wing, from the men under Rhys ap Thomas's banner. These south Welshmen never forget that the longbow was their invention, and nothing stops them practising, even in time of peace.' His voice echoed weirdly from under the bascinet helmet, but Francis could see that, inhibited by his steel gauntlets from fiddling with his rings or dagger, he was busily chewing his lower lip. Richard was not a nervous man; it was strange that he had so many nervous-seeming mannerisms.

The arrows flew back and forth and, in due course, the cannonballs and the bullets from Richard's serpentines and hand-guns, but the range was too great, the guns' aim too unreliable, and the enemy lines too slender for much damage to be done. The air, however, began to smell chokingly of gunpowder and the noise was ear-rending, earth-shaking.

The thousand armoured knights and mounted men-at-arms surrounding Richard were becoming restive, their mounts snort-ing and snuffling and pawing the ground at the smells and the

414

noise, and the whiff of freshly spilled blood. Richard raised a calming hand, but it had no perceptible effect.

Francis, intolerably hot and uncomfortable in his plate armour, could feel the perspiration trickling down his temples despite the sweat band he wore under his helmet, and wondered whether everyone else was feeling the same. After a while, he found himself thinking of peace, and quiet, and Constantia.

What was Richard thinking of? The battle, Francis knew. Only the battle.

And then he was aware of Richard's eyes on him, and Richard's hand indicating the coronet that ringed his conical helmet, and Richard's voice, raised but not loud, saying, 'Power is a bauble. Today, I would exchange this for Anne's life, without a moment's hesitation. I wish I had known sooner.'

Francis struggled in vain for something to say, and in the end came out with the bravest words he had ever uttered. 'I am afraid.'

'Only stupid men are not afraid.' Richard hesitated, and then went on, 'Francis, whatever today's outcome may be, you *must* survive and go back to Constantia. Do you understand me?'

'I understand the words, but whether I survive or not is hardly under my control.'

'We can do . . .' Richard broke off and raised a silencing hand. 'Wait! I think Oxford is advancing! You have the advantage of height. Can you see?'

And Oxford was indeed closing up his ranks and beginning to move forward, clearly intending to bring his full five thousand men uphill and into action, despite the continued and increasingly deadly rain of arrows and cannon balls and serpentine shot from Jocky Howard's fifteen-hundred-man vanguard.

Jocky's trumpeter sounded the charge.

An explosive sound broke from Richard's throat, part expletive, part negative, wholly furious.

Francis glanced questioningly at Ratcliffe beside him, who opened tightly compressed lips to say, 'Throwing away the advantage of our position. Madness. I suppose Jocky's hoping to break the enemy line.'

They had to wait and watch as the archers handed the arrow lads their bows for safe keeping, drew the battleaxes and mallets from their belts and, with the men-at-arms, charged down on the enemy.

Francis thought, 'Why doesn't Richard sound the recall?' and then realised that worse confusion would inevitably follow. At least the vanguard's charge would clear the hillside and allow Richard to take the heavy contingent into action. Wouldn't it?

But Jocky's charge failed either to break or drive back the enemy lines and the first impetus disintegrated into fierce hand-to-hand fighting, with Jocky's men, all too clearly outnumbered, gradually being forced back up the hill. The whole hillside became one vast, confused mêlée, mallets striking on armour, swords driving into leather-jerkined chests, battleaxes whirling everywhere.

Seething with frustration, Richard sat his great white charger and watched. The minutes passed, became an hour, and more, though only the sun's movement in the sky gave any sense of time. Otherwise, it was an unchanging, ever-changing vision of weapons rising and falling, of men swaying and righting themselves, or staggering and collapsing.

And then came disaster. The big figure of Jocky Howard, striking out mightily, his visor up as he rallied his men, his chin-piece knocked aside by some glancing blow, took an arrow through his throat and, his hand clutching at it despairingly, fell to the ground. It was the worst of bad luck. When a captain died, his men always lost the will to fight.

His mind working furiously, Richard scanned the field and the horizons. The two Stanley contingents were still showing no sign of joining in the fray, but the small band of men surrounding Henry Tudor, no longer protected by the line-up of his main force under Oxford, was on the move, not towards the battle on the hillside but towards Sir William Stanley a mile away to the north.

Richard reached out to clasp Francis by the arm. 'Go and tell Harry Percy to bring his men round by the south of the hill and take the enemy in the rear. Explain the situation.'

'Yes.'

It was not easy to work his way through the press of the main army, an army restless and anxious for action, and when Francis at last reached Harry Percy that gentleman was less than cooperative. He was so far back from the leading edge of the hill that he could not see what was going on there, and when Francis explained, he replied coolly, 'Easier said than done. Taking my men down the hillside would mean having to re-form them on the plain and then march them a mile to the attack, exposed at every stage if that Stanley contingent over to the south should decide to move.'

'But,' Francis began, and got no further.

Sharply, Harry Percy exclaimed. 'God's life! Richard has thought of a better way. Look there.'

Francis looked, and saw a body of about a hundred men, with the royal standard at its head, pounding across the plain to where Henry Tudor was.

Instinctively, he pulled his charger's head round to scramble down the hill and ride after them, but, 'No, Francis, my friend,' Harry Percy said, taking a forcible grip on him. 'Stay where you are. You can do nothing. You would be too late.'

So Francis, held in the unrelenting grasp of two of Harry Percy's men, had to stand motionless far away and watch the last desperate act of the drama being played out. The act in which Richard had ensured that Francis himself should play no part.

RICHARD KNEW that, during the decades of war between the houses of York and Lancaster, no army had ever gone on fighting once its principal commanders had been killed or captured.

And there was Henry Tudor under his banner of the red dragon, separated from the main body of his troops and cantering towards Sir William Stanley's force, probably to ask for reinforce ment, but still some way away from Stanley's protection.

The opportunity was too good to lose. One short encounter could put an end to Henry Tudor, *and* the battle, *and* Henry Tudor's cause.

As soon as Francis was safely out of hearing, he gathered the knights and squires of his household around him and told them what he proposed.

Ratcliffe exclaimed, 'It is too dangerous for you. Let me do it!'

But Richard shook his head, his steel gorget squealing in protest, and said, 'No. This is personal.' It wasn't quite true, but it was a reply he knew that Ratcliffe and the others would understand and accept.

There was no time to be lost. Their horses scrambling and slithering down the north west hillside, Richard took his little squadron of a hundred men round and beyond the mêlée to their left, to go racing out over the plain – racing madly, crazily, relying on their chargers to negotiate hummocks and rabbit holes and scrub and all the other hazards of open grassland.

For Richard, after the months of physical inaction, of trying to counter slander and forestall treason, of thinking and planning and waiting for Henry Tudor to take the initiative, the sense of release was almost too great to be borne. All the unquiet thoughts fled from his mind. He knew that, tactically, he was doing the wise thing, the sensible thing, and the thing he *needed* to do, but none of that mattered in comparison with the wild exhilaration that possessed him. The moment of decision was at hand, and whatever the outcome, he would live — or die — as king of England.

Henry Tudor, seeing him come, hesitated and recoiled, then drew the hasty screen of his bodyguard around him. But the weight of Richard's charge carried straight through it and with one huge sweep of his battleaxe Richard felled Henry's standard bearer and then, with scarcely a break in his swing, succeeded in unhorsing the seven-foot figure of Sir John Cheyney, who landed with such a crash that the ground shook.

Or so it seemed.

Richard was so concentrated on reaching Henry Tudor that he failed to connect the vibrations in the ground with Sir William Stanley's force leaping to horse and thundering over from the north to the aid of the pretender. He did not recognise it even when he felt a tremendous blow to his back as Stanley's archers came within armour-piercing range. There was no pain, not yet.

Then his magnificent wounded white charger faltered and, slowly, slowly, began to collapse by the knees. He was able to slide out of the saddle and remain upright. If he had fallen in all his armour he would have been like a lobster, lying on his back, waving his claws helplessly.

But now he was surrounded by men striking and hacking at him, and he could no longer try for Tudor, because now he was fighting for his own life.

Distantly, he heard Ratcliffe's cry of, 'Sire! Richard! Diccon! You need a horse! Take mine! Take mine!'

But he would not.

The numbers were too great for him, and he knew it. He wielded his sword and brandished his axe and did an amazing amount of damage before he was brought down, the wound in his back pouring blood inside his armour.

Grounded he lay, still striking out blindly against the tens, scores, hundreds, thousands, millions of men intent upon his end. He was past the stage of fighting back when, brutally and systematically, they slashed the ties that held his armour in place, and removed it piece by piece, and stabbed him, and stabbed him again, and again.

As he cried out to God in his agony, in his head he heard the tolling of the Passing Bell, and Anne's voice saying, 'You will come and join Ned and me soon, my dearest love.'

And then, at last, the killing blow was struck and everything was over – the life, the drama and the dream.

Historical Endnote

1

Fact or fiction?

THE POET Paul Valéry once complained that historians of the French revolution spent all their time bombarding one another with severed heads.

If, to severed heads, suffocated princes are added, much the same might be said of biographers of Richard III.

Thanks largely to Shakespeare, Richard has come down through the centuries as one of the most alluring villains of all time, one who remains an icon of iniquity even after five hundred years and despite vigorous modern attempts to rehabilitate him. Sardonic, self-aware, spectacularly evil. A man who is prepared to murder his way to a throne, and a man who does it *with style* . . .

The truth was almost certainly not like that, but no one knows what the truth was.

History is always, to some extent, a work of fiction, its actuality filtered through the minds, attitudes and cultural preconceptions of succeeding generations. Shakespeare, writing four generations after Richard's time, was reflecting Tudor orthodoxy, an orthodoxy that had sprung to baleful life within hours of Bosworth. Henry Tudor, with the worst claim of any English king since William the Conqueror, was as much a usurper as Richard had been, and a far more ruthless one. He could not afford to tolerate any other view of his predecessor than the one he himself proclaimed – that he was a villain guilty of 'Perjuries, Treasons, Homicides and Murdres,' of the 'shedding of Infants blood, with manie other Wronges, odious offences and abominacions ayenst God and Man'. Henry even dated his rule from the day *before* Bosworth, so as to enable him to execute for high treason anyone who had fought for Richard on that day.

The real Richard remains opaque. The modern historian has to depend, for what he did, how he behaved, and what his motives were, on a small handful of contemporary or near-contemporary sources, some of them outsiders who were none too well informed, others of them better-informed insiders writing with hindsight and the virulent dislike that was politically correct in Henry VII's time. Such material has to be approached with care, and so, too, do the government records, signet letters, patent rolls and the like which are now being systematically studied by scholars. Even here, interpretation is not always as coolly analytical as might be expected. In his time, Richard was one of those charismatic personalities whom people either loved or hated. Curiously enough, they still do, and it shows.

Insufficient and biased information leaves the non-fiction biographer with a number of intractable problems, commonly resolved by reducing events to a political narrative and tacking on a chapter entitled 'The King in Person' or 'Richard the Man' – as if, in an age of personal rule, it were possible to detach the man from the events. And since it is academically unrespectable, as well as irritating to the reader, to use such phrases as 'he may well have thought', 'perhaps he assumed', or 'no doubt it occurred to him', the odds are stacked against any attempt to give the subject the psychological plausibility that turns a lay figure into a believable human being.

This seems as good a reason as any for resorting to a fictional format. In *The Seventh Son*, I have taken Richard through the authenticated events of his adult life on the assumption that he was tough, charming, self-seeking, and very much a man of his time (though more competent than most). Given that he was far from perfect, but also far from being the double-dyed villain of tradition, I have tried to make sense of how his situation might have developed.

I have invented only two episodes in the saga, both of them hinted at in the record but generally dismissed as being entirely dependent on Richard's own evidence – unjustly, one feels, since other single-source evidence is accepted without a murmur. These episodes are the attack on him at Northampton, and the attempt by Elizabeth Woodville to bribe Hastings into betraying Richard.

Furthermore, I have left Richard innocent of murdering the princes in the Tower, since there is no proof whatsoever that he was responsible and their deaths would have been of no particular benefit to him. But they were crucial to Henry Tudor's claim, and it may be indicative that Henry's mother, Margaret Beaufort, that pious and implacable lady, was rewarded when her son came to the throne far beyond what might reasonably have been expected on the basis either of family feeling or her known involvement in his affairs. Much the same may be said of Reginald Bray, who also reaped massive rewards. There is nothing to prove that he took such an active rôle in promoting Henry's interests as I have awarded him, but *someone* did. Richard lost the Battle of Bosworth mainly because he had already lost the propaganda war.

Bosworth itself is scarcely less of a mystery than the rest of Richard's career. The numbers involved, the battle plan, even the location are all matters of debate. I have in general followed Ross (see under *Further reading*) while taking due note of the wider military expertise of Philippe Contamine in *War in the Middle Ages* and Sir Charles Oman in *The Art of War in the Middle Ages*.

As far as the secondary characters are concerned, almost nothing personal is known about Richard's wife, Anne Neville, or about Francis Lovell; *The Seventh Son* being a novel, I have given them both a likely life of their own. There are one or two small hints in the records that imply warmth in the relationship between Richard and Anne – in the unexpected context of an estate account, for example, Richard refers to her as his 'most dearly beloved consort' – but no more than that. Francis's adored Constantia is entirely fictional. Much of the dialogue between Francis and Constantia is there to illuminate the opinions that were being widely expressed at the time.

All of which having been said, it is worth repeating that no biography of Richard III, whether non-fiction or fictionalised, can be definitive. Where *The Seventh Son* is concerned, it makes no other claim than that, 'It might well have happened like this . . .'

2

Richard's appearance

GREAT ACTORS have always revelled in the Bardly hump and dragging limp but, in truth, there seems to have been nothing remarkable about Richard's physique. After his death, it was claimed that he had been two years in his mother's womb and that he had been born with a full set of teeth and hair down to his shoulders, but it took Sir Thomas More to establish the 'crookback' image. As he had it, Richard was 'little of stature, ill featured of limbs, crook backed, his left shoulder much higher than his right, hard-favoured of visage'.

Richard was not tall in comparison with his spectacular elder brothers. Where they were well over six feet, he was probably nearer five foot eight and looked smaller when set beside them. Recent research has it that the more sons a woman bears, the less favoured they become, which might partly account for Richard's lack of his brothers' striking beauty – although George, the sixth son, appears to have suffered from no such disability. There is also a long-standing belief that a child born after his/her mother has suffered a miscarriage – as was the case with Richard – is susceptible to developing a slightly humped back.

However, the surviving portraits of Richard, which date from more than thirty years after his death and were probably copies doctored to suit the Tudor political climate – of an original painted during his lifetime, suggest no abnormality. Indeed, modern examination of the portrait in HM the Queen's collection shows that the right shoulder was at some stage crudely overpainted so as to suggest a deformity absent from the original.

Though Richard's brother Edward IV was considered to be the best-looking prince in Europe, the standard portrait of Richard – after a little computer manipulation to remove the worry lines – shows a face appreciably handsomer and more interesting than his brother's.

3

After the curtain...

FRANCIS LOVELL

Francis escaped from Bosworth to sanctuary at Colchester in Essex. He was attainted by Henry VII, and many of his lands were granted to Lord Stanley. By the Easter after Bosworth, Francis had broken sanctuary and was trying to raise a Yorkist insurrection. It collapsed, but Francis escaped to Flanders, to return a year later with a force of German mercenaries financed by Margaret of Burgundy, the sister of Edward IV, George of Clarence, and Richard III. With John de la Pole, earl of Lincoln – Richard's nephew and, after the death of Ned, chosen successor – he raised the standard of rebellion in Ireland in favour of the twelve-year-old earl of Warwick, the orphaned son of George, duke of Clarence.

Unfortunately, one of Henry's first acts as king had been to seize the young Warwick from Sheriff Hutton and imprison him in the Tower (where he was to be kept for the next fourteen years before being judicially murdered). The 'Warwick' being hailed in Dublin was actually a well-trained imposter by the name of Lambert Simnel, although it took some time for this to be discovered even by his supporters. In June 1487, reinforced by Irish levies, Francis and Lincoln's army confronted Henry's at East Stoke in Nottinghamshire in a hard battle, which Henry won. It was the last battle of the Wars of the Roses.

Francis Lovell was never heard of again. He may have been cut down on the field or drowned in flight, swimming his horse across the River Trent. There is, however, a persistent legend that he succeeded in making his way back to Minster Lovell, there to die, possibly of wounds or starvation, shut up in a secret chamber. He was the last of his line.

RICHARD'S ADHERENTS
Jocky Howard, Ratcliffe, Brackenbury, Ferrers of Chartley, Robert Percy and John Kendall were all killed at Bosworth.

Catesby was captured, and executed (for treason) two days later.

Harry Percy, whose force had not been engaged, made his submission to Henry and was sent to the Tower for six months. He was generally thought to have betrayed Richard at Bosworth. When he returned to the north, he acted as a servant of Henry's and in 1489 was lynched when attempting to quell a peasant uprising against Henry's taxation policies.

Sir James Tyrell was absent from the battle, being then captain of the castle of Guisnes near Calais, and was to serve Henry there and elsewhere until 1502, when he was accused of treason and condemned to death. As it happened, two of Henry's three sons had recently died, leaving only the none too robust ten-year-old who was to become Henry VIII. The king, who had already had to deal with two pretenders to his throne – Lambert Simnel, claiming to be George of Clarence's son, and Perkin Warbeck, supposedly the younger of the princes in the Tower – grasped at the opportunity to lay the ghosts of the princes for ever. To that end it was announced that Tyrell had confessed to their murder before he died. This lonely little 'fact', elegantly and heart-rendingly improved on by Sir Thomas More, became the accepted solution to the mystery of the princes until very recently.

HENRY TUDOR'S ADHERENTS
Thomas, Lord Stanley, received many benefits from his stepson's succession – the title of earl of Derby and a steady flow of royal

patronage bringing him many new lands. But he lost almost all control over his wife, who was granted the status of *femme sole*, which effectively made her mistress of her own destiny. He died in 1504 at the age of sixty-nine.

Sir William Stanley also benefited from Henry's victory, becoming chamberlain of the household and recipient of several other important offices and numerous grants of land. But, powerfully entrenched though he was, ten years after Bosworth — where he had saved Henry's life — he made the almost inexplicable error of becoming involved in the Perkin Warbeck conspiracy. After a show trial, he was executed on Tower Hill on February 16th 1495.

Jasper Tudor, who had been Henry's unofficial guardian since his childhood, was created duke of Bedford. Fifty-five years old at the time of Bosworth, he had never married, but a bride was soon found for him — the dowager queen's sister, Katherine Woodville, the widow of Harry Buckingham. Other honours were also heaped upon him.

Lord Oxford did equally well, having restored to him all the family estates of which twenty-year-old Richard had relieved that 'helpless old lady', his mother. He became Admiral of England, Ireland and Aquitaine, Constable of the Tower and, appropriately, Keeper of the lions and tigers therein.

Bishop Morton, with characteristic astuteness, had stayed away from England in 1485, but was welcomed back in 1486 to become Chancellor of the realm and then Archbishop of Canterbury. In 1493 he was granted a cardinal's hat. He died in 1500 aged eighty.

Reginald Bray became one of Henry's leading counsellors and one of the most influential men in England. A principal financial administrator and property manager, he served on numerous commissions, was created a Knight of the Bath,

Knight of the Garter, high steward of both Oxford and Cambridge universities, in the process winning for himself a considerable reputation and large personal profit. He died in 1503, probably in his late fifties or early sixties.

MARGARET BEAUFORT

Margaret outlived her son, though by only two months. Throughout his reign she had been the greatest and most revered lady in the land, a sore trial, no doubt, to her sweet-natured daughter-in-law Elizabeth of York (who died in 1503 at the age of thirty-seven, having borne her husband eight children of whom only three survived to maturity). Margaret travelled widely with Henry, argued with him, dictated to him, worshipped him. She visited him every day during his last illness at his new palace of Richmond, built on the site of Sheen, which had burned down in 1497. He died on April 21st 1509 aged fifty-two and Margaret survived long enough to give her grandson, the eighteen-year-old Henry VIII, instructions about his coronation, marriage, and the composition of his council, before dying herself at Westminster on June 29th 1509 at the age of sixty-six.

ELIZABETH WOODVILLE

Although Elizabeth was mother to Henry's queen, she did not greatly benefit. Henry indulged in negotiations to marry her off to the newly widowed James III of Scotland, but James was still trying to lay down conditions when he was assassinated in 1488. In the meantime, although initially restored to her properties, Elizabeth was deprived of her widow's jointure and removed to a convent at Bermondsey. This may have been from choice. The only other explanations advanced, both difficult to sustain, have been (a) that she was thought to be sympathetic towards Lambert

Simnel, and (b) that she was suspect because of her reconciliation with Richard in 1484. She died at Bermondsey in 1492, aged about fifty-five.

4

Further reading

MODERN PROFESSIONAL historians and biographers who alike reject passionate defence and venomous criticism of Richard III (and those two schools of thought continue to flourish vigorously both in and out of the groves of academe) are still inclined to be offended by him.

Not, it should be said, for his reputed deeds of violence but for his attitudes of mind.

Although it is likely that Richard no more wrote his own proclamations than world leaders today write their own speeches – he had an experienced, hundreds-strong secretariat to do that, sending out between thirty and forty thousand letters and documents a year – he is held to be intolerably sanctimonious. Also, it is thought rather shocking that (five hundred years ahead of his time) he used character assassination as a deliberate instrument of policy.

Omitting specialist studies, of works currently in print the standard and most reliable biography is *Richard III* by Charles Ross, but perhaps more accessible for the reader looking for a straightforward account of events is *The Life and Times of Richard III* by Anthony Cheetham, which is well produced and informatively illustrated. A useful selection from the source material is provided by Keith Dockray in *Richard III: A Source Book*, which includes an excellent rundown of the history of attitudes to Richard since his own day. A.J. Pollard's lavishly illustrated *Richard III and the Princes in the Tower* also covers the historiography and even takes it beyond the 'respectable' into modern comic-strip and bodice-ripping territory. Bertram Fields' *Royal Blood* is an American lawyer's investigation into whether the case against Richard would stand up in court.

All these are works which take a balanced view of their subject. For readers interested in the unbalanced view, there is Desmond Seward's *Richard III: England's Black Legend* – a prime exemplar of Mark Twain's dictum that fluid prejudice is the ink with which all history is written. Seward writes very readably indeed, but his impassioned hatred of his subject frequently leads him into defiance of probability and, indirectly, into such historical and clinical absurdities as, 'Not even the wildest legends of the Borgias contain so exotically cruel and inhuman a killing' as the duke of Clarence's drowning in a butt of Malmsey. Nor is he above the cheap gibe. The Holy Roman Emperor's ambassador, Nicholas von Poppelau, noted that Richard was slender and three fingers taller than he was himself, 'but no doubt Poppelau was a barrel-chested dwarf.'

England's 'Richard III Society' and its overseas branches do much valuable work in originating the specialist academic studies which have in the last three-quarters of a century contributed so much to knowledge of Richard III's time, but at the other end of the scale and strictly for fun – the history nowadays looking a trifle shaky – there remains Josephine Tey's 1951 detective classic *The Daughter of Time*, in which a hospitalised policeman solves the mystery of who murdered the princes without moving from his bed.

For subjects other than Richard, the following may be

recommended: *Edward IV* by Charles Ross; *Henry VII* by S.B. Chrimes; *The King's Mother [Margaret Beaufort]* by Michael K. Jones and Malcolm G. Underwood; and *False, Fleeting, Perjur'd Clarence* by Michael Hicks.

Now you can buy any of these other
Review titles from your bookshop or
direct from the publisher.

FREE P&P AND UK DELIVERY
(Overseas and Ireland £3.50 per book)

Summertime	Raffaella Barker	£6.99
The Catastrophist	Ronan Bennett	£6.99
Of Cats and Men	Nina de Gramont	£6.99
Two Kinds of Wonderful	Isla Dewar	£6.99
The Alchemist's Apprentice	Jeremy Dronfield	£6.99
Earth and Heaven	Sue Gee	£6.99
Tales of Passion, Tales of Woe	Sandra Gulland	£6.99
Shadows on our Skin	Jennifer Johnston	£6.99
In Cuba I Was a German Sdepherd	Ana Menéndez	£6.99
After You'd Gone	Maggie O'Farrell	£6.99
A History of Insects	Yvonne Roberts	£6.99
Kissing in Manhattan	David Schickler	£6.99
Girl in Hyacinth Blue	Susan Vreeland	£6.99
The Long Afternoon	Giles Waterfield	£6.99

TO ORDER SIMPLY CALL THIS NUMBER

01235 400 414

or e-mail <u>orders@bookpoint.co.uk</u>

Prices and availability subject to change without notice.